INCUBUS

by GIUSEPPE BERTO

Translated from the Italian by William Weaver

New York: ALFRED·A·KNOPF

1 9 6 6

L. C. catalog card number: 66–10028

THIS IS A BORZOI BOOK,
PUBLISHED BY ALFRED A. KNOPF, INC.

FIRST AMERICAN EDITION

Originally published in Italian as *Il male oscure*. © 1964 by Rizzoli Editore, Milan.

It was the obscure disease whose causes and behavior the histories and laws and the universal disciplines of the great University chairs continue to ignore; and the victim carries it within himself, along the whole blasted descent of a lifetime, heavier every day, untreated.

C. E. GADDA, *La cognizione del dolore*

What oppresses me cannot be cured: it is my cross and I must bear it, but God knows how my back is bent from the effort.

SIGMUND FREUD, *from a letter of 1900*

Painful are these things to relate, but silence too is painful.

AESCHYLUS, *Prometheus Bound*

Ever since Flaubert said, "Madame Bovary c'est moi," *everybody realizes that a writer is always autobiographical. Still it can be said that he is a bit less so when he writes about himself, that is when he takes up more openly the theme of autobiography, because then narcissism on the one hand and the joy of narration on the other can lead him to a downright malicious distortion of people and events. The author of this book hopes that his natural narcissism may be forgiven him, and as for the joy of narration he is confident that it will be appreciated by those who might recognize themselves as characters in this novel.*

INCUBUS

I think this story of my long struggle with my father, which I once believed unusual if not unique, isn't so extraordinary after all since apparently it can comfortably be catalogued according to established psychological systems and theories; in a sense, it could even constitute an appropriate demonstration of the validity, the rational validity at least, of these systems and theories, and therefore, though personally I don't get a thing out of it, I might claim that my purpose in writing the story down is to furnish further support for the doctrine of psychoanalysis, which still needs it more than they think, but such an assertion wouldn't then jibe with a suspicion which more than one reader could have, the suspicion that the present narrative is nothing but a forced surrogate for certain aims and intentions of which I shall necessarily have to speak a bit later; they concern what I might call my literary ambitions and on this score, naturally, everyone can think what he pleases, but for myself, since I am on the point of taking leave of all human ambition and I suppose also of life itself, I feel it would be highly incorrect to attribute specific artistic intentions to this narrative, and indeed I have the impression that the story in a way is writing itself, a feeling that involves no serious contradiction of the doctrines just mentioned, or at least not of so-called parapsychology, and to tell the truth, it so happens that events and thoughts do arise to a great extent automatically from those obscure depths of my being where first my illness then its treatment went rummaging until they finally aroused this immoderate desire for exposure of which I seem to be merely the passive agent, in the sense that all I do is lend to this desire my expressive diligence, and if you'll allow the word, my style, which in less painful circumstances might have taken me who knows how far, I mean along the road to glory. Anyway, this struggle with my father which I can now assert is nearing its unexceptionable conclusion, that is the final identification of the two opposing terms, so that you can't really tell whether the final step will be a defeat or a victory, lasted for sixty years and four months at the very least, and really you could without exaggeration include the prenatal period, that is the time I spent in the maternal womb, if you want to admit, and it's not such a stupid idea, that in those surroundings there existed a however ill-starred opposition to my destiny to come into the world, and this not in any conscious sense, I mean not that my father and mother didn't desire my appearance, on the contrary, after me, with the aim of having a second son they happily produced five daughters not to mention several completely involuntary miscarriages in between, so that since they couldn't then foresee the meager pleasure they were to derive from it, it is inconceivable that they were opposed to the birth of their first and only son, so if we accept the thesis of opposition, we must believe in an autonomous resistance of my own to my birth and to the successive confrontation with my father, and this would indeed be extraordinary since it would posit the formation of an embryonic consciousness and will in me in that foetal state, which is I should imagine fairly rare, not denying however that with an intuition of this kind you could explain, though this isn't my case, a number of involuntary miscarriages which in the present circumstances of scientific progress are I would say otherwise inexplicable.

In any case, even if we leave out the prenatal period, my struggle with my father seems to me varied and prolonged enough to serve as the subject of a story, and with this aim in mind, but more for convenience in handling it than for any other reason, the struggle can be divided, roughly of course, into three periods or phases, which I would call simply first, second and third phase, the first extending from my birth to my eighteenth year when I had the fine idea, a necessity really, of going off into the army, and this phase is characterized, at the beginning at least, by an overpowering paternal domination, exercised both symbolically and physically and with various means such as, for example, his tall stature, and his weight which exceeded two hundred pounds, his cloak perhaps of olive drab, and his baldness which, whether through association with the other qualities or for some independent reason, I have always considered a sign of potency, though even when I was very young I was not unaware of my father's singular attempts to encourage his hair to grow back through the use of Migone Quinine, so that now I am led to believe I had an organic incapacity, or at least, an obtuseness in correlating different and contradictory data referring to a single subject, and in fact I have never been very sharp in these matters, nevertheless by discovering contradictions and defects in my father, I gradually succeeded in freeing myself from his great power and with my headstrong act of signing up as a volunteer I managed to pass into the second phase in which, frankly, I was able to get the upper hand with this father to such an extent that at times I was downright sorry for him, I gave him all kinds of satisfactions and even money not infrequently, a situation which lasted more or less to my thirty-eighth year, when he had the misfortune to die, giving rise in this way to the third phase which dates from his death on, and it was at this point that things again took a bad turn for me, a very bad turn.

My doctor knows all this well, better than me you might say, and in fact at the beginning of my treatment, interpreting in the most correct way a dream I happened to have, which I have classified as "the dream of Rossetti's bookstore," he was the one who gave me, well not the idea of this struggle with my dead father, since I had known for some time I was fighting with the deceased, but he furnished me with the probative starting-point thanks to which we later arrived, little by little naturally, at the proper or scientific explanation of this struggle, freeing it from all its superstitious or mysterious quality, giving it not only a logical order but, above all, human dimensions which, it seemed, could be borne. I believe everybody, or almost everybody, by now has some idea of this kind of psychological treatment which is beginning to be fashionable everywhere and therefore even in Italy, but mind you, I want to make it clear right off that it wasn't out of snobbishness that I began my cure, in fact I would happily have done without it, because of the expense if for no other reason, but at that period I was at such a low ebb physically, to say nothing of spiritually, that practically speaking, if I excluded suicide and the sleep cure which was then going through an unfashionable period, the only two solutions, according to everybody, were electroshock and psychoanalysis, and while it's true that I rejected electroshock out of a perhaps excessive respect for my brain, it's equally true that my choice of psychoanalysis was inspired not only by the hope of intellectual benefits as will become clear in due course, but also by a secret need to replace my dead father in some way so that the battle, if there had to be one, could be joined with a living, rational being and not with a memory or something similarly indefinable and elusive, like a dead father in fact, and though at the beginning my secret needs weren't very clear to me, the transference-phenomenon was precisely the first thing that worked, that is, the transference of my affections and not, as some might imagine, the elimination of the dead father and his effective and convenient replacement by another person, since psychoanalysis doesn't aim at this, and couldn't do it anyway, and in effect the treatment simply wants to make us aware of the problems and conflicts buried in our unconscious so that when we unexpectedly have to face them, maybe in quite different guises, we are not scared out of our wits.

Being psychoanalyzed is, at least apparently, the simplest thing in the world in the sense that the treatment consists in going to the analyst two or three times a week and maybe more depending on the case, then lying on the special cot or couch invented by Doctor Sigmund Freud to make relaxation easier, and telling quite freely everything that goes through your head, above all, whenever possible, your recent dreams, and this freedom of expression which is absolutely indispensable, should be all the easier since the cot or couch is arranged in such a way that the client can't see the analyst in order to spare him all embarrassment and other inhibiting feelings because, except for the paying part of it, psychoanalysis is a little like going to confession, that is it's no use unless you tell the truth, and since we tell the truth more to ourselves than to others that's why the priest is hidden behind the grating and the analyst sits behind the patient, to make everything simpler even if sometimes the patient becomes distracted, trying to guess what the analyst is doing while he is facing the other way, relaxing and telling, and as for me, I think that, at least to judge by the sounds, my man used to toy with the keys to his desk drawers and often had trouble lighting his cigar with his lighter because he had to flick it five or six times before getting the cigar lighted or else giving up the idea of lighting it.

Doctor Freud was beyond doubt a great man inasmuch as he was the inventor of psychoanalysis, so that many people have no hesitation in placing him, with Jesus Christ and Karl Marx, among those few geniuses who opened new doors to mankind, and I naturally have no objection to this view, but with that relaxative cot or couch of his, to my way of thinking, he was wide of the mark. I never once got good and relaxed, I always lay there with my knot of tension in the stomach, with the usual worry about giving a strict order to my thoughts, and besides, an increased discomfort in one of my most unfortunate spots, I mean the five lumbar vertebrae which, I have a feeling, one remote evening provoked the whole disaster, as I will no doubt be telling later, and though from that evening on I discovered unfortunate spots at every turn, I never forgot that first one, rightly enough, and when I stretched out on the Freudian cot or bed my five lumbars, under a special strain because of the general position of the body, began to feel warm and turn numb and have other unpleasant sensations all harmful to relaxation as well as to my tricky psychic equilibrium, creating fear and tension, which in themselves could be the reason why I never mentioned to the doctor this vertebrae problem, even if, from another point of view, I may have kept quiet so as not to hurt his feelings, since I'm sure that he believed in the relaxing qualities of the cot or bed, and I wouldn't have liked to grieve him, or even arouse doubts in him, by revealing that his contraption, at least with me, didn't work.

I would have done anything rather than grieve my doctor-analyst, and this was one of the things that regularly infuriated my wife who would insist I cared more about a character who was taking a pile of money from me while I chattered to him than I cared for her, a statement quite untrue in an absolute sense, but all the same, my wife, inexpert in matters of psychoanalysis, was also very much in love with me, or so it seemed, and in reality was possessive, egocentric, and impulsive, as the doctor made clear to me, and she was annoyed by any person or even thing or activity which took me from her however temporarily, and in the question of psychoanalysis, she sensed that, thanks to the transference phenomenon, I had finally got myself a proper father whom I could love without reservations since he wasn't always getting on my nerves like my real, though dead father, and was on the contrary a man who was glad to forgive my every sin, also because on top of everything else it seemed that sins didn't exist, at least not mine, or rather it seemed that in my bad actions I had always been conditioned, which meant that under the circumstances I couldn't have acted better than I did, so the analyst said, and I bet he would have said the same even if I had, to give you an example, raped all five of my sisters, unlike my real father, and also unlike my wife of course, but in this story the most important character is my father and not my wife, and he, especially in the first phase of our struggle, had always been prone to discover, in the various things that went wrong around us, some guilt of mine, though many of these things, especially those concerning our family life and his business, went badly without my having anything to do with them. God only knows what he thought of himself, I mean, whether he connected himself with me, partially at least, in the numerous faults he attributed to me, or whether this attributing gratuitous faults to me was an evasive maneuver of his to relieve, even with fictions, his own conscience too heavily burdened with feelings of responsibility. To tell the truth, for a long time and even after his death, I thought he considered himself an upright and wise man par excellence, and therefore exempt from all sin like a god, but later I wasn't so sure of this, in fact I wasn't sure at all, not so much because I had discovered previously unknown documents or because new evidence had emerged, but because, as a result of the vicissitudes of my illness, I was forced to upset, you might say, my whole point of view, even excessively, since if through a process of comparisons it turned out that I resembled my father, it also followed beyond a shadow of a doubt that my father, when alive, must have greatly resembled me, also in the exorbitant sense of guilt therefore, but I am aware that in this question of resemblance the identification still going on plays a big role, and I also know I run the risk of identifying myself with an absolutely imaginary father, or perhaps even with an idealized projection of myself, but then, to support me in my faith and my effort, there is an unquestionable and frightening physical similarity, an objective fact, and that leads me, just for an example, to cite the story of the photographs.

The time my father died I arrived, naturally, late, namely when he was laid out on one of the five or six marble slabs in the morgue, all neatly shaved, wearing his black wedding suit, forty years old but still almost brand-new, you could say, partly because, like me, my father was parsimonious and always wore his worst clothes, and partly because just after he was married he put on a tremendous amount of weight and the suit never fitted him, and to tell the truth they had to rip open almost the whole seam behind to get it onto him even after he was dead, but this wasn't very noticeable since he was lying on his back, dignified and solemn in his definitive peace, and for myself, in those days not yet ill with my death obsessions and other such things, I wasn't unhappy to look at him that way, I felt that, as dead men go, he was one of the handsomest dead men I'd ever seen, and that's how I got the idea of having his picture taken. Now, when I say it like that, the explanation is perhaps even too clear, but far from exhaustive, and in fact it isn't that I wanted, as you might think, to have souvenir photographs or some other unseemly thing, but in having his picture taken, I wanted, shall we say, to pay him homage, though in my unconscious I aimed at other results then still nebulous, but today obvious and strictly connected with that diffuse sense of guilt which, as is only too apparent, has developed in me out of all proportion thanks especially to paternal influences, so that, in this case, I would have said to hell with it, if I had known, although, since on that occasion I arrived late, there does exist a concrete guilt on my part, because I had had presentiments and all the rest of it, assuming, of course, that there's something guilty about arriving late in a situation of that kind, and to tell the truth, my doctor was of the opinion, for instance, that there was nothing wrong in arriving on the scene when your father is already dead, but of course the doctor had to lend me a hand in freeing myself of my outsize guilt complex, so he made an effort to convince me of my innocence even when, as in the case of my absence at the moment of the paternal decease, the guilt existed, and how.

I'd like to make myself clear on this point, which is a capital point in the whole story inasmuch as it marks the beginning of the transition from phase two to phase three in the struggle with my father, in other words his return to power, and it may even mark the beginning also, though still remote and mysterious, of the obscure disease that developed in my soul, indeed we can say for sure that this horrible disease was born out of this, since the verification of an objective guilt, as my absence in fact was, was the temporarily unnoticed jolt that set in motion all my other guilt feelings, stored away in the unconscious, waiting to harm me. In fact, at the time my father became so mortally ill, I was just fine in both soul and body, living in Rome, out of the family's way, I earned enough money working for the movies and I was always involved in trouble with women, because unlike plenty of other men I never liked having more than one woman at a time, so when I found a new one I had to get rid of the one before her, and this caused trouble, but interesting and basically pleasant troubles, the kind that concern women. As a rule I wrote my father twice a year, first at Christmas to say that I was sorry I couldn't get up to visit him but we'd see each other at Easter, and again at Easter to say the same thing, that we would see each other at Christmas, and both times I stuck a check into the envelope, which was very little compared, for example, to the cost of getting rid of one woman and taking on a new one, but it was plenty if you rightly consider what little need my father had of money since, on top of everything else, he received two pensions, small ones if you like, but two all the same, and if the amount I sent him seemed downright ridiculous, say ten or even five thousand lire, then to pacify my conscience all I had to do was remember something about him that irritated me, I don't know, his obstinacy in signing things with his last name first, for example, or the airs he gave himself when he attended patriotic ceremonies carrying the banner of the local chapter of the National Association of Retired Carabinieri, since all things considered there's nothing so splendid about having a carabiniere for a father, even a retired one.

So when my oldest sister telephoned me to say that my father, poor thing, wasn't too well, that he'd had something or other wrong with his intestines, maybe only constipation, but with terrible pains, and in short, on the advice of the town doctor, they had taken him to the hospital in the city, they had special rooms for patients with first-category pensions, about three thousand lire a day including heat, they wanted to see if he could get rid of this awful bellyache, which in fact he had already got rid of somewhat, however they still had to see why he had had such an awful pain in the first place, and so, she was speaking also for my other sisters and our mother, it wouldn't be a bad idea if I put in an appearance and quickly too, in short when my oldest sister called me with all this jolly news I dropped everything, my work and my women troubles, took the fast train to Venice, and all during the trip I kept thinking that the old man's days were numbered, all right, or rather, not to feel like such a crapehanger, I thought indirectly about what might change, in my family and personal life, in the sad event that he was really washed up, and it seemed to me that substantially nothing or very little would change, except for my mother poor thing who would be left a widow with the problem of the two pensions which might or might not be transferred to her, at least the smaller one, the one from Social Security, was apparently transferable, but not the other one, not yet anyway, and in reality from the letters that my father wrote me every week or so signed naturally with the last name first and with all the curlicues underneath I knew that he, also in the name of the local chapter of the National Association of Retired Carabinieri, had been fighting for years with uncertain outcome to establish the transferability of the pension in the case, which was his own, of a non-commissioned officer who had married after retirement, anyhow considering the small amount of this second pension which was large only if compared with the first, it seemed to me that not much would change after all even for the widow, and also from this point of view my father's death, at present merely foreseeable, appeared a completely natural event, nevertheless the trip I was making wasn't a pleasant one, and besides it was winter, February to be precise, and my town which is in the low country around the Venice lagoon is cold and foggy and depressing in winter, and as if that weren't enough I wasn't going up there alone because at the last minute to assist me on this sorrowful occasion, the woman I had been living with for a while *sub eodem tecto* and *more uxorio* had clung to me, a widow of French origins still fairly young and I'd say attractive but with a downright passion to get married again, and I didn't dislike her, in fact I was in one sense grateful to her since she had helped me overcome several prejudices of a sexual character, I mean being a widow and French into the bargain she had taught me to make love properly, but when it came to matrimony I kept telling her that the two of us were more than husband and wife inasmuch as we lived together by mutual consent and not because of obligation or contract, and she had been waiting for just this business of my father's illness to exercise her rights and duties as more-than-wife, which as I rightly foresaw, was going to cause me plenty of trouble of various sorts.

My first move obviously was to take a room in the city's best hotel, and there I left her and went to the hospital to the private room where my father had been put as a paying customer, and I saw that by now death had got its hooks into him, I was surprised first off by how pale he was, and then that he had pajamas with blue stripes whereas I had always seen him go to bed in a nightshirt or even more often wearing his undershirt, a cotton one if it was summer or wool in winter, and then I was surprised too by the way he looked at me, without any great interest to tell the truth, but I bet he was thinking why is he here I must have one foot in the grave already, naturally he could have had this same notion also for other reasons, but the substance of it had to be the same, I suppose he already knew he was going to die, or maybe he didn't know it yet, but in his eyes he had that same slightly recalcitrant look of alarm that oxen and cows have when you take them to the town slaughter-house, and you don't know if the oxen and cows realize where you're taking them, but judging by their look they surely realize that they're not headed for anything beneficent, and in general therefore this meeting with my dying father was a fairly unsuccessful not to say painful event, so he began drumming his fingers on the turned-down sheet now looking the other way, and my mother said that here in the hospital with the central heating he was much better off than at home and so they mustn't think of the expense, and besides he had to have X rays and all the tests, and anyway what counted most was that his bellyache had almost gone, only he had a bad taste in his mouth, but this happened to him because of his digestion nearly all the time, and she would have given him liver salts the way she always did but here in the hospital there were doctors and professors and they were the ones to decide, and my father let her go on saying all these things while he drummed his fingers on the sheet and every now and then pursed his lips as if to say hm, in short he didn't make even the slightest effort to believe what she said, he simply left himself to her and my sisters and the other relatives there in the room, and this turning himself over to the womenfolk could be a sign that he knew he was going to die, because when men die a Christian death they always have women around them, and for that matter women are more familiar than men with diseases and bad smells, just think of how they give birth, and it seems that they have a special tolerance and even a certain attachment for these unpleasant things, and in fact there were often arguments involving my five sisters and even my mother, each claiming the privilege of being closest to the dying man, but as for me the stink that came from his mouth or from somewhere or other was unbearable, so I spent most of my time in the corridor, a bit ashamed of feeling this disgust at my father, but especially thinking of the French widow, of the trouble she was bound to get me into, and sure enough a little later, with the excuse that I was tired from my trip and from the emotion of it all, I wanted to go back to the hotel, but my mother told me to wait because in a little while the doctor would come by and it would be fitting for me to speak to him since I was the only son and besides I was educated and could understand better than the others what the doctor might say about my father.

As it turned out my conversation with the doctor was fairly frank, however the main problem wasn't the conversation but the doctor himself, that is it was hard to reach an adequate estimate of him as a person, assuming that we can judge offhand a man who has chosen as his profession cutting up stomachs bladders and lungs, and in fact we always oscillate between two extremes, one consists in considering him a kind of priest inspired by a desire to succor his neighbor, while the other and more banal notion is that a man who chooses that path may not be inspired so much by missionary-like motives as by sadistic instincts, and anyhow he makes you pay through the nose for his succor, and certainly after a morning of handling the gallstones and cysts and tumors of suffering humanity, he goes home and eats spaghetti maybe followed by mixed fry of brains and artichokes as if it were nothing at all, which we wouldn't be able to do, but luckily this surgeon in

whose hands my father had ended up possessed an open face, a
confident manner, and beneath his white tunic you could see a
blue-striped shirt and a tie that didn't look the least provincial, and
all things considered, the only detail that struck me as out of place
about him were his yellow shoes all full of holes and seams with
thick soles, though these shoes cost plenty, English-style they're
called, but I've never been able to stand them, and obviously
though involuntarily a bit of the dislike I felt for his shoes finally
was reflected on their wearer, but with this man I wasn't to let
myself be influenced by shoes or anything else, I was to feel
affection towards him and trust, and to think, maybe forcing myself a little, that my father couldn't be in better hands, and in
reality maybe they weren't so bad since what he was telling me
was very simple and sensible, for the sick man, according to him,
had an intestinal occlusion, the X rays had shown this much with
absolute clarity, and to be precise, the barium couldn't get past
a block that had formed right at the point where the colon changes
direction and from being transverse begins to descend, and as to
the causes of the occlusion, well, it could be just a simple twisting
of the guts to put it crudely, but it could also be a tumor, maybe
a malignant one, cancer in short, and anyway it would all be
clarified tomorrow morning since he had decided to operate the
next day at nine to be exact, and he said this with great calm and
logic, and when things are explained in such an appropriate way
they never scare you, though there was that possibility of cancer,
and for a layman which I was after all the word cancer is always
connected with the idea of an inevitable and particularly unpleasant death, and in fact when you read in a death announce-
ment that some character has died of an "incurable disease" you
can bet nine times out of ten it's cancer, and my father for years,
ever since a cousin he was very fond of died of cancer, had got the
idea he was going to go the same way, and so I now found it
especially cruel though in a sense inevitable that his intestine
should be blocked by a damn cancer, and I said to the doctor that
it was all right, that he should go ahead and cut up my father's
stomach if he thought it necessary, but he was to do me a favor

and if by chance inside he found the feared cancer, well, I didn't mean he was to pack the old man straight off to the next world, but at least arrange things so he could go promptly without even waking up from the anesthetic. When you consider the shoes he was wearing, maybe I shouldn't have made him such a suggestion which apparently wounded his professional dignity, but I believe he was also thinking of the poor show a surgeon seems however wrongly to make when a patient dies under his knife, as they say, anyhow he acted as if I had suggested he kill a healthy person, whereas all I had really done was ask him to abbreviate the sufferings of a man who was headed for the next world anyhow, that is, I had proposed euthanasia, without any risk on his side because it's only very rarely that they make an investigation to see why patients die under the surgeon's knife, otherwise it would be tough on them, on the surgeons I mean, but this one wouldn't even allow euthanasia to be mentioned, and since his attitude was not only legal but also a matter of legitimate personal conviction, I went so far as to apologize, forget I ever mentioned it, I said, and since at heart he was a good guy, we were friendly again at once and he explained to me with glowing optimism that the operation in the eventuality of cancer would be a bit difficult but not absurd as I who knew nothing about it might think, because in elderly people cancer developed very slowly, and therefore once the present cancerous growth had been removed it would take years and years before another one developed, and my father in the meanwhile would die of old age and not of cancer, and as I listened to him I was almost persuaded, I imagined the operation as a trifle, a cut, out with the cancer, and then the two parts of the intestine sewed up again, then the wound sewed up, and in a week or a little more the old man would be strong as ever and ready to live out his life, but the doctor no sooner got a whiff of the way I was feeling when he said, all offended, that no, no, it wasn't such a simple task that just anybody could do it, first of all the tumor had to be exposed, at least I think that's what he said, and then left there sort of to dry up, and then cut it off, and in the meanwhile the intestine, opportunely sewed to the edge of the abdominal skin, would be strengthened a little to allow evacuation, all this being called an artificial anus, and as soon as I realized that, in the best of hypotheses, my father would evacuate his faeces through a hole in the middle of his belly a couple of inches from his navel, I was filled with a great pity for him and a sense of rebellion against the whole moral and social order, and I told the doctor that to my way of thinking anybody who kept a poor old man alive so he could expel excrement from a hole in the middle of his belly was a criminal or almost, and I went off angry, I went off naturally to the hotel, because the sight of my father now upset me more than ever, knowing what I did about his future artificial anus.

In the hotel, the woman, I mean the widow, was grumpy, she had been out and had spent a tidy little sum to buy some things but without any pleasure because there aren't any good shops in that city, and she wanted me to take her to Venice that afternoon where there are all the nice shops you could want, but when I told her how I had found my father in bad shape she started crying, and as she sobbed she said half in French that she didn't know him but it was as if he were her own father since he was mine, and she sobbed harder and harder until to comfort her I drew her to me and started hugging her, and a little later we even made love because that's how she worked, she liked to make love often and especially when she was sad, and then while she was asleep all relaxed in the big bed, I stayed on my side right at the edge as far as possible from her and I felt lousy, despite the sexual progress achieved thanks to the widow I still felt lousy and dirty after making love, but this time more than any other time even before the widow, because I had fornicated while less than ten minutes' walk away my father was proceeding towards his horrible cancerous death, and therefore, in an attempt to feel a little less miserable, I began to think that maybe it wasn't cancer, and in any case I could hope that the fairly optimistic doctor was right, and in the long run an artificial anus might even be preferable to death, you can never judge these things until it's your own skin you have to decide about, however, all things

considered, this line of thought wasn't too consoling, and I wondered who could give me a hand to boost my morale, surely not
the widow sleeping there with her body all satisfied, and then I
thought of telephoning a friend of mine who is assistant to a
famous surgeon in Rome, and in less than an hour the call came
through and the friend hardly let me finish explaining before he
started asking how old my father was, and when I answered that
he was over eighty, he said right out that since it was a laparotomy
he had maybe one chance in a hundred of pulling through, and
a slim chance at that.

So this was a fine consoling phone call, now I was so filled
with disgust at myself and everybody that I made an effort to
think how eighty is a considerable age, I'd have signed a pact
right then and there to live that long, maybe even a couple years
less, and generally speaking my father had had a far from unhappy life, never any sickness and plenty of satisfactions, from
nothing he had risen to become First Sergeant in the Carabinieri,
and then once he retired he had started selling hats, umbrellas
and caps, which for him was something, and then he had had an
affectionate and faithful wife and not all of his children had
turned out bad like me, and a house with a garden in front of
it which was his passion, and the games of bowls at the village
wine shop and latterly the card games because when he was almost
eighty his back began to hurt him and he couldn't bend down to
pick up the balls any more, and in short his life had been modest
but full and happy so now it wasn't all that unfair that he should
go, but God knows why, as I kept thinking all these basically
consoling thoughts, I got a lump in my throat, and infinite compassion for myself and for my father, so I began to think with all
my might I don't want him to die I don't want him to die, as if
the whole business depended on me, and finally I started to cry,
and I cried for a long time silently until I had almost forgotten
the reason why I was crying, and when the widow woke up because she was hungry she saw me in tears and seized the occasion for a cry, too, so then we had to make love again.

So, all in all, this operation of my father's wasn't a pretty or a simple thing, and since you could foretell how it was going to end, it seemed best for me to take precautions against any future remorse, that is, best for me to make my peace with that surgeon who was going to cut him open, and for this purpose I took my place early the next morning outside the door to the surgical wing, but when he arrived he didn't even remember who I was, he was so full of his own narcissism that the rest of mankind was a little hazy to him, however, after I had explained that I was the son of the retired carabiniere in room number four who was going to be operated on that morning for intestinal occlusion he really didn't show any signs of bearing a grudge, he even put his hand very affectionately on my shoulder and promptly walked on saying we've got it all under control, all under control, leaving me however very dubious though I don't see how I could have done anything else, especially since I was now convinced that from my father's point of view dying under the knife was less desirable than an artificial anus with which he could still, if not work the garden, at least play cards and read the *Gazzettino*, and this was why I wanted to make peace with the doctor so that any resentment he may have felt toward me wouldn't cause him to screw up the operation more than he could help, and now that I had done what I had to do, we were all together in the sick man's room to wait, with a certain solemnity, for something to happen, they had given him an enema the night before and even shaved his pubic hair so he was all ready, but the nun in charge of these matters came in to say that the doctor was doing another one first and we'd have to be patient. I don't know about my sisters, but I and perhaps my father too had a feeling that this operation was the final click of a mortal trap, and therefore a thing to be postponed as long as possible, however, since we had now reached this last waiting stage I think we were all in a hurry, it irritated us to be patient, even my father, I bet, who was drumming his fingers on the sheet and staring at the door to see when they'd appear to take him away, although from time to time he also looked at the numerous relations surrounding him, and seemed to be asking each one at least to explain the disaster that had befallen him, but strangely, when it came to my turn to be questioned, his eyes skipped me and went straight to the next person, so I almost wanted to ask him if he was angry with me by any chance, but of course this wasn't the time to ask such questions, given the circumstances and the other people present, especially because if queried on the subject of the disaster I could only have said that one way or another we all have to go when our time comes, and besides I hadn't got used to that stink he was giving off, and God knows how I would have managed if he'd asked me to come closer so he could say something to me or just to wet his lips, and therefore, after all, it was what you might call a stroke of luck that he didn't want me, however it was also a bit disconcerting to be treated like an outsider, me, his first-born and only son.

So it was a big relief when they came with the stretcher to carry him off, taking him to the operating room which was at the end of the corridor, beyond a pair of doors with frosted glass, and though he hadn't asked me, I walked all the way inside with him, staying next to the stretcher and then beside the operating table where they laid him, and now that I was the only familiar person around he was forced to look at me rather than anybody else, and he did look at me, but in a way I'd call hesitant and maybe also cautious, not very different from the way he looked at the surgeon and the other doctors and orderlies who were bustling around, and God knows why I remembered that the thing he'd said to me most often in my life was the prophecy that one of these days I'd end up in jail, however, this wasn't a nice thing to remember at that particular moment, so with a bit of effort I began to think maybe he'll die under the knife, maybe this is the last time my father and I will be together, never again never will we be together, we understood each other so little in our life and now it's too late, and with these and similar reflections I was better able to bear the awful smell, however, tears came to my eyes and a sense of mounting unhappiness, so I was almost comforted when they finally gave him the injection which knocked him out on the spot, and since I could then be of no more help to anybody in there I went out into the corridor where my sisters and the other relatives were pacing up and down sighing, and I soon realized that they were giving me dirty looks which they did without any regard or restraint, and wondering why they looked at me like that I decided it must be envy, they had always been envious of me because according to them I had a high old time in Rome earning plenty of money, and though this surely wasn't the best occasion to express such dishonorable sentiments I let them think what they pleased and I went to my mother who was in the old man's room. They had already remade the bed and laid out neatly on it were pajamas with a starched collar, again with blue stripes, which would presumably be of no use, and my mother was sitting on the little couch crying, so not even in the room could I feel relieved with my mother there crying, but that's life, and after a while I tried to console her patting her head and saying that Saint Anthony would help her, but devoted as she was to Saint Anthony she still went on crying and paid no attention to me at all, and one of my sisters who had followed me into the room intervened to say I was to leave mother alone because she wasn't only crying for our father poor man but also for me, who made her suffer, and by God this was more than I expected, that is her crying there on account of me, as I had nothing to do with the disaster that had befallen us, nor with any concomitant disasters to my way of thinking, but as soon as I tried to say something to invoke justice my oldest sister shut me up by saying that it was a shame and a scandal that I came from Rome to the bedside of my dying father bringing a fat slut along with me.

Now, to tell the truth, the widow I had brought up with me from Rome had her defects, but she wasn't a slut, you couldn't say that about her, no, she really loved me and would have been happy if I'd married her, and actually two or three times a week I was seized by the fear, only momentarily, that I might marry her, though I was opposed on principle to the institution of marriage, that is to say I would never get married and she knew this too, still there was a big difference between our situation and calling her a slut, even if to see her in certain shall we say culminating moments of love-making you might think she was a bit of a tramp, but I believe all women are like that, I bet even queens and princesses and my five sisters in the culminating moments of love lose their self-control to some extent, however, to hear them say in cold blood while only a few feet away they were cutting open my father than she was a slut was unthinkable, and above all unfair, and in fact I replied almost at once that this woman whom my oldest sister had called a bad name was my fiancée, and I could hardly have thought up a more unfortunate clarification because my mother started crying with greater grief than before, while my sisters with increased animosity hastened to speak their minds, one for instance saying that a fiancée who has any self-respect doesn't take a double room in a hotel with her intended, and that she couldn't see what I found beautiful or interesting in a woman like that with crooked legs, that I let myself be taken in like a fool because she gave herself airs and swallowed her *r*'s pretending to be a foreigner, that the fur coat she had on must have cost at least a million and a half, that now at last they knew why for almost a year I hadn't sent a penny home, and on and on, that the hospital expenses and the costs of the disease would be mine to pay, that the house needed urgent repairs or else it would tumble down and naturally I would have to take care of it, et cetera et cetera, and obviously I couldn't let them say all these thing to me without rebuttal, I answered that the fur coat was nothing to do with me, that she had it before I knew her and it came from Paris in case they didn't know, and they returned to the fray saying who knows what fancy man bought it for her, and I said I liked her as she was even a little bowlegged, and I had only met her three months before so it wasn't her fault if I didn't send much money home, I didn't send money because I was fed up with keeping the whole family, that I might take care of the hospital and the doctors, but not the house where I hadn't set foot for years, and I didn't care if it did fall down, and then the girls came back saying I was no better than a bum to talk like that about the house where I was

born, and they just would wait and see in event that, God forbid,
our father didn't survive this present disaster, whether I would
renounce my share of the inheritance seeing as how I didn't give
a damn about the house, and in short, we had a rambling, interminable argument and, under the circumstances, an inopportune though perhaps prophetic one, and therefore, before it could
degenerate any farther, I went out into the corridor where, thanks
to the presence of distant relatives and outsiders, they left me in
peace a bit, but meanwhile they had filled me with such fury that
I had a hard time thinking about my father there under the knife,
or rather I could just bet he was giving me dirty looks because
they had persuaded him that the widow was getting all my money
out of me, which above all would have been a stupid thing in his
dying state, and in short, more than anything else, I was thinking
that to have a family is by and large a big nuisance, it really
was in my case at least, and as for the house, just to spite them
I would demand my share though I honestly didn't give much of a
damn, one day maybe they'd put a marble plaque on it because I
had been born there but I didn't give a damn at that moment, and
would care even less the day when they put the plaque up. Meanwhile, as my mind skipped here and there, and in pondering on
the great ability my five sisters had for discovering the many
things they had discovered about the widow, I had almost forgotten what they were doing to our father poor man, for over an
hour he'd been in the operating room and we didn't know a thing,
but the fact that we knew nothing in a way was a good sign, because if he had died surely somebody would have come out to tell
us, anyhow it didn't seem such a bad idea for me to stick my
nose into what they were doing inside there, and instead this was
one of the worst ideas that had ever come into my head since the
day I was born, maybe the very worst even counting the idea of
my voluntary participation in the war and similar errors, however
I could hardly have imagined it at that moment, so without the
slightest suspicion I slowly went into the antechamber and then
into the operating room where they were already taking huge
stitches in the wound, finishing up the job as planned, and I saw

all those people terribly stained with my father's blood, and as I went forward I also saw the tumor exposed on his belly, I had always imagined that a cancer must be something disgusting but not as disgusting as it turned out to be in reality, nothing could have made me imagine that, big and disgusting and bloody, like the guts of a dead dog set on my father's belly and connected to him indissolubly by a mortal knot, and I felt like saying my God what an ugly death this is, isn't there some better kind, a death that is more suited to an honest, just man like my father, he was honest and just, he didn't get rich selling hats and umbrellas, and even when he was a carabiniere he didn't do any harm, when I was a kid I kept asking him how many robbers and bandits he had killed and he hadn't killed a single one, and though at the time this was a disappointment he really hadn't killed anybody, and now this honest and just man was there with all his fearsome disease exposed, his face and skull yellow, and his slack mouth gasping, he breathed with a deep rattle, filled with pain, and to hear him you couldn't believe he wasn't feeling pain, though the doctors assured me he wasn't, and the surgeon, his face sweating, and with all that blood on him, was very happy at the way things had gone, pleased with himself as he showed me the finished job, the tumor brought out, the intestine sewed together, the place where in due time, namely when the resection had been performed, the anal orifice would be so to speak moved, and he was satisfied because he probably didn't get many chances to perform a fine job of this sort, but I felt only pity and grief for the bloodless old man, I wondered what he would wear at that place, a little rubber sack no doubt, or maybe plastic now that they used plastic for everything, and what will become of the true orifice the rectum and the lower colon which will be superseded, and I was thinking above all about myself, if I'll have to die in such a cruel way, of all the deaths I had seen in peace or in war none was so cruel, and it had to be my own father's, and if it happened to him who was honest and just, God only knows what would happen to me, neither honest nor just.

Afterwards they took him back to room number four and at

least a dozen relatives crowded around him, and he was breathing
with a little less rattle than before but still with difficulty, and
his color was a more cadaverous yellow than ever, so much so that
if it hadn't been for his all too evident breathing he would really
have seemed dead, instead he was only unconscious because of the
anesthetic which would last they said another couple of hours,
and since I only remained in that room because of a tie of blood
and affection with the dying man, while all the others, including
my mother who kept crying and I began to wonder if instead
of my father's present catastrophe she wasn't weeping because I
had brought from Rome a foreigner that I was fornicating with
in violation of the sixth commandment, all the others, I say, were
indifferent to me, at least temporarily, I slipped out unobtrusively
and went back to the hotel, though I was going only from one
hostile atmosphere to another equally hostile, because that woman
was bored to distraction and wanted me to take her to Venice,
and when I said firmly that I hadn't come all the way from Rome
to entertain the likes of her but to assist my dying father, then
she answered that she too wanted to be at the side of my dying
father, along with me, of course, and she couldn't understand why
I hadn't yet introduced her to some of my family, at least to one
of the many sisters I had, and the more she wondered the more
she began to think that maybe I felt ashamed of my family in
front of her who came from the best Parisian society, but I was
stupid to think that because she would be nice to my family
even if they were humble people, it wasn't their fault they were
that way, and as a result I left her too there in the room and went
out into the foggy February day where you couldn't tell if it was
still day or already evening, with the people clumsily bundled up
in scarves and overcoats or raincoats, while in Rome at this hour
there might still be sunshine and pretty girls in the streets and
no thought of a bloodied father about to go up to heaven, if he
hadn't already gone up there.

I walked along the streets only to calm down, obviously, in a
state of nerves and without looking where I was going, the city
had nothing new to say to me anyhow, I had gone to school

there and also been in the army there for a while, I knew where
it was beautiful and where it was ugly, and I didn't give a damn,
I just walked around thinking a bit about my father and about all
my other troubles, and a bit also about when I was a boy and went
to high school, about a chaste and interminable love of mine for
a girl in teachers' college and God knows what had become of
her poor thing by now, almost forty, I suppose, whereas the next
woman I got involved with I wanted to be young, maybe even
one of those completely stupid girls who come to Rome to get
into the movies, but young, and in the meanwhile, maybe without
meaning to, I was going along a street where there was another
little side street that led to a brothel, and I suddenly felt like
going to see if it was still there, I remembered my embarrassment
and nervousness when I went there as a boy for the first time to
corrupt my innocence, maybe I still had a bit left, and anyway
then I was deathly ashamed turning toward the side street,
whereas now I had a skin like a rhino's and wasn't ashamed at all,
and the house was still there, there was the freshly painted door
and the brass plate with the name on it, and the little peephole
where they looked out at you before they opened, and I thought
to myself you want to bet I go inside, I want to feel that sense of
unlimited power that you feel when you go in and you have before you five or six girls who after all are human beings and you
can say I'll take this one or that one or that one over there whichever you want, it ought to be like that with all women and not
only with the professionals, in short I was about to go inside because I really needed a bit of that feeling of power, but then I gave
it up and I felt fairly praiseworthy for this sacrifice and I went
into some movie house, but then I realized what a terrible thing
it is to have a father who's dying, and instead of seeing the actors
on the screen I saw him with his mortal growth tied to his belly,
and I thought also in self-defense of what a faint tie united us,
me and him, yes, his seed had fertilized the egg from which I
had been formed in the maternal womb, but this had happened
almost forty years before, and God only knows how absent-
mindedly, maybe he didn't want to bring a son into the world at

that moment, or maybe he wasn't thinking about it, and as for me I have always preferred non-life to life, so it's no use discussing it and therefore this tie that binds us is a pretty casual one and not at all binding at least not from below so to speak, but meanwhile the thought that he was dying made me suffer so much that I had to leave the theater and run to the hospital to see if by any chance he was already dead.

He wasn't dead, he had waked up from the anesthetic though and was one big groan with his eyes shut, aah aah aah he kept saying, only the women could bear it, I was overcome by the idea of all that pain, so I went to the nun on this ward to see if something couldn't be done, but she had her own opinions about suffering, she thought very religiously that if a man suffers enough here below he spares himself God knows how many years of Purgatory in the next world, and my father had of course been to Confession and Communion before going under the knife but, in the past, he had lived outside the Church, as my mother had confided in her, so now he couldn't expect to go right straight up to Paradise, he was bound to have a spell in Purgatory, though with this suffering, provided he offered his pain up to Our Maker, as she hoped, he was storing up incalculable grace, and in any case, since I was fairly firm in dissenting from such theories, she said she wouldn't give pain-killing injections without orders from the doctor who had gone off without leaving any such order for patient number four, and he wouldn't be back till tomorrow morning, and there I said to myself what a lousy bureaucracy a man lands in if he isn't lucky enough to kick off suddenly, which on top of everything else is also economical, so I went to look for the doctor on night duty, a young man who when asked stated that he didn't attach any significance to Purgatory or Hell, still he didn't think morphine was at all necessary for my father, naturally a laparotomy wasn't an operation to be sneezed at but I needn't be scared if the patient groaned a lot, this happened so to speak automatically in a kind of torpor and he certainly wouldn't say my father was enjoying himself, quite the contrary, but surely he wasn't suffering as much as you might think he was suffering when you heard him groan, so it was best to leave him alone, in fact while we were on the subject he would take the liberty of saying that in room number four there were perhaps too many people, but since it was a first-class room there wasn't any regulation or limit in this matter so I should handle it myself if I felt like it, but what could I handle with all the ill will my sisters aimed at me, and as for my father I was all too painfully aware of my helplessness in the face of his agony, so I might just as well go on back to the hotel.

Naturally I didn't hope that going back to the hotel would relieve me of my troubles, however when I first arrived there I thought things could have gone even worse, in fact the widow was lying on the bed in the midst of a mountain of illustrated magazines, she had bought herself every magazine published, even German and Swedish ones I mean, as well as of course French, and her mouth was wide in a constant yawn, and clearly she had it in for me because I had left her alone in the hotel she would never have imagined that I was so provincial, the type to leave her alone in the hotel, but now she had had more than she could take, she had slept all afternoon and the idea of also spending the evening there frightened her, so I had to choose, either take her to my house or at least to the hospital where if nothing else she'd feel she belonged to the family somehow, or take her to Venice, she didn't care if I thought it was too late by now, and so to go to Venice we caught the bus in front of the Central Post Office, and the trip never seemed to end even if the lousy driver raced like a madman against the wall of fog over the highway, with a sound on the damp asphalt that seemed made by the poor souls in Purgatory, and headlights of other cars and trucks coming out of the milky darkness, this is it, I thought, now we're going to have one fine old accident, and me and this foreign widow will end up in the *Gazzettino* with our full names to the delight of my five sisters, but it pleased God to let us arrive safe and sound at Piazzale Roma, and there we took a *vaporetto* with the windowpanes dripping with condensed steam, and outside them the fog in which the *vaporetto* started wandering from one stop to the next, to load

or unload some lost soul, and after quite a few of these stops it
unloaded us too at the Rialto and then we realized what a silly
idea it had been to come to Venice, even she realized it obviously
but she would have died sooner than admit it, and I was thinking that it would be a long time before I took up with another
French woman, or French widow to be more precise, anyhow we
started walking along the Mercerie, deserted and full of fog,
and for her information I told her that the people who go to Venice
in the summer have no notion of what a stinking city it can be,
with the Piazza and the narrow streets which at fixed times fill
with people and at fixed times are emptied, just like Corleone
or Tropea or any other hick town in the province of Catanzaro,
but she replied that I was an ignorant provincial because that was
the real Venice full of fascination and mystery, though in the end
she too began to grumble because the windows of the famous shops
were either dark in which case she said *merde* because she couldn't
see anything or else they were lighted and then she said *merde*
why do they keep the lights on if you can't buy what you feel
like buying, and she wasn't entirely wrong unless she was planning
to insist on coming back the next day, but in the meanwhile we
had come to the square through the arch under the Clock Tower,
and there the fog, borne by a cold wind, came at you in tons
as if the Stygian swamps were facing us instead of the glorious
basin of Saint Mark's, since the only living being nearby seemed
to be a poor devil huddled behind a column with a pack of the
Gazzettino evening edition that he was hoping to sell God knows
to whom, so considering also what was happening in room number four in a hospital not too far away this was one of the most
desolate moments of my whole existence, and in fact when she
said why don't we go eat something I couldn't think of any objection, especially since I hadn't had anything but coffee since
the night before as near as I could recall and now my stomach
was all twisted up with the need for food, only I had to be careful not to order rare beef or anything else that might remind
me of an exposed carcinoma.

I ordered a seafood *risotto*, which is the only thing that makes

me homesick for Venice when I'm far away from it, but despite
its good smell of mussels and parsley and its absolutely inoffen-
sive color I still couldn't drive from my mind the sight of that
thing perched on my father's belly, so I wasn't able to swallow
more than a couple of mouthfuls and then I stopped and looked
at the plate with such sadness that she asked me if I was thinking about my father, and though at that moment it was a completely private feeling I answered yes and then she stopped eating
and stared at me her eyes brimming with emotion and held out her
hand affectionately to take one of mine and at the same time she
rubbed her knees and thighs against me under the table, and I
said to myself I bet this widow will want to make love on the
spot and maybe will force me to take a room, but after a little
while she dropped the tenderness and with a great sigh resumed
eating her *risotto* which was very good, and after the *risotto* she
ate a heaping plate of fried fish, and then an apple, and when she
had finally finished and I said now it was time to go home,
she wanted to go to the movies, but even if I had been willing we
couldn't have gone to the movies because it was too late and
afterwards we would miss the last bus, and the best thing was to
go straight home, however, she wouldn't hear of having come all
the way to Venice for nothing, and if it was downright impossible
to go to the movies then we had to go to the Casino, which was
surely the right place for me to free myself for a half hour at least
from the thought of my father.

Now I don't want to say I'm all that used to casinos or in general to places where high society amuses itself, in fact I had
never been inside a casino before then, nor did the present situation strike me as the best under which to take new steps of this
sort, but basically I was tired and submissive on that day so
crammed with wearisome troubles that I felt it had begun far
back, I couldn't even remember when it had begun, and in the
last resort it made no difference to me what we did so long as
we didn't miss the last bus which left I think just a bit before
midnight or a bit after, but when I saw how she stared wildly

at the little roulette ball and how greedily she waited for the croupier to give her the chips when she won and how sadly she saw them taken away when she lost, then I realized that the damned widow had one vice more than those I had before then suspected with some justification, so I soon dropped the idea of the last bus, resigning myself and summoning all my energy to defend the dozen ten-thousand-lire notes which were all I had left in my wallet. I wandered around the various rooms, far from her, praying in my heart not to meet any acquaintances who might later go and tell my sisters how the night when my father was dying or even already dead I was whooping it up at the Casino with the widow, and I also prayed *Non nobis Domine non nobis*, if for no other reason because these are the words which, God knows why, are written outside the building where the Casino is located, also wondering why the man who had thought of writing them hadn't had them put the whole verse which goes on to say *sed nomini tuo da gloriam*, which maybe means that this character was a bit like me who had prayed the Lord not to give me pestilence and famine and war, and if possible not even my father's death by cancer, but glory, that's what I would like, it was for glory that I had fought all my life ever since I came into the world you might say, though what I'd like to know is if a man starting out with a father who sells hats and moreover is President of a local chapter of the National Association of Retired Carabinieri can easily achieve any kind of success after all, so in the end I might just as well have gone on and prayed sincerely *sed nomini tuo da gloriam*, and meanwhile the widow at irregular intervals came to look for me and to ask each time for another ten thousand which was, above all, an embarrassingly low sum in a place like that, until about three in the morning when we had a nasty fight because after having given her seven ten-thousand-lire notes I didn't want to give her another, I didn't care so much about the hospital and the probable funeral but I couldn't borrow money to pay for the hotel and the return trip to Rome, so we ended that horrible night in the cold waiting room of the

station until they opened up for the first train which at four twenty
I think could take me away, and I kept thinking that if by chance
my father in the meanwhile had died or was dying it served me
right, it would teach me to get myself into lousy situations, which
were the very ones that had kept me from achieving glory so far,
not that I will ever achieve it now, I fear.

In any case my father wasn't dead, he was you might say arrested in the same condition as the previous evening only it was harder than ever to believe his groaning was merely automatic, if he kept groaning like that he must surely be suffering like hell, and in fact the only words he managed to say were it hurts Oh God how it hurts, and we were all in there suffering with him waiting for the surgeon who was supposed to arrive any minute, I with my sisters and relatives because my position in the family group had unexpectedly improved when they all saw my exhausted-looking face, and I really hadn't shut my eyes all night and this meant if nothing else that my vicious way of life hadn't stifled every last spark of decency in my heart, or in other words my father's suffering after all was causing me a bit of torment as was only right, and though undeserved this new condition of acceptance was in my best interest also because it would have been quite unwise for me to confess how in fact I had spent the night with the overall expense of almost eighty thousand lire, a sum which God knows why in my roster of griefs forced itself into an important place along with my father's death agony and my extreme weariness spiritual as well as physical, in any case thank God around eight the surgeon arrived still wearing those unfortunate yellow shoes, maybe he only had one pair of shoes or maybe several pairs but all alike, and he glanced at the temperature chart, and glanced also at my father who was clinging to him with his eyes and his soul, having even stopped groaning, and he said everything was going well as far as the general condition was concerned, he even congratulated the old man who had a physique many a youngster could envy, as he put it, and then he went off in his puppetlike manner, that is with every movement of his legs and arms and even his smile worked by invisible strings, and after he had gone out our father looked at all of us with knowing dismay, in the absence of the doctor he wanted to cling to each of us even to me, but since there certainly wasn't much to cling to he said that fellow can say what he wants about everything going well but the fact was he felt he was dying, and he asked all of us for the love of God to help him in this situation because there was too much suffering, Oh Lord, how much suffering there was before the end of it.

Now it wasn't easy to stand there inert and dazed with sleepiness before a man who was complaining like that, especially seeing him yellow and cadaverous when you remember how strong and heavy he was and practically invincible, it was really painful and too full of suffering this ending of his life, so I ran after the doctor or rather I waited for him at the door of number two and when he came out I asked him in a polemical tone if it was really necessary to make a human being suffer so much before letting him die, that for me his conduct and that of the other doctors not to mention the nuns who were so-called nurses bordered on sadism, or on a pathological pleasure in making your fellow man suffer, but that doctor really was good-natured he didn't take offense at all, and even said he excused me because I was obviously worn out and I loved my father but the patient wasn't doing at all badly according to him, he was a hearty oldster who would still fight more battles, but in the meanwhile, yes, if I really wanted, he would have them give him an injection of morphine, in fact he immediately instructed one of his assistants to see to it, and so things were a little better for the old man his groans gradually seemed to come from farther and farther away, until he even dozed off a little his carcinoma also sleeping on his belly, and to tell the truth at this point I would also gladly have gone off to sleep, my head was spinning with fatigue, and I wanted to vomit all the coffees that I had drunk since the day before, in addition to the sofa there was also a second bed in the room where during the night my mother rested taking turns with whichever of the five sisters won the fight to stay with her father, and now that bed was full of seated relatives whom I would happily have shoved aside if it had been possible for me to lie down and sleep, but of course it wasn't possible or rather not without causing grave scandal, so I sat there on a very uncomfortable chair, my head swaying first this way then that, waking at times with a start and always with an unpleasant sensation at seeing the place where I was in case I had forgotten about it, and finally one of my sisters I don't now remember which but God bless her anyhow came and said why don't you go home and sleep, and she really meant home and not the hotel since she gave me the long key that opens the door of our house, and to tell the truth this fitted in precisely with my own ideas because I didn't have the least wish to go back to the hotel and the French widow, since she had made me lose a night's sleep plus about seventy thousand lire at the Casino.

So I took the bus and in less than an hour I was in the fog of my home town, with my overcoat collar all turned up against the cold and also so people wouldn't recognize me and force me to tell them how I was and how the old man was and how things were in Rome, and did I by chance know some cardinal or senator or TV actress or better still announceress, but luckily the fog was really thick and not a sign of sun in the sky though it was almost noon, and I walked along the road to the house all mud and puddles being careful to set my feet in the driest spots, when I was in Rome or anywhere else it never occurred to me to think of my town in this lousy season, I always pictured it in the spring or summer when it isn't so damn ugly, but this is natural since

I thought of my town only at times when in desperation I couldn't do anything else, or at the times when I realized that for me any glory or even lasting security was far in the future, and maybe it had all been a mistake for me to leave the place where I was born, and to make the despair at my mistake even worse I pictured the town as less ugly than it was, while in reality it was ugly, and even the house was ugly with its four trees dripping fog in the garden inside the wire fence, and the bare vines growing wild, and the abandoned garden where only a few cabbages grew born at random and some grass which seemed burned by the frost, and in short nothing you looked at with a bit of relief, and finally the house itself which couldn't be said to have any architectural nobility, in fact our father had had it built a little at a time beginning when he gave up being a carabiniere to please our mother who would never marry a carabiniere again, so it was quite mistaken to demand any architectural nobility from all this, and in the final analysis it wasn't one of those houses which look well with a marble plaque saying here was born a famous man, and this is another thing that should be taken into account by me and by everyone else before judging me too severely as a failure on the road to glory.

The key to the gate was in its usual place on top of the post, as my sister had reminded me, and the key to the house as usual didn't work, and while I stood there in the fog and cold sweating until I found the right spot to make it turn a cat came out to rub its bastard fur against my pants, the house cat of course which hadn't found anything to eat for four or five days, obviously not the same cat as when I was at home, but it was all one to him, and to me too really, for he helped me establish a difficult sentimental equilibrium as I was after all returning, if only through a sad accident, to the house in which I was born, moreover taking with me that presentiment of definitive failure which lingered in my mind after the thought of the plaque. Anyhow before giving way to emotion it was best for me, with some Saint's intercession, to help that damned key find the right point in the lock which nobody had bothered to replace, but if they didn't change it I was damned if I would, and heaven only knew when I would be using it again, and in any case, thank God, the key found the right spot and we went into the house, the cat and me, in the house as cold as an icebox, straight to the kitchen where there was a smell of spent fire to look in the cupboard for something to eat, we found a plate with some cooked greens and a piece of cheese almost all crust and a couple of slices of polenta, and the cat wouldn't touch the greens but he ate the cheese with a hearty appetite, and then he began to eat the polenta keeping me company, while I looked around trying to establish a relationship however uncertain between myself and the walls and the old objects like the cupboard and the table and the sink, but it seemed to be too cold for any such attempt to succeed, and meanwhile the cat had eaten all the polenta and was meowing because he wanted something more, but when I didn't give him anything he went off to meow in front of the door which I then had to open and let him out, and I remained alone in the house immersed in all the chill accumulated over so many winters since it had been built with the money saved up, coin by coin, by the man who was now dying, and to tell the truth a bit also with my money on certain later occasions, but anyway the house was his because of the meaning he had given it: family and hearth and food eaten together on the solemn holidays, while for me it had chiefly been a kind of trap from which I had to escape at all costs if I wanted to get anywhere, and now obviously it wasn't the same in the sense that my escape had led to precious little when you thought about it, however, it wasn't a refuge either or a place to go back to after you've made too many mistakes and for that matter I still hadn't made that many, so the house, birthplace though it was, didn't mean anything substantially, not even the upper floor where there was the magnificent bathroom, crystallized in the frost, with its pink mosaic tile and the gleaming fixtures, nor in the bedrooms especially since my own room didn't exist any more apparently, the desk had vanished and the shelf of books and personal objects which, in any case, I had abandoned there, it had become the room of my oldest sister or the one after her with a dressing table with mirror and ribbons and plenty of cosmetic jars, only right after all since they certainly couldn't keep a room at the disposal of somebody who showed up every five years and always in a hurry to get away again, still when I saw my room gone I suddenly felt more rootless than a minute before when I still didn't know I was without it, and moreover now I didn't have a bed to fling myself on, I was trembling with cold and my head was spinning and I felt my mouth burning from the smoke of I don't know how many cigarettes, and yet I wanted to light one more, so then I picked out my parents' double bed and lay on it in my overcoat pulling the featherbed up over me, lying on my father's side because there on his bedside table was the old ashtray of rusty metal where he set the butts of his Virginias, and then of his Toscani when he decided to change his brand of cigars because nowadays you couldn't find decent Virginias any more, I had always heard him grumbling about his cigars except for two very special ones that had been given to him by the Soldier Poet at the time of the First World War, because it was my father himself who commanded the Carabinieri guarding the Casetta Rossa and one day D'Annunzio, as a reward and encomium, made him a present of two fancy cigars, so fancy that my father had never had the courage to smoke them, and singing their praises he preserved them in the first drawer of the dresser until one day I stole them to smoke them myself under rather unfortunate circumstances connected with my scanty supply of ready cash, but the cigars had become awful full of holes dusty and moldy, they couldn't be smoked. I thought of this funny matter of the two cigars as an episode revealing how unwise my father was in practical matters, for him one of the most delightful of pleasures was to postpone to some vague future the satisfaction of sensuous needs, and in this respect he was right to feel I was different from him, and in fact in the end I was the one who smoked or tried to smoke his cigars, however I didn't hide from myself the fact that in those days, that is when my father was still alive and even for a little while afterwards, I preferred to recall the aspects of him that could show how different he was from me, and not the aspects that made him resemble me, or rather me resemble him, to be exact inasmuch as he had preceded me in this life and indeed I descended directly from him thanks to an operation which in all likelihood had been performed in the very bed where I was lying and where in fact I had been born, I like my five sisters who had followed me, so this was a fairly important bed, within the limits obviously of our family history, and now I was in it fighting sleep and cold, and at the same time I was thinking I wonder how many times the old man has made love in this bed, maybe thousands of times if he was endowed as I believe he was with normal glandular efficiency, unless making love was one of those satisfactions he believed better postponed to a future date, but he was surely too physically healthy to believe such nonsense, and all things considered, I was busy imagining that my father had been a robust lover so he could close up the books of his life in the black at least in this respect, which isn't a minor detail in the final summing up of a man's existence, though when we're on the point of death our past sexual activity isn't much of a consolation, and in addition I always had some trouble in picturing my father in the act of possessing my mother, and this derived from my disappointment on the day when somebody explained that I couldn't claim I was born under a cabbage plant, or brought down from heaven by a stork, or by any other acceptable system, but like all the other people in the world I came from certain things that my father had done in bed with my mother, except that I didn't give a damn about the other people in the world and apart from the diminution of my self-importance that derived from this system, I couldn't bring myself to approve my father's doing such things with my mother, and therefore I hated him then with all my might, and even now I almost hated him a little when I thought of my tribulations at that time, though it was ungenerous to think of this particular thing while he was about to pass on, indeed he had already passed on as far as these problems were concerned, in the sense that it was unlikely he would now be able to add anything new to the knowledge we had one of the other, and it was a poor knowledge to tell the truth, so before I fell asleep I had reached the conclusion that I knew little of him and he almost nothing of me.

When I woke up there was fog outside the window and night and I didn't know what time it was because I had forgotten to wind my watch, under the featherbed it was nice and warm now and I was feeling good except for a slight headache and the taste in my mouth from smoking, but the first thing I did was light another cigarette and lie there smoking it, thinking of my father, thinking of him calmly I'd say that is bringing up rationally the main question which was if he would live or not, though this wasn't exactly the main question which was the other one would he accept or wouldn't he the artificial anus if he did survive, and according to me he wouldn't accept it he had too high an opinion of his health and physical strength to accept such a mess, he certainly feared old age and illness more than death I knew this well especially because of an episode I now remembered vividly though it had taken place many years earlier, in the last stretch of our struggle's first phase, a period when I was think-ing with secret bitterness what does this old bore want from me just because he brought me into the world, and a big favor that was, nothing I do ever suits him, and at least four or five times a day he would prophesy that I was going to end up in jail, and though I swore to myself I wouldn't pay the least attention to him nevertheless I couldn't shrug off those prophecies without feeling a slight annoyance, also because I was young and not yet sufficiently wise in the ways of the world, I was in my second year of *liceo* then, or maybe my first, and it was during the summer vacation, I had to take a make-up exam in October in chemistry or physics or mathematics depending on which year it was, any-way it was only one subject and not even a very important one in view of what we might call my literary bent, so I didn't need to wear myself out studying anyway they wouldn't be such bastards as to flunk me in October for a single subject, but my father had it in for me especially because I got up late in the morning, and to tell the truth I did get up a little late, around ten or maybe even noon depending on how late I had been out the night before with my friends, whereas my father on the contrary had a mania for getting up at dawn, in the summer at four or a little later, and he had another mania for tending the garden, I had always heard him complaining that it wasn't worth the trouble that it was a waste of time and labor that you couldn't get a goddam thing from that ground which was clay for making bricks and not gardening land, but every spring he started hoeing all over again, lining up the furrows scientifically, fertilizing them with stinking liquid from the cesspool, planting and transplanting and watering when summer came especially, and in short this business with the garden was a true though to me incomprehensible passion. So at four or a little after he would start drawing water up from the well making a hellish racket with the pulley and chain, and then cursing in a loud voice that the buckets were heavy as lead, and to be precise they weren't buckets but old kerosene drums fitted out with handles, so his cursing wasn't entirely unjustified, but he also shouted at my mother who was always beside him, he shouted that he was tired of killing himself to support certain people who slept until noon, he shouted that he had had enough of feeding certain bums who would surely end up behind bars to the dishonor of the family, he shouted that certain sons who had no conscience would find themselves kicked out of the house one of these days, and obviously he had it in for his first-born, he made the noise on purpose and shouted to wake me up, but even if I woke up I didn't give him the satisfaction of showing it, I rolled over on the other side and tried to go back to sleep asking myself what right he had to nag at me like that just because he had achieved the great feat of procreating me as they say, until one morning came when instead of curses and shouts I was waked up by a great racket of tin drums and moans and groans, I bet he's broken his neck this time I thought, and I rushed to peek through the shutters which I left slightly open because of the heat, and I saw him sprawled out on a little path between two furrows, with my mother in despair because she couldn't pull him up, get up she was saying, don't frighten me so, get up man it isn't anything, and he lay

there with a groan as if he had broken God knows what, finally
he pulled himself to his knees all covered with mud because the
water from the two buckets had spilled all around on the path,
he knelt there looking at his hands and his undershirt and his
pants stained with mud, and all of a sudden he started crying,
really sobbing loud without any shame, saying I'm an old man,
look at the state I'm in, Oh Lord Lord I'm old, and with part of
my mind I was amazed that he had only now become aware
of this since to my eyes he had seemed old for ages, but with the
other part I understood what a terrible thing it must be to feel
the way my father was feeling at that moment, and I almost wanted
to run down and start crying with him and maybe carry the
buckets of water for him, but with a father like him you couldn't
dare do such a thing because he was capable of saying get your
ass away from me, or he might have called me a bum, the way he
always did, so I stood still and watched this pitiful scene through
the crack between the shutters, then I went back to sleep, and
when I faced my father at the midday meal he had the same
grumpy face as always, so the whole business earlier that morning might never have happened, however I remembered it now
as I lay there on that bed of his long life, and I remembered it
to convince myself that if he found himself still alive with an
artificial anus halfway down his belly maybe he would wish not
to be alive, and in reality I was praying he was dead, there was a
Saint Anthony of silver-plated nickel on the other bedside table,
my mother's, and I said to him, Saint Anthony let him die without knowing about the artificial anus, if you have any influence
try to have him go without suffering too much pain and humiliation and decay, but maybe Saint Anthony couldn't do anything
about it or maybe I wasn't able to exert any pressure on him in
questions of such dubious propriety, for the fact is that when I got
to the hospital around ten that night my father was still alive and
struggling against his death, but so painfully that you could
only hope he would have a sudden stroke, I ran to the nun on the
ward and then to the doctor on night duty raising hell because
they wouldn't give him morphine even at the risk of sending him

straight to the next world, so they gave him some and after a little while he dozed off, he even managed to snore with his mouth slack in a frightening gape, however, all in all, it seemed to me that I had done a good thing about the morphine, but my mother and my sisters either refused to look at me at all or if they did they glared at me with reproach and ill will, and I said to myself rightly just look at this family I've found again, why couldn't I have been an only child or better still a foundling, at least I wouldn't have to sit up with dying fathers and get reproaches from the others for my trouble, what have you got against me now I couldn't help asking at a certain moment, and as if I had committed a new crime, my mother started crying sadly and then my oldest sister took me by the arm and dragged me out into the corridor and said to me show some respect for your mother at least with all the sorrows she has already, that woman had the nerve to come to the hospital looking for you, shameless that's what she is, and you're shameless too to bring such a person up with you, all painted up till she looks like a streetwalker, you were such a good boy when you were at the Salesian Fathers' boarding school, now you're ruined and you don't give us a thought even when we are in need, and on and on like this though with an occasional hint of hope that I would see the light, until when I was finally able to have the floor I said to her, why don't you mind your own business, all of you, it would do you good, why don't you take a look at yourselves, you bunch of beauties, and then I went off while, embittered by my attitude, she continued to explain that it was their business and that foreign hussy wasn't to dare show herself again at the hospital because she would tell her to her face that our family didn't want whores like her around, and this finally was a slightly consoling revelation because if the matter was still in the threat stage I could hope she hadn't said as much already, and therefore the situation with the widow wasn't yet completely ruined, maybe.

In reality when I got to the hotel I found an unusually considerate note from her in which she said that she had slept all day and therefore she was going to the movies to see I forget what, and if I wanted to I could join her there or else I should go straight to bed so when she came back she would find it nice and warm, in fact this was her advice to me darling darling, so if she was thinking of making love the clash with my oldest sister at the hospital couldn't have been too serious or at least she didn't think it useful to recall it, so on that front thank God I could foresee a calm night, but as for making love she could go to hell, and yet not knowing what else to do except go to bed, I did, thinking I wouldn't fall asleep since I too had slept practically all day, and yet I fell asleep almost at once though I wanted to stay awake and think calmly about this big mess of my father which was a mess whether he lived or died, and in fact I think this was the very reason that I fell asleep, namely to escape all these thoughts with no solution, and when she came back about one she began to wake me up by tickling my face with her hair and saying in French darling darling like so many other times, and besides she had brought me a little packet of chocolates which I ate right away one after the other because I suddenly discovered I was terribly hungry, God only knows how long it had been since I had had anything except coffee and this last day only orange juice because with the coffee I was afraid to vomit, and maybe vomit blood because of my duodenal ulcer that was hurting something awful, and meanwhile without even hinting at visits to the hospital and family encounters she began to undress, dropping her things here and there at random since she was in a hurry, and in fact as soon as she was naked she lay down under the covers with her make-up on and everything, saying how nice to find the bed warm, and then we made love of course, I went through with it having only death in my mind, my father's death and my own too when it was to come, and right after love she fell fast asleep while I remained wide awake with my thoughts of death, poor old man I thought of my father and tears came to my eyes, he might even have died at the very moment when I was thrashing around over the widow senselessly or in any case with only my sex, here it was two in the morning and I had done that business at about one thirty, and all of a sudden I was sure that to my eternal remorse the old man had died precisely at one thirty, after all these cases of telepathy do occur by which a person knows exactly what is happening at a distance, in fact I could imagine I was my father and could feel the cold and stiffness of death in me, my God now I absolutely had to know the truth whatever it was, so I took the telephone and called the hospital to learn if number four surgical ward had died by any chance at one thirty, and somebody at the other end half-asleep kept asking what what, and I skipped the part about the precise time and said I was the son of number four surgical ward and I wanted to know please how was he, and the other person said all right and went off and after an infinity of anguish he came back and said that number four in the evening had a temperature of ninety-nine, had rested quietly the first part of the night, but now he was fretful and restless but this happened with all patients after an operation and there was nothing to worry about, and as I listened to these things I felt a bit relieved but I also saw with extreme clarity the unhappy calamity I had fallen into, namely a father who wasn't dying but who wasn't going to live either, and suddenly I felt I couldn't stand this family situation any more with my five sisters and the widow I had brought with me, I didn't want to go crazy or even fall ill since now the chocolates were weighing on my stomach like so many bricks, and the duodenum a little farther down was writhing in spasms, and a little farther still the memory of that disgusting growth was concentrating, so finally when it was seven in the morning leaving the widow to sleep the sleep of the just I got up and went to the hospital to have a frank talk with that damned doctor, I had to catch him before he started his rounds and was distracted by other treatments, and I did catch him and said that to my way of thinking a man who had lived for eighty years had lived more than enough so I wasn't going to make a tragedy of it if by chance my father was to kick off in the present situation, but he was to tell me without any hemming and hawing if he thought the old man was about to die or not because my father himself thought he was on the point of death since nobody could suffer what he was suffering unless he was going to die, and though I was a layman as I watched him and heard him I had come more or less to the same conclusion, and moreover I had had a good look at that big exposed tumor, and with a thing like that going wrong and growing inside him it seemed to me a man was bound to die, maybe even a younger man than my father, but he was the doctor and surely knew better than we did how things stood only he was to tell me without any fear of scaring me because I didn't scare easily, what with one thing and another I had had five or more years of war so I was pretty familiar with death, and he answered without acrimony that he was surprised that I had so little faith in him or at least paid so little attention to what he said since I kept asking him the same questions and saying the same things, everything was under control and what more did I expect, my father's temperature had never gone above a hundred and his pulse was steady and his blood pressure good too, of course the pain was great but we had to be patient because it was best to go easy on the morphine, and as for the tumor properly speaking tomorrow or the next day he would resect it and then when the artificial anus which was all ready and waiting went into operation my father would be fixed up better than before you might say, and when I heard him talking like this I almost kissed his hands, because you see, in Rome I left a lot of business matters untended to, work and engagements and deadlines, and naturally if my father were in the slightest danger I wouldn't leave, to hell with business and the rest, but since things are the way you say they are, I can go back to Rome with a clear conscience also because I know that I'm leaving him in good hands.

Now the hard thing was to explain this to my father, during the three days I had been there he hadn't seemed to take much notice of me, which was no more than right since he was all taken up with his mortal suffering and hadn't any time to devote to a superfluous being such as I was basically, or maybe not so much superfluous as encumbering, if for no other reason than the foreign widow, but now that I said to him look I'm going back to Rome he suddenly seemed interested also in my presence, I even had the impression that with his almost exhausted gaze he was saying I wish you wouldn't go, you help me too in this desperate pass, only his breath stank horribly and God knows so did the filthy growth on his belly, and then I said you see my going is a good sign, I had a long talk with the doctor and you can be sure I wouldn't leave unless everything was under control, and stopping his groans for a while he started drumming his pallid fingers on the sheet which was at least a symptom of hesitation, but also of vitality all things considered, and I said to him that I would never be leaving him if he weren't really out of danger so he wasn't to worry, and besides I would take care of all the hospital expenses present and future, nobody was to worry about that since after all I was the oldest and the only son, and anyway as soon as I could, in a week or two, I'd run up to celebrate when he went home all cured, and then I hurried out because I didn't want to see whether or not he was believing the lies I was telling, basically I was responsible only up to a point if he didn't believe them, for God's sake, the doctor himself had told me the same lies only a moment before, not to mention the fact that while they were lies for me for the doctor they were scientific verities, and they could very well be the same for my father, so I could go off without great problems on my conscience or anything else, and when my mother walked with me to the door of the wing I said don't worry Signora Augusta everything's going to be all right, and to the pair of sisters who were assisting my mother I said let me know how much the hospital costs and I'll send you the money from Rome, and then good-bye, never on leaving my homeland and family had I felt such urgency as this time, Manzoni wasn't in it with his farewell, mountains rising from the waters and such nonsense they teach you in school, but I hadn't even got to Rome so to speak when my oldest sister telephoned me to say he died last night at four o'clock, no he didn't ask for you, he didn't look for you, yes he suffered terribly poor thing he was conscious right up to the last minute they even gave him Extreme Unction, how should I know, the doctor said everything was going fine only his heart didn't hold out, she said these things with great difficulty because she was crying a lot and I answered quickly I have to wait until nine when the banks open and then I'll take the first train, and in fact before that evening I was back again in that smelly little provincial hospital, not in the surgical wing but in the icy mortuary cell, and I gave a five-hundred-lire tip to the doorman or gravedigger or whatever he was, five hundred lire to leave me alone for a few minutes with my dead father, and somewhat puzzled he left me alone although maybe it occurred to him that I might dramatically hang myself over my father's corpse, but I wasn't thinking at all of suicide and actually though a bit moved I hadn't yet any notion of how things were about to change because of this death, in fact I felt fairly peaceful and I said to him forgive me for leaving you alone when you were dying but tell me what was the use of my staying, and besides if you ask me it's a sign I loved you otherwise I wouldn't have gone off, another proof is that in the war plenty of times I stayed easily enough with people who were dying though they were strangers who didn't mean much to me, and anyhow so it goes old man what can we do about it now, of course there is that business of the lousy smell and you might say that if somebody really loves you he can swallow the stink and more besides, when you love a person you stand everything, sure you're right but on the other hand you had plenty of satisfactions in life, except for this last week of suffering life went very well for you, so don't complain old man, and anyway you'll see, I'll end up much worse than you, but there wasn't much point in my reasoning with him as he lay there dignified and remote finally at peace, and I wasn't at peace, no, despite my efforts to make myself think so, my God my whole life had been nothing but a series of lazy evasions of my father up to this last flight at the moment when he was about to give up the ghost, after all male children can be of some use at the supreme moment, but then even if I hadn't been of any use my father was old-fashioned enough to want a fine patriarchal death with all his offspring around and instead, his first-born and only son had sneaked off at that very moment, and so as I subtilized about my various sins especially recent ones toward my father it occurred to me to have his photograph taken, after all it seemed a pretty good idea because as far as I know they only photograph dead people when they are fairly important, Lenin or Marconi for example or the President of the United States, and after having attached scarce importance to my father all through his life now that he was dead I made an act of reparation setting him on a plane with the most illustrious figures, which I think must have given him great satisfaction in the event, however improbable, that he found out about it, but here it was more than anything else a question of easing my own conscience so I had a man come with a Rolleiflex and flashbulbs who shot a whole roll of film full-face and profile as I directed him, giving him rather good directions in general, and I felt a certain bitterness at the thought that for many years I had pursued the mirage of becoming a film director and now here I was directing a provincial photographer snapping my father in his black wedding suit waiting to be laid out in his bier or coffin or whatever.

Then there was the funeral in the village with a first-class hearse since I had told my sisters to do as they pleased and not to worry about the expense, and there were a couple of sprays and various wreaths, and the pastor in person who followed the bier with both his chaplains, and a number of sincere mourners because my father was a true gentleman of the old school, they all said as much and especially the six or seven members of the National Association of Retired Carabinieri who were there in an official capacity with the banner of the local chapter, and in other words the whole thing was more than decorous and even the deceased would have found nothing or very little to criticize, and also the place of burial had been appropriately chosen, one of the niches in the new wing of tombs where all the people of a certain social standing were put, and I thought well old man you'll be happy now that you have somehow achieved your middle-class ambitions, here you're in the midst of doctors, lawyers and landowners, rest your soul, and forgive me if I didn't have them carve on the stone Citizen of Great Worth, upright and honest, and not even Retired Sergeant of the Royal Carabinieri, and not even Respected Merchant which was the title that for want of any other you set great store by despite your lack of success, and besides you had sold the shop some years ago making your last ill-advised business transaction so to be strictly correct you weren't a merchant any more, but to you it seemed terrible not even to be a Cavaliere, and I know that you thought that being in Rome I could have had you made at least a Cavaliere without any effort, you thought that I was on intimate terms with senators and maybe even cabinet ministers, whereas I really don't know anybody who can make a man a Cavaliere however upright and honest he is, or to be frank I have never bothered to get to know even the undersecretaries or the administrative chiefs of the ministries, so be content with just your first and last names written on the stone, first name first and not last the way you used to write it, but never mind, a man belonging to the professional class doesn't sign his name that way, although you would never get this simple fact through your head.

Then there was a private family reunion for the reading of the will since our father was an orderly man and kept his last will and testament scrupulously up to date, it consisted of a document long and complicated like all the writings of carabinieri sergeant-quartermasters even retired ones, with many turns of phrases and maxims of a moral nature in which the syntax was finally altogether lost, despite which we managed to figure out that our mother was to keep everything that is the house and two million eight hundred and forty thousand lire remaining from the sale of the store which was safely deposited in an account at the local Savings Bank, and though some of the sisters raised the objection that in leaving things this way the former sergeant-quartermaster was violating the law and depriving his children of their legal share, in the end we all agreed that our mother in substance at least if not in form would inherit everything, excluding personal objects and clothing which my sisters could take to ingratiate themselves with their respective husbands or in-laws, while with great discretion I took possession only of a necktie that I had given the old man myself five or six years earlier, and he had never worn naturally, nor have I ever worn it obviously, to tell the truth I don't even know where it's ended up, however I'm sure I took it, and in fact I believe I must have been a bit sorry the old man had died inasmuch as I did more than one useless thing like the tie and the photographs, in fact in my haste to leave after the agreement on the will I had completely forgotten about those photographs and now, in the train heading for Rome, I was thinking of quite different matters, thinking for example that old Signora Augusta with two million eight hundred and forty thousand lire was richer than I, who had never seen that amount of money at one time and was unlikely ever to see it, so for the moment she could look out for herself, especially since I had a rather skimpy period ahead of me economically speaking, and I went on to think, secondly, but it could also have been firstly, that once I was in Rome I would take a new apartment because I honestly couldn't put up with the French widow any longer, we had quarreled again before I left because she had got it into her head she was coming to the funeral, so now I would promptly take a new apartment telling her that from now on if she wanted to go to the movies with me from time to time or have dinner somewhere that was all right, and even if she wanted to make love once in a while I'd be glad to, at my house or at hers whichever she preferred, but no more living together, I had realized that I just wasn't cut out for these things, and besides I had to be alone to increase somehow my working output and obviously my income, since I had been left so to speak the head of the family, and maybe it was this idea of being head of the family which was connected however loosely with the death of my father and reminded me of the funeral photographs, so I said to myself that I must write to the photographer to send them to me C.O.D.

And less than a week later the photographs reached me at the address of the hotel I had given, after fleeing somewhat brusquely from the widow's house, and I took the heavy envelope to the new little furnished apartment I had rented meanwhile in the Parioli district, not chosen because I was putting on airs but because the widow lived in Monteverde Nuovo and Parioli is one of the sections of Rome farthest from Monteverde Nuovo, and with this I don't want to deny that maybe hidden inside me there might have

also been a fundamental desire to change my way of life, that is
to make it less sad with the sight of pretty, well-dressed young
girls which you happen to find before your eyes more frequently
in Parioli than elsewhere, so to the new house I took the envelope
with the photographs and along the way I thought how in just a
week my father's death had become remote as if it had happened
three or four years before, maybe for a whole day I never happened to think of it, and then when I did think of it I always told
myself the old man had led a full and happy existence if it hadn't
been for that last, unfortunate week of suffering, but what is a
week compared to a life of more than eighty years, so all in all
I was in a fairly comforted mood, therefore it would be wrong to
say that the photographs' arrival aroused any special emotion in
me, even when I looked at them I didn't feel anything special although there were the ones taken with Mantegna-style fore-
shortening which were a complete mistake, as a director in fact I
was ridiculous since I hadn't noticed that the deceased's left eye
wasn't completely shut which in the foreshortened pictures gave it
an unexpected importance not at all attractive, while the other
photos, the ones taken from above and especially the ones in
profile, weren't bad, however I wouldn't have sent them to my
mother or my sisters who would have been capable of shedding
God knows how many tears over them, and so there I was the sole
owner and so to speak beneficiary of those photographs, but what
the hell could I do with them for God's sake and where could I
keep them, now finally I realized that the photographs of a dead
father are a useless thing and even more annoying than they
might seem, and in short this was the first act of open hostility and
let's go ahead and say vengeance that my father performed
against me after his change of condition, but at the time I wasn't
even thinking about this possibility of our struggle's being perpetu-
ated, I imagined that once dead and buried he was all finished, so
when I had put the photos back in their envelope I stuffed them
into the bottom of a drawer without much thought, and then a few
months later when by chance they came to hand again and I had
the curiosity to look at them I was already ill, and then they did

make me feel at once their subtle and treacherous potency, I mean that they were the start of or at least an extraordinary stimulus to that process of identification which at present is having its natural and inevitable fulfillment. It's obvious that at the beginning, especially because of my inexperience and ignorance of modern psychological doctrines, that identification was feared in a purely physical and phenomenal sector, physiognomical to be more precise, I mean it was little more than the banal tendency of a son to resemble his father, but this tendency developed on a substratum of primordial and mysterious fear whose chief manifestation was that I didn't want to look at those ill-advised photographs but still I wasn't able to throw them away, and so I kept carrying them around with me in the various houses that I kept changing, always shut up in their envelope and shoved to the back of the deepest drawer, but there was certainly no need for me to look at them to know that, especially in the profile ones, a kind of predestination was portrayed in them connected in obscure ways perhaps with an intestinal block and with what little can be left after that, and from then on in fact I began to examine my profile more carefully making use of two mirrors and at times even three carefully arranged, studying with a hostile attitude the fatal resemblance, clutching like a shipwrecked man at every possible difference, and since the chief difference consisted in the sparse hair still on my head what I can only call a fanatic care for my remaining hair began with the use of all the lotions ever invented, excluding obviously Migone Quinine which had disappeared from the market long since, but in any case in view of the dubious preservative merits of any hair lotion I directed my defensive strength also against the photographs in themselves, as if their material existence and nothing else determined the relentless process, so that more and more I pondered the notion of destroying them, maybe even burning them up with an appropriate ritual, in the middle of the night for instance and with the envelope sealed, in some sparsely settled place, some sacred place like the Via Appia with its crumbling tombs and dark cypresses, however I could never find the right moment to do this, and then years

later when I began my psychoanalytical treatment one of the first
things I told the doctor was in fact this story of the awkward
funereal photographs, confident that he would tell me to burn
them up giving me the courage I lacked, and instead he said
simply as if it had been nothing at all no no why burn them, maybe
I hadn't made myself clear or maybe he wanted to lessen the
importance of the photos to avoid my making a fetish of them
which was what I had already done, anyhow those early days of
my analysis weren't at all easy since I remained as a rule anchored
to actual things and events, when he wanted me every time to tell
him some dream but I rarely had any dreams to tell, either I
didn't dream at all or else the minute my dream was over I forgot
it, and sometimes I even dreamed I was dreaming and then forgetting because in reality I was rather worried about this lack of
dreams which might also be attributed to inadequate diligence,
as if I weren't applying myself sufficiently to my analysis despite
the money it was costing, and really when I went to the doctor
without any dreams I felt guilty like when I used to go to school
without having done my homework or studied my lesson, whereas
I was overjoyed when I did have dreams to tell, even though they
were fairly wretched little dreams, like the time I dreamed that
before an audience of about ten thousand people I was denounc-
ing in a loud voice the defects of *La dolce vita*, achieving a huge
success and embraces even from Fellini, or the other time at a
cocktail party of successful people Gassman put his hand on my
shoulder and asked me when are we going to start work together
and although reluctant I had to explain that I had a splendid idea
a story taken from the Gospel which was bound to be a hit for
us both, anyhow dreams like this were better than nothing at
least they could be discussed, me offering my interpretations and
the doctor his which sometimes agreed with mine and sometimes
didn't, and in those cases I clung to my opinion since I can't say
that Freudian interpretations convinced me all that much, until
one day I happened to go to the doctor with the dream known as
the Dream of the Rossetti Bookstore, which I considered a poor
little dream still connected with my contingent problems like the

dreams I'd had up till then, whereas the doctor made a different interpretation very original and convincing, and I'd say not convincing just by force of logic but also because of a strange emotional flux that seemed to strike me as he spoke, and because of some images that flashed forth from God knows what mysterious depths in me, and psychoanalysis is really a fine thing when it reaches what you might call this fermentative state, but I only reached it with difficulty because I lay there with my hands numb on my stomach, or to be less vague on the curve that the colon makes from transverse to descending, and moreover I had my miserable five lumbar vertebrae in their pins-and-needles state which for me was the equivalent of the thought of death, rather of suicide, for reasons which I won't be able to avoid illustrating later on if I manage to get that far.

So this basic dream which had stayed in my mind perhaps because of its simplicity and perhaps because of the apparent ease with which it could be interpreted consisted of the following events, I was in a place not at all unfamiliar probably it was the Rossetti Bookstore in the Via Veneto or probably not, I say Rossetti Bookstore because it was a place where I wasn't fond of going not even before I was sick since it was frequented by big shots of that superseded intellectual period coinciding first with Fascism and immediately thereafter with antifascism, and they were vain maybe involuntarily but you never knew whether to say hello to them or not always running the risk of being snubbed, at times when you ran into them you had the impression they didn't even see you, and the same applied to whatever somebody different from them did or wrote, I mean for them it just didn't exist, so you ended up thinking they only existed for themselves and maybe a dozen of their similars, an opinion not so farfetched and indeed supported by the poor results they achieved when they tried to go into politics and form a party, anyway in the dream it wasn't clear if this was the Rossetti Bookstore exactly or whether the people in it were the radical party, but what was clear was a little low table like the one that stands in fact in Rossetti's, and there at that table was a very important man with a long cloak who was holding in his hand a very beautiful reproduction which he had made himself, and while I stood a bit to one side to watch the scene the very important people who were in the store went up to admire and even to touch the reproduction saying oh how beautiful and oh how delicate and other things of that sort and the man in the cloak allowed anybody to touch it pleased by the flattering remarks everybody showered on him, until after everybody had gone up to admire and to touch the reproduction I ventured to move from my secluded corner to go up and admire and touch it, curious to feel if it really was so delicate to the touch as the others had proclaimed it, and inside myself I may even have been prepared to express some compliment, but the man in the cloak said curtly no he wasn't going to let me touch it or even look at it, and thus with my great humiliation the dream ended.

Now when I told a dream the few times that I happened to tell one I understood immediately whether or not it interested the doctor behind my back, sometimes it didn't interest him at all especially if the dreams were made up of leftovers from the day, but other times he was deeply interested, and then he stopped playing with his keys and asked one question after the other, he wanted to know this and that, the associations as they're called, and so it happened with the Rossetti Bookstore dream I had to explain in fact the place where I was in the dream most likely the Rossetti Bookstore in the Via Veneto, and the people there could very well be the leaders of the radical party, writers, journalists, playwrights, essayists, critics and so on, all people who at least in my opinion had more fame and success than they deserved, and all because they were all tied up with one another, and it's true that when a book came out by one of them or by some friend of theirs at the Rossetti Bookstore they kept it in the window for years like it was the Bible or The Divine Comedy and so at this point the dream for me was very clear and closely related to the wretched little dreams I was just talking about, only these latter ones had a shall we say vendetta quality whereas in the radicals dream there was a directly anecdotal form about the sense of inferiority and frustration that has persecuted me

since birth or at least since I was aware of my unfortunate relationship toward the Venetians, and in a particular way since I
became aware that I would never have any connection with glory
at least not while I was alive, and naturally this could depend on
me and on my lack of ability for bringing off masterpieces but
more than that it could be attributed to the lack of attention
from others, from the male and female or in-between organized
groups who are too busy advertising one another, giving one another prizes, dedicating essays and highly flattering reviews to
one another, recommending one another to publishers and newspaper editors even abroad, and obviously I couldn't hope to com-
pete with them because I was isolated and very proud of being so,
and I was sure anyway that the radicals would never welcome me
into their group, and naturally not even the women or the queers
for obvious reasons I'd say, so in the end from my point of view
my position in the dream was completely clear, and so was the
position of the others, all corresponding to reality, but the doctor
wasn't satisfied with my associations and he insisted on knowing
who was the man in the cloak, and I kept saying I didn't know, it
was as if he didn't have a face only a sturdy physique and an
extraordinary capacity for arousing my dislike and yet awing me
at the same time, and the doctor kept on and on asking with whom
I could associate the image of the man in the cloak and I was
racking my brains until I finally dredged up a couple of names
of writers who I have the impression are not too fond of me,
Moravia for example or Bonaventura Tecchi, the latter however
chiefly because of his heavy physique and in fact I didn't believe
he had anything to do with the radicals not ideologically-speaking
anyhow, they even said he was a Catholic and this could very well
be true, but the doctor wasn't satisfied even with these clarifica-
tions he wanted more associations with the person but I couldn't
satisfy him, I couldn't get beyond Moravia or Bonaventura Tecchi
or if you like Goffredo Bellonci, and then he got obstinate and
wanted to know at least what was depicted in this reproduction
object of so much longing and my God how could I answer him,
I hadn't paid much attention to the picture itself because whatever

it represented the facts didn't change that is the result was always my defeat and humiliation at the hand of my enemies, still the first figures that came to me were the rather enigmatic lady with a child at her breast like the one you see in *The Storm* by Giorgione or any Madonna by Raphael though it was strange that Moravia should start reproducing Raphael Madonnas, and in this particular case the person in the cloak might more suitably be Bonaventura Tecchi, but as soon as I had told the doctor what I supposed might be represented in the delicate reproduction they wouldn't let me touch he was delighted and gave the dream its correct interpretation according to Freudian doctrine, that is the grim man in the cloak far from being Moravia or Bonaventura Tecchi was my father, and the delicate reproduction was my mother whom he was keeping for himself and maybe even for others while he prevented me from touching her, and though in a way I still wondered what the radicals had to do with my father and my mother there was something irrationally convincing in the doctor's opinion, I felt his idea fill me and run through me as if erasing my every concern with the curves of the colon or the five lumbars or with the other points of the body where the fear of death or of worse nested, making me feel completely drawn into a search for the past until I could see my father the first time I really saw him, before then he had been only things and symbols and smells, but now he was my father though still without a face who held my mother in his arms on the landing of the steps of our house, he tall and heavy and she little, she wept in his arms because they had just had a quarrel over some jealousy business, but she belonged to him perhaps even happy to be maltreated or hit, and I who was standing there watching from below didn't exist for her as I didn't exist for that superhuman force who was my father, looking on I felt my first loneliness I discovered the wish to die or to kill that grips a child when he feels alone for the first time so alone that nobody even notices his wish to die or to kill.

Now I know that all this was a kind of fairly tendentious game that I wasn't directing but was being run by the doctor behind my back although naturally he didn't furnish me the images or even suggest them to me, but it was he who gave me the courage and the will to dig among these forgotten things to find all the evil my father had done to me, since I wasn't to feel so over-powered by him in this struggle I was carrying on against his dead image, and in other words what I was supposed to do chiefly was to find reasons for hating my father, hating him after I had with the best of intentions abandoned him at the moment of his horrible death, and after I had thought of all the things I could have done to give him at least a bit of satisfaction and which I hadn't done, and I didn't care if this was a very unspecific feeling which afflicts anybody when somebody close to him dies, I knew the infinite number of things that could have given him some satisfaction and I hadn't done them, sometimes on purpose, so my present sense of guilt wasn't absolutely without foundation although I did understand that a sense of guilt was a bit out of line directed toward a man who had so bound me to himself with this identification business that I could already imagine how my death was going to come and take me, or rather how it will come and take me since the problem still hasn't been overcome, only I think it will come to me with greater haste than it came to him, I mean that by now I have no desire to reach his eighty years and before then I'll be carried off by that damned death nesting in the curve of the colon, unless it's that other death connected with the pins-and-needles in the five lumbars, or else suicide to speak openly, although thanks to the reflections to which psychoanalysis has made me all too accustomed a number of doubts have risen in me about death's being the end of our troubles, since if you consider it for example as an end of power you risk making a mistake, as my father proves since when alive he didn't count for anything but as soon as he was dead or a short time afterwards anyway he started dominating me again, and still if I explicitly gave up suicide I wouldn't want to give in to him, that is, to allow time to complete this process of identification in its worst aspects which are weakness, old age, illness, suffering and only at the very end, death. Obviously, at the time of my psychoanalysis, these weren't things on which the doctor could agree with me, suicide I mean or mortal identification, but we didn't talk much about them to tell the truth, or rather at times I may have hinted to him of the temptation toward suicide not as an escape from fear and suffering, but as a preventive maneuver to keep my father from making me identical with himself even in that monstrous and shameful business they exposed on his belly but as I recall we never discussed this at all, and for that matter it wasn't a question of constant suspicions although they weren't so rare either, which came to me when I was in the state of fluctuation, with nothing secure inside or outside me, no straight line, so to speak, or no concept of it, that is to say when I was assailed by all the doubts and fears and anxieties of this world and the next, and I was alone except for the active and surely far from benign presence of my dead father, who was only waiting for me to lose a bit more hair and to have a few more wrinkles on my neck to make me identical with himself in the death he had achieved after so much pain. Now I don't know that this is acceptable and fair, indeed let's say that it's absolutely unfair because for example you can't say that my father struggled with his father as much as I've struggled with mine since birth probably, to tell the truth I don't know much about these facts and I never even knew his father that is my paternal grandfather, nor have I ever heard anything about him except for the fact that he was a peasant, however all in all he must have been a man of good sense without excessive ambitions about sending his children to school, whereas my father was downright sick with these ambitions at least in the case of his first-born son, and he really did make many sacrifices so that I could study, many painful sacrifices, but here the doctor interrupted and said firmly it wasn't true, or rather once and for all I ought to stop thinking of those many painful sacrifices, however I had been as they say traumatized by that business, by the fact I mean that when he decided to send me to boarding school my father told me I had to study hard because he was making many sacrifices to keep me there, so when I still wasn't nine years old I found myself faced by the monstrous necessity of making a good showing and always being smart to repay in that way at least my father's sacrifices, I thought of him working all day for me and maybe not even eating enough, he and my mother and my sisters who were little then and of whom there were only three, all of them ate too little and to be precise took the bread from their mouths to save every penny in order that I could study, so just imagine all the responsibility he had placed on my weak shoulders, all because he wanted the satisfaction of an educated son, he was thinking of making me an accountant in those days and out of love for my father and my family which was going hungry for me I studied like a madman, I always tried to be first in the class although I didn't always succeed, and when my mother and my sisters came to see me on Sundays at times also with my father when he didn't have to play bowls, I told them that I didn't like chocolate and not even candy and not even jam to put on my bread, for a snack at four they gave us only a piece of bread, but I couldn't have eaten bread and jam like the other boys or bread and chocolate even though I liked it very much with the thought of my family taking the food from their mouths to keep me at my studies, my God I felt such great joy in eating dry bread and repaying with a little sacrifice of my own the great sacrifices they were making for me at home, however the matter naturally wasn't as simple as I explain it now, and in fact this detail of the dry bread, which wasn't even very good bread, in fact abandoning all regard for the reverend fathers who ran the school I might as well say that often the bread was bad, made with sour or moldy flour, through this dry and disgusting bread then, which I had a hard time swallowing, I also gratified some exceptional mystical impulses which had seized me between the ages of nine and eleven, and it was a mysticism tending in absolute forms to the mortification of the body and my final annihilation in the Eternal Father, you could say that after that time I never again experienced such a vivid aspiration toward non-existence, not even in the period when I had what seemed spiders crawling around in my five lumbar vertebrae and was constantly tempted to end it all throwing myself out of a sufficiently high window, only in my school days my wish to die had the value of a transfer of myself

into God all light and blissful eternity, whereas my later tempta-
tions to suicide had only that limited escapist significance which I
have already mentioned above.

Now for my doctor it was an easy matter to say that the fact
of putting me in boarding school before I was even nine years old
was downright cruelty, especially since I had clearly told him the
kind of school it was, nowadays we can hope such schools no
longer exist, at least not paying ones, and in fact you entered at
the beginning of October and didn't get out until the first days of
June and you could never go home not even at Christmas or
Easter, and if the bread was bad the soup was even worse, as was
the milk-and-coffee in the morning which was obviously more
water than either milk or coffee, and then you suffered from the
cold terribly because in the winter you washed with freezing water
and sometimes thank God you didn't have to wash at all because
the water had frozen in the pipes, but the fact was that I had to
be content because it was a school that didn't cost much, although what little it did cost was a huge sum when compared to
our family's economic possibilities, however it must also be admitted that for what strictly concerns the struggle between me and
my father, thanks to this story of the sacrifices made to allow me
to study he suffered a sharp drop on the scale of what we may call
mythological values, since from the position of absolute
supremacy and power which for better or worse he had maintained
until then he slipped I won't say to the rank of poor dumb bastard,
for this was a subsequent achievement on my part, but in short he
was neither more nor less than one of the many men who had to
drudge to keep alive, however this detail also brought him a little
closer to me who was nobody, it brought him nearer symbolically
and maybe sentimentally I mean, for as far as physical nearness
is concerned I think he didn't like the school much, and for the
most part he came to visit me only when a clownish uncle of mine
came too who made everybody laugh with his jokes, for example
he would take the paper splattered with whipped cream or custard
from the cakes that the other students in the parlor had been
brought and he would make as if to wipe his bottom, and then he

would lick the paper so that everybody laughed at times till tears came to their eyes, whereas I wanted to sink through the floor at the shame of having such relatives, I hated them with all my strength and in my heart I was praying that they would die and then they wouldn't come to visit me any more, I even hated my father who was also laughing, but I didn't want him to die, still I would have to perform all sorts of exploits covering myself with glory to redeem the vulgarity of my origins.

These circumstances according to my doctor cast some light on many aspects of my life that are otherwise inexplicable, they clear up for example how an individual like me, basically lazy and timid and alien to violence the way nearly all parsimonious people are, should have gone off to fight in every war that it was possible for him to get into, disastrously wasting many years and also losing the respect of the radicals who rightly do not approve of such things, and from another point of view these facts clarify also the obstinacy with which I always wanted to be first in the class, and they explain above all my endless solitude, since now that my father had come down from his mythological pedestal and was approaching me emotionally with the business of the sacrifices, at this very moment I couldn't love him because he laughed at the coarse jokes of my uncle, I was ashamed and suffered at not loving my father but I simply couldn't, I would have preferred him to be remote again as he had been before, a mere symbolic presence as he had been at the beginning, an occult power inside a military chest which contained coffee, sugar, rice, pasta, oil and condensed milk, and that was my father, things nobody else could have because the war was on, but we had them my father sent them to us from Venice where he was on duty right at the Casetta Rossa which was where princes lived and now instead there was the Soldier Poet, my father was great therefore and powerful and knew everything, and when Caporetto came along and people were running away for fear the Germans would cross the Piave we didn't run at all, and there were the medical officers billeted in our house who asked my mother why

aren't you running away since you have small children, and my
mother answered grandly that if there was any danger her husband would have let her know and even at the last minute he
could even give her a truck to escape in, and how old could I have
been then maybe not even four but I could perceive my father's
vigilant power, without doubt he was more powerful than the
major and captain of the medical corps, while my mother at that
time wasn't so much, she always made me wear a striped smock
which was exactly like my sister's, and when she couldn't make
us obey her she had the major or the captain scold us and they
both had moustaches, besides she was terrified of horses afraid
they would rear up or run off and knock us down, and then
once when there was a column of German soldiers in the town
and they wouldn't let them take water from the fountain, they were
forced to drink the dirty water from the ditches, then my mother
protested to some corporal or maybe a sergeant, but he answered
signora you don't know how they make our men suffer on the
other side, so the corporal or sergeant was right and my mother
wrong, but she was a woman and what could she know about
war, whereas at home I had reeds and sticks that were so many
bayonets and guns, and stones that were handgrenades and I made
war with them just like the Arditi who went by singing on trucks
to go into action on the Piave and then the ones who didn't die
came back full of glory to get drunk and sing and make love with
the girls, and in short war was downright beautiful for a man
could even go with a dirigible, or he could be like my father who
didn't go up in a dirigible but was with the Soldier Poet who was
also a hero, and then he sent us condensed milk so we could say
all the bad things we wanted to about the peasants who wouldn't
give us cows' milk out of envy because we weren't peasants like
them, we weren't peasants at all, we even had a maid because
my mother had to keep the shop open though there was almost
nothing to sell because of the war, however this didn't matter
because my father sent almost his whole pay home and in addition
coffee, sugar, rice, pasta, oil and very sweet condensed milk, and

even cans of meat, all things that only we had and nobody else, because nobody else had a father powerful like mine, who could have anything he wanted.

Now, strange as it may seem, but then it isn't so strange if you think that he was mostly a chest, I don't have any visual memory of my father at that time, certainly he came home to see us often taking the train, or else first the vaporetto to San Giuliano and then the tram, but I don't remember him in uniform as he must have been, I don't even know for example if he had a great mantle or dark cloak the way carabinieri usually do, or whether it was olive drab because of the war, all I knew about the uniform was that the three-cornered hat of the carabinieri makes them lose their hair and that's why my father was completely bald though they said he wasn't at all old, however here too the whole business is confused since the word they used to describe his hat, *lucerna*, also means lamp and I couldn't see what lamps had to do with hair, and anyway the real image of my father was in such contrast with the abstract image embodied in the chest of provisions that I could erase it altogether to the advantage of the abstract father-power idea, which however had a voice, and in fact I knew from his tales of when he commanded the station at Occhiobello or at Perarolo, so in addition to everything else he was a stationmaster that is he made the trains go only if he felt like giving the order with his trumpet otherwise they wouldn't leave, or else even more wonderful tales about when he went to Bellolampo hill to catch bandits and slept on the ground with one eye open and keeping his gun ready, but he was surely joking when he said this because he couldn't have been afraid since it's the carabinieri who frighten bad men and not bad men who frighten carabinieri, and then when dawn came they went down into the Golden Bay, they walked along the little roads amid gardens with orange trees and all you had to do was reach up and pick all you wanted and not paying anything that marvelous fruit which doesn't grow in our parts, and so Sicily was the happiest and most beautiful place in the world and I would surely go there just as soon as I was grown up, and Sicily also had something to do with spaghetti *alla car-*

rettiera which I loved, and my father was always getting mad because nobody in our house knew how to make decent sauce and then sometimes he would go about it himself since he had been in Sicily as a carabiniere and he would make the sauce with garlic, oil and tomato, called *alla carrettiera* because the wagon drivers in Sicily make it like that since it doesn't take long to cook, while the spaghetti is cooking the sauce cooks too my father used to say, but at that time the great war must have already been over, by then he was the man without a face who argued with my mother on the landing of the stairs because he was jealous, and naturally I had no idea what jealous meant, still the thing may have had some connection with the fact that my mother had once taken us to watch the people dancing, they danced on a wooden platform under a great tent like a circus with the band playing waltzes and mazurkas and at the end of the dance they drew a rope so that all the couples that had danced had to go under an arch where the men paid two centesimi but the ladies nothing, and then there were wires going from one side to the other with little tricolor flags hanging from them because we had won the war, and my mother with our aunt had taken us to watch because it was pretty to see, and after a while the two of them had also started dancing with two gentlemen who had come to invite them, my mother was really happy to dance you could see in her face how happy she was, and she seemed beautiful to me really the most beautiful of all with her dress that came down to her ankles and the gold chain with the watch on her breast, and then when we were going home she warned me and my big sister not to say anything to our father about her going dancing or else he would be angry, and our aunt said if my father wasn't so grumpy there wouldn't be any need to go dancing on the sly, and I disliked her when she said this but all the same I would have died rather than tell this thing to my father, but then somebody must have told him, I won't say my oldest sister but maybe some acquaintance who had seen mother dance, this was possible since the town was small and the people envious, anyhow maybe this was the reason why they were fighting like that on the landing of the stairs, my fa-

ther still without a face, merely a heavy and threatening figure
with a bald head because of the hat or lamp, and when he was in a
good humor he would sing Come with me sweet flower of May
come with me upon the hay, and Mamma would laugh because he
couldn't carry a tune, but most of the time he wasn't in a good
humor and he didn't sing, and when he was mad he would say
goddammit to hell sonavabitch and our mother didn't like him
to say bad words when we were around, he took the Lord's name
in vain and even the Madonna's, and since I went to catechism class
then on Sundays I knew that if he dropped dead on the spot without time to say My Jesus have mercy he would go straight to hell,
however if I had dropped dead on the spot I would have gone to
hell too because I still hadn't made my first confession and I was
already looking at the little girls who climbed up in the fig trees
without any underpants on.

At that time I was very curious about little girls who were
different from me in that part of the body which is usually hidden
by underpants, but my curiosity was so hindered by shyness and
by the awareness of committing sin that I hardly ever looked
unless it was to follow the example of the other boys who did or
unless it was with a girl who was named Lucia who liked to be
looked at and even touched so they called her Dirty Lucia and I
also looked at her and touched her but only when we were alone,
and obviously I felt pleasure when I touched her but immediately
afterwards my remorse and shame were all the greater, nobody
should ever know this, especially my parents who were absolutely
pure and apart from those curses of my father's both were absolutely deserving of Paradise, whereas I wasn't so pure since I sometimes touched Dirty Lucia there where she was different from me,
being the same everywhere else inasmuch as I had to wear a striped
smock and had long, pageboy hair which many people liked to pat
because it was blond and curly, and they asked me if I was a little
boy or a little girl and I would shut up with my head down and my
teeth clenched, and my mother would tell me not to be rude why
don't you answer, but I wouldn't answer because at times after I
did answer that I was a little boy these people would say I can't

tell that show me where you're a little boy, and I knew they were talking about that shameful thing between my legs which I wasn't supposed to show to anybody, I hated them because they talked about that thing right in front of my mother, and my mother of course knew I had that thing, she even used to help me when I had to make peepee, but not any more because I was big and could do everything by myself, but if I was big why did they make me wear that smock and keep my hair long like a girl when I would have liked a forelock or at least short hair if a cropped head wasn't possible since only nasty little street boys wore their hair like that, and I wanted a cap with a shiny vizor or else a sailor's hat with a ribbon with *Italia* or *Andrea Doria* written on it, naturally I didn't know how to read, I could only hold the pencil and make strokes, however I could see where *Italia* was written or *Andrea Doria* words which had no meaning whatsoever, I always asked what they meant but nobody could give me an answer I could understand so they remained names with no sense, but still they wrote them there so you wouldn't make a mistake and put the back to the front, the words had to be in front, however there was also the ribbon with its two ends hanging all the way to your cheek, and the two ends were supposed to be on the right, that is on the same side with the hand that you held the pencil with, while the other hand had a different name that I could never remember.

My father at that time was still without a face, but already had a moustache, or else he didn't have it because sometimes he let it grow and sometimes he shaved it off since moustaches weren't in fashion any more, just like long hair on women wasn't in fashion any more, nor skirts down to the ankles like before the war, and not even my mother wore long ones any more though she was cross, she said that it was committing a sin to show your legs to everybody like that, but my aunt who was her sister and some other women friends of hers joked and made fun of her saying she was against short skirts because she had crooked, ugly legs, but it wasn't true, I could have killed them when they said that, indeed I would definitely kill them just as soon as I was big enough, including my aunt who thought she was prettier than Mamma only because she was younger, and sometimes I heard them say that my Mamma was jealous of her sister and maybe this and not the dancing was the reason why she and my father had quarreled that day on the landing of the stairs, anyway nobody in the world was more beautiful than Mamma not even the queen who was tall, all right, but who looked funny beside the king who was a short little man, instead my mother was tiny beside my father who was tall, and this was right. My father then being without a face was still to a great ex-

tent void, that is to say he consisted almost exclusively in his be-
longings, especially the ones contained in a little drawer to the
right over the commode next to the mirror, where there was the
Migone Quinine which had a nice smell and his hairbrush which
instead had a nasty smell, and nothing else, whereas in the chest
of drawers on the other side which was my mother's there was
always a great confusion of combs and hairpins and clips for the
hair and some larger combs that were never cleaned and had long
hairs sticking in them, because my mother was never going to
have a boyish bob, while my aunt probably would have one because she had to find a husband, in fact she had been engaged to
a lieutenant during the war who said that in civilian life he was a
great gentleman but then once the war was over he disappeared,
however this was something we were never to mention when our
aunt was around because she would get mad or else she would cry
at being so unlucky, but I was almost happy to see her cry since
she thought she was more beautiful than Mamma, and especially
if it was true that Mamma was jealous of her, and this must have
been true because a maid we had whose name was Romilda used
to say that my father was a handsome man and women liked him
only it was too bad about his bald head, and in fact my father at
that time always took great pains when he brushed his hair he
stayed a long time in front of the mirror particularly when he was
in a good humor and sang Come with me sweet flower of May,
and he would take the sparse hair that grew at the sides and the
back of his head and brush it carefully forward, and my mother
would tease him about this, saying it was no use his taking so
much trouble with those four hairs on his head because no matter
how he brushed them he was still bald, and when my father was in
a good humor he would say he was worth any four youngsters
with hair, and then he hadn't gone bald because of his age but
because of his hat, and besides with Migone Quinine and then
also with Longega Oil for restoring fallen hair he still had some
hope, obviously if the government permitted all the advertising
that those products printed in the newspapers there must be some
truth in it, otherwise it would have been fraud and there were

laws made especially to prevent frauds, although these post-war times weren't too good for the laws what with the subversives and the strikes and the no-goods getting ahead on all sides, at times you were afraid even to go out of the house, and thank goodness I had a father who had been a stationmaster and First Sergeant of the Carabinieri before he took to selling hats so it was the others who were afraid and not him, but I of course wasn't afraid of him because he was my father, when he let me I would climb on his knees and touch his bald head, however it didn't often happen that he allowed me to climb up to that place I liked so much, so when he wanted to see my notebook with my pencil-strokes in it which are the most important thing in the world because an educated person can always get on in life whereas an ignoramus can be shoved around by anybody, when he wanted to see the notebook I'd let him look at it only if he would let me climb on his knees and afterwards I never wanted to get down again of course and I would stick my fingers in his eyes and even rumple the few hairs on his head until he would lose his temper and say wife take this demon off me, and my mother would come and take me but then she wouldn't be able to keep me because she always had something to do especially at supper time when they came back to the house from the shop.

The shop was under the arcades in the square like the other shops of the village, on one side we had the household goods shop where they sold dishes, glasses, pans and kerosene lamps for the peasants out in the fields who still didn't have electricity, and on the other side there was the Venezia Bar and Pastry Shop which was the finest shop in the town and maybe in the whole world all white and gold stucco, and there they sold cakes, chocolate, and candy, things that cost money and gave you a bellyache, and I absolutely didn't want to get a bellyache otherwise they would try to give me castor oil whereas I knew I couldn't take it because once Mamma had tried to give it to me with sugar and lemon and she said you couldn't even taste the oil and instead I did taste it and couldn't get it down, it was really something I just couldn't do, but Mamma didn't understand this, she thought that I was like good little boys who maybe do take their oil if they're told to sharply, and so she had pinched my nose to make me open my mouth and swallow it by force, and then I had spat it all over her dress, not on purpose but because I had strangled, however she believed I spat it out on purpose and this made her so mad with me that she gave me six of the best on my behind, and then left me alone in my room to cry in the dark in pain and bewilderment at this injustice, and after that when I felt bad I never said so, not even when I had a terrible bellyache because I had eaten too much bean soup, I put up with the pain and didn't say a word to anybody for fear of the castor oil, that Mamma would get mad if I couldn't manage to take it, and anyway it wasn't just fear of the oil that kept me from insisting that they buy me cakes or chocolates but also because they were filth that cost an arm and a leg, that's what my father said whereas for me filth was what Dirty Lucia and I did in secret, and so I was sorry that my father used this word for the cakes and the other things they sold at the Venezia especially the Jordan almonds, however there were times when at the shop they sold a brand-name hat and then they went to the bar to drink an *americano* with the customer, and if I was there they also had to buy something for me even though my father had to pay, and then I would say that I wanted a pastry called a creamcake although my conscience prompted me to ask for a candy which cost less, and in fact many times I said a candy instead of a cake, and sometimes nothing, because my father loved me more if I said I didn't want anything at all.

In any case to go to the shop was a wonderful thing, there under the arcades the whole town went past and they told me I was a fine-looking little boy when I was seated next to my mother at the door while my father was playing bowls and came back early or late according to the seasons, but in summer though he came back late it was still daylight whereas in winter it got dark early, and then we waited for him inside the shop and not outside even though inside it was colder than outdoors and probably we waited for him half in darkness, with only the lights of the window lighted, because anyhow unless it was Saturday no customers came to buy hats or caps and so we might as well save on the lights, and we waited maybe Mamma and I alone in the shop without my oldest sister or the other little one because if there were two of us we only made trouble, whereas taken one at a time we weren't so terrible, so it was nice to stay there just me and Mamma inside the shop in the half-light, however it wasn't entirely nice because my Mamma was always worried about my father at the wineshop playing bowls or cards if the weather was bad, she used to think of him and be afraid that maybe there would be an argument or something worse because those were bad years, my father knew how to keep his mouth shut all right and never said a word unless he had thought about it first but the socialists were bad, they sang red flag against the king and the pope and they wanted strikes to make trouble so my mother wasn't happy until my father came back, she could hear him coming and tell his footsteps and if he coughed she could guess that it was him from even beyond the Venezia Bar because my father had a way of coughing all his own, or rather he didn't cough but cleared his throat, and I of course wasn't able to recognize him at a distance but my mother could, she was another person the minute she heard him coming, and then he would take the money from the drawer if there was any, marking it in the ledger and they would shut up shop, turning out the lights in the windows and pulling down the shutter and we went home and there was a long walk till we got home, more than a kilometer, and at times I was tired and wanted them to carry me but my father said I should be ashamed at my age, and if I cried he got mad with mother too because the kids ought to be left home, and then I wouldn't cry but would let Mamma secretly keep me under her arm, and holding tight to her I would walk along with my eyes shut thinking I wonder where I am now if I've already passed the first telegraph pole or the second or the gate of the Traldis house, and I always made myself think I was a little farther back than what I really believed, so I would discover that I was nearer home when I opened my eyes and this would make me happy.

However I wasn't allowed to go to the shop very often, almost always it was my oldest sister who went because she knew how to recite her poem and for this reason there was always somebody who gave her a candy or bought her a cake, whereas I didn't know how to recite anything I was really a dunce and always shy in front of people, so nobody ever bought me anything and it was better for me to stay home with the maid, but I wasn't a good little boy when they left me at home with the maid, I misbehaved and hid in the rooms upstairs or at the end of the garden without answering her when she looked for me, and in fact my life's only consolation was the siren of the pepper factory that blew at five o'clock, because after it had blown the working girls walked along the road going to their homes and there was one I used to wait for, standing behind the wire fence, I waited for her with a kind of frightening emptiness inside me because at times if she was with some boy and was talking to him she went by without even noticing me, instead when she noticed that I was standing there behind the fence she stopped to say I was handsome and she would pat my face or my hair, and then that emptiness was suddenly filled with blood racing faster in joy and alarm, and at times I was sad because my mother had left me at home and I would have liked for this girl to be my Mamma, but then I became frightened at such a thought I surely didn't want a mother different from the one the Lord had given me, however I also loved this pepper-factory girl all the same so I would marry her as soon as I was big, but I would never talk to anybody about this of course, not even to the pepper-factory girl for the moment, in my soul I needed more and more space to put all the things that nobody was ever to know, also my bad thoughts or my impure actions with Dirty Lucia, however since I really loved the pepper-factory girl it was shameful in an entirely different way, maybe it wasn't even a venial sin though it did have to remain secret, and when I said my night prayers I wasn't sure if it was something I had to repent for and ask the Lord's forgiveness, anyhow it was never sincere repentance because the next day I would be standing there again behind the fence, but in the winter when it was cold and I had chilblains and chapped places on my hands and feet, or when it rained they wouldn't let me go outdoors in the yard and I could see the girl go by with her umbrella a little after the five o'clock siren had blown, but she couldn't see me because I was in the kitchen beyond the window so when it rained it was nasty but to make up for it it was nice to see the milkman arrive in his buggy, I could hear him in the distance blowing his horn like the stationmaster, and then the women would come out into the street with their umbrellas and their change counted out and the pan where he would pour the milk, and he didn't care about the rain because he had a great cloak and a hat and a cigarette in his mouth, and after he had served the women he would say gee-up horse slapping the reins and the horse would go off and he would smoke, he surely didn't feel the cold with the cigarette in his mouth and his hat and cloak, it must have been one of the most beautiful things in the world to go out like that in the rain whereas I had to stay in the house, and I couldn't wait to grow up so that I could sell milk too, however when they asked me what I wanted to be when I was big I was ashamed to answer that I would be a milkman, and instead I would say I was going to be a priest be-cause of all jobs being a priest was the one that pleased Mamma most, but my funny uncle when I said I would be a priest made them all laugh with the things he said, I certainly didn't under-stand them but I could hear him talking about the housekeeper and this was the thing that made them all laugh, even my mother a little though she scolded my uncle for saying such awful things in front of innocent children, and I was innocent all right, how-ever if at that moment I remembered about Dirty Lucia then my innocence was already thoroughly lost and maybe the Lord wouldn't even let me go off to be a priest, and anyway I didn't always think that I would be a priest there were for example some evenings when after supper Mamma wasn't too tired and we weren't too sleepy, and then she would read poetry, we had three big books in the house with illustrations and the poems of Fusi-nato and also *I promessi sposi*, however nobody ever read that whereas the poems of Fusinato were really beautiful and my father had been right to buy them even if they cost a lot of money, however he never read aloud, it was my mother who read them and she had a marvelous reading voice. The Student of Padua or Over the Bridge a White Flag Flies, or another poem which was the best of all and told about a poor knight who went off to the wars afar against the infidels, but first he rode beneath the balcony of the fair princess that he was in love with and after telling her good-bye he rode away and never came back again because he died in the war, every time we had to cry at this sad end of his, and still at those moments there was nobody I wanted to be more than that doomed knight and the princess on the balcony to whom I went for a last farewell was Mamma, or sometimes the girl from the pepper factory, certainly never Dirty Lucia who was only good for doing filthy things with, and Mamma's voice was so beautiful and pure while she read the poems that the thought of Lucia was all wrong at that moment, and if by chance she came into my mind even without my wanting her to, it was like insulting the beauty and purity of my Mamma, it was like not deserving a Mamma so lovely and pure.

However there was also something very ugly about the fact that we had a shop, and that is that while the other children whose fathers worked on the railroad or were masons or salesmen had Mammas that always stayed at home, mine had to go to the shop and twice a week she had also to go to the markets, so she left us at home with the maid, and often to keep us from crying she tricked us telling us to go somewhere and bring her this or that and while we went off then she would secretly leave, and then when we discovered Mamma was gone it filled us with sorrow and anger and I would have liked for the maid to die because if she wasn't around then Mamma would be forced to take us to the square, and one day I hated the maid so much that I put an iron into the fire until it was red hot and I wanted to burn her with it, and she cried and screamed with fear saying put it down for the love of God, but as soon as I did put the iron down she whacked my hands and bottom soundly, and then she shut me up in the chicken house where I sat crying with grief and dismay my mind a confusion of wicked deeds that the others had done to me and I

to the others, a tangle from which however all my sins loomed
greater and greater until this time my mother on coming home
would never forgive me, nor would she prevent my father from
giving me a thrashing, sometimes she came between us and
stopped him saying that his hands were too heavy and he didn't
realize how much he was hurting me, and then my father didn't
give me a thrashing but his face was grim and full of reproaches
for me who had been bad to the maid or to my sisters, or else I
complained because I didn't want to eat the cabbage soup and
even the saints in heaven would have lost their tempers to hear me
whine, or when I deserved punishment because I had torn my
sailor hat, but this business wasn't too clear because everything
cost money and there wasn't any money and what little there was
my father had to sweat blood to earn, however he had plenty of
sailor hats there in the shop and he didn't have to pay for them,
and still he got mad just the same if I lost my hat or more often
when I tore it because under the leather band inside it was made
of plain cardboard, and then it wasn't true what Mamma said
that those sailor hats were handsome because rich people's sons
wore them, whereas the caps with vizors that I liked so much
were worn only by nasty little street boys, and in short the world
was becoming larger especially through these obscure and unfair
things, and maybe this was what growing up meant, suffering
and expanding, experiencing pleasure and shame in touching
Dirty Lucia, feeling alarm and sweetness when the girl from the
pepper factory stopped to smile and pat me, and feeling inside me
such rebellion against Mamma who had gone away and left me
that I gave another woman some of the love that should all be
given to Mamma, and then being old enough to go still farther,
and here I am sitting at the first desk of the first grade and there
is a pretty young teacher that I am looking at spellbound, she's
even more beautiful than Mamma maybe almost as beautiful as
the Madonna I might even say, and how can she know that I love
her but she does know, she stops in front of me and combs my
blond pageboy locks, caresses me and sometimes even kisses me

on the cheek, and I don't know what's happening to me but I know I'm committing a mortal sin because when she kisses me I feel a little like the pleasure I feel when Mamma kisses me and a little like the way I do when Dirty Lucia touches me between the legs if I'm not too afraid and let her do it, and now it's clear what an abyss of sin it is to think of these things while the teacher is petting me because I'm the best in the class in penmanship and vowels, this is the only reason she's kind to me and I must thank the Lord that I have a father able to teach me penmanship and vowels even before I start the first grade, my father who had commanded the stations of Occhiobello and Perarolo, who was Sergeant-quartermaster and guarded the princes' house where the Soldier Poet stayed, my father who is goodness and who defeats evil, and he never never even more than mother must never know the sins of thought I commit sometimes when the teacher pets me and combs my hair and clasps me gently to her, my God how many things I already have to hide in my life I can't wait till they let me start preparing for my First Holy Communion so I can confess all my sins, and then if I die suddenly in the night I won't go to hell anymore but to Purgatory or even to Paradise if I happen to die right after going to confession without time to commit a single venial sin, and this is without doubt the most desirable thing in the world to die and go to Paradise, although there is a great problem involved and that is in Paradise I will surely meet my mother but it is almost equally sure that I won't meet my father who says goddamit to hell and curses and doesn't go to church on Sunday or receive the sacraments, and so how can my father be perfection if he isn't in a state of grace, and then I also discover other things to his disadvantage and this is that the stations he commanded at Occhiobello and Perarolo weren't train stations but in some way carabinieri stations like the carabinieri barracks in our town, and I discover that he went up on the Bellolampo hill over the Golden Bay of Palermo to earn twenty centesimi overtime, and then I discover that in the summer when the city people come from Venice for their holiday there are children whose fathers have clean clothes every day even on workdays and who earn money without sweating blood, and these children call me some times to play with their marvelous toys but then as soon as they are tired or when some important visitor comes they send me away, and these are children who can say when I'm big I'm going to be an engineer because they have the number five Meccano set, and their houses inside are beautiful they have bathrooms with water that comes down when you pull a chain, and then another bathroom upstairs a big one where there's a tub to take a bath in, whereas we have just one toilet on the ground floor and you have to throw water into it with a bucket and when we have to take a bath we do it in the laundry tub in the kitchen next to the stove in the winter, but in the summer time out in the shed where there's more room, and one day I go into the shed opening the door that was already ajar and I see my father standing naked in the tub and that thing between his legs is sticking straight out and is monstrously big, maybe grown men have it like that but I didn't know and I stand there looking at it terrified, certainly it was only a moment but I remember it as a very long time until my father starts shouting at me angrily to get out, and then I hear him shouting against my mother who doesn't mind the children, maybe he's never been so angry in his whole life, and I don't know why, I only know it isn't fair because if he didn't want to be seen he ought to have shut the door with the chain from the inside, and so the fault was his and not mine or Mamma's, instead he was shouting against me and against her and when he was so angry my mother paid attention to him and not to me, so in my unhappiness I naturally had to think about something else about the pepper-factory girl for example, or even better about the first grade teacher I could also have married when I was big, whereas the pepper-factory girl I couldn't, not anymore because those little boys who came from Venice for the summer said that they would never marry a girl who worked in a factory, however when I was in the second grade they gave me a different teacher, this one was old and ugly and stern, not as stern as the man who taught the fifth grade who if he was mad hit the students' hands with a stick when they made a mistake and my father would have been happy if I had landed under a teacher like him because my father thought that was just how teachers ought to be, however even my old lady teacher was plenty strict, and she was also a bit frightening because she had tiny little eyes and her skin was all wrinkles like my grandmother who was dead and I couldn't remember anything about her except that wrinkled skin and the fact that when she was dead they laid her out on a table in the hall, and then the carpenter came with the casket and shut her up in it which was only right because she was now dead, and nobody cried because my father was a man and a man must never cry, and my Mamma didn't cry because it wasn't her mother who was dead but my father's mother and Mamma hadn't even been too happy to have her in the house, she would have preferred to have her own Mamma who did in fact come, or maybe even my aunt who however was younger than she and so she was jealous of her, I now knew a little what jealous meant since we had on the wall some pictures of Othello or the Moor of Venice where first you saw that the two of them were happy in a magnificent garden, and in the next picture you saw her already dead on her bed and he in despair about to kill himself with the dagger or so it seemed, and she was very beautiful on her deathbed very different from my grandmother, and different too from my grandfather when he died, and this time Mamma cried a lot because grandfather was her father and she took me up to see him in the room where he still was, and without any fear I looked and saw he had his eyes shut and his skin all yellow and you could almost see all the bones of his face under the skin, so that now I understood about death's-heads like the skulls embroidered on the funeral draperies in church or else on the banners of the Fascists who didn't give a damn about dying and had daggers and grenades like the Arditi in the war, still as far as my grandfather was concerned I didn't feel any great sorrow that he was dead, he had been paralyzed for years, always sitting at the door of the house with his cane and his hand shook and he smelled of snuff and even worse because they said he did his business in his pants and it was really a great trial to take care of him, so thank God who called him to Himself all the better for him and for everybody else they said, however my mother cried and told me to kiss him on the forehead poor grandfather because afterwards they would shut him up in a casket and nobody would ever see him again, and to make her happy I gave him a kiss on the cold forehead, he smelled and even tasted like death, and the only thing I felt was a profound disgust and desire to run away from that room, however if I had run away everybody would have thought I was heartless, my mother would have thought that especially if I didn't cry after her father had died, so I said to myself cry you've got to cry because grandfather is dead, and in fact forcing myself a bit I managed to start crying, and so they took me away and luckily the day of the funeral I didn't go because since it was the fourth of November they celebrated the anniversary of the victory, and there were Fascists about in black shirts with banners full of ribbons, gold borders and medals, I liked the Fascists a lot when they shouted We don't give a damn and they weren't afraid of dying, once when I was in the shop with my Mamma the Socialists had gone through the square with red flags and hammer and sickle, and my Mamma secretly made the sign of the cross because she said that if those men won they'd send away the King and even the Pope, however according to me the big red flags that flapped in the wind while everybody sang The workers' flag is deepest red were rather beautiful, but not even half an hour later a truckload of Fascists arrived singing *Giovinezza* with death's heads embroidered in front, they had revolvers, daggers and iron-spiked clubs, there were hardly more than twenty of them and they went into a theater where at least three hundred Socialists were holding a meeting and they drove them all out like so many old hens, the next day there were a lot of Socialists around the town with bandaged heads, they said that the Fascists were pigs and cowards but all the same they had taken a beating, and secretly I was on the side of the Fascists who were braver, and my mother said that a person who's in business needs everybody and can't afford to have either side against them but in her heart she was more afraid

of the Socialists than of the Fascists, and my father didn't come
out for either but it was well known that he was for respecting the
laws and the monarchy, Faithful through the Centuries being the
motto of the Royal Carabinieri, and so as long as the monarchy
was safe the rest was all the same to him, and anyway it was better
to wait and see what happened whereas the way I looked at it it
was better to line up right away with the Fascists especially because once when there was a strike the Fascists started driving the
tram, and if you wanted to take it you could go all the way to San
Giuliano and come back without paying a thing because the
Fascists didn't make anybody pay for a ticket, and in short one
day I took a piece of coal and over the door of the chicken house,
since that year my mother didn't keep hens as she kept them every
other year, the year she did keep them she always argued with my
father and was upset because it wasn't worth the trouble to keep
them, but then after a year of being without hens, she let the old
desire for them take her again, what shall we do with the leftover
polenta she said and the crusts of bread better to raise a few hens
they don't cost us anything and then we have our own eggs and
the hens to eat when they're fat, however it wasn't true that they
didn't cost us anything, behind my father's back my mother
bought semolina to make them mash or corn to throw into their
pen at the foot of the garden, and when they did lay eggs it was
the season when eggs were practically being given away, and
often before they managed to get fat they got some disease and
all or almost all of them died, so Mamma would say this is the
last time after this I'm not going to keep any more, well anyway
this was a year when she wasn't keeping hens, and with the piece
of coal I wrote over the henhouse door Fascist Headquarters, with
the *s* of Fascist backwards, and then with an old cardboard shoe-
box I made a big oval badge painting it red white and green the
colors of Italy, and I also tried to draw the *fascio* in the midst but
it didn't come out well, however the letters P.N.F. which stood
for *Partito Nazionale Fascista* I wrote correctly, and I hung that
big badge around my neck with a piece of string and in this cos-
tume I not only stayed inside my Fascist Headquarters but also

walked in the streets with some fear of the socialists if I had run
into one of the ones that hit people, but instead I ran into a boy
who was only two or three years older than me and wore a black
shirt and a real badge because his father was a Fascist and he
also was enrolled in the Young Guards, seeing me he said take
off that badge you aren't a member and you haven't the right to
wear it, and I said take it off me yourself if you have the nerve, and
he ripped it off me and also hit me a lot with his club, and I swore
vengeance but I stayed a Fascist anyhow thinking that as soon as
I became chief I'd kick him out of the party, for the moment however it was best for me to keep my mouth shut because he was
bigger than me and his father was a gentleman with lots of money
and had to be respected, and I caused enough trouble in those
days and ran around with bums and beggars from the streets so
my mother said that when I grew up I'd be a bum too, and I
caused her all kinds of worry when I ran away from home to go
to the river where I might fall in and drown, because the river was
beautiful, it was like going to America or the South Seas and the
most adventurous places on earth, when I could I ran off along the
railroad and in ten minutes you were at the river and then I didn't
do anything I just stayed there and watched the older boys and
even kids no bigger than me all of them naked and diving into
the water from the railway bridge, and when they told my father
he said steps would have to be taken you watch out he said or
we'll send you to boarding school, and I answered proudly send
me away then I don't care, so that time I also got a healthy slap
the kind I could cry over for a couple of hours and long to be dead
and have all of them sobbing over me repenting for the bad way
they had treated me, and in short gradually they began to give
serious thought to boarding school, according to my father the
only difficulty was the tuition which cost too much however making some sacrifices they could manage it, and he had two or three
schools send him their prospectuses with the expenses and he saw
which school cost least of all, too bad that they didn't have an
accountant's course but only the regular courses, however I could
go to the fourth and fifth grades there and then maybe they would

transfer me to another school where they did have accounting which in a few years taught you a profession you could earn a living with and have a proper title, whereas with an ordinary high school education you don't have any title because you have to go on to the university afterwards, but where could they ever find that kind of money with my father who was already giving his life's blood for his children, and so when the month of October came they bought me a rather large rubber ball and my mother took me to the school, put me at the gate and showed me some boys playing at the end of the yard, she was crying poor thing at the thought of leaving me but all the same she said go and play with those boys with your playmates, and I didn't want to leave her seeing that she was crying, however at a certain moment she vanished and then I went to where the boys were playing tag, they were bigger than me they were ten or maybe eleven or twelve and one of them saw I had a ball in my hand and said give it here and we'll play ball, but I didn't want to, I had to swallow the lump in my throat before I could start playing, but he hit the ball when I wasn't looking and it slipped from my hand and with a kick he passed it to another boy who passed it to still another, and it was no use my chasing the ball I could never catch up with it because the others kept passing it kicking it from one to the other, until one of them gave it too hard a kick and it went up on the roof and wouldn't come down, maybe it rolled down on the other side or got stuck in a chimney pot or a rainspout, anyway it didn't come down again and without my ball I was suddenly facing the whole unhappiness of my new condition, until then I hadn't clearly understood that boarding school meant being without Mamma and without the possibility of looking for her or calling her when I needed to, and now finding myself alone in the midst of a wicked world I started sobbing desperately against the wall of the church, and after a little while a priest came to see what in the world I had to cry about but meanwhile in those few minutes that I had been crying against the wall of the church I had become grown up, because I had known a quantity of grief that no child can bear and still remain a child.

Now according to the doctor all these vicissitudes that happened to me in infancy were more than enough to explain the shadows so to speak in my character and also a good part of the woes I carried around with me, and among other things they also threw some fairly convincing rays of light on certain details of my spiritual life such as to name one the serious difficulties in defecation that often disturbed me psychically, which difficulties had their probable root in the little castor oil episode, and also my avowed antipathy for the radicals and the dreams I kept having so insistently where I was making speeches to ever greater applause before vaster and vaster gatherings of successful writers had their origin more than anywhere else in the sense of inferiority I had acquired in early childhood by coming into contact with the children from Venice, but all things considered the important fact that emerged from a first and still crude examination of my fairly remote past was my father's unremitting cruelty towards me, and now it's not as if this revelation could suddenly eliminate the many sensations of guilt that assailed me as a rule unexpectedly, at times connected with the events of his death but more often without any apparent cause and yet so strong that they plunged me into anguish without the satisfaction of knowing even remotely why I should have to suffer so much, however on thinking it over calmly then every guilt feeling whose sense seemed impossible to find could without difficulty be connected with a colossal debt I would never succeed in paying, that is the business of the many terrible sacrifices my parents and sisters had made to keep me in school, and obviously with a debt like that weighing on my conscience my every guilt however small became a gigantic sin of ingratitude, which remained as much even if I had arrived by myself at the point where I understood there was a great amount of exaggeration in this story of the sacrifice, because while you can't say they hadn't made any sacrifice at all, no that would be going too far, they certainly hadn't made as much of a sacrifice as I used to think when I was away at school picturing them without enough to eat, maybe only polenta and milk or polenta and cheese in the evening, and in the winter their overcoats all threadbare and maybe they even had holes in their shoes which let the rain in and they couldn't buy new ones because every three months they had to pay the bill from the school, whereas the only really true thing in all this story was my father's suffering when he had to shell out the money to pay my tuition at the end of the quarter, however my father always suffered when he had to pay out money, he suffered even when he bought shoes or paid bills at the shop, and every time he took out money even a modest sum he would always say that he couldn't keep the damned circus going much longer, by which expression he meant the whole complex of his activities and relationships both family and commercial, however I think that the circus would have gone on just as well without so much worry on his part, even better I would say, and I know this not only through plain logic but also because of our fatal resemblance, in the sense that I also suffer or rather used to suffer at having to shell out money to pay anything and I worried even when it would have been right not to, with the difference however that I for example tried to prevent my daughter from knowing how I felt, she was never to know the apprehension and uneasiness her existence caused me since I could never forget that I was responsible or shall we say guilty for her life, and this burdened me with a whole pile of duties that would never be exhausted until my death, or at least I thought not until my death before a certain event that to my way of thinking made all my thirst for further expiations wholly superfluous. Now surely my father never had this kind of thought, he felt that it was to his credit not otherwise to have brought me into the world, this at least was his constant attitude which was illustrated also in phrases that often recurred like you show no gratitude to the man who gave you the gift of life and others on a similarly bombastic level, however who knows this may simply have been an assumed attitude of his a kind of fiction to mask sentiments that perhaps unwittingly were the same as mine, since of course everything I have so far written and argued about my father is only one aspect of the truth, or rather it is only the crust of the events, and under the crust there existed another truth that I was gradually discovering through my relations even the most casual ones with the daughter that in the meanwhile I had brought into the world, singing to her baby baby pretty baby to the tune of an elementary ditty while I bounced her on my knee, or else teaching her to say the word Papa, or else holding her hand and helping her to write on the lines in her first-grade notebook, or else on many many other occasions when I suddenly saw myself as my father and heard his voice in mine, these were true illuminations of an absolute identity, and I though Oh Lord Lord if my father really loved me the way I love this daughter of mine then my whole life has been nothing but a series of unpardonable sins, to tell the truth I never thought my father loved me except in the coarse way that was natural to him but what does coarseness have to do with questions of love, wasn't I even more crude and cowardly letting him die without ever realizing the love he may have felt for me, and in this fashion I could easily have enclosed myself to the end in an endless sense of guilt, however examining without any sentimental agitation the relationship between me and my father through the experience of the equivalent relationship that had come to be created between me and my daughter I then understood very well that the love relationship between fathers and children is not necessarily reversible so to speak, that is all the quantity of love a father may have for a child is compensated for by the very fact that the child exists, in other words a father can't demand that his child love him with the intensity of his love for the child or with the same kind of love, a little child loves in a capricious way he can cry because he wants to stay on his father's lap or because he wants to get into the big bed between his father and mother, and he can stick his fingers into his father's mouth or even his eyes, or else he can start studying his father's head though not all fathers have one as interesting as my father's bald head was, this is how a child loves and the next minute he forgets and runs away drawn to something else that attracts him more, and the father must realize that this is right and that it will happen more often in the future, more and more often until the child won't need to sit on his father's lap any more and give him clumsy caresses, he will go off one day on his own completely detached from his father as is right without any concern about loving him or not loving him whereas the father will always feel the need of loving the child, and then if I imagined my daughter behaving toward me as I had behaved towards my father I didn't see any guilt in her, and still I always carried about with me this incurable guilt at not having realized the love of my now deceased father, and this could very well have been the root of my illness, although on the other hand I could also explain how by another simpler and apparently more plausible path I had arrived at the knowledge of the worst anguish and fear, even close to the final disintegration of my very self.

In reality, in the first months after my father's death I didn't care very much that he was dead, or rather I was sorry but at heart I thought how it's only in the natural order of things that fathers die before their children, so there were no big problems about this indeed there weren't any problems at all, and since I remembered my father always grumbling about something when I happened to think of him after his death I still imagined him grumbling, and I said to him what are you complaining about old man you always complain you lived more than eighty years isn't that enough for you I'll be lucky if I get anywhere near that, yes all right you didn't make money whereas all the others who had shops like you under the arcades in the square made bucketsfull at least during the war and the years afterwards, and you say that it was hard luck but just be reasonable a minute and admit that in the first place you weren't really cut out for business, you had even picked the wrong article deciding to sell hats just when everybody was beginning to go bareheaded, and the same thing applies to umbrellas when you consider raincoats, so thank God that despite everything you still managed to make a living for yourself and your numerous family, that may not seem like much to you but if you only knew all the worries I have even being a bachelor, and besides let's be frank you had too many defects to be able to make money, you boasted for example that you found a way of saving right up to the last cent, well according to me this was just stinginess and harmful to everybody and to business too, and in fact just to give you one example when somebody bought an expensive hat you put it into the special paper bag with the name of the shop printed on it in big letters, but if somebody bought a cap or a cheap hat you wrapped it up in any old paper just to save the two centesimi that the bag cost, and the customer was maybe offended and the next time he would go and buy his cap in Mestre or even at the market in the square on Mondays, instead you should have wrapped any purchase in the bag that had the name of the shop on it, can't you see how in the town if they had seen on a Saturady afternoon or better still on Monday morning at the market eight or ten people walking around carrying bags with the name of the shop on them everybody would have thought why look how much business that shop does I must go there myself, instead only seeing one or two they might have thought that you didn't sell much because you cheated people whereas you didn't cheat anybody I'm sure, unlike your wife who if she could gyp somebody especially a peasant she gypped him happily and if you found out you got mad because it wasn't fair trade, how could you expect to make money with the ideas you had, and then it was another mistake to light up the window always after all the others to save electricity, this also gave an impression of poverty to say nothing of the mirror which had cracked straight across when they put it up the first day and so it had remained, and it hardly helped trade having the shop always filled with four or five retired corporals and sergeants all busy writing protests to the Ministry about their pensions, or even direct appeals to the Duce with scant hope they would reach him because he of course was an honest man who would right all wrongs but the men who surrounded him were a pack of crooks who did everything they could to hide the truth from him, so when somebody came in to buy a cap or an umbrella the atmosphere was all wrong and you yourself were so taken up with the arguments about the rights of pensioners and the art of governing Italy honestly that you looked at the customer as if he were an intruder and you waited on him reluctantly, in short you have no

reason at all to complain if the others have become rich while you
reached the end of your life almost poorer than you had been at
the start, but I don't mean to overlook your hard work in keeping
your head above water especially before you got your rheumatism
and the other ailments of old age, when twice a week you left
the shop in the hands of our aunt and went to the markets with
Mamma, Wednesdays to Casale and Thursdays to Roncade, I
haven't forgotten the few times you took me with you to Casale,
certainly Roncade would have been better because it was farther
away and besides there was the Sile that you crossed on a barge
however I was happy even with Casale especially in the winter
when we got up and it was still dark, the mud in the road had
frozen hard and we walked all the way to the stables behind the
square to hire a quiet horse that wouldn't scare Mamma, and
there was Uncle Rodolfo who hitched the horse to the cart which
was loaded with big boxes of hats and caps, and long boxes with
umbrellas, and we went off with Uncle Rodolfo holding the reins,
once upon a time at the time of the crusades Uncle Rodolfo had
been an English baronet knighted by the king, he still had the
papers he showed everybody, but then he had lost everything and
he had a moustache waxed with tallow like the Germans since
he had been born and brought up under the Austrians and it
seemed that he had even fought on their side in the war, and my
father had him drive the wagon out of charity to let him earn a
little money since he was the husband of a cousin of my father's,
but to me Uncle Rodolfo was interesting, and he didn't scare me
not even when he had had a bit to drink, it was nice to sit beside
him on the box all bundled up in my overcoat with my scarf wound
around my neck and head because the sailor hat didn't cover my
ears, there was the horse that went on and on over the frozen road
his mouth and even his back steaming, every now and then Uncle
Rodolfo touched him with the whip and said gee and for a little
while the horse would trot a bit faster but soon he would go back
to his slow resigned walk so Uncle Rodolfo if Mamma wasn't
watching would give me the reins to hold, and of course I could
have driven us all the way to Casale if my father hadn't grumbled

that it was late and we'd miss the whole market because the good
hours are the early ones when the peasants still have money in
their pockets, and then Uncle Rodolfo would whip the horse and
say gee and the horse in his efforts to go faster would sometimes
make noises with his behind that weren't nice, I hoped I was the
only one who heard them and that at least Mamma didn't hear
them, but instead Uncle Rodolfo would imitate them with his
mouth and laugh, and to tell the truth this was the only thing
about Uncle Rodolfo that I didn't like so much. Then there was
the market with the peasants who came suspiciously over to the
goods where they were displayed on the stand and even on the
ground on some canvas since the stand was too small, and my
mother kept her eye on them trying to figure out which were the
ones who wanted to buy and which were the ones who only
wanted to waste your time for you, and also making sure that
nobody stuck something in his bag and then slipped off in the
confusion, and when the right moment came she would accost
the possible client in a loud voice now then lady can we help you,
or else sir or even my fine sir if it was a man, and then the hard
part of the sale began you had to convince the peasant that the
object was beautiful and good and a bargain, in no other place
could you find goods like this and still less in the shops where
the owners had to pay so much taxes and were bound to become
thieves, and I stood off to one side to watch reciting a variable
number of Hail Marys and ejaculations like Sacred Heart of
Jesus make me love You more and more, offering up to Jesus,
Mary and Saint Anthony many future good deeds if only those
people would buy the umbrella and my father would have a few
less worries, and then when the market was over around half past
twelve we started putting everything back in the boxes and cases
and then in the wagon, and while Uncle Rodolfo who ate only
bread and cold meat not counting the wine stayed on guard we
went to the Trattoria alla Speranza which was all warm and
steamy, and full of confusion of farmers and livestock traders
who ate and drank, and voices and the smell of wine and fried
fish, and then we ordered eels with polenta which was the best

thing in the world, so father I don't understand why you complain, maybe your horizons of adventure were limited however
yours was a simple life Holy God, and you don't know what a
great gift simplicity is in this complicated and precarious world
of ours, and I don't want to argue about your intentions now I
know by making me study you thought you were giving me a
good start, instead you would have done better to leave me simple
and ignorant as you were, and better still to leave me in the mind
of God without situating me in the terrestrial condition through a
thoughtless act of yours.

One sure thing in any case is that I didn't think a lot about
my father in those first weeks after his death, I was too busy earning money because the expenses of the hospital and the funeral
had upset my budget, and then I had to deal with that French
widow who wanted me to come back and live with her or at least
pay the rent on her apartment, and I also had to deal but much
more pleasantly with a young girl I had happened to meet one day
by the fountain in Piazza del Popolo, a really extraordinary young
girl after all who wasn't yet eighteen and to tell the truth looked
even younger but she was in a great hurry to learn everything I
could teach her in matters of love, until one day she had the bad
luck to lose her virginity however she said it didn't make any
difference so long as I had enjoyed it, and to tell the truth I had,
without having to lie as so often happens I could say that making
love with her was better than with any other woman I had ever
known before, so she concluded softly good that means that from
now on you'll make love only with me and I don't care what you
say one fine day you're going to marry me just you wait and see,
so in other words I had my hands full with this teen-ager too, and
on top of everything else it seemed that she couldn't live without
me even in minor matters like going to the movies or the swimming pool or a restaurant and so on, so I had less and less opportunity to think about my father, I had the impression I had settled
him for good in the most respectable middle-class fashion in the
new tomb, let me live I said to him when by chance he came back
into my thoughts, and in effect he did let me live, certainly before

then I had never in my life had a period as beautiful as this almost forty with a young girl barely eighteen capable of inventing for her invisible family the most complicated deceits in order to spend whole nights in my bed, and then since summer had come we went to the pool at the Foreign Ministry Club where there was no lack of pretty girls or at least well-groomed ones which is another quality that has its importance, and although mine was the prettiest of all I wasn't sorry that I also appealed to the others, however there was a catch because the atmosphere was a rather athletic one, those girls and mine especially flung themselves in the water with the greatest of ease in marvelous dives from the high board and then they swam the crawl all glowing with youth and mine was also indescribably in love, but I have never had what you might call a natatory vocation I didn't know how to swim or even how to stay decently afloat, so to avoid cutting a poor figure I told her in the mornings that I had to see people on business and instead I went to the public pool at the Foro Italico to take special lessons, and in two weeks I could manage not to drown and could jump in to the pool from the edge without smacking my stomach, at times I even succeeded in getting my head in first with my legs a little arched, then frog-style I crossed the width of the pool under water it was seventy-five feet by twenty-five and when you also consider how often I was making love with the teen-ager at that time it was a fine case of over-exertion especially physical, however I didn't even think of that indeed I felt like something halfway between a movie idol and an athletic champion, and what's more I was dangerously convincing myself little by little that the real flavor of life was what I was then tasting, I bet I've got it all wrong from the very beginning I said to myself, this is the life taking what you like without so many worries, and in fact things had never gone so well for me since I was born, except that one of those evenings while I'm urinating in the bathroom I happen to look down and I see a dark brown liquid coming out of me and though I felt no pain or disturbance that surely wasn't the proper color of urine, my God what was happening to me, and instead of keeping calm and

imagining a simple mechanical disturbance in my urinary apparatus I start thinking what have I done wrong why should such
a thing happen to me, in short as soon as I got scared I realized
I hadn't yet rid myself of notions of witchcraft and occult powers,
and for that matter even the religion of my forefathers wasn't too
far off if I started thinking of some divine punishment, after all
sacred history and even secular at least the way you study them
in boarding school are nothing but a series of divine punishments,
and when in Italy they say God doesn't pay on Saturdays they
don't mean necessarily that he has to pay only on the other days of
the week, God knows why I thought this was my payday, I mean
that my sins had reached the stage of ripeness for the punishment
to fall properly, not too soon and not too late, and on the other
hand I didn't have to rack my brains to figure out what sin I had
to expiate with such scrupulous punctuality, it had been lying
there all the time under my skin, under every thinking membrane
of my brain, and shall we say also in the folds of my conscience
assuming that I had one in that period of dissolute behavior, in
short it was my father's end that was coming to the surface, my
lousy cowardice in leaving him alone with his cruel death, and I
now had to pee blood, you thought you had skipped out on your
old man but you have to pay for everything in this world, he who
does evil receives evil as he always used to say to you, and I with
the awareness of my sins was also ready to pay if it couldn't be
avoided however I didn't want to drag the innocent down with
me in my ruin, and for example I told the girl I had a headache
and so it would be a good idea for her to take a taxi and go to her
Mamma, I wanted to be alone with my overwhelming thoughts
about this hematuria and its metaphysical causes, lying down appropriately on the bed I waited for the desire to urinate to return
even though I was scared stiff, it can't be true just wait and see it
was all a mistake, I said to myself consolingly, and in fact late
that night or rather towards dawn when I make up my mind to
urinate again the liquid comes out nice and yellow as mother
nature decrees it should be, you see I said to myself you got all
worked up over nothing, but just the same I hadn't just dreamed

that dark brown color of the night before, if it wasn't outright punishment it was certainly a warning, and in this sense I also felt ready to make some good resolutions for the immediate future, still I couldn't assign the whole business completely to supernatural motives that is, on sober reflection, it would be wise to take what you might call a clinical glance at it, and for this my friend the famous surgeon's assistant was just the person, as soon as I get up then I go to see him in the de luxe clinic where the celebrated surgeon operates at frightful prices and naturally I wait in a chair in the entrance hall because they're operating and my friend can't be called out, my God what a beautiful clinic there's even a doorman who looks like the doorman of a hotel just the right place to come and kick the bucket without worrying about it, but I wonder how much it would cost in my case and anyhow I better not think about that, then finally around one o'clock the friend appears and I'm kind of embarassed to talk to him about brown urine, why don't we see more of each other I say to him, I also say I'm happy for him because he must surely make a pile of money here, he laughs and says it's the boss who makes all the money, and meanwhile it's clear that he's a bit annoyed wasting time with me, so perhaps a bit brusquely I tell him I urinated a brown color and I notice a moment of bewilderment in his expression however this may not necessarily be connected directly with my hematuria, it may even stem from a different thought more or less like look who's here getting in my hair with his urine and I won't make a cent out of it because we're friends, anyway we'll see, meanwhile I follow him through a hall, then along a corridor, then in the elevator, and finally along another corridor on the fourth floor where he tells me to wait for him, I see him go into one room and later into another giving me the general impression that his goings and comings have nothing to do with my urine, however this is also psychologically effective in a double sense first of all because it shows me how busy he is and in the second place because it establishes the principle of my absolute dependence on him within the limits of clinical questions obviously, but still clinical questions are the only ones that count in this desperate period of my life which is just beginning, in any case here he comes back to lead me into a kind of chemical laboratory where there is a rather cute de-luxe-clinic-style nurse who with inconceivable charm hands me a kind of cuneiform glass and tells me to put a bit of urine in it, and I stand before her with that chalice in my hand thinking she surely doesn't mean for me to do it before her eyes, until she says to me the bathroom is at the end of the corridor and I go to the bathroom and with all the good will in the world I put the urine in the chalice and then come back to the nurse encouraging myself with the thought that after all this is her job, who would ever have thought that after all my accumulated sexual experience I'd be so shy in front of a nurse even a pretty one, but it isn't so much the nurse who intimidates me as this billionaire's clinic where if you think about it I with my limited earnings really have no right to enter, anyway the urine is nice and clear and the right color so I'm almost disappointed, and when finally my friend comes back I explain to him that the urine that scared me was very different from this, with urine it must be like teeth that when you got to the dentist they stop aching, but the friend tells me not to give it a thought and to come back tomorrow.

With my teen-ager naturally everything changes you can't go to the swimming pool or make love when you keep thinking how you urinated blood or maybe something worse the other night, so you sit there peacefully in an armchair allowing yourself to be gripped by melancholy thoughts like my God she's so young and especially so healthy, she should live on happily even after my death, and in this fashion the sentimental vein comes out and since she really likes making love but according to her she is even more pleased when I show that I love her now she rubs tenderly against my shoulder as she sits on the arm of the chair, and from this position she tells me that she was downright lucky to fall in love with me I'm her first man and I'll also be the last because she'll never ever want anybody else, and I have feelings of indescribable tenderness thinking if that's true what an unlucky girl you are poor little thing, you don't know it but I'm

heading for a nasty end, and by a ghastly coincidence she says
you never talk to me about your family what did your father do,
and I realize that by dragging out this subject she is trying by
a thousand subtle ways to approach the idea of family and specifically of matrimony, and at this moment I would even marry her
if I didn't feel sentenced to an untimely death, so to lighten the
conversation I drop a cheap witticism and say that my father was
a cavalry colonel, in fact the body snatcher of a lovely town in
the province of Treviso, and there carelessly or rather like a fool
I hit on the cemetery right where my father is lying in his sacro-
sanct bourgeois tomb, and I say to him take it easy father in a
little while I'll be joining you, and he seems to agree so I see
myself almost dead or rather in a position now to reveal to her
openly how desperately and sweetly I love her, though as to matrimony she'd better not count on it for various reasons, and as I
say this to her I feel at peace at least as far as she is concerned
free of guilt though she says you'll end up marrying me I tell
you, and I guiltily allow her to cherish this illusion.

The next day we learn that the urine sample so innocent in
appearance contained numerous red blood corpuscles so it seems
a good idea for me to have a nice radiological examination, but
only if I want to my friend says because strictly speaking it
wouldn't be necessary, having numerous red blood corpuscles in
your urine when everything else is in order with only traces of
urobilin and of albumen is nothing at all really, in fact from the
way the friend talks to me it seems that peeing blood is one of
the most popular disturbances among healthy men of forty, still
when it's a matter of your health you can't be too careful so I'd
be wise to have this examination fairly soon, and I decide to do it
and I make an appointment with the radiologist of the de luxe
clinic hoping that when the time comes to hand me the bill they'll
remember that I came there out of friendship, and so the next
morning on an empty stomach I go back to the clinic where the
day gets off to a bad start because the nurse in the X-ray department who is naturally cute at least as cute as the other one wants
to give me an enema, if you ask me she's crazy, I'll do it myself

even if first I'd like to know what the connection is between an enema and a hematuria, anyhow though with plenty of difficulty I manage to carry out at least in part that painful and demeaning operation and then when my turn comes they make me lie down on a table which is evidently part of the X-ray machine, it's really a handsome new and complicated machine that costs God knows how many million lire which I too will contribute towards paying let's hope to a not too exorbitant degree, good heavens every time I think of the sad necessity of coughing up money I'm reminded of my father, who however doesn't need pecuniary thoughts to reveal his powerfully active presence in the midst of these gadgets which I'm sure in a much more economical version must have dug around in his belly hunting for the death that was nesting there, what do you say old man you must be pleased now that you've got me prematurely following in your footsteps, in accordance with my guilt obviously I'm not denying it, for that matter just look at me, see how resigned I am, how I let them do whatever they want with me, they've injected God knows what into my veins to make my urine opaque so they can follow its course through my kidneys and the urethra into the bladder, and they've taken measurements with a plumb-line attached to the lens of the apparatus, marking the various spots on my skin with a pencil, see how reasonably I take everything imagining that you did the same thing when it was your turn, we're very reasonable, aren't we father, now they've turned off the lights and are trying a radioscopy to see if that opaque substance has already reached the kidneys, and sure enough it has, they load the film and then one moment hold your breath, you hear the buzz of the current and at that same moment without anybody seeing them the rays go through the body, and although this is at least the twentieth time that I've been X-rayed especially because of the duodenal ulcer I'm still afraid that these invisible rays may produce ter-rible consequences after a short or a long while, I ought to be more careful and not let my father screw me so to speak with my own hands, anyhow I can't behave like a savage and show that I'm afraid I have to let them make all the X rays they want, at a certain moment the table I'm stretched out on rises automatically and I find myself in a vertical position, my God I wonder how much this supergadget costs and how much of the cost I'll have to pay, maybe it would be better to go to the Municipal Hospital or to the poor ward in San Giovanni or some other public place where I hear they make you pay very moderate fees, in any case we're here now so let them go ahead and photograph my kidneys and bladder on this side and that and in horizontal and vertical positions, but what a lot of X rays they're making after all, expense is obviously no concern around here since they're used to handling billionaires, there, now they've finished but we have to wait and see if the plates were properly exposed, and after a certain while they say that everything is all right so I can go, but before going I still have time to make a huge gaffe with the X-ray doctor asking him much does it cost, and he is offended and says ask the business office as if money stank and evidently this is how rich people behave, and in fact after a couple of days I find at the business office a reasonably enormous bill but I'm glad to pay it because in the meanwhile my friend has already taken me to look at the thirty-some X rays displayed in a little room against illuminated screens, and has said to me well you really had me scared with that urine of yours you know hematuria is usually a symptom of very serious diseases like tuberculosis or even cancer, instead in your case it's nothing really nothing at all and leading me from one of those mysterious images to the next he illustrates the general condition and working order of my urinary system, the right kidney has the major calyces a bit dilated but it isn't anything when you're forty you have to expect a few troubles, however the passage of the urine is perfectly easy and now see in this X ray you can notice that the right kidney is considerably lower, and this is one of the X rays they made when I was in an erect position, and what does this mean it means that I have a floating kidney, nothing to worry about because almost all women after childbirth have one and sometimes even two and while it's perfectly clear that I haven't been giving birth recently still I must have been overdoing things maybe working too much, so now all I have to do is put on a bit of weight and the fatty padding which is supposed to keep the kidney in place will form again, meanwhile if I feel any inconvenience the best thing is to lie flat or, even better, have a carpenter make two wedges to put under the legs at the foot of the bed so that the body will assume and maintain an inclined position and in that way the kidney is unable to get out of its place, because the business of the blood in my urine is explained precisely by the fact that the floating kidney when it moves down presses on a little vein along the ureter and the bit of blood comes from that vein and is found in the urine, and when the matter is explained in this way it becomes a mere nothing, as for the cure all I have to do is eat plenty of spaghetti and mashed potatoes so I'll put on a few pounds which won't do me any harm even from the aesthetic standpoint, and all in all my friend manages to be fairly convincing although he committed the psychological error of telling me he had had a big scare when I first went and talked to him about that brown-colored urine of mine and he had been able to hide his fear pretty well, and God knows maybe this time he's hiding something too let's hope not, still even if it's nothing as he says I have to change my life a bit the way I did ten years ago when they discovered the ulcer in my duodenum, at first I was gloomy from morning to night I had almost given up smoking and I felt I had to bid life farewell and then a couple of months later I paid no attention to it at all except when it really hurt, when you think about it the first attack of old age and until now the worst was one I had had at eighteen when I had spat a bit of blood and hadn't told anybody about it and it took several months for me to convince myself that it was from my throat, you get used to everything in this world I had got used to my ulcer and if need be I'd get used to tuberculosis, and I'll also get used to the floating kidney especially if, as it seems, it's only a passing trifle, and to tell you the truth if I hadn't happened to see that brown urine myself I would never even have been aware of the thing whereas now I can tell myself it's nothing till I'm blue in the face but I still keep thinking about this damn kidney, anyhow I'd better telephone the teen-ager be-

cause if eating spaghetti is good for me then we can at least eat
it together, however I have to go a bit easy on the love-making
and not do it too often like before and I'd better skip the swimming
pool too, anyway it's October and I'd have had to stop going one
way or another. Behind all these unpleasant events obviously
there was my dead father lying in ambush, I was fully aware of
him even though I couldn't foretell the horrible pass to which he
would lead me, in fact after the friend's explanations I surmised
that the deceased chiefly meant to call a halt to my social pleasures
and to make me think of him a bit more often, and to tell the
truth I now did think of him frequently associating him with
my floating kidney and the sense of decline connected with it, I
remembered above all that morning when he fell flat on the
ground with the buckets of water and started crying like a baby
because he was an old man, and while he cried he finally was
made flesh this symbol of a father I had been stuck with, this
man all duty and strictness and royal carabiniere there he was
revealed as a human being in all his weakness though a bit ridiculous he was about it, how old could he have been when he tripped
and fell, between fifty-seven and fifty-eight I suppose, but Christ
what did he expect at fifty-eight if he carried those huge drums
of water which I fear I'll never be able to carry, not to mention
the fact that his fall was only a fleeting incident because afterwards he started carrying drums of water as if it were nothing
and also drums full of sewage when he emptied the cesspool to
fertilize the garden, but anyway father you had a full life almost
right up to the end, believe me if it had been up to me I'd have
spared you that last terrible week I had every intention of sparing
you, if it hadn't been for that snide surgeon so full of himself we
would have shortened that terrible last week of yours by a few
days, and don't be angry with me if I ran off instead of staying
with you at the final moment you stank unbearably my God, and
then there were my sisters around those pains in the ass to say
nothing of the French widow who caused one disaster after another, and still I swear to you if that doctor with the yellow shoes
hadn't given me all those fine guarantees you know about I

wouldn't have gone away, I would have stayed with you to help you as best I could in your going, so let me live father all I have is a floating kidney and if I put on a little weight everything will be as it was before, after all I have a right to enjoy a bit this late maturity remember the childhood and adolescence I had, partly through your fault, too.

When the girl saw a couple of big dictionaries in the middle of the room under the legs of the bed I had to explain more or less the business of the floating kidney and the basically elementary mechanism through which at a certain moment a bit of blood had ended up in the urine, and though after all we were pretty intimate when you consider that in the last five or six months we had made love abundantly I think if she had told me such a thing about herself I would have been a little disgusted by it, but instead the organic deviations taking place in my body aroused in her a complementary maternal sentiment, after all it was sweet to be spoiled by a young girl so fresh and so in love, she said from then on we would make love only once every two weeks and I felt this was exaggerating, once a week was all right that was what my doctor friend said I insisted lying, but she was obstinate about the two weeks and as we argued about it we were taken with a great desire to make love right away and though she hypocritically said no no please think of your floating kidney, we did it though we repented immediately afterwards but this is natural it used to happen to me even before the floating kidney, anyway that evening I would eat a double helping of noodles with extra butter plus a Florentine steak with a side dish of mashed potatoes, and as you can clearly see the psychological adaptation to the floating kidney was costing me less time and effort than I would have foreseen, and in consequence also my father's immortal soul went back to stay in the grave which all things considered represented the apex of his social aspirations, until finally in a single night that disaster which was to happen happened.

During the day preceding that night to tell the truth I had had a few unpleasant presentiments like listlessness and a vague sense of uselessness, and towards evening I had also noticed a bit of swelling of the stomach or of the floating kidney one might suppose anyhow nothing to worry about, I telephoned my girl whom I was supposed to take out to dinner and told her I had some work to do and I went to bed after reinforcing the dictionaries under the bed with another pair, thinking to myself you want to bet that goddamned kidney has got out of place, but now it'll go back by God yes it will, and I lay on my belly with my fist thrust into my abdomen to help that filthy gadget go back where it belonged, after all this was the first time it had hurt me and it wasn't a really unbearable pain, however I had the impression that things were taking a rapid turn for the worse and maybe it would be a good idea for me to take some kind of sedative, all I had in the house were some headache pills but anyhow they couldn't do me any harm, so I get up and take them by my God what a hard time I have moving I even have to walk bent over because of the damned pain that has gripped my right side, although now it is also moving to the left, to tell the truth if I had to say with any precision where it was and what the pain consisted in I wouldn't be able to, all I know is that it's monstrous and unfair, unfair even when compared with my boundless cowardice in abandoning my dying father at the very moment when he was passing on to a better world, yes because it really seems to me that this pain is overdoing it if it hasn't already gone beyond all proper proportion to the guilt that created it, in any case it surely isn't a good idea for me to think of my father in these present circumstances when I have plenty of my own affairs to think about, it hurts Oh God how it hurts I feel the words escape me exactly what he said after they had done that great job of bringing out his tumor, how can this kidney hurt so much, assuming it is the kidney and not some other misfortune much worse and incurable, anyhow best for me to keep calm and still it's only eleven and if the pills get rid of it a little I can sleep and tomorrow morning I won't even remember it, to encourage myself I summon up the numerous occasions in my life when I displayed a certain amount of manly courage in the face of pain and even of death itself, like when I was on the point of going up to heaven thanks to a tertian fever under a military hospital tent in Gondar or when, also for the greater glory of the King Emperor and the Duce Founder of his Empire I caught a bullet in my foot and it almost went into gangrene, or when I was in prison and they operated on me for double hernia with enough anesthetic only for a single hernia so that when they started on the second one I could feel how they were yanking at my guts and muscles and tendons, in short I've been through too many big things in my life to let myself get scared by this business but my God I could swear I've never been through anything this bad before, I wonder what's happening because I really feel bad Oh God how it hurts, and this isn't any exaggeration because about two in the morning I can't take it any more and I call my friend the assistant to the famous surgeon, I hear him over the phone dazed with sleep say for Christ's sake why are you calling me now if you've been like this for three hours, I didn't get to bed till after one and tomorrow morning at eight I have to be in the operating theater, believe me the pain isn't anything and you mustn't worry about it, get yourself an injection of morphine and it'll pass, tomorrow morning at seven-thirty before I go to the clinic I'll look in on you and good night, so there I am again all alone with my illness as cruel as the one that sent my father to the next world, now what to do now what can I do, and I think of telephoning the neighborhood doctor the one I use for sore throats and vitamin shots, but I bet he hasn't come back to Rome, I just bet he's still at Chianciano where in the summer and in the autumn too he makes his living by squeezing the livers of ladies over forty, Oh Christ I can't stand these pains any longer, help me help me I can't stand it, God he is up in Chianciano all right making money with livers so I'm told by his sister-in-law or sister or whatever she is, and now what can I do Oh Lord Lord all this pain I feel, what have I ever done wrong I didn't kill my father after all he would have died even if I had been there to count his stinking breaths day and night, my God if I don't find a doctor I'm going to die for sure, I know plenty of doctors why can't I remember the full name of one of them or even just the last name, and finally I do remember one

who was a good friend of that French widow, maybe he even went
to bed with her or had before me anyhow this is of no importance
in a civil and organized society, now I'll call him and I do call
him, he's on the other end of the wire strangely willing to help
me, right away I'll come right away of course I'll take a taxi, and
now I can calculate how long it'll take him from Piazza Mazzini
where he lives, I don't know what kind of doctor he is however
you don't have to be a specialist in surgical pathology to give an
injection of morphine I'd do it myself if I had some, anyhow I
suddenly remember that this character who is rushing to my aid
is an anesthetist in a clinic so we can hope that he knows how to
give an injection, in any case I would almost let myself be injected
even by the janitor this suffering has plunged me into such despair,
too bad that janitors don't keep morphine handy, meanwhile I've
managed to count up to seven hundred and ninety-two counting
slowly and finally in the now almost silent city I hear the taxi
stop the door slam here he is thank God, I throw him down the
key to the building and a little later he is coming toward me with
his silly eager face, a feeling of perhaps instinctive defensiveness
causes me at that moment to feel less pain but unfortunately for
me this doesn't last, a moment later I am in the grip of torments
even worse than before so I ask him bluntly if he's brought the
morphine, and he says of course he's brought it however you
can't do things so casually as I think, at least as a formality he
has to take a look at me, in fact he asks me to collaborate and tell
him where it hurts, of course where does it hurt at first it seemed
to be in the neighborhood of my back but then I felt the pain
moving forward like it was walking towards a preestablished point
which is exactly the curve that the colon makes when it stops
moving transversely and begins to descend, but this may very
well be an impression of mine due to metaphysical influences I
hasten to say, the only unquestionable fact is that about a month
ago I had a hematuria, and about ten years ago thanks to careful
X-ray examinations they found a duodenal ulcer in me, not very
big about the size of a pea but in the meanwhile it may have grown
and so it may be at this point the ulcer that's hurting me, and to

conclude I hurt everywhere and so the best thing is for him to hurry up and give me the morphine, and he answers yes of course however first he wants to know if I have vomited and good God I hadn't even thought about vomiting but now that I do think about it I seem to want to, I have an idea that I don't lack any of those fierce and disgusting things that collaborate to kill a man, now it isn't that I want to live at all costs it doesn't mean a great deal to me although this has been a favorable period for me in general at least before that lousy wrong-colored urine, but my God why doesn't he give me the injection he seems to have no wish to do it instead he stands there poking at my stomach with a face as serious as a gravedigger's, he presses here and there wanting to know where it hurts when I've already told him it hurts everywhere what more does he want to know, let him give me the injection and have done with it, but he picks up the telephone and dials a number and at the same time tells me to take it easy it's nothing, I know it's nothing myself and death after all is less than nothing however I don't want a horrible death like my father's who if he is fair should agree with them to kill me without making me suffer too much, still I wonder if he's all that fair because this effective instrument of his vengeance isn't paying the least attention to me, he is talking into the phone God knows to whom, he says arrogantly that if you ask him it's abdominal but what's abdominal if you ask him isn't clear, he is saying yes, vomiting, hurry up, and then he explains that he has called the assistant in the clinic where he works as an anesthetist and I'm thinking they're all crooks in this thing together they call each other till they've fleeced me naked, or else I think well it must be something serious if this doctor calls another one for help, naturally I was stupid to think it wasn't serious with all these pains, but why doesn't he give me the morphine I ask him in a nasty tone now and this man who above all must be a coward answers in a minute in a minute, but it's a minute only after a manner of speaking because this idiot has to boil the syringe, and while he's there in the kitchen I try to make a rational summing up that is leaving out any idea of avenging ghosts, to begin with I look at the time

and it's five to three, what can have happened to me with this
illness which above all seems a new kind to me, never experienced
anything like it before, from what I understand it must be like
labor pains thanks to a vague sensation of having something to
bring forth, except that with labor pains you know where they
end and in my case nobody knows this, least of all this eager
gravedigger that I was kind enough to call, he looks like the man
who makes great decisions maybe at the moment of following his
medical vocation he dreamed of saving at least one life with his
prompt intervention, and now here is his big chance only I'm not
very sure he's capable of saving a life, so thank God he's called
in that other one, the assistant I mean, let's hope he's better
than this one who now comes from the kitchen with the syringe
all ready in one hand and the dab of cotton soaked in alcohol in the
other, I roll over on my stomach myself to hurry him up and there
he gives me the injection and now I am lying there trying to deceive myself about the degree of the pain, moaning at times and
saying ow ow or else ugh ugh interminably, it seems to be dulled
and I seem to feel these frightful pains less, and in any case all I
have to do now is be patient because he's given me the morphine,
in a quarter of an hour at least it should take effect, that time
that I caught the bullet in my foot and there was danger of gangrene they gave me morphine and the effect came in fifteen minutes
if I remember rightly, but now the minutes pass and it keeps on
hurting the same as before if not worse, I bet this is a kind of pain
morphine can't do anything about maybe there are such pains,
I almost ask this doctor but I can't stand his smug manner,
so I stay here turned towards the wall on purpose so as not to
see him with his serious, sepulchral look, and the pain doesn't
pass my God it doesn't pass at all, and then I begin to suspect
can this man have injected something into me that wasn't morphine, he's capable of anything, but why would he have done
that, he doesn't look like a degenerate after all or a sadist he
only looks stupid because he acts so important, what did you give
me I ask him and he answers hastily morphine morphine, however
he isn't a very good liar and I'd bet anything that it wasn't mor-

phine, suppose this idiot starts making experiments on me now no it wasn't morphine I say to him, and he says yes, I am all sweating with the pain and the agitation like a woman in labor I say it wasn't morphine and I tell him to get out who do you take me for I'm no quinea pig, I always pick the quacks this is just what I say to him, but he isn't the least offended in fact he wipes away my sweat telling me to take it easy and it'll pass in a minute, and I would like to not have these pains just for a moment so I could stand up and spit in his face, but my God how it hurts and all I say is that he's a shit and a pervert, and this definition makes him stop and think it almost seems we're going to have an argument, but then the door buzzes and it's the second doctor arriving who surely can't be worse than the one I have already.

But when I see him I tell myself I was probably wrong, maybe in serious circumstances like these a poor bastard wants to see Jesus of Nazareth in person walk in with his sweetness and goodness and above all with a certain talent for working miracles, whereas this new doctor doesn't know much about miracles at least to judge by his personal appearance which has nothing to do with the Jesus of traditional iconography, in any case he looks several years older than the anesthetist and this may be a point in his favor, but a moment later I think if he's still only an assistant at his age he's surely no ace, anyhow we'll wait and see now he too has started poking earnestly at my belly and doesn't ask me anything but turns towards his colleague the anesthetist and says oh yes it's taut all right, and the other one's face glows with pleasure as if he had guessed all the right answers on the football pool I only wish he would have these damn pains for a minute, in the end the assistant condescends to ask me something too if I've vomited and I reply that I'm not too clear on the vomit question however I feel so awful that my bile has come up into my mouth, and so he turns towards his buddy and says oh yes it's perforated, and I ask him for the love of God to give me some morphine because I can't stand it any longer but he brutally answers no, no morphine or any other analgesic because by attenuating the sensitivity to pain the clinical situation is changed and the venerable

Professor-surgeon when it's his turn to intervene must have all the information in the natural state at his disposal, and for that matter I don't have to wait long since even without the final agreement of this luminary of science there can't be any doubt about the fact that my old ulcer has dug into the wall of the duodenum until it's perforated it, and therefore the surgical operation known as laparatomy is urgent if I want to save my skin, and in consequence they had better arrange for me to be conveyed at once to the clinic where the first doctor is the anesthetist whereas the second succorer is the assistant to the venerable professor-surgeon.

Now one thing is finally clear namely that they're going to cut my belly open according to a procedure all too familiar to me, and another thing is equally if not more clear and that is that there's nothing I can do about it, I simply lack the spiritual strength to oppose such a sinister event and while it's a good idea to establish the fact that I am now going off where it was my fate to go thanks to a series of circumstances all clearly pigeonholed in a logical and materialistic order nothing can drive from my head the thought that my father is enjoying his legitimate revenge, especially since I am not at all persuaded that these two champions of science who at present have me in their power aren't making a big mistake, in matters of this sort a little margin of error should always be calculated and this is precisely where the intervention which I would call metaphysical could plausibly come in, but on the other hand physical suffering has one good thing about it which is that when it reaches a given intensity it makes you wish for any way out even the worst, not excluding demise in some special cases, and my case to all appearances was precisely one of those both because of the intensity of the pain and because of the faces the two gravediggers pulled allowing for their triumphant satisfaction at the exploit they had begun, and also because of the rights that my defunct father had to assert from his middle-class tomb where I had fooled myself into thinking I had buried him forever. So now though I never cease my groans and my invocations to the pair asking them for pity's sake to give me a little morphine, I prepare myself as best I can for my grim and horrible decease with moving farewells to everything I could have done and now will do no more, for example achieving glory in some way, and also to everything I possessed and now obviously will lose, walking through the streets at night for one thing or eating spaghetti *all' amatriciana* or naturally making love with the teen-ager, in fact it is the girl who seems to sum up in herself all the marvelous properties of the universe I am about to lose, I feel so sorry for myself at the thought of her that I am moved to tears, and to tell the truth it would be no small comfort to break down and cry in the present situation but I'm prevented from this by the very cruelty of the pains which leave no room except for a firm desire to end it all, but before dying I'd like to see her one more time, once more my living little girl, I'd like to see her in despair beside my deathbed, when I was a little boy and they hurt me I always thought of dying and then I saw myself dead lying on the table in the hall like my grandmother with my father and my mother and sisters and the maid all gathered around weeping over my death, and so now I wanted the girl but I wanted her to get there while I was still alive because I wasn't at all sure I'd be in a position to enjoy the scene once I was dead. Anyhow it wasn't easy to get in touch with the girl at three forty-five a.m., the two or three times I had tried to call her even at more respectable hours I had always come up against a voice that displayed toward me a sentiment I'd define as repellent and besides they had always told me that she was out, so just imagine calling her at three forty-five, so I don't call her house but I wake up a girl friend of hers, they're about to take me to the hospital I tell her it seems serious and anyway I feel like death, so call your friend right away and tell her to hurry, I'd like to see her one final time but if she doesn't get there in time tell her that my last thought will be of her, and dammit I'm overcome with self pity which is just as well because I was about to say that if the girl did get there in time I'd marry her *in articulo mortis*, and this is always a risky business because it isn't absolutely sure that I'm going to die, despite the obviously unfavorable situation and the evil forebodings the instinct of self-preservation hangs on, and all in all if I'm going to survive I'd rather survive as a bachelor. In any case it seems this matrimonial event *in extremis* isn't included among the designs of Providence or my father's, before anything else can happen the ambulance arrives, two men in white coats come up with the stretcher, they carry me down the stairs with consummate skill, and it is this unusual thing of being carried down the steps in a litter that shows me the extent of my helplessness in the face of what is happening, I'm no longer the one who guides the final events of my life somebody else must do it even this petulant and wiseacre anesthetist who is enjoying the triumph of having been the first to diagnose peritonitis correctly, he must even consider me his personal prey because after climbing into the ambulance with me he sits down at my side and wipes away my sweat and tells me to take it easy we'll be there in no time, be where I want to ask him just to establish the difference in our points of view as to final destinations, for me it's obvious that the farther we go the worse it is, and the pains increase and the nausea and the taste of bile in my mouth, Oh Lord Lord the pain's even worse how can that be, and still shut in that truck that smells of fresh paint and of carbolic acid I think that I am making my last journey on this earth and the situation deserves some attention after all, these damn jolts are the tracks of the tram at the Piazza Ungheria or maybe the Number 3 line in the Via Bertolini, and now these lamps that every now and then make the milky windows brighter must be the Viale Liegi, now I remember it even as being beautiful in the summer when the plane trees almost make an arch over the street, farewell to you too Viale Liegi, I feel all tender like when I used to read *From the Apennines to the Andes*, too bad my death is so banal that is to say entirely without glory, if I'd thought about it sooner it would have been better to die in the war, but it's too late now and in a little while we'll be at that fatal clinic and the girl, my God the girl, will surely not get there in time for her nuptial and funeral march combined.

I thought that in a city with already more than two million inhabitants the nighttime arrival of a dying man didn't constitute

a particularly unusual or solemn event, but instead I was wrong
at least about this clinic where at the entrance I am being awaited
not only by the assistant who had preceded us in his car but also
by three or four nuns and as many orderlies with a bed with
wheels on to which they transfer me groaning from the ambulance's stretcher, and in the meanwhile they all look at me with
deep interest both nuns and orderlies, I wonder what's so interesting about me it's only a perforated ulcer, the rest is known only
to me I alone know the intensity of these terrible pains and the
score I have to settle with my father, naturally when you see yourself being looked at like this you have the impression on the one
hand that you're farther gone than you suspected and on the
other hand that you're an important customer without any public
health insurance, that is to say a private citizen obliged to pay in
one lump a pile of money which is the usual amount charged in
these disasters, and when you think about it our medical and
sanitary organization is a colossal fraud at the expense of professional free-lance writers of scarce means and so here too they
should do the way they do in England where you don't have to
pay for doctors or hospitals, however on further reflection here
if things are already bad even when you pay just think how much
worse they would be if you didn't pay, and on the other hand it
looks as if this will be the last money you spend old boy so stop
crying over it and regret instead that you haven't made a will so
you could leave the girl that broken-down car you have or at
least some money to buy herself a Seicento maybe which would
satisfy her in the absence of anything better, oh well face with
manly courage your tortured solitude, they've left you all by yourself to groan on the little bed in an icy and ill-lighted corridor
with a bulb that's five watts at most and set what's more in front
of a plaster statue of the Madonna with fake flowers according to
the bad taste that nuns display as a rule, but in the meanwhile as
they light the corridor however dimly they also procure for themselves the benevolence of the Mother of God, and anyway that
faint light is more than enough to let you read over a door the sign
Operating Theater my God how similar even with its differences

this place is to the one where they butchered a certain person, but
he at least had plenty of people bustling around him whereas I
don't have anybody, they've left me alone with my frightful pains
in an icy corridor, Christ why doesn't something happen I can't
stand these pains any more now the vomiting is coming that'll
satisfy them, and in fact I do cough up some foul bitter muck
nothing but bile obviously my guts must be all turned inside out,
why don't they kill me off in a hurry instead of abandoning me to
my agony in the garden, and now a nun comes along and then an
orderly who wipes up the muck I vomited and they also clean
my mouth with a cloth and the nun puts a basin beside my face
and says I must try to vomit into it if I feel like vomiting again,
and she asks me if by any chance I want a priest in order to go
to confession and I almost am rude to her, I say where's the surgeon and why don't they give me something to ease the pain, and
she says that the professor can never be waked before six because
he's very old and besides it's apparently bad manners to wake up
a famous surgeon unless it's for a case that gets him illustrious
publicity which certainly isn't my case since whether I live or die
won't arouse much interest, anyway I realize that everything
was a mistake and I should at least have called back that friend of
mine who's assistant to another famous surgeon to warn him
look here they've got it into their heads that they have to cut my
stomach open, but because of my hellish pride I didn't call him
because instead of rushing to my bed of pain he had answered me
crossly and said I ought to sleep, and I wonder tomorrow morning how he'll feel when he comes to see me at seven thirty and
finds they've rushed me to the hospital an emergency case, after
all this is another satisfaction though admittedly a macabre one
and especially insufficient in my present misfortune, if he were
here maybe they'd give me the morphine even over the phone he
said as much that morphine was all that was necessary, instead
those two grim gravediggers have brought me here with all my
pain to this premature appointment with my forefathers, and suddenly I'm reminded of the god Huitzilopochtli who sniffs your
blood and though the poem doesn't seem so beautiful to me at the

moment though I loved it as a boy here there is somebody who is sniffing my blood, and my only defense against such a disaster is my weak desire for them to hurry up and get it over with.

However now that they have managed to leave me in that squalid corridor where my sufferings and my mortal presentiments take on a tragic consistency, it seems they have no more haste to get on with it, at long intervals the anesthetist or the assistant makes a fleeting appearance and they say everything is proceeding well that I mustn't worry it's as if I had a headache or at most a cavity in my tooth, and they clear out quickly because obviously they themselves despite the scarce sensitivity with which they're endowed realize that the endless waiting in that pre-funeral place is a disaster for which I could reasonably blame them, therefore they abandon me in solitude until the first nun reappears and asks me if by any chance I've changed my mind about confession, to face severe trials with a clear conscience is always an advantage even for the body you might say and in fact the Lord is more of a mind to help those who turn to Him than those who turn their backs on Him, but I say where's the surgeon for Christ's sake where is he, and at the first whiff of blasphemy she runs off with her habit rustling toward the chapel no doubt where she will start praying to her omnipotent God to open my eyes in time, and in the meanwhile a horrid window at the end of the corridor has become light there it's day what day is it in November, I don't know but according to any reasonable conjecture it's my last day and I care so little about it that I think this gray dawn has been granted me by mistake or as a punishment, but why won't they free me from these pains Oh my father let this cup pass from me, I say father who art in heaven and art not in your walnut casket which cost me an arm and a leg, you see how you've got under my skin earthly father if I start thinking about money even when I'm in my death agony, and I doubly regret not having made a will because I would also have expressed the wish to be buried with the least possible expense in the potters' field at Prima Porta, whereas now I'm sure that somebody will have the bright idea of shipping me God only knows at what expense up to my home town maybe even to set me in a definitive middle-class section next to you, as if we needed such material nearness to prove the relationship that binds us in sickness and in health, but more in sickness than in health apparently, and anyway it's high time this damn demiurge of my expiation arrived, now that I have admitted my sins there is nothing that ties me to this world except for the feeble hope that the girl should come, but for that matter poor wretch that I am what could she do against these terrible pains, so it's best for the surgeon to arrive and end the whole business.

However when he does finally arrive and I see him all of a sudden I change my mind, I really wish he had been struck down in the street before getting to me, and this enables me to see how much play-acting there was in my supposed resignation to death, or rather I was resigned all right but not sufficiently at least as far as the way was concerned, and now that I see this man before me pressing my belly and moving his jaws as if he had something quite different on his mind I see how old he is maybe the oldest man I've ever had anything to do with, and he's examining me with the indifference toward death that a man must have when his own death is long overdue, my God I wonder how old he is at least a hundred, at his age you won't find a house painter or a train conductor or a schoolteacher that's still on active service but instead with this man who cuts open the bellies of living people there isn't anybody who tells him he's too old to go on doing it, and he had to happen to me, despite my mortal sufferings I would like to yell at him to get his ass out of there it would even be amusing to use such a crude expression with an old man that many would consider deserving of respect, however he is only the instrument of destiny eh father, in reality for a demiurge I could hardly find a better specimen than this so we may as well keep him, only let's ask him for the love of God to let us have an injection of morphine, and from his remote senility he says yes now they can give it to me now that finally this lousy old Methuselah has ascertained how taut my abdomen is and how I am all huddled up in pain, maybe not even my father with his monstrous visceral carcinoma had suffered so much, anyhow we are at the end a man comes and gives me the injection and I see that it is the more-than-triumphant anesthetist and I tell him not to try to cheat me this time, and he swears that he hasn't that this is really morphine they always give it before the operation, the venerable doctor has decided that they must operate *illico et immediate*.

So now the pain is little by little dispelled by the morphine and goes off toward other subterranean zones of my being leaving me free to meditate on these last moments of life while I calmly follow the preparations for the operation after the orderlies have pushed me into the theater and shifted me onto the table under the lights, all around me they bustle silently and I would like to hope also efficiently, nuns and nurses and doctors with a solemnity as if they were making ready for a religious function, and this I suspect also a bit because of the presence of the nuns and a bit because the Holy Mass is also a sacrifice, indeed it's the sacrifice par excellence according to what I was taught in boarding school, and naturally without any intention of comparing myself even remotely with the Son of God I too feel a bit like a victim, strange that among these busy nuns there isn't that first one who kept bothering me with untimely suggestions about confession, I felt too awful before and exceptional suffering in general does not stimulate a religious feeling which may have been long neglected in fact it inspires you more than ever to blasphemy, not everybody can be Jesus on the cross although even he kept saying Father if it be thy will, which in a certain way might mean that when sufferings pass a given limit they are hard to reconcile with any idea of religion, anyhow now that my sufferings are back within the limits of toleration if that nun should reappear with her devout proposals I wouldn't be too averse to making a quick over-all declaration of my more important sins, but she doesn't show up and it doesn't matter what counts now is that a man should approach his own extinction with a spirit of adjustment, a few hours of searing pains as rather rightly they're called and an injection of morphine have sharply devaluated that possession of great price which is our life, anyway I wouldn't have achieved glory even if favored by more propitious circumstances probably, in any case it's late now the old man is approaching all masked for the cruel job, funny that he can walk by himself that is not supported by anybody but merely surrounded by the veneration of his assistants and disciples, God it's almost beautiful this appropriate ceremony, my father into thy hands so far from piteous after all I commend my spirit, *in manus tuas commendo spiritum meum*, but then that dope the anesthetist ruins the solemnity of the ritual because at the climax he drops a little tube making my blood spurt brightly forth from a needle he had previously stuck into me near the wrist, and the poor bastard tries to carry on as best he can but he trembles before the ultraterrestrial eyes of the old man, keep calm young fellow I manage to say to him fraternally, but at the moment he doesn't even know what the word *calm* means and he sweats and his teeth chatter and he trembles especially his hands, however before he manages to kill me through loss of blood his patron saint helps him to connect needle and tube again and there he is more triumphant than ever injecting into my blood something that whirls me back toward nothingness, this is real nothingness as I understand it, there is dark dark dark and then it isn't even dark any more.

A few hours later one comes back from nothingness and to tell the truth life is a gift of dubious satisfaction since in his toilsome emergence towards consciousness the poor bastard before he arrives at the assertion why I'm alive passes through phases in which he is aware more than anything else of a headache and a bad taste in the mouth and all in all without much desire to progress toward complete awareness, anyhow despite this lack of desire coming back is inevitable unless the doctors and surgeons have caused important and irreparable damage in the organism, and since at least for the moment this isn't my case here I am with my eyes still shut vaguely rising toward the surface of consciousness, and finally I open my eyes and prepare myself for the assertion by God here I am again, however my eyes first of all see something that contradicts foreseeable reality that is to say on one side of the bed there is a widow probably foreign of my ac-

quaintance and on the other side a young girl also of my acquaintance both tensely observing my reawakening like a pair of creditors, so the first thought that comes into my head is a dead man's
thought I must have passed on and one of these is the angel of
God while the other has come from hell and now they're going
to fight for the possession of my soul, to tell the truth at the
moment of my farewell I had felt some religious feeling however
vague, I had even been thinking in Latin as near as I can recall,
in any case at present I don't myself know whether to hope for
salvation or damnation since I couldn't decide which of these
two must be the angel of God and which the one from hell, my
Lord is it really inevitable having to go on like this even beyond
the grave, anyway now little by little I have to abandon the comforting idea of being a bodiless soul and I have to face as best I
can the hard situation, after all I had invoked the teen-ager myself,
whereas the other one was no doubt informed by that wondrous
anesthetist and now here they both are and perhaps they'll try
to force me as soon as possible into the position of having to choose
between them, and these situations are always difficult and painful for me even when I can enjoy every prerogative of flight and
subterfuge so just imagine now how painful it is in my shattered
condition, so all in all my best course is to put it off as long as
possible and play dumb that is accept as the most natural thing
in the world the presence of both of them at my bedside, and so
with my mouth thick with narcosis I ask what time it is and the
girl says eleven and the widow says ten to eleven as if ten minutes
had God only knows what importance for me who after all am
returning from a kind of eternity to which sincerely I would like
to be restored as soon as possible if the first gift of daylight is to
be the fine mess I see myself in, thank God those two must have
understood that this would not be the ideal moment to engage in
a struggle for supremacy and they seem to have decided on what
you might call a period of armistice, and the one says that I look
fine whereas the other completes the sentence informing me they
didn't find anything wrong in my stomach, and at this last piece
of news I'm in a cold sweat I think father this would really be too

much and I fearfully move my hands over my stomach to look for the exposed growth, I manage to touch the gauze there it is I say to myself however thank God there isn't that terrible mountain of death that they pulled out of his belly, here there doesn't seem to be anything but the bit of gauze which normally covers a surgical incision, but before I even have time to heave a sigh of relief I start thinking of another of those things that surgeons always do when they find a nice cancer they don't know how to deal with, they sew it back in again and let nature take its course, I bet that's my situation I have this fatal cancer sewn back into my stomach, my God I had already taken my leave of the world and all my woes and now here I am starting all over again, God only knows in what terrible way the person who wants my death has arranged for me to die, but what evil did I ever do him after all, yes I abandoned him on his deathbed however he obviously didn't know what to do with me when I was there at his side, and then let's make one thing clear he didn't die of a stroke or of a broken heart but of a collapse following a terrible operation that was no responsibility of mine, I got there when all the decisions had been made, and my only spontaneous gesture ineffectual as it proved was when I suggested the idea of having him die under the knife, naturally not to deprive him of life before his time but to spare him useless suffering in the event that dying was inevitable for him, he ought to have granted me this at least in all fairness I mean let me die before when the worst was over, and not now again with who knows what more pain.

Anyhow if this is the truth I have to discover it right away and I have to be sly with the doctors who generally employ lying tactics and even praise them as a form of treatment, and in fact falsehood is what they're best at and rather than fall into their hands a man should wish to die by drowning or to be snuffed out in an automobile accident, however I'm not the biggest idiot on earth to let myself be taken in like a nitwit now I'll manage to find out if they've sewn my death back into my stomach or if they really did make a mistake in cutting me open as my two angels agree in affirming, and now when the decrepit old butcher arrives with his assistant but thank God without the anesthetist I drop a witty remark for exploratory purposes, I say well you made extra work for yourselves this morning eh, but they are impenetrable to humor and for that matter I would like to see them laugh about this, in general I think doctors who have cut a belly open by mistake don't feel much like laughing, at least not in public, so the fact that they remain as serious as undertakers supports the notion that they cut me up when they could perfectly well have avoided it, well I say a little less provocatory how did it go then, however apparently a distinguished old man of such huge fame must be treated with greater respect, he doesn't answer a word and goes right off leaving his assistant to explain that all the symptoms pointed to an intestinal perforation and that it was therefore their duty to operate urgently, but all things considered it's better this way since here wasn't any perforation and not even any irritation of the appendix so I should be pleased, and as far as the duodenal ulcer goes I must have dreamed it up, it's well known that there are some people who convince themselves they have diseases they don't have, I must be one of those and for him I remain one even after I explain to him that thanks to that ulcer I was rejected after a military examination once when they wanted me to take a special course, all right all right he says smugly he doesn't have too much respect for the Army Medical Corps apparently, and so he insists in his opinion that I should be happy now I am certain my intestine is all in order, they examined it you might say inch by inch, oh yes I think I can just imagine how happy they would have been to find something wrong no matter how small to justify their operation even to the eyes of a layman and instead they didn't find a thing.

Summing up at this point it seems that I've had my belly cut open and sewn up for nothing and it may be that now I can go on for a few more years in peace, now that I'm sure I don't have an ulcer I can just see all the spaghetti *all' amatriciana* I'm going to eat, however now through a process of logical parallelism the spaghetti reminds me of my right kidney which is floating because of my excessive thinness, God only knows what must have happened to my kidney in this big shake-up, my God I hardly have time to ask myself this question when I'm immediately reminded of the terrible sufferings of the night before, so I say to myself what were all those sufferings if there wasn't any perforation they must have been something else because they really existed in all their undeniable horror, this however the doctors didn't explain perhaps the clowns never even thought about it, and now I'm here with this fresh incision in my belly and as the anesthesia wears off I begin to perceive its pain, but also that other sorrowful mystery that almost knocked me off to all appearances still hasn't been resolved, my God what evil can I have done to deserve such misfortunes, these are calamities that have no justification not even in a moral world like ours which first of all brings us into the world already burdened with original sin, here they must have established to my disadvantage measures and standards different from the ones accepted till now. Oh Mother of God here comes last night's terrible pain back again, every minute that passes it becomes more and more the unspeakable thing of last night, to my lips come even the words of my dying father why don't you help me for the love of God help me I'm suffering too much, but who can I say these words to for God's sake there are the two women and I can't say it to the one without turning the other against me, timidly I make the suggestions that they take turns I'm not too badly off I try to lie, but neither the one nor the other seems to have anything better to do at the moment they don't even seem to be hungry though it must be long past noon, and anyhow I decide I don't give a damn about these two because I'm too sick, oh Lord Lord how sick I am I start to moan, so one takes my right hand and the other the left and both of them with special expressions of sympathy do what they can to console me, however there's no use sympathizing the pains get worse and worse, now I'm back in the same fix as last night and with my stomach cut open for nothing into the bargain, angels and saints of heaven help me, however it isn't as if this outside help came about very often, and besides I know that it's highly unlikely the celestial powers would make a move in favor of a sinner like me who among other things has at his right hand and at his left two excellent occasions of sin, so abandoning all other hopes I call for the nurse but it seems that she has no authority beyond enemas and bedpans, so she calls the nun and as my own past experience should have instructed me the nun can't do anything without specific orders from the head of the ward who anyhow has gone to lunch and after lunch he sleeps which is only right since he didn't get any sleep last night because of an urgent case namely in the final analysis myself, and here I am body and soul in the monstrous machinery of pain and suffering, poor me but where can I turn, I even think of calling my friend the assistant to the other famous surgeon, maybe he is angry but he might also want to come and enjoy the petty satisfaction of seeing my belly cut open for nothing, so I have him telephoned by the girl whom he also had occasion to meet in the guise of my fiancée , and she goes off into the corridor to telephone, reluctant to leave me of course, and she isn't wrong because the minute she's outside the widow hastens to tell me that a little while ago she saw the girl rummaging among my things no doubt looking for my wallet you never can tell, she also tells me she can't understand how I could lose my head over a girl like that pretty of course but so insipid poor little thing that when you take away her silly prettiness she didn't have anything left, but I didn't have much desire to listen to this foolishness racked as I was by pains, so I let her rattle on and in the meanwhile I was thinking I wonder if my friend will come to help me, the widow insists that in this life a person also has to have intellectual interests for heaven's sake and as best I can I indicate to her that I agree with her completely, and then at last the girl comes back to say my friend will be right there and sure enough he does arrive in a rush a little later, what have you done without saying a word to me you could at least let me know before you let them do a laparatomy on you, he's cross with me for this reason and God only knows how wrong his reasoning is at least as far as my active participation in the matter is concerned but what the hell, telling him he's right I invoke him as if he were Saint Anthony of Padua in person begging him to lend me a hand in this colossal disaster, and he says of course he will why do I think he rushed here except to lend me a hand, and in all confidence he adds that I need one too because in this clinic where I've chosen to come they are all dogs so after all I've really been lucky, but I say I don't see how I can be so lucky since I'm dying of pain, and he says of course you're suffering you poor devil however the thing in itself is nothing at all, and he explains it to me at once saying that the floating kidney as usual slipped down this time flattening the ureter itself that is to say the duct through which the urine passes into the bladder, and obviously when the natural outlet is blocked the urine started to press against the kidney swelling it, and of course the pain is terrible but it's a trifle practically speaking, too bad they cut my stomach open otherwise he could have yanked me by the feet and with a good shake he would have put everything back in place, anyhow now since this is a cheap-skate clinic where they've never even heard of an adjustable bed he'll make them give him a couple of wedges or wooden supports to put under the legs of this bed, and in fact after a somewhat brisk exchange of views with the doctor on duty he has the wedges brought and in no time I am back in the now habitual position with my head inclined backwards, I bet you feel a little better already my friend says to encourage me and I don't know whether it's politeness or hypnotic suggestion but I say yes, so he can go off somewhat relieved, in fact he goes off obviously content, what's more seeing there are two women he asks if either of them has a car and would she drive him because he came in a taxi, and the widow though reluctantly offers to take him leaving me alone with the girl who eagerly informs me that this woman isn't driving the doctor off in her own car but in mine, and the first thing she did when they told her I was in the hospital was to rush to the garage and make them give her my car, and she was able to do this because of my own lack of will power since I hadn't made her give me back the car keys at the time of our break, but if I was a man as she hoped I was I should report that woman to the police for theft and I ought also to report the men at the garage, however when she thought about it a minute and about how I generally behaved I surely wasn't a real man except for

the sexual side strictly speaking, but as for the rest I could allow
a common slut to get the best of me and one who on top of everything else pretended to be French though if you asked her she
came at most from the Val d'Aosta and not Paris and she probably
had been there on some gold-digging trip, and it wasn't certain
she had married a French film director the way she said, and anyhow the director had died right after the marriage apparently of
a stroke so it was no exaggeration to call her a tramp, but if I didn't
take steps to throw her out after having got my car back from her
then personally she would have nothing more to do with me because naturally she couldn't share her fiancé with a decrepit bag
like that who tried to pass herself off as a journalist, and my God
how low I've sunk she sighed but I felt so awful that I couldn't
arouse much interest in her troubles, and besides I certainly
couldn't abandon myself without any self-control to sentiments
of pity because from one moment to the next that Jeremiad could
turn into a proposal of matrimony perhaps *in extremis*, and I swear
I would have done anything at that moment to make the pains go
away however I realized full well that the institution of matrimony
bore no relation even accidental to my suffering state, so marriage
was useless as well as inopportune, however I was really sick
poor me, the illusion of improvement had vanished with my friend
the assistant now I was worse than before if possible, and it was
really inconceivable that such a huge disaster could be remedied
with a couple of wooden supports under the bed's legs, only a fool
could believe that, my father would certainly not have been
satisfied with so little. Therefore I now have to face my present
pains in all their cruelty, or rather last night's pains plus the ones
derived from the incision and the confusion that ancient surgeon
caused in my guts, and the funny thing is that I am no longer so
worried about the cause but rather about the motives so to speak
of these sufferings namely whether they have an expiatory or
punitive nature, and though these terms are related it seems to me
that the first allows some room for survival whereas the other
would bring me inevitably to my tragic end, anyhow at the present
moment I don't care so much about living I only care about going

off without suffering so much, so I start cursing and saying I want
an injection of morphine and I go on swearing until God knows
what time in the afternoon and the famous assistant comes in
obviously annoyed with me because I made him make the wrong
diagnosis and what's more he doesn't conceal his disgust at the
supports he sees under the legs of the bed, on the other hand he
has a rather ingenious theory on the subject of my pains that is he
says they are a mere fiction or to be more benevolent the fruit of
my imagination, since he has gone over my hapless intestine inch
by inch as he never tires of repeating and in my intestine there
is nothing that could cause me pain absolutely nothing so according to him an ordinary sedative for headaches suitable also for
periodic pains in women is more than enough for me, in fact he
gives orders for me to have two pills and he leaves me there to
meditate, of course I don't understand these things too well or
rather my knowledge doesn't go beyond the vague recollection of
the name of a play entitled *Le malade imaginaire* whose author
on the other hand was probably killed by it, anyhow apart from
the fact that so-called medical science for better or worse must
have made some progress since Molière's day and then according
to what you hear the thing that leaves me unconvinced in this
self-styled gentleman's opinion is that he continues to talk about
intestines in the strict sense whereas I was saying kidney, and I
could also have said any other entrail that can cause pain which
they all can or almost all so far as I know, still while I'm here
waiting for the menstrual sedative to produce some effect I think
it is also hindered by the girl who continues to tell me what
I would do if I were a real man also insinuating that if you asked
her by now the widow is making love with my friend the assistant,
I then think as much as I can about the business of the imaginary
sick man, I suppose I invented those pains, I also make a great
effort to convince myself of this fact certain that it would be to my
advantage and indeed it would be the finest thing in the world to
get out of this tremendous suffering through a serious control of
my imagination, however it doesn't seem probable that such heavy
and substantial pains could originate from the working of the

imagination at least my efforts in this direction bear no fruit what-soever, and so at a certain moment I start yelling that I want an injection of morphine and I don't stop until the assistant reappears with a face like an offended god which is apparently fairly common in this clinical Olympus, anyhow I don't let his contemptuous manner intimidate me and with the most effective terms I can find I speak to him of the physical reality of my pains, and in his turn he smugly explains to me that I'm a mythomane and a morphine addict like all artists, and then at last I understand into what imbecile hands fate has cast me, he must be a delinquent unless he only is simple-minded, I who hesitate before taking an aspirin I who have inherited a sesquipedalian prudence from a sergeant-quartermaster of the Royal Carabinieri who have ab-sorbed from a largely religious education a completely eschatologi-cal concept of pain here I am called a morphine addict by a com-mon nincompoop, lucky that this immediately foils their plot to drive me crazy, now I have reality in my grip again, the sense of reality they were trying to make me lose, I suffer therefore I am, and so in perfect freedom I can tell this doctor what I think of him and the wild ideas he pulls out after he has collaborated in cutting open my stomach for nothing, *errare humanum est* I say to him *sed diabolicum perseverare*, I also ask him if they have decided in this clinic to do their best to thin out the overabundant population of our peninsula, but since he doesn't understand the irony I confess to him that according to me he and his colleagues and the old man are all gravediggers, how many people do you kill per day I ask him straight out, but I'm not ready to let myself be killed any farther than you've already gone, I want to go home while there's still time, in fact I tell the girl and the widow who has meanwhile come back to resume her place that they should get busy and find me an ambulance, so thank God the assistant is at last persuaded I'm a desperate case, nothing can save me now steeped as I am in vice, so he tells the nun to give me the morphine or anything else that I decide I want, and in fact the nun gives me this longed-for injection with the same look that Pontius Pilate must have had on the well-known occasion, that is making it quite clear that in my alkaloid damnation she is playing no part, and meanwhile what with one thing and another it is night and after the pains recede with great effort burying themselves in my butchered body I am dozing off, I sleep, and then waking up when it's still night I see the girl asleep all dressed with a blanket over her on the other bed which is in the room so that the relatives of the victim can rest there, thank God I say to myself they've come to an agreement about taking turns, instead when she wakes up in the morning thanks to a big cup of coffee and a homemade bun that a nun kindly brings her I find out that in the late evening there was a memorable row between her and the widow, a fight to the finish with no holds barred especially in the defamation department and apparently she has come out the winner, which pleases me pretty much for understandable reasons, however a moment later I become frightened thinking my God if this girl has managed to put the widow out of commission she's a power to be feared, and the motives for fear obviously increase after she explains to me that she managed to win thanks to the support of the nuns of the ward who joined in the battle after she had won them over by leading them to believe the widow was a Protestant whereas as far as I know she was simply an atheist or nonreligious.

And so thanks to this maneuver which was basically quite simple I had become virtually the exclusive possession of the girl who had told her mother she was going to stay with a cousin in Minturno and instead she stayed at my side night and day supported by the nuns in a body since she had also invited them all to our imminent wedding, and the first time I heard this business mentioned I wanted to protest fairly firmly but she motioned me to behave myself, and then when we are alone she illustrates to me her theory that people have to be taken as they come if you want to get any good out of them, and in fact now when those terrible pains came back to me the nun didn't make such a fuss about the morphine and on the other hand not even the doctors made any fuss perhaps because they were now convinced that in my case one couldn't speak of downright addiction to drugs, I think that their giving in derived above all from the fact that after what had happened they didn't like me and more than anything else they considered me an unwanted guest, but if they didn't want to keep me there I wanted even less to stay in that unlucky place although now it wasn't such a good idea for me to get out too soon because since I was there through their fault they couldn't make me pay for my period of hospitalization, and instead, after two weeks when the moment finally came for me to leave they handed me a bill I won't say how big, with everything specified so much for the room and so much for the medicines and so much for the operation subdivided among professor and assistants and anesthetist, in short the whole gang that had taken part in the fine exploit, and father I only hope you know how reluctantly I shelled out that money which was a lot since it seems that a mistaken operation costs no less than a correct one, and when you reflect a minute it couldn't be otherwise because then in order to spend less money everybody would start investigating his operations to see if they were mistaken or correct, and I believe they're almost always mistaken at least to judge by my personal experience.

So now I was at home convalescing and most of the time lying on the tilted bed and when I felt the approach of the all too familiar pains I immediately telephoned my friend the assistant of the famous surgeon and without a moment's delay he would come and give me a yank by the feet which he could do now since the wound on my stomach had healed beautifully, and when the yank didn't resolve the situation then an injection of morphine would fix everything up though only temporarily of course, in fact since the yanks can't be said to have been efficacious very often I sometimes didn't even telephone to my friend who had so to speak invented them but to the neighborhood doctor who had finally come back from Chianciano in great good humor after his long season, and this doctor was one I surely didn't tend to overestimate but he was very kind and then he was better at giving a morphine injection than anybody else, but after all I couldn't go on like that forever with the dictionaries under the legs of my bed and being shaken by the ankles and with more and more frequent injections of morphine, in the long run even the person who had the greatest responsibility for the whole business namely my friend the assistant of the famous surgeon began to betray some uncertainty saying he had

absolutely no doubt about the diagnosis that had been made and
the deductions from it, but at the same time if by chance and just
to make sure I went and had myself examined without being
hospitalized of course by his famous professor I surely wouldn't
be doing any harm, anyhow it seemed the professor didn't take
more than fifteen thousand lire for an office visit, and this way I
would feel reassured and he too would feel reassured, and moreover the girl agreed too and I could hardly oppose the suggestion
under the circumstances, and to tell the truth after having thrown
away all that money another fifteen thousand more or less didn't
make much difference, so towards Christmas after the inevitable
appointments and waiting I found myself one day face to face with
the medico-surgical celebrity who without putting on the slightest
airs asked me and noted down on a special kind of filing card everything that can be asked about my physiological mishaps and also
those of my father and mother and if possible of other ancestors
back to a fairly remote degree except that such things weren't
generally recorded in our family so I knew very little about the
ancestors, and then he looked with suitable attention at the X rays
of the kidneys and especially of the floating one and finally he
told me to go and have other X rays made of my liver and my gall
bladder and my entire intestine, and a week or more later I went
back to him with that packet of new X rays and he studied them
and reread with great concentration my personal and family re-
miniscences, and finally he said I had to have an intensive course
of antibiotics for a month after which if there was no improvement
he would remove my right kidney since from the X rays it was
unmistakably clear that there was nothing wrong with my intestine
or my liver or my gall blader, although I had a cavity of an obviously tubercular nature precisely in my right kidney.

Perhaps tuberculosis of the kidney isn't so tragic as it seemed
to me at that moment when the luminary informed me of it, however you have to bear in mind that I was just emerging from
particularly depressing vicissitudes and also it was difficult for me
to attribute this new calamity to destiny or chance or to other
forces which in their blindness are impartial or at least without

any specific will to harm, here if I was not mistaken the god
Huitzilopochtli was at it again or else it was a new manifestation
of hostility on the part of you know who, and clearly I couldn't
go on forever struggling with a dead man who had at his disposal
means far superior to mine, in reality these were the problems I
was thinking of while the girl who was walking with me along
the lovely streets around the Villa Massimo wanted to know
everything the luminary had told me, and I couldn't tell her because if I talked about it I was bound to burst into tears in view of
the justified pity I was feeling for myself, and perhaps understanding the gravity of my reticence she walked pensively at my side,
worried I believe also about her own fate namely thinking about
our relationship in the event that it didn't end up in matrimony in
which case her life would prove pretty well screwed up, but on the
other hand it was also presumable that at the present moment
marriage with the grim and taciturn figure at her side didn't
appeal to her so much any more so I could very well tell her about
the cavities eaten away by tuberculosis in the calyces of my right
kidney what did she care about it all now anyway, I did tell her
in fact while she was walking along with her head down looking
at her shoes and I also expounded to her my intention to evade
further disasters by throwing myself into the Tiber, there was
nothing else for me to do, and since she didn't say a word where-
fore one might also have thought that she was basically in agreement then who could have controlled the waves of self-pity
while I saw myself in the act of jumping off the Ponte Cavour
or the Ponte Margherita without anybody in the world feeling the
slightest interest in my gesture, and it's only natural that with
thoughts of this kind the tears which were already in my throat
should rise rapidly to my eyes, you want to bet I start sobbing in
the street like a fool because there is nothing ahead of me but
death I was saying to myself, but when a person says these things
it doesn't mean that this stops his tears on the contrary it's like
flinging open the gates, so I then say quickly to the girl go away
and leave me alone when by now the tears are coming from my
eyes, and she really does go away or rather with her head down

she dawdles behind, then I turn and I see her standing there looking at her shoes, and after a little while I turn again and she's gone,
there I am alone in the world sobbing with real desperation paying
no attention to the people going by who stare at me, I really would
go and throw myself in the Tiber if the expression hadn't only
been a figure of speech in view of my repulsion for diving into the
water especially in the bad season, anyhow drowning isn't the only
way to kill yourself and I'll easily find another one more suited
to my tastes.

So here I am again lying in the tilted bed meditating on the
various ways of taking one's life, of all of them the least complicated I think is surely barbiturates although I don't happen to
have any barbiturates in the house, if I did have some however
I wouldn't hesitate to take an abundantly mortal dose to make
sure not to get stuck halfway like so many attempts, what's the
point of life now if even my young girl has gone off, they say
rats leave the ship when they sense a wreck coming and I am
really finished, I don't even have the strength to take the dictionaries from under the bed even though by now there can be no
doubt of their scarce value, it's not conceivable that you can cure
a kidney tuberculosis with a pair of dictionaries, a disease of that
kind can be met only with death maybe through gas when there
aren't any barbiturates around, however how sad it is to die alone
abandoned by everyone, just look at the condition I've been reduced
to by him who wanted to avenge my abandoning him, it's the
system of retaliation apparently, anyhow I can't persuade myself
that absolutely everybody has abandoned me and in fact in a little
while I hear a ring at the door and it would be marvelous if it were
the girl so I could bid her an appropriate farewell from the brink
of death, instead not without disappointment I find that it's the
neighborhood doctor whose abandoning me to tell the truth
wouldn't have made much difference, in fact he's a man without
any special qualities if you except a vague mildness and on the
other hand I have the impression that he hasn't actually come for
my sake but to hear the reply of the luminary and to feel himself
thereby connected however indirectly with the most illustrious

circles of modern medicine, I almost feel like not telling him anything to teach him a lesson not to exercise his vanity at my expense, but instead I suddenly start spilling everything, you might even say that in the absence of anybody else I can make do even with him, I tell him about the consumptive and cavity-ridden kidney which they mean to rip out of me after the antibiotics cure has proved useless as it's sure to prove, and for a while he stands there either meditating or sympathizing I can't tell which, you know where he can shove his sympathy, then suddenly reviving he wants to see the X rays though he has already seen them at least three or four times, he starts studying them with a connoisseur's manner against the desk lamp since in my house we don't have those special fluorescent screens, and after a while he has the goodness to admit that the major calyces of my right kidney are dilated, yes quite dilated this meat-head says after he has had the diagnosis of the big professor to help him figure it out, anybody can discover America once Christopher Columbus has been there, but this one obviously wants to do something more than just discover America and in fact he has started meditating again as if he were going to extract God only knows what ideas from his head, until finally he gets his nerve up and says no he isn't convinced by the big professor's diagnosis, how can it be with all the examinations of the urine that we made not even one bacillus turned up, this is really strange too strange he wants to look into this more closely before beginning an antibiotics course that might run me down even worse than I am now, in short he says he wants to culture for bacilli which is something that doesn't cost me any pain because you do it with rabbits or guinea pigs, but I tell him that even if it doesn't cost any pain it costs money and I certainly don't want to go to any further expense over my life which apparently isn't worth a lead nickel, and he says if you won't pay for it I will because this culture absolutely has to be made, and though I always feel a certain distrust of this sort of mania I tell him yes anyway I don't feel like having them stick pins in my behind with streptomycin when I've already made up my mind to kill myself, so we'll wait these few days for the culture and then the liberating leap into the dark there's always time for these things, and in fact if I had killed myself on that occasion because of the kidney tuberculosis I would have made a big mistake, because the culture proved I didn't have tuberculosis of the kidney, what I did have only God knew, but it wasn't tuberculosis.

So presently I was back once more where I had started from, with the theory of the floating kidney considerably weakened but still in force for lack of anything better, in fact I had replaced the dictionaries under the legs of the bed and as for the yanking when I felt the pains coming on I tried to administer it to myself by raising my feet against the wall, and to tell the truth at times it did seem as if the pain receded with this treatment primitive as it was but at other times and I would say more often than not I didn't feel its influence and then I had to fall back on a morphine injection in general given me by the neighborhood doctor who poor thing was so far the only one who had got anything right about me, it was something to see how justifiably pleased he was and he always came to examine me even though he was aware that my current economic condition didn't permit me to pay him, and the girl had come back too in fact she had come back in rather special circumstances which is to say because she was afraid that she was pregnant, and according to me that was all I needed Holy Christ didn't I have enough troubles without adding another one that important, which wasn't so simple as it might seem at first glance because every time I dared suggest the only possible solution from my point of view the girl started yelling I was a criminal and a monster and a murderer, according to her the baby was already alive in her womb and she wouldn't kill it for any reason in the world, still after some insistence I manage to send her to be examined by a good obstetrician who if required could also do me a favor if sufficiently recompensed for it, and after a little while she comes out in despair saying that there isn't any baby and the obstetrician has told her she can never have one because she has an infantile uterus, and I try to console her as best I can in her desperation which I really can't share in fact I consider this the only decent piece of news I've had in the last four or five months,

also because it isn't nice to make love with all the precautions you
have to take to keep from making babies, now I can finally do
it without racking my brains over the cycles calculated according
to the Ogino-Knaus calendar, it really is a great relief although
the neighborhood doctor when I tell him the story says how can
that doctor say such a thing an infantile uterus has never been
any guarantee a woman can't become pregnant, not to mention the
fact that with sexual exercise the uterus can also be developed, in
short he tries to fill me with doubts this spoilsport however I decide
to pay no attention to him, he's not a specialist after all in these
things and even as a general practitioner in the final analysis you
can't say he exactly shines, and the fact that he was right about
the kidney tuberculosis and the big professor was wrong doesn't
so much demonstrate his medical intelligence as it does the professor's colossal stupidity, assuming it is stupidity because we all
know that there are characters whose hobby and pleasure is to dig
their knives into the human body even when it's not at all necessary. So now at least one good thing has happened to me, and indeed I can finally hope I have reached a beneficent turn in my
existence, even those horrible pains don't come as often as they
used to, maybe I have placated the manes with so much suffering
and maybe I can now manage to have a slightly less calamitous
period, I even start working here and there when I can trying to
put together a bit of money to pay at least a small part of the
debts I've run up with my medical expenses, to tell the truth debts
are an obsession with me and they could hardly be anything else
with everything my father taught me on the subject, he always
used to say I had to pay attention to him when he said that a
gentleman must never be in debt to anybody, and to tell the truth
there was an infinite number of other things about which he used
to say I had to pay attention to him not that I absorbed them all
however this business of debts both material and ethical I did
absorb almost I'd say in an exemplary way though I recognize
it's one of the most fallacious lessons a father can teach a son
especially nowadays, and in point of fact I myself used to run
around with plenty of people who didn't worry about debts at all

not even about the ones they owed me, and generally they lived
a lot more happily than I did in my best moments, anyway apart
from the nuisance of the debts I could easily imagine I had already
overcome the worst of my troubles and was heading towards
health because whereas troubles come on their own that doesn't
mean they have to go away on their own, however when you think
about it another thing that bothered me at that time was the fact
that the girl talked too often about marriage although I told her
she had to get the notion out of her head, moreover when a man
has a girl inevitably he has some nuisances too, so apart from the
debts and the girl and to tell the truth also a certain urinary
incontinence due probably to a prostate inflammation or a slight
ailment of the entire kidney system down to the sphincter of the
bladder, apart from these little things I didn't seem to have any
other current ills and for almost two weeks I hadn't had any bona
fide kidney attacks, looks like you've made it this time I said to
myself with mounting confidence, and instead one of those evenings was the very evening that was to give a new and particularly
calamitous dimension to the rest of my whole life.

The events both in the manner and the order of their occur-
rence are only too clear, so their interpretation if one wants could
be equally clear, it's all a matter of believing it, however since
uncomplicated things cannot possibly exist in this world apparently, though when you reflect a moment the most uncomplicated things are the ones that don't look that way and vice
versa, and truly the business of making distinctions and classifications even with a philosophical basis is almost always a waste of
effort, anyhow for the moment the best thing is for me to report
the events with that modicum of logical sequence which naturally
links them on the condition that I may explain them differently at
a later date if my strength holds out so that anybody can see the
double aspect of these mishaps, the traditional phenomenal aspect
and what you might call the psychoanalytical, with everyone
then free to choose the one he likes best, since for my part I don't
want to force anybody to accept my preferred interpretation, assuming I have one now after having remained uncertain for so

long. Anyhow that evening I was in bed as for that matter I was every other evening during that period because I surely wasn't going to the movies or out walking with the enuresis that afflicted me, but enuresis isn't the exact term and in fact it was an almost continuous discharge or dripping caused by the prostate inflammation or by a mysterious pain like a pricking that I felt at the pubic orifice something which in effect also caused an incessant stimulation, so that I had to apply to myself constantly a fairly unpleasant apparatus vulgarly known as a parrot perhaps because of its shape, and when I think about it I can't understand why the girl wasn't disgusted by all this stuff and why she didn't go off without even a good-bye, this demonstrates a strong maternal element in her love despite her youth, anyhow that evening I didn't have the parrot and the girl wasn't around either, I was I would say unusually serene there in bed with a big pile of magazines beside me to glance through looking for some rather strong story that with a bit of camouflaging and retouching might be sold as an original idea to one or the other of our movie producers, in fact more than a few script writers and idea men managed to sell stories of this kind and the fact that I hadn't succeeded before didn't exempt me from paying these magazines proper attention, so then glancing through these magazines I feel myself drawn to the unusual story of a girl who after various unsuccessful attempts had finally succeeded in reaching the next world by throwing herself from the window of her house, and I read this event with some enjoyment since there was a rumor around that the girl had killed herself because of what we might call a sentimental relationship with a writer who at that time was having a big success both with sales and general popularity and the radicals found very little to criticize in him, anyhow I read that otherwise sickening story adding a bit of malice of my own although when you think about it how could the writer be held responsible if the girl had such a stubborn inclination toward suicide, who hasn't had some experience I asked myself with one or more girls who have turned on the gas at home or tried out razors on their wrists in the bathtub, and so maybe the writer in question wasn't really responsible after all even though he was a writer famous among other things for his offhand way of getting rid of his women when he tired of them, anyway for this reason or for another I was reading with some pleasure despite the subject, and in particular I read how the first time she had tried to drown herself at Ostia and they had fished her out, and then a second time with barbiturates and the third with gas and almost miraculously somebody had always intervened to drag her back willy-nilly into the world of the living, until she had decided to throw herself out of a seventh-story window and here it was hard for even the best-intentioned person to intervene in time, in fact in the magazine there was a fine picture of her splattered on the pavement with her bath-robe flung up all a mess except for her legs which were long and white, and the article also went into some detail describing this beautiful girl turned into a pulp, and when this description was over then came the best part namely the conjectures on the whys and the where- fores of this lovely girl's fatal leap, and then I suddenly feel a warm sensation towards the base of my back where there are the five lumbar vertebrae, that is at the very spot which from then on I call for good reasons the suicide spot, and that warmth exactly as if it were warm water suddenly gone mad begins to climb up my spine all along it rather hastily and ends up right in the cerebellum where it produces an inconceivable tumult, all of a sudden I feel overwhelmed with terror, my God this is death I say to myself without thinking that death can't be something so terrifying, in any case I jump down from the bed as if death or rather that other and worse business were there beneath my back, but by jumping from the bed and standing up I cause even worse harm because as always when I stand up abruptly my head swims because the blood at that moment flows from the brain, usually it's a trifle but even with trifles it depends on the moment when they happen, anyhow my head swimming and my eyes clouded I throw myself on the floor and then dragging myself along like a dying cat I reach the door of the apartment and manage to open it and I start yelling toward the stairs up and down help help as loud as I can, maybe what comes from my dry and half-paralyzed throat isn't even the word *help* maybe it's only a rattling and horrifying shout, anyway a little later people come the concierge and some of the other neighbors I had never seen in pajamas before maybe convinced that they were going to find thieves, and instead they find me looking at them with my eyes popping and what's more stricken with motor aphasia though only temporarily so as I try to explain what's happened to me and what is still happening I get confused in a series of inarticulate sounds that produce a bad impression, and in fact a naval captain seeing also how pale I am and how I'm trembling from head to toe suggests calling an ambulance to take me to the hospital, but I'm not crazy enough to end up in a hospital again after my recent disasters, so partially regaining the power of speech and for the rest complementing it with gestures I explain that I don't agree about the hospital and then I show somebody a telephone number in my book, and it's obviously the number of the neighborhood doctor who at present is the only guardian angel I can turn to in fact I make an effort to convince myself that he's not only the only one but also the best, and in fact since he was right about the kidney tuberculosis he may even manage to understand something of this new and terrible disaster which however really does show every sign of being of metaphysical origins, my God until this moment in all my mental disorganization I hadn't thought of my father and instead here he is with this frightening new weapon of his, indeed I find a resemblance to him in that navy captain who wanted to call for an ambulance and so I sit with my back to the wall you never can tell, and then the neighborhood doctor when he arrives out of breath with his first-aid bag has some difficulty in pulling me out of the corner where I have huddled down like an antelope stalked by a lion, first I insist he send away all those people or at least the male ones, then I obey him and lie down and he feels my pulse and then with the proper implements he listens to my heart and measures my blood pressure and while he does all these things I calm down a bit because I entrust myself entirely to him in the hope he may understand something though I wouldn't want him to understand the only true thing which is the spiritual presence of my father, anyhow he seems fairly far away from similar deductions and actually he is asking me where does it hurt but God only knows where I hurt, it's difficult enough to figure that out when it's an ordinary pain that you feel on one side or the other or vaguely on both as I have learned to my cost so imagine this business now which is completely different from the sufferings I felt when the kidney was swollen, in fact this isn't really pain but a kind of sickness in an immeasurable quantity although practically without pain, truly the only physical thing I seem to have felt was that warmth around the lumbars and its rapid rise to the cerebellum and the rest is only exorbitant terror moreover without any cause or reason as far as I can figure it out, and the doctor poor man can't figure it out much better, and so after thinking it over carefully and seeing that the heart is all right and the blood pressure normal and seeing also that I don't have any specific pain in any anatomically existing organ he declares that the only thing that's wrong with me is a bit of nervous exhaustion and I will surely have to take a cure to build myself up with phosphates, calcium and vitamins, for the moment in any case the best thing for me is to take a sleeping pill and get some rest, so the neighbors who had stayed snooping by the door go off clearly disappointed at this denouement, in fact everybody suffers from a bit of nervous exhaustion nowadays, and so they all feel it wasn't worth making such a fuss over a trifle, but whatever they may think I surely do not allow myself to be convinced it's all a trifle, I've really never felt a fear like the one I just had not even in the worst moments of my life when I was about to die, and now I don't want to be left alone because I'm afraid it will come again, and the nice doctor says I'll stay here with you and he really does sit down there on the chair waiting for the couple of pills he has given me to take effect, and in the meanwhile I have regained perhaps completely the power of speech as well as the ability to connect my thoughts and I talk and talk to him about that warm stuff that formed in my lumbars and then raced up to my cerebellum and upset not only every sense of moral strength and decorum but also all the other achievements that my ancestors in the course of several hundreds of thousands of centuries had made in the field of ratiocination.

Well, this incident which was after all rather banal at least in its external aspects, and really somebody might be thinking of the commonplace hot flashes that especially in the last century used to attack maidens who needed embraces and which were generally cured with balm-mint water how ineffectually one can easily imagine, so practically speaking those who insisted that in my case it was nothing but a manifestation of nervous exhaustion would be quite right if serious science did not properly avoid such a simplification, and in fact people ought to be a lot more careful about using the word *nerves* all the time which has a bad sound to the ears of the qualified, this banal incident as I was saying which took place while I read about the successful suicide was in reality the event that completely turned my existence around, endowing it as I think I have said with a new dimension and also with an infinity of refined sufferings never imagined previously, since from then on I found myself in constant contact with a world of fear into which I risked plunging at any moment without being able to realize the causes which made it happen, as if on a sudden caprice a kind of bizarre nervous or maybe even electric contact took place by which on the one hand I was I as far as capacity of suffering was concerned while on the other hand I was no longer I as creator so to speak of that suffering, and truly one could also believe that this evening and often afterwards if I didn't arrive at the disintegration of the Ego as it is properly called I wasn't far away from it and in any case I surely reached a kind of splitting of the personality though only temporary, so in conclusion there is no one who cannot see how the banal incident taken as a point of arrival for one series of misfortunes and as point of departure for a series of even greater misfortunes can also be a keystone in the story that I am narrating, and in truth up till now one could also have thought that I had passed through such a rich and extraordinary succession of misfortunes that in the end I could hardly help losing my mind, a prospect which is not at all contradictory to the science of psychoanalysis since Freud himself at least at the beginning admitted the existence of traumatic events or in simpler terms some fine knocks on the head such as I had abundantly received, anyhow though up till now I have limited myself to what might be called an objective narration and exposition I certainly haven't neglected the metaphysical and even religious aspect of my calamities, insisting even too much perhaps on the hypothesis that they were directly related to the will of a certain deceased person who was angry with me for his own not entirely baseless reasons, and with this I don't mean that I don't accept the validity of humanity's progress in the knowledge of reality thanks especially to positivism, but it can happen that in certain particularly unhappy moments a man allows himself to be gripped again by the superstitions of the past, and in fact more than one positivist on the point of death makes his peace with his Maker according to canon law, but even when a person isn't on the point of death however he can find himself as was my case buried under an avalanche of God's punishments hard to explain rationalistically and then a certain atavistic urge drives him to discover the root of his ills outside himself and outside the tangible world, and this backward leap of several centuries can be a mistake if you like but it can't be more mistaken than a mere positivistic and phenomenal point of view, and in fact the correct explanation at which I arrived through psychoanalysis learning among other things that my exhaustion had the grander name of anxiety neurosis, or *Angst*, however I like anguish better, as I was saying this explanation also involves the figure of my father not of course as a spirit from the other world or in his last resting place from which he was sending me vindictive disasters, but as something substantially similar, that is a maleficent force that acts inside me, disastrously.

Anyhow it isn't as if I reached the correct explanation of the phenomenon then and there, to tell the truth it was quite a while before I happened upon psychoanalysis, and in the meanwhile that business which in our ignorance we conveniently call nervous exhaustion diminishing it with this term and almost reducing it to feminine vapors, that business I was saying certainly hadn't as was only right furnished the key to the preceding ills mostly of the kidney which were unquestionably of a physical nature even though still mysterious, indeed it had so to speak exalted them enriching them in their supernatural nuances, which explains also how at that time which I could crudely define as the period of weeping since often whatever happened to me I suddenly realized I was a failure and what's more a fatherless orphan and then I would start sobbing disconsolately as if my father had died yesterday instead of a year or more ago, and this thing obviously created great difficulties in all my relationships both social and business especially with movie producers who as a general rule mistrust those who start crying for no good reason unless they are pretty girls which certainly wasn't my case, so this also explains why at that time I wandered a bit here and there as far as medical treatments were concerned, and in fact while on the one hand I don't neglect the wedges under the legs of the bed and the yanks when I feel one of those awful kidney attacks coming on, nor do I lose touch with the neighborhood doctor whom I keep so to speak in reserve, on the other hand I seek out certain kinds of doctors whose activities border on magical practices, and they thump me on the back on the upper vertebrae which they say are out of place insinuating that also the famous lumbars might be mechanically in disorder and it might be a good idea to fix them up except that this would require a special appliance, or else they give me something called Chinese acupuncture and my girl who witnesses these scenes then assures me that they stuck pins this long in my knees and elbows while I was lying down with my head back and I didn't feel a thing, or else they make me take a homeopathic cure which consists in not brushing my teeth with the usual tooth paste and in giving up the use of vinegar I believe and at the same time at fixed hours I have to place under my tongue certain substances contained in papers that have to be kept away from light and odors, in other words I did a lot of crazy things and at times I was almost ready to listen to friends who advised me to consult the Wizard of Naples or of Mondragone, but then I let it go because that mental outlook which basically is also a paternal inheritance drove me in the opposite direction to consult recognized luminaries who taught at the university at least as assistant professors if not as heads of departments and on their prescription blanks they had all sorts of degrees and titles, and normally they prescribed Valerian and then one said I should sleep with the window open and another that I should have cheese and pears in the morning instead of coffee and a third that I should give up my car and buy myself a bicycle, but all agreed on one particular which was that as far as the exhaustion was concerned I had to pull myself together and cure myself, and from my point of view this was downright nonsense because if I had been capable of curing myself on my own I wouldn't have gone to them for them to screw money out of me since they were all expensive as hell, so in the end it was better for me to try the acupuncture again, which I finally did even though it cost five thousand lire and I suspected it didn't do much good. Strangely enough however in this disease that might be called twofold that is with one part that concerned my body and another my spirit, there were some things that did bring relief however temporary, and they were morphine in the case of kidney or intestinal pains when I couldn't stand it any more, and in the case of those attacks of fear that overwhelmed me without any apparent reason there was the girl whose therapeutic effect was vague but unquestionable, in the sense that when she was around I was more able to keep from being swept away by my fear or to recover my senses if by chance they had already gone, and on the other hand she wasn't frightened at seeing me tremble and turn pale and stammer out a few painful words generally obscure to those who listened, nor was she surprised that I had a constant lump in my throat as they say and in fact when she saw tears in my eyes she said go ahead and cry it'll do you good, and moreover she wasn't disgusted by the parrot when in those attacks the annoying dripping of urine also turned up, in short I believe it was her charity and my faith in her that kept me in one piece as far as possible and on the other hand I had seen that on many occasions things were much worse without her, so now as soon as I felt a warmth at my lumbars or cold sweats or pains in that damned curve of the colon which had already screwed my father, and in short as soon as I felt in any physical or metaphysical region of my body a current of illness warm or cold about to attack my Ego with the aim of disintegrating it I would call her first of all, in fact I called only her in a city that abounds in doctors and clinics for the mentally ill, and so when she can come she does, sometimes even in the night she comes and lies down beside me on top of the blankets with a lap robe over her and she holds my hands and tells me I'm not all alone in the world because there's one person who will never abandon me, and with her at my side I feel that maybe I won't lose my identity, and so little by little I'm not trembling any more and I don't feel the need to rub my hands or bite my fingers or massage my neck where the cerebellum is, and I am moved to tenderness at my own uselessness and un-happiness and solitude and I start crying, and then I also feel like making love and the girl undresses and comes under the covers all ready and close and I can penetrate into her with gentleness and aggression, and though afterwards all the remorse of the world falls on me for what I have done, this kind of remorse expects quite a remote punishment, and in the meanwhile I fall asleep in her young arms. So the girl has become as necessary to me as morphine even more so since these crises of the spirit are much more painful and terrifying than the attacks connected with the floating kidney or the guts in general including the urinary tract, and she knows of course how necessary she is to me I would say that she has an extraordinary intuition and perspicacity in grasp-ing anything that in some way can be useful to her, although in the present instance I can't see how her capacity to help me in my sufferings can be of any use to her, in fact for the moment it seems to me that this situation is all to her disadvantage and in my favor, but then it happens that once when I'm sick and I call her she isn't in, and another time she's in but she can't come because she's afraid of her family, and there's a third time when instead of coming herself she sends her best girl friend who however doesn't possess the shall we say thaumaturgical powers that my girl has in helping me so I suffer frightfully the whole attack of fear with phantoms of madness which assail me in my inner being, and then I cry with my face in the pillow saying I want to die and I don't let the best girl friend so much as touch my hand, all alone and orphaned I drain the cup of my agony to the lees, and afterwards when in the end I have calmed down a little the friend tells me that my girl has had serious troubles with her mother on my account and so she can't come as often as she did before, and besides it seems that she's found a very serious young man with a good position who's fallen in love with her and though she isn't very much in love with him she's fond of him after all, and moreover this young man apparently a lawyer is only thirty so between the two of them there isn't any great age difference as for instance there is between her and me, but above all this lawyer is prepared to do things properly that is to say going to her house and asking for her hand the way respectable people do, and while these fine things are being revealed to me I am thinking why that little bitch leaving me like this now just when I need her she seemed so sincere and nice and she turns out to be a worse tramp than the others, however if I get my hands on her just once more I'll fix her, in this world you must never feel sorry for anybody that's the long and short of it, but naturally I don't let her girl friend see any of these thoughts in fact I tell her that the girl is absolutely right from her bourgeois point of view, after all she wanted to make somebody with a steady income marry her and I wish her all success, I don't hold anything against her and I would like us to remain good friends even after she's married, so everything is working out for her however I don't see why this clarification has to come through a third person, after all even though it was a bit irregular ours was a marvelous love story so it's only right that if we have to say good-bye to each other we should say it face to face, or at least like civilized people if we don't want to get sentimental about it, so I ask her friend if she doesn't feel the girl and I should meet one of these days as soon as I'm a bit better, and as it turns out the girl shows up at my house again the next day with a face like a plaster saint which looks fine on her in view of her new decision to take the sacrament of holy matrimony, and I obviously treat her with all the respect the situation demands I even apologize for being in my pajamas but as she knows my health isn't too good, and once I'm back in bed with her sitting beside me I tell her that there couldn't exist in the world two other people who loved each other the way we loved each other but then love is one thing and life is another, therefore she had herself to consider and her future I could understand her perfectly, on the other hand I was too old for her and what's more sick with this humiliating and mysterious disease with no end in sight, now I couldn't even manage to earn the pittance necessary to make ends meet not that I had much wish to go on under the present conditions, so all I could do was wish her every happiness in her new life with this young and brilliant lawyer, and as for me she wasn't to give me a thought I had found a way out since there is always one way at the disposal of desperate cases, and on and on like this until I realize that I've got her really stewing in emotion and then I draw her closer to me and I caress her hair and her forehead, then I also caress her breast outside her blouse, then I try to slip my hand inside and she defends herself, weakly however and at the second attempt she lets me do it also because she is sobbing like a faucet inasmuch as in the meanwhile I haven't stopped describing to her how alone and poor and wretched I'm going to be without her, and since her weak point is her breast in no time I find her stretched out full length beside me with a wild desire to make love, and I start in and when I see her almost melting I begin to say to her you lousy whore I'll show you, I'll get a baby into your belly and that'll teach you to act like a pig with me and then act coy with others, and as I say this I'm not really thinking of making her pregnant, I feel a bit like a man who announces he's going off to the war to die but really hopes not to die at all, this was the mood I was in as far as making her pregnant was concerned, in fact I must say I was almost certain I wouldn't because of that infantile uterus, though I wasn't of course forgetting the discrepancies expressed on the subject by that wet blanket the neighborhood doctor, anyhow I was only meaning to frighten her and make her face her responsibilities, and instead in less than a month she comes to me and says well I am, and I am promptly seized with a terrific desire to run away because new situations always frighten me and I say but I thought you had an infantile uterus, and she shrugs and I shrug too and I say it must have been the lawyer, and she catches me off guard with a powerful slap and then like a fury she also tries to scratch my eyes, and keeps saying coward and criminal and she also says that the lawyer never existed but she and her girl friend had invented him to see if I wouldn't make up my mind and come to some serious decision, it was all too easy to take advantage of her day and night without ever giving anything in return, but this was the end I could die with my crazy attacks and she woudn't lift her little finger to help me, and as for matrimony she wouldn't marry me not even if I went down on my knees and begged her, and in short after this complicated tirade I manage with some difficulty to make peace, and then we take out the papers in a big hurry and with a scanty attendance of relatives and friends we are hastily married at five in the afternoon in the Romanesque church of Santa Maria in Cosmedin, where they have the Mouth of Truth, whereas only God knows through what sequence of lies and tricks that girl managed to make me put the ring on her finger, which for that matter had been her goal both secret and declared since the day when destiny caused us to meet by the fountain in the Piazza del Popolo.

So now I find myself with a wife who's expecting a baby in addition to my other familiar troubles, that is to say the nervous exhaustion as we may as well go on calling it so long as we are clear about it, and the floating kidney which we will also go on calling that even though by now nobody believes such serious and obstinate ailments can derive from a floating kidney, otherwise women after childbirth who generally have one would certainly never have more children and run the risk of pains like mine compared to which the suffering of birth pangs is laughable inasmuch as that at least ends after delivery, whereas I who fail to give birth an average of once a week fall into one of these monstrous attacks which are beginning to worry me also on account of the morphine because a bit today and a bit tomorrow I'm likely to get addicted and then wouldn't those gravediggers at the hospital have themselves a good laugh, in short the theory of the floating kidney and the remedies both pharmaceutical and empirical connected with it are falling out of favor also because the teenager who is now my wife and who has in consequence changed her attitude says she is suffering from nausea from her pregnancy and so she doesn't agree with the business of sleeping with the dictionaries under the legs of the bed which make her sleep crooked and then maybe the baby will come out wrong, and anyhow I have to give up this and the other practices which in addition to being ineffectual make her think of Zulus and witch doctors, and this is rather odd on her part since if I remember rightly at a certain point in the story when I was hesitating between the Wizard of Naples and the professor of I don't know what at the University of Rome she was rooting energetically for the former, but when I remind her of this she says it's time I grew up now that I have a family, and to begin with since I have kidney trouble why don't I go to a specialist in that field a urologist in other words, in the meanwhile however spring has come so I am also suffering a great deal from another old illness namely the duodenal ulcer which always acts up at every change of season and on this score in addition to suffering with the ulcer I also have to fight with my wife who says but they just cut your stomach open and they didn't find a thing so why do you insist on believing you have an ulcer it's a mania with you no go to a urologist, but I answer that I'll only go to the urologist if she has faith in me and believes me when I tell her that my ulcer is hurting me, and at this point she begins to regret marrying me she says she hoped I would settle down and instead less than a week ago I secretly went back to the acupuncture man, which is true but I went there out of pure chance that is because a lady I met at some friends' house had told me that before the war she had had a terrible disease of the stomach maybe cancer and a man had cured it for her through acupuncture, and in short at a certain moment I remember that I'm an orphan and that matrimony certainly hasn't remedied my suffering state so I start crying and my wife inconsiderately says I'm crazy but to please me she'll go with me to a radiologist provided we can find one through friends so we won't have to pay so much, and in fact after a short while thanks to the generous collaboration of the neighborhood doctor who now for some reason is all on my wife's side we find one who makes me swallow the usual disgusting muck, and then he stands there with his big rubber apron and presses my belly to make the barium stick to the walls of the stomach and the intestine, and he does this with absolute reluctance since he has already told me in private that he's making the X rays but it's no good because it's all in my mind, and instead all of a sudden he says aha by God there is an ulcer here all right I'll say there is, and then from the X ray it turns out that I have an ulcer almost as big as one of the new 5-lire coins, so my wife realizes I'm not all that crazy and when I say I'm sick it means I'm sick, and she says forgive me darling I'm really not worthy of you and she starts crying because she also can start crying over nothing now that she's married me and is expecting a baby, and as you can imagine I don't miss this opportunity for a fine dose of sobs and tears and so we enter a period of weeping and love, and I promise her that as soon as one of these producers I'm planning to work with gives me an advance I'll place myself in the hands of a serious urologist, and in fact a short time later with the help of fortune I go to one of the most serious urologists in the city and without wasting any time he slaps me into his clinic, and here we are again I think this time they'll really skin me alive like Saint whoever-it-was, and I also do a lot of thinking about whether or not it'll be a handicap for my son to be born already half an orphan, judging by my own experience I would say no, anyhow this is one of the thoughts that encourages me most while I start off on the usual round of X rays under a machine that thank God is not so expensive and complicated as the one in the billionaires' clinic although we will see if in the end they don't take the shirt off my back here too, and then they inject into my veins the liquid that makes the workings of the kidneys visible, and since my exhaustion I am occasionally afraid that even the water I'm drinking is poisoned so now my heart is in my throat as if I were going to blow up any minute, and thanks to such thoughts I almost have one of those big attacks that upset me so, luckily this radiologist who is a Tuscan luminary suddenly exclaims something in dialect and shows signs of great interest, and I ask him if by any chance it's tuberculosis or on the other hand cancer, and he answers idly no no and a little later when the X rays are developed he comes to me all pleased with himself and says I'm lucky because at the very moment they were making the plates I was having an attack, that is you could see the ureter swollen with liquid that couldn't pass through because the passage was blocked right at the entrance to the bladder, in other words according to him my long disease came from a very ordinary little stone which I was already passing on my own, however he couldn't make a definitive diagnosis since this was the job of the great urologist, still it happened that the professor after looking at the X rays was in agreement with the radiologist, and seeing how things stood in order to facilitate my cure he decided to perform a cystoscopy which naturally wasn't any fun, however while he was inside my bladder with those tiny instruments he started to nudge the stone that was about to descend into the bladder and he made it fall there all things considered at a very modest expense, and I must say that since then my right kidney has never caused me severe pains again or serious concern, but it had already brought about enough disaster with that nervous exhaustion which every now and then still hurled me into the realms of terror and tears.

So all in all this satisfactory clarification of my bodily ills which if it had come at the right time would have been providential now I would say caused more harm than not, in the sense that it left isolated and more evident than ever the unsolved extralogical problem of my nervous attacks, that is to say what was the cause and the origin of the fearful seizures that every now and then made me lose contact with external reality and at times even with internal namely with my self, but to understand anything about them was apparently a highly complicated business given the variety and the instability of the concrete symptoms and the com-

pletely subtle technique that the disease adopted in assailing me,
since as I believe I have already said it didn't always employ the
five lumbars and the idea of suicide, sometimes it also came
through common stomach-aches or simple movements of intestinal gas things which for me are connected with the concept of
cancer, or else with little pains in the left side of the thorax and a
tingling sensation also in the left arm which obviously can be connected with the idea of myocardial infarction, or else with a banal
headache or rheumatic pain, or else with certain mysterious pins
and needles in the reproductive glands, but most often to tell the
truth it didn't make use of anything at all, nothing I could sense
or pin down concretely, and really it could even be the malefic influence coming from the tomb where rested so to speak that father
with whom I had it seemed an ethical debt beyond all paying,
however in my better moments I considered these spiritual con-
structions mere imagination as is only right, and in fact having
inherited and later enriched with experience a strong sense of
reality I was led to attribute my disease to some imperfection or
rather some chemical disfunction in my bodily make-up especially
in the nerve department, and it is really easy to imagine that the
nerves too are made up of cells and very delicate ones with established chemical components maybe very numerous of which a
great part I think have not yet been discovered or properly investigated, and it may very well be that some lack or excess of one or
another of these elements can provoke a disorder minuscule in
itself and even imperceptible with the techniques at our disposal
but disastrous in its overall consequences given the extent of the
nervous system and above all its importance in our general health
both physical and spiritual, in short after all this thinking about
my troubles I had worked out a fairly satisfactory theory as everyone can see and I didn't give a damn that the doctors of my
acquaintance and even the neighborhod doctor didn't agree, from
what I could tell medicine still had a long way to go before it
reached a respectable level, however this theory which we can
properly call chemical had one defect in that it kept me in a constant state of alarm because everything we eat and breathe is

chemical, and since there is probably something chemical even in what we look at and who knows maybe in what we think, I was upset by the infinite possibilities of disorder I was constantly on my guard against everything I ate and drank and looked at and thought, a highly tiring state as you can well imagine, so little by little I tried to neutralize at least in part the chemical theory flanking it with another theory that I called the physical theory, different though not entirely unconnected with the first, in fact with some overlapping areas, as for example the mysterious though widely diffused influences that atmospheric conditions have not only through pressure as such or through the speed or provenance of the winds but also because of the presence of chemical elements like oxygen and hydrogen and infinite other combinations and compounds, and anyhow in a purer physical field for example the field of colors there are some colors that at times but not always arouse a sense of bewilderment whereas others on the contrary give you the sense of belonging to the external world, and finally moving on to the purest physics I can affirm that the straight line in a special way gives me a sense of security thereby contradicting what the majority of doctors and their sympathizers believe namely that nervous cases should go to the mountains, I have always suffered unspeakably in the mountains, whereas at the sea I suffer less precisely because the line of the horizon gives me a sense of stability provided however I don't remember that the earth in the last analysis is round otherwise not even the line of the sea is any good, and this happens when I'm sick and I see everything crooked without being able to decide whether I'm sick because I'm seeing crooked or vice versa, and this mess also happens in connection with cancer of the intestine or heart disease or any other ailment when that disastrous confusion takes place inside me I can't understand whether it's cause or effect or both together, in the sense that it is a sequential reaction through which the physical illness exacerbated by the spiritual illness accentuates it and then is in turn reinforced with a movement that could also be a kind of constant turning of the screw if for example the victim became crazy, whereas in general the movement is a conic spiral and culminates in a crisis that is a shattering or at least temporary splitting of the Ego, which in two or three days' time settles down again and resumes its functions.

Now anybody can see how basically difficult it is to work under such conditions and really putting all justified ambition and all vain desire for glory aside in those terrible times I had to content myself with very humble jobs so long as they were paid quickly, trying in addition to take them casually although not too casually otherwise the ghost of my carabiniere father sprang forth with all his load of transmittable rectitude to say mark my words you begin like this and you end up in jail, he always used to say I would end up in jail and I would really have been sorry to give him also this final satisfaction after all the others that I had been giving him since his death, in any case under this paternal vigilance I worked as best I could in order to make money since my wife even somewhat ahead of schedule it seemed had grown a spectacular belly which caused her some awkwardness both esthetic and psychological which could only be handled with little dresses called *prémaman*, and then I have to send her to a chic obstetrician who has all the pregnant ladies of high society under his spell, so that he rightly makes them pay the earth, and in addition I have to furnish her money to buy the baby's layette as well as an enormous amount of English yarn which is knitted by a whole raft of female relations who spring up a few at a time, and finally I also have to think of myself a bit and I have to continue my desperate search for a doctor who is able to find the key to this disease of mine which gets more and more complex, and to tell the truth just recently I've discovered for example that my blood goes as it should from the heart down to the legs and to the feet but then it doesn't come up again or rather it has trouble coming up even though there isn't any swelling or reddening, and therefore I always have to stay with my legs raised but maybe this is just a bad habit I picked up in the days of the dictionaries, the fact remains that now we're in late spring and the neighborhood doctor has gone off to make money in the thermal station with his liverish middle-aged lady patients and I tend to wander from one doctor to another, and following the suggestions of my wife who in any case prefers specialists I go to have myself examined by some psychiatrists even if I'm convinced that my disease at present consists in poor circulation in the lower limbs, or in proven premonitions of cancer or heart disease, and these psychiatrists like all the other modern doctors for that matter want to write down a whole lot of things about me that is to say they want to compile my personal history as it's called, and though I am already experienced in this business I can't remember all the misfortunes of my life from mumps on, and in fact once one of those semi-witch-doctor doctors looking into my eyes with a little flashlight says were you once wounded in the left arm in the past, and I say not on your life, and then he falls back on the right arm, and again I say not on your life, and then he gets cross and says that I must have been wounded at least in the leg or the foot at some time in my life, and to tell the truth he's right on this score since during the war in Abyssinia I caught a bullet in the foot, the right one to be precise, only afterwards when I'm on my way home I remember that once, and not so many years ago after all, when I was racing with a motor scooter I fell off like a fool and fractured my arm my left arm to be precise, and then I rush back to this semi-witch-doctor to express my esteem and to have him cure me since he possesses such outstanding divinatory gifts, and I imagine also thaumaturgical, but later it becomes evident that except for some peculiarites like that business of the wounded arm he isn't up to much, and then the following week as soon as they pay me an installment on my work if any money is left over after dealing with my wife and the expected baby I go to a real doctor, and we're off again with the personal history and the list of my troubles, and then as a rule he takes out a little hammer and hits my knee hunting for reflexes, and the leg reacts however I am never sure whether it moves on its own or if I'm not the one who moves it just to please the doctor who wants it to move, and since it also seems that when the reflexes are in order the rest also is pretty well off, in the last analysis it turns out that all I need is to build myself up and of course come to the office for regular check-ups, which is all more than enough to fix up both my soul and my body on condition of course that I make a sincere effort to rid myself of the morbid fantasies in my mind, and with the term morbid fantasies they are generally referring to my struggle with my father and then with all the politeness I can muster I say thank you doctor how much do I owe you, and he says no hurry we can settle next time, but I screw him because the next time I go to somebody else which will teach him not to believe me when I tell him about my war with my father, however there are also the ones who don't let themselves get screwed because at the door I find a nurse who says with determined charm sir that will be five or ten thousand lire.

So to sum it all up
this exhaustion of mine was a big mystery though everybody
knew all about it I mean not only the ten-thousand-lire doctors and
the five-thousand-lire doctors but also both my friends and my
wife's all of whom had either already had a nervous exhaustion
or still had it, and also many people we ran into at the café or
coming out of the movies had had the same thing or at least a
close relative had had it, and in this great abundance I hardly have
time to tell them some of my phobias for example to name one
my elevator phobia or ship phobia or football game and concert
phobia before somebody turns up who had the same thing or his
uncle had the same thing, even when I'm inventing some phobias
just to put on airs, like for example the sixth-floor phobia which
allows me to go to the fifth or the seventh but never to the sixth,
even in this case somebody turns up who swears he went through
exactly the same nonsense, and naturally he knows how to cure
it or else he can recommend exactly the right doctor, and so after
all this groping around at a certain point I happen on a specialist
who attaches enormous importance to sport, *mens sana in corpore
sano* he says explaining that all or almost all nervous disorders
stem from a neglect of this principle which maybe goes back to the

ancient Egyptians or Babylonians, people are driven crazy by the automobile and the elevator he says, and after this preamble which still leaves unanswered the question of how there happened to be crazy people also in the times of Lucretius and Christopher Columbus he asks me if I go in for any sport and summoning up my courage I say no, I don't even tell him about my swims in the pool at the Foreign Ministry Club because apart from the fact that they are a pretty miserable and ridiculous affair I am also reluctant to remember them since my kidney got out of place precisely on their account I imagine, and the ruinous little stone no doubt took advantage of the situation to make a few moves on its own, so I tell the doctor no and he says too bad because on top of everything else it seems I have a fairly athletic physique, but better late than never and besides if I want to get well I have to take up sport, but an all-round, elegant sport since social prestige is also something not to be underestimated, horseback riding for example he says, and at this point I have the impression that I'm not the one whose brain needs treatment, but to tell the truth this is an impression I often have on first encountering a new doctor and it isn't necessarily always mistaken, anyhow this one as soon as I remind him of my floating kidney falls back without any hesitation on tennis or swimming which are also fairly all-round sports, and obviously I decide on tennis and so at my age I get myself into white shorts and T-shirt with a Spalding racquet which the man in the store insists is really the racquet of champions, and I go out and find the most secluded tennis court in the city and there with the pro at first I learn the positions and the preliminary movements and then he throws me the ball with his hands and somehow or other I catch it with the racquet and knock it over the net, it really looks as if this tennis is cut out for me and in fact after a dozen lessons or so except for the fact that I start to pant too soon I manage to move easily and gracefully, by God I say maybe if I'd thought of it in time this was the right career for me to win glory I could have been another Canepele or De Stefani or some other champion forgotten today but famous in their time, however even starting so late I take it up with a will sometimes hitting five or six balls in a row with forehand and backhand, except that at a certain point my right leg takes to hurting and I can't move it well, it's that rheumatism I tell myself you picked up in Abyssinia where you were fool enough to go instead of staying home and taking up sports, however it isn't exactly rheumatism and in fact my back starts aching too I mean the notorious five lumbars or just below them, so I tell my wife I have to have my spine X-rayed and this is one kind of X ray that is no bother because you don't have to take anything either orally or by injection, and my wife who in her position as a visibly pregnant woman is now without any inhibitions says you're crazy to have yourself X-rayed again haven't you had enough of that already, and obviously I answer that I'm the one who makes the money it's mine and I can spend it any way I like and she says not any more now that you have a wife and soon a child as well, in short we have a big row because I can't allow my wife to fling in my face the money I spend on my health when she squanders almost everything I earn and neither she nor I knows where it's gone, and since it is always during our fights that I display the most energy and will to be independent I go out slamming the door and just to show her that I wear the pants I go straight to the radiologist, and he discovers that the space between I forget which vertebra and the one either above it or below it does seem in fact a bit reduced, maybe there is a beginning of a hernia of the disc or in other words a squeezing of the cartilage of the disc that then presses on the sciatic nerve and this would also explain the pain in my leg, and in conclusion he says that I have to wear a corset, my God that's all I needed, and I am excessively frightened since after all a corset isn't that kind of iron and plaster armature I thought but instead a little girdle with iron ribs which is made to measure and costs twenty-seven thousand five hundred lire, and moreover they tell me that in the old days fifty per cent of the cavalry officers who wanted to have trim waists and their entrails in order despite all their jumping on horseback used to wear corsets like mine, so I am quite happy to put it on, first two hours a day then three and four until I get attached to it since

I feel completely at ease supported by the braces, I can do pirou-
ettes and knee bends easy as pie and I am thinking of having my
pants taken in which at present are loose at the waist, but the
marvelous and really extraordinary fact is that I begin to feel well
also in spirit, I wouldn't be surprised I say to myself if all this
endless disaster and the exhaustion came from a slightly displaced
vertebra, it was pressing on a little nerve and click everything was
upset, my God why couldn't it be true since all the other troubles
from the hematuria and the wrong operation and the countless
kidney attacks came from a tiny stone that you couldn't even see,
and so the exhaustion too was caused by a trifle, in short I really
feel fine also because in these nervous ailments it so happens that
if the patient thinks he feels fine then he really does feel fine, except that one day with the corset on and everything I have an
attack worse than any I've ever had, to make matters worse it
comes on me right in the middle of a square I think it was the
Piazza Barberini full of people and of course the people don't help
me at such moments in fact I feel even worse because of my agoraphobia, and not knowing what else to do in desperation I grab a
traffic cop who is about to take offense but then seeing how pale
I am and upset he leads me into the pharmacy there at the corner
of the via Quattro Fontane where they give me a tranquilizer or a
stimulant God only knows which it doesn't matter anyhow, but
despite their care I feel like I'm suffocating and it's that damned
corset with its laces and stays that gives me this suffocating sensation, I have to go to the back of the shop and take it right off, and
so I also acquired a corset phobia then which I think is a kind of
subspecies of claustrophobia, twenty-seven thousand five hundred
lire down the drain, plus the money for the Spalding and the
complete outfit, all that money wasted father, however don't you
start saying it's my fault she's already saying that to me, and just
see the mess I got myself into by marrying and having a baby I'll
be forced to incur more debts father and that'll give you yet another reason to feel bitter toward this your unworthy son, but can
I help it if I'm unlucky, what's more I married this kid who lets
money slip through her fingers and makes all sorts of demands,

when the time comes she has to go to a de luxe clinic of course because her beloved obstetrician only operates in clinics of a certain standing obviously, and I really want to lay eyes on him this pig who flirts with women eight or nine months gone putting his hands in the midst of all that filth that it's best for me not even to try to imagine, otherwise I'll never be able to make love with my wife again.

Now it so happens that one morning while I'm sleeping on the single bed in my study in the new house that we've taken not in Parioli any more but in a cheaper neighborhood under Monte Mario where however we pay more since the apartment is bigger, and in fact we have to remember that we will soon have a baby and moreover my wife has a program which I would define as vast since naturally with the baby we have to have a Swiss nurse or at least one from the South Tyrol or Upper Adige depending on how you look at that particular section of our country and this is one of the many little questions we disagree on, anyhow that isn't so much the point the fact is that as far as I'm concerned there will be no nurse not even from Rome and environs, and my wife who is secretly prepared for these narrow ideas of mine says all right then I'll get my mother to come, and this is her real goal the Swiss nurse being merely a feint as I believe they say in the artillery, so that explains why she wanted a bigger house however at the moment we don't have any furniture since we rented our previous apartment furnished and this one unfurnished, so we have a surplus of space so to speak with these rooms where there are only a bed and a chair used as a bedside table and in my room obviously also a table to work at, and there is then the baby's room with laces and crib and bathinette and the little table and the little scales and the little cupboard and the pictures of Mickey Mouse on the walls because naturally when you bring a child into the world you have to give him everything he has a right to expect this is my wife's line of reasoning and she seems to ignore the fact that some babies were even born in a manger also to give us an example of moderation, and naturally for these and other reasons we argue often so she with her big belly sleeps in the master bedroom and I in the study, and then one morning she enters my room with that common-sense manner she assumes only on state occasions and she tells me to keep calm and not to get upset, it seems that the great moment has come that is the bag of waters is broken or God only knows what has happened along that line, the fact is that without even wakening me because despite what I think she is full of consideration for me since I work and have this disease which of course is nothing but still it is after all a nervous ailment, so without wakening me she has already telephoned the clinic and has prepared her suitcase with the few necessary things including the special nightgowns of white muslin with short sleeves to seem more proper and little buttons in the front so she can nurse the baby herself, and now if I feel like getting up and driving her to the clinic that would be fine otherwise she won't cause me any trouble or annoyance and can call a taxi and go by herself, and I would almost let her go alone which would teach her to make certain hypocritical suggestions except that afterwards she would throw it in my face daily for fifteen months or even longer if in the meanwhile I haven't committed some other worse misdeed, in short I get up and take her to the smart clinic where they say that Ingrid Bergman had a baby and it also seems one or more wives of the king of Jordan, the day isn't all that festive to tell the truth because since we're almost in the exact center of a low pressure zone it's pouring rain and is cold which after all is only right since it's early November winter practically speaking, but in Rome God only knows why when winter comes many people believe the city enjoys a tropical climate so that in the apartment houses except for those in Parioli and a few other de luxe zones the tenants are divided into two factions, the one that wants the heat turned on immediately and the faction that says the Roman summer lasts right up till Christmas, and naturally we live in a building where democratically the Christmas faction is in a majority and therefore in our apartment we shiver and things get moldy whereas here in the clinic with the heaters turned on it's delightfully warm, and the room has lovely cretonne curtains at the windows and a big easy chair covered in the same cretonne and instead in our house there are neither curtains nor easy chairs, and they also say this is the very best room where Ingrid Bergman or some other movie star of equal importance stayed also for reasons of childbirth, and my wife likes it a lot and I also like it although there are other little rooms at the back of the clinic where they take women who have health insurance and these cost less of course, but my wife says our child has to come into the world in comfortable surroundings because that way he'll be luckier in life, and I find this thought very beautiful but all the same I wish the whole thing would be quick at least and instead with births what normally happens is that you break your neck getting to the hospital and once the expectant mother is there she goes to bed and waits, how long she has to wait only God knows it seems there have even been cases where after waiting a week or a bit less the pregnant woman has gone home again because she was a month off in her calculations, at least this is what the nurse tells me who among other things is also a cute girl, but in my present mood my heart is entirely concerned with the cost of the clinic with what could also be called per diem tariff and so I can't think about the beauty of girls or of rooms, my wife on the other hand has got into bed quite content in her de luxe maternity nightgown and now she is waiting for the famous professor who will come God knows when, he's a professor who doesn't have a schedule since his work depends on these women who as a rule don't give birth at set times, anyhow it seems that the majority of them prefer the night so the professor sleeps late in the morning they say he never gets in before eleven, and so my wife says to me why stay here and be bored go browse around the book-shops which you enjoy so much or else go home and work, but this is one of her familiar traps since if I agreed all hell would break loose almost as if I were abandoning her in labor on the street with the rain pouring down outside, so I tell her that the only thing I want to do now is to stay beside her and she is grateful to me for this attitude which for that matter isn't a complete fiction and she says why don't you work here where there's the radiator on, and this suggestion saddens me not only because it reminds

me of the radiator in the modest little hospital room where my
father died but also because it proves once again that my wife
understands nothing about me or my method of working if she
thinks I can work anywhere maybe even in a lying-in hospital
where there is a constant coming and going of nurses, nuns, and
orderlies, and mind you I don't protest so much against the thing
in itself in fact at the price we're paying it's only right that they
should go to extremes in caring for the patients but I would certainly not be able to work in all this commotion, whereas my wife
is of the opinion that the best screenwriters that is to say the ones
who make a pile of money generally write their scripts at the little
tables at Canova's or Rosati's in the Piazza del Popolo, or at the
Caffè Greco the ones that like a more old-world atmosphere, or at
the Via Veneto cafés the ones who want to show off so people
won't forget them, but as for me even on unimportant jobs like
scripts and other things for the movies or TV I have to have seclu-
sion and privacy and maybe this is why I can't earn much, well I
won't contradict her that's how I am and certainly in the hospital
room where my wife has come to have a baby I couldn't write
anything good or bad, so she sends me out to buy the weekly
magazines and then we start leafing through this mountain of
magazines which at any rate don't tire the mind since they all report the same events in the same way, except of course for the
radical magazines which report the same stories as the others but
in a different and all things considered better way so that often
you can't figure out what they want, I mean whether they're for
or against the vote of no confidence or Sophia Loren's marriage
or the alienation phenomenon so typical of neocapitalism. What
with one magazine and another noon comes and with it the famous
professor, a handsome man no denying that with a white jacket
which is perhaps like all the other white jackets in the world but
on him it looks as if it had been tailored by Caraceni or at least
bought in Regent Street, these obstetricians who deal with movie
stars and queens and other very wealthy pregnant women present
company excepted of course have to have their secret weapons
among which beyond any doubt sartorial elegance must be num-

bered, and this one besides really knows his business since he goes
in for the psychological method known as painless childbirth, and
besides he has a special charm of his own as he says well let's see
how the young and lovely Signora So-and-so is today while he feels
her stomach and her legs and whatever he wants, and the young
and lovely Signora So-and-so is beside herself and devours him
with her eyes as if he were a well-balanced mixture of Padre Pio
of Pietralcina and Laurence Olivier, and these things can also
slightly annoy certain husbands even those who don't go in for
jealousy here it isn't a matter of jealousy but of decency and also
of an objective judgement on a character who earns a pile of
money feeling our wives, the fact is that after he's gone out I don't
express any direct consideration on the matter of the feeling but
I hazard the opinion that my wife has come to the clinic a bit prematurely attracted there more than anything else by that dude of
an obstetrician, and this is unquestionably an imprudent remark
for many reasons but especially for the veiled allusion to a pre-
sumed dishonesty however passive so to speak in the prophet of
painless childbirth who at present enjoys unconditioned prestige
in my wife's mind, so in the end we have a fine row also raising
our voices despite the surroundings, she accuses me of mental
cruelty and stinginess and I tell her she's made a big mistake if she
thinks she's here on a holiday with what this place costs, she cries
and says I'm heartless and I go off hurling defiantly the suggestion
that she call in the doctor to console her, and I really do go off
and have lunch in a restaurant from my bachelor days since the
woman we have who comes in by the hour thanks to her legs
afflicted with varicose veins would depress even spirits that always look at things optimistically so imagine my spirit, however
in the restaurant there isn't joy unconfined either with a waiter
who recognizes me and tells me the story of his life from the end
of the war to the present, anyhow after a while other people come
in and also a friend of mine comes well more an acquaintance than
a friend, but since he has two fairly good-looking girls with him,
rather one beautiful and one so-so, I flash him a smile and naturally since two girls are one too many he smiles at me, and

we settle down at the same table and I'm of course predisposed towards the pretty one who is a divorced lady from Puerto Rico with sugar plantations it seems, and she speaks French with charming nonchalance like a person accustomed to moving in the smartest international circles, and I say to myself now why didn't I marry this one who has mountains of cash and so could go to clinics that cost ten thousand a day or even more with two obstetricians instead of one to pat her here and there, but no my wife shouldn't have done it, I try as hard as I can to feel a justified bitterness towards her so that if the occasion demands I can make this Puerto Rican, it would serve my wife right she does everything she can to exasperate me so any revenge would be fairly legitimate and I could go to bed with another woman, still I must add that as a general principle she has made the idea of being unfaithful to her pretty frightening and in fact when the moment comes I keep thinking my God I wonder what a row she would make if I was unfaithful to her, anyhow it's certain that by disposition I am what is commonly called a faithful husband but it is equally true that when I have a fight with my wife I ponder the idea of being unfaithful in reprisal, and now that we've had a fight I have an opportunity like this with the Puerto Rican from the international set and it would be a crime to let her get away, good heaven can it be that I just don't have the nerve to cheat on my wife, maybe I really don't and anyhow it seems that the sugar queen has reached an understanding with the dope who brought her here whereas the other girl isn't the kind that makes it worth your while to get into trouble with your wife if she should find out, so I say I have a business appointment around three and I go off, I go off but I don't know where to go I would even go back to the clinic if I weren't sure of giving her an undeserved satisfaction, so I start looking in the paper for a movie and it seems impossible that in a whole page of movies there isn't one to be seen, and then they talk about a depression in the film industry these idiots of course there's a depression with the producers we have, anyhow let's pick any old film chosen with the criterion of convenience since it's still pouring down rain, it's been raining like

the great flood since seven this morning when she pulled me
out of bed as if the baby were coming that minute, and instead
God knows how long they'll drag it out in that smart clinic with
that chic gynecologist who enjoys touching other people's wives
whereas it would turn my stomach to touch even Liz Taylor if she
were in her ninth month, and for that matter I bet that not even
he does it out of pleasure but only to charm those nitwits whose
husbands then shell out ten-thousand-lire notes, the fact remains
that nothing I do amuses me not even going to the movies at three
in the afternoon, I had forgotten what a second- or third-run
theater was like at three in the afternoon with students and un-
employed and soldiers on a three-hour pass and five or six ugly
girls who keep busy in the dark, it certainly isn't a consoling
atmosphere also because of the barracks smell that the soldiers'
uniforms give off after they've soaked up the rain, I remember
the years and years in the army all wasted, in any case now that
I'm there I watch a lot of ads then a documentary on poverty in the
south and a newsreel that maybe was once funny but is now too
old, and then more animated ads and finally a film that is really
idiotic like almost all the films about the Far West, and still I sit
there watching it almost twice through since I certainly don't
want to give my wife the satisfaction of going to visit her before
six or six thirty, and in fact it's well after six when I turn up at
the clinic and I find her with a long face looking at the TV set
she's had them bring into the room and she promptly informs me
that she asked for it on purpose to make me pay five hundred lire
extra per day because that's what it costs, and I don't say a word
of course what could I say, and then she changes her tone and tells
me it's not true she only wanted the TV because she felt too lonely
and unhappy without me, and I tell her it's all right what's another
five hundred lire more or less, and sinking into the easy chair I
also start watching TV which seems to be explaining how you
raise chickens and since this subject allows me plenty of free time
in my head simultaneously I'm thinking that if I were a decent
husband I too would write film scripts on the Via Veneto or in the
Piazza del Popolo and I'd have a house with curtains and sofas

and handsome antiques, basically I'm a lousy husband and this
poor girl here is right when she gets mad at me however she
doesn't understand that I'm stingy because I don't have the money,
if I had it I wouldn't be stingy and therefore I'm not really that
way even if I must surely have inherited a certain prudence in
spending, and then I also think of my mother that sainted woman
who produced a son and then five daughters in her own double
bed with the help of a neighbor woman or midwife spending all
told less than a tenth I'd bet of what this wife of mine is going to
spend to produce just one baby, and not to make comparisons
which are always odious but I would like to see how my father
would have behaved with my mother if she had insisted on the
hospital and the rest of it every time, although on thinking about
it when I came into the world people didn't go to hospitals and
most women had their babies at home whereas today with all this
nonsense about the psychological painless childbirth method we
start spending money you might say even before we knock them
up, and I really have to laugh about this painless childbirth of my
wife's, she says she's studied the manual and done the exercises
and the self-hypnoses, but as far as I know she hasn't done a damn
thing except maybe look at the pictures in this manual and browse
through it casually because my wife isn't the type who applies herself seriously to anything in fact I would say that her main charm
at least for those who aren't her husband is her almost infantile
thoughtlessness which includes among other things the notion that
she can learn without applying herself, take English for example
she's gone around I don't know how much to institutes like the
Cambridge School or Marymount and the Scottish nuns on the
Palatine and maybe the Canadian sisters in the Via Camilluccia
without learning a damn thing but she thinks she knows English
better than me and lots of other people because she can sing a
couple of Frank Sinatra songs mimicking his accent but mauling
the words she doesn't understand which are practically all of
them, so I will have the laugh on her now with this painless birth
which she thinks she's learned and in the meanwhile the TV has
given up chickens and has started on a travel documentary about

the Salento region rich in fine baroque churches resembling that cheese with holes in it, and my wife follows it carefully because she's good at art history and to tell the truth one of the few occasions when she beats me is when she sees a picture or a reproduction and she says right off that's such and such a painter of the fifteenth century and this is from the eighteenth century maybe even fairly unknown painters like the Cossas or Pesellino whereas I never can guess a single one, so she looks at the documentary intently and I can foresee that when it's over she'll give me an earful on Apulian Baroque to show me that in at least one field she's superior to me, and instead she says softly what did you do today and I say movies and she says what did you see and I say nothing and she says I love you you know and she wants me to take her hand to show her I'm not mad because of the five hundred lire for the TV, and I take her hand and tell her that I love her too and inside myself I am very pleased that I wasn't unfaithful to her with the Puerto Rican sugar heiress although to tell the truth it isn't sure I could have been even if I had wanted to, anyhow she sighs tenderly and says why didn't you bring me some *marrons glacés*, and I think Jesus Christ just look at what she demands how in the world could I have thought of bringing her *marrons glacés* instead of chocolates or *petits fours* or candied violets, anyhow I don't feel like fighting since apparently we have just made peace and I say I'll go out and get you some, and she says no it's raining and I say I don't mind the rain it's just a minute I'll come right back and she says be sure to get them from Moriondo on the Corso, and I go off secretly grumbling because of this whim about Moriondo on the Corso, couldn't she think of an easier place to send me, I know she's pregnant and you can't reason with pregnant women but to drive into the center of the city at seven p.m. in this downpour would try the patience of a saint, and in fact it's almost an hour before I get to the Corso and find a parking place within a radius of half a kilometer, and the return trip of course is quicker because there isn't the parking problem but all the same it's after eight when I come into her room with the little package of *marrons glacés* and I find her already in labor it seems these are the cyclic pains that is they come in waves every so many minutes, and when the pains seize her she moans and digs her nails into my hand, and then when the pains pass she says I'm really happy now you won't say I came to the hospital a week ahead of time, and then when the pains come and she moans I think some painless childbirth you're working up to, and it turns out that a couple of hours of these pains have to go by before the nurse decides to phone the professor-gynecologist, and he shows up looking well fed after his supper and he says well let's see what's happening to this lovely little signora, this time they even send me out into the corridor to wait, and then I see them all rushing around and orderlies come with a stretcher obviously she's ready to bring it out, but at times like these she really is a grand girl and as she goes by on the stretcher she says I don't want you to stand around here waiting go to Pasqualino's, and obviously I am a bit moved and besides when a man's in love with a woman these are the very occasions when he feels it most deeply even if by chance he's a bit irritated because it's clear that my wife became so serene once the painless childbirth man appeared, but I don't want to think about that now and I press her hand as she goes by and I say remember I want a girl with blue eyes and blond hair, and she says yes and smiles when she has already half-vanished inside an elevator and I say to myself look at this wife I've got the heroic exhibitionistic type I mean the kind who shines on great occasions and the rest of the time is a pain in the ass, and instead if anything I would have preferred the opposite since great occasions are rare whereas occasions for being a pain in the ass are constant, anyway once my wife has vanished it seems I have no function in the present juncture and I certainly don't want to start chain smoking outside the delivery room like every expectant father, so all in all the best thing is to go off to Pasqualino's who's a great friend of hers inasmuch as he has often said terrible things about the French widow when my girl was still only my girl and this widow turned up again now and then like a menacing ghost capable of upsetting my future wife's plans, and with Pasqualino I start chatting about this and that while he gives me something to eat and of course we chat also about the days when I wasn't yet married and the widow every so often tried to regain her lost position and he lets me know that on one of these occasions he even went to bed with the widow, so when you come right down to it he was a real bastard if I am to believe him, in short we talk about a bit of everything except the most important and immediate event namely the fact that I'm about to become a father, but I don't know why I don't feel like talking about this though naturally I'm thinking about it all the time even when I'm talking about the widow and other things, really this business of becoming a father seems inexplicable to me I mean why anybody does it instead of not doing it, or rather in my own case I know very well why I did it and when and how but I find myself in an uncertain position with regard to the general problems as for example the principle of the perpetuation of the species, and since I don't see what need there might be of me for this great mission my personal position appears a little shaky and in other words though I am past the fine age of forty I feel completely unprepared for fatherhood and if I could I would gladly forego the opportunity but it's too late now because before I expect it somebody calls from the clinic maybe a nurse who in an important voice says everything has gone just fine and I say thank you very much and her tone becomes even more important and unctuous like somebody accustomed to making a living off tips and she says don't you want to know if it's a boy or a girl, and I feel like answering something on the order of what's the difference to you however I remind myself that the difference to her is nothing whereas I am the father and it ought to make a lot of difference to me within certain limits, but rather than give her any satisfaction I say it's all the same to me and I hang up and then while I'm on my way to the clinic under a kind of cloudburst with the water coming into my rattletrap little car whose windshield wipers aren't worth a damn and you can't see where you're going, I say to myself just like me to lose my way now and never get to the damned clinic at all, or else have an accident and kick off just when my baby is born at last they would write about me at some length in these papers because a man who dies while his baby is born is always news despite the cynical times we live in, however I wonder if it's a son or a daughter not that it would change the newspaper's interest but all in all I would like to know before I die, and at the same time I figure that if I don't die and it's a girl I'll have her on my back for a good twenty years but if it's a boy for even longer, and in these last few days I've been amusing myself by calculating more or less what it will cost and it seems that by and large it'll cost about a million per year without taking into consideration inflation, so this still unknown descendant of mine has already settled into what will be his chief function for the coming years namely the job of inspiring worries about money and fear of death, anyhow for the moment I get to the clinic safe and sound although pretty wet and I find my wife in bed a little pale but so pleased with the professor-gynecologist who has come to see her after her trial and says what a brave lovely little signora, and I think you want to bet the painless childbirth worked after all my wife is really capable of anything, on the other hand she's obviously beside herself at this praise received from on high and when the doctor finally goes away she wants to take my hand and she looks at me all moved and tells me she wants another one right away, and I burst out with the hell you say we're not completely nuts and I would like to tell her to take it easy, but then I realize what she said was another girl and this means that it was a daughter so I say it was a girl wasn't it, and with her exhausted eyes and mouth smiling as if she had never done anything but love me and love me without causing me a moment's annoyance she says you wanted a girl, and then she says but she doesn't have blue eyes and blond hair I wasn't good enough, and I tell her don't be silly and I almost start crying, luckily a nun comes in and when she learns I'm the father she congratulates me heartily and says it's really forbidden but if I want to peep at the baby she'll let me, to tell the truth I don't care all that much today or tomorrow it's all the same the way I feel in fact rather tomorrow than today then at least for one more night I can pretend she hasn't been born, however it seems that there are fairly rigid conventions governing the behavior of new fathers and one of these consists in his looking with satisfaction and emotion at his newborn baby so I follow the nun down the hall and she motions me to wait and a little later she brings me my daughter, dressed in muslin and laces like a princess but otherwise exactly like all the other babies in the universe who are surely not beautiful, indeed I would say they're ugly and red-faced and my daughter is no exception, however I note that her little hands are white with very long fingers I wonder if it's normal for her to have such long fingers being just born however if it isn't normal so much the better my daughter must have something exceptional about her after all, so I begin to feel the required satisfaction and desire to touch one of those hands to feel the skin of this creature still a bit alien as far as I'm concerned, and then I don't know how but she grabs my finger she's only an ugly little monster who moves her mouth and hands without knowing it and yet just by grabbing my finger she has completely established a natural relationship also of love that is indissoluble, in short she has caught me for all my life placing me at her service, a fine business when you think about it, for the next twenty years or even twenty-five if not more my work and my efforts will all have one purpose, God help me.

And so this barely born daughter fills my mind and soul with a sweet effusion of love and also a considerable increase of responsibility obviously and so I start working with great energy in the cold house where the maid with the varicose veins is omnipresent and my God how she makes me think of physical decay and the decline of the whole human race this maid with varicose veins, really there ought to be a remedy for these things and for example my daughter will never have varicose veins to begin with, anyway fighting the discouragement coming from the cold and the maid's legs I work hard for a couple of days so I can go to the producer with a sheaf of paper and collect an installment on what he owes me, and I go to the hospital when I can always in a rush with the car that is moldy after all the water that got in it, one day I'll tell my daughter how much water fell from the heavens in the first days of her life with a north wind that blew

down a lot of leaves so all of a sudden winter has come, in fact I
think that I should keep a diary of these details like the bad
weather and the gesture she made in taking my finger right after
she was born and also intimate reflections like to name one if I
am worthy of what has happened to me and sufficiently responsible, and when she's twenty I'll give her this diary and it will be a
marvelous gift I can imagine, because I don't know anything
about when I was born and now that I think about it I regret it,
my father with his decided graphomania could easily have kept a
diary instead of writing infinite appeals and petitions to headquarters and ministries, after all keeping a diary doesn't cost
anything just a bit of patience and perseverance, so I decide to
begin tonight starting however from the evening when she was
born because it could turn out to be a nice piece of writing with
the confused feelings I had and the cloudburst over the city and
my speeding through the night as if summoned by my child even
though I didn't then know if it was male or female, I really must
write it in a diary otherwise you always end up forgetting these
things, and since I only go to the clinic when I can manage it with
my work my wife grumbles that they all leave her alone although
to tell the truth in these first days of motherhood her room is always
full of relatives who say how pretty you look and how brave you
are, and this is another pain in the ass these relatives since I rarely
tell my wife she's lovely and brave, and anyhow while I'm on my
way I think that maybe I'll find her in a bad humor and it occurs
to me to take her a present to pacify her, flowers would be ridiculous and besides they are even overflowing into the hall outside
her door because her girl friends and relatives who love her have
sent her so many, so I think maybe it's best to take her some *marrons glacés* however when I have this idea the Corso is a bit out of
my way because I am near the Piazza Fiume and if by chance I
did want to turn back and go to Moriondo I then wouldn't have
time to go to the clinic so all in all the best thing is for me to buy
these *marrons glacés* in any old shop I'm sure that she's just
putting on airs saying she wants the *marrons* from Moriondo and
I bet if I gave them to her with her eyes shut she couldn't tell

one from the other, in short I get the girl in the shop to wrap them
in tissue paper with no name on it so my wife can't tell where I
bought them and then I rush to the clinic and I find her with a
long face and her eyes glued to the TV, today it seems she felt
terribly abandoned because neither parents nor girl friends have
come to see her but how could I know that, she says she called
home all afternoon and I was never there and I tell her I was at the
Hotel Excelsior for three hours waiting with my fifty pages ready
for the producer hoping he would pay me an installment and instead he's going to pay me tomorrow and meanwhile he also suggested I go to Paris with him next week, and still very cold she
asks me if I've been to the registry office to report Michaela although she knows full well I haven't gone and that the subject
makes me nervous and at this point I say Michaela hell I'll castrate
myself before I call any daughter of mine Michaela, and looking
up only for a moment from the TV she says surely you don't want
to name her Augusta after your mother and I say my mother's
name isn't Augusta it's Ottavia, but they call her Augusta my wife
says and this is true God knows why because everybody does call
her Augusta, in any case I can't see anything wrong with the idea
of my daughter being called Augusta it's a nice name and besides
my mother is her grandmother after all, of course this isn't the
first time that we quarrel over these names we've already done
it many other times even before the baby was born without either
of us managing to convince the other, and meanwhile she has un-
wrapped the *marrons glacés* without paying much attention to the
paper thank God because she's arguing about the name and also
watching the TV, and then she puts in her mouth one of those
sugary things which by the way certainly aren't any cheaper
than Moriondo's and she immediately looks up from the TV and
stares at me with hatred, where did you buy this muck she says
with hatred, and I can't bear being looked at and spoken to with
hatred, muck yourself I say, and without thinking twice she takes
the little paper dish with all the *marrons* and throws it in my face,
and a moment later I am out in the corridor with all my dignity
as head of the family shattered, and I go to look through the win-

dow of the room where they keep the babies, there are about a dozen in there in their cribs and naturally I don't know which one is my daughter so I choose a crib at random and say ah daughter of mine if you only knew how unhappy I am God only knows if you'll ever forgive me for bringing you into the world unhappy and mixed up as I am, however you'll see I'll make that mother of yours pay for this and just for a start I'll be unfaithful to her so help me, and then tomorrow morning right away I'll go to the registry office and give you the name Augusta and to hell with Michaela she makes me laugh with this Michaela of hers, and in short I cheer myself up a bit with these prospects of revenge and I manage to get into the car but after a little while I have to stop because the windshield wipers aren't working and then I start crying, I cry and think all together of my dead father and my newly born daughter and my wife who is so demanding even when it comes to *marrons glacés*, and then after this fit of weeping is over I go to the restaurant in the Via della Croce imagining I won't find anybody there at this late hour but with the secret hope that there'll be the Puerto Rican woman of the international set, and in fact there she is with that idiot friend of mine and the girl who's only so-so and they say why don't you come out with us this evening we're going to have something to drink in a studio nearby, and I say sure of course I'll come and in fact I eat a plate of spaghetti *alla carbonara* in a hurry and then we go to this studio in the Via Margutta with my friend who during the short walk tries to pass off the ugly girl on me whereas I play dumb and never leave the side of the Puerto Rican, and in the painter's studio there's a record player and dim lights and when we start dancing locked as close as two people can get I realize that she's game but at this very moment when I feel her soft body against me and her panting in my ear I seem to get over my anger with my wife, of course there are some ugly scenes between my wife and me however it's also true that we love each other though in a confused way, and if I cheated on her it would spoil everything she is always telling me that if I was unfaithful that would be the end so imagine if I did it now while she's in the hospital after having

given me a daughter, however a woman who throws a package
of *marrons glacés* in your face deserves to be cheated on I'll say
she does, and in fact this conclusion gives me strength and I whisper
in the Puerto Rican's ear why don't we sleep together tonight
but she whispers back into my ear no not tonight I'm busy but how
about tomorrow we can have lunch together but don't tell Enrico
about it, you can imagine how much I want to tell Enrico among
other things I had forgotten his name was Enrico till this moment,
we arrange for me to telephone her tomorrow at the hotel
and then I go off because some character with a guitar has started
singing French songs and although all the others around are
listening and enjoying it a lot I feel it isn't worth losing more sleep
since the preceding night I hardly slept at all in order to get the
fifty pages ready for that lousy producer who then didn't cough
up a cent, and if he doesn't pay me how am I going to pay the
clinic, anyhow I go to sleep still brooding chiefly on the injustice of
those *marrons glacés* in my face and even in sleep I can't get over
it and in fact as soon as I'm awake I jump in the car and in the
rain I drive to the registry in the Via del Mare and there at five
hundred lire a head I take two witnesses since the law demands
witnesses for these transactions and so these characters make a
living witnessing as much as they can, in short when my turn
comes I sit there before the registrar with a witness at my right
and another at my left and making use of my paternal legal authority
I arrange that this daughter born to me in my wife be
given the name of Augusta, and that isn't all because the official
asks me about her legal residence and I say what's that she was
born here in Rome and therefore presumably she resides in Rome
but he answers oh no it isn't that simple a baby can perfectly well
be born in Rome and be registered as a resident of Milan, and then
I remember that on this detail of legal residence my wife and I
have never seen eye to eye because I have always scorned taking
out Roman citizenship whereas she of course has the opposite
view also because having been born in Rome and having Roman
citizenship which seems to have been a great privilege for more
than two thousand six hundred years she has no intention of

giving it up to take out legal residence in a hick town like mine, so since I haven't forgotten the insult of the *marrons glacés* in the face again taking advantage of my legal authority I arrange for my daughter Augusta to have her legal residence with her father and not with her mother which will teach the latter a lesson, and I'm sure that these bureaucratic formulas will start a fine row but so much the worse for a certain party.

Naturally this is only the first and after all the less entertaining part in my program of revenge, now I have the Puerto Rican before me, however in the meanwhile I hurry home to work because that lousy producer said he wouldn't hand over a cent if I didn't bring him at least another twenty-five pages, anyhow I can write them easily enough since it's notorious that he can't read, and my wife is right when she says the world belongs to the smart implying that I am dumb, I am really dumb as far as the profit I extract from my work is concerned when you consider the effort and time I put into it, but what can I do if I've inherited a conscience that's never quiet even now when I have to concoct a script on *The Count of Monte Cristo* which I had always heard mentioned but had never read and now at last I fill this gap in my culture finding the book generally a disappointment, in fact I am amazed that a rather sophisticated person like James Joyce if I'm not mistaken considered the work admirable I forget from what point of view, though it doesn't seem much to me surely I'm mistaken since I'm reading this book aged forty whereas you should read it when you're twelve or maybe younger, anyway if that louse hadn't given me the script to write I would never have read this *Count of Monte Cristo* at forty or any other age, in fact when I think about it I could have managed without reading it even though I have to do the script since this is what the smart ones do they read resumés or else a line here and a line there to save time whereas I conscientiously swallow it down to the last syllable of the learned and edifying conversations of the Abbé Faria, in any case as soon as I get home the woman with the varicose veins informs me that the signora has telephoned twice and wants me to call her and I think like hell I will and I start dashing off a few pages trying to stifle my conscience, but meanwhile my wife calls again from the clinic and I don't have the courage not to go to the phone, I go and she tells me she hasn't slept all night because she was thinking of those *marrons* she threw in my face she says she cried and she's still crying and can't stop and we have to make peace or else her milk will dry up and then God knows what a wet nurse from Brianza would cost or even one from Ciociaria, and I think lousy whore listen to the reasons she thinks up to persuade me and I hold out and she says darling why don't you say something let's make peace at least for love of our daughter Michaela, and I say to her listen I went to the registry and your daughter's name is Augusta in case you want to know, and with a couple of sighs to swallow this bitter pill she manages to say meekly I'm glad you told me because this afternoon I'm going to have her baptized here in the clinic it only costs five thousand lire which is a nice saving don't you think and that way we avoid the refreshments and just think what a mess it would have been if I'd had her baptized with one name when she has another one at the registry, in other words I have the sensation that she's giving way all along the line maybe I could take advantage of this atmosphere and confess the little detail of the hick-town residence, but better postpone that to the next opportunity, and meanwhile she says why don't you come and eat with me here in the clinic now they bring me lots of food enough for two, in the end it seems to me that under the present circumstances I don't have any good reason for being unfaithful to her, it always happens like this before I can do it she somehow or other achieves a reconciliation, and if I go on like this I'll remain monogamous unless I change my character, but how can I change my character at my age well you can become dumber but not less dumb, so skipping all considerations of a general nature now I have to call the Puerto Rican at the Hotel Inghilterra and think up some excuse, however I don't know what excuse to invent really I'm not very good at these maneuvers and in fact I telephone before I have an excuse in mind, I'll tell her the truth I mean that I can't and that's that or else I'll tell her I have a head-

ache and she can go jump in the lake, but when I ask for Signora
Maria Cordella which is naturally pronounced Cordelya they tell
me they haven't a guest by that name so I must have got her name
wrong or the hotel's name or both or else she made a mistake unless
she did it on purpose that bitch, these international-set women are
capable of doing as much and the thing irks me obviously although
on the other hand it solves all the problems concerning my wife,
and in fact I set out for the clinic but first I go by the Excelsior
where naturally the Commendatore isn't in but I wait to keep him
from screwing me, sometimes he makes them say he isn't in when
if you just wait in the lobby sooner or later he has to come down,
and in fact here he comes after half an hour or a little more, but
he really does come in from outside and he say's he's been out at
Cinecittà with Abbe Lane and I say Commendatore I came for
that money you're supposed to give me and he says of course
let's go upstairs and when we're in his suite he starts talking about
Abbe Lane again which is certainly a worthwhile subject but
I've come for the money and I repeat it to him and then with
great effort he pulls out twenty thousand lire of the two hundred
he's owed me since last Saturday, but what use is twenty thousand to me I've just had a daughter and I have to pay the clinic,
and he says that children are the most important thing in the
world a real blessing a man feels more self-confident when he
has children, however he doesn't have the two hundred thousand
not till the day after tomorrow, and I say but the day after
tomorrow it'll be three hundred because another payment falls
due and first he says no, then he gives way in the face of the evidence but asks me what do you do with all this money you're
a writer, and I say Commendatore I had a daughter five days ago,
and he says oh yes I forgot yes children are our only consolation
in this life the most important thing in the world, anyway he
wants to know if I can go with him to Paris on Tuesday because
we have to work together on an idea that is all his which takes
place in the next world and so it will need subtle dialogue the
kind only I can write, and I say Commendatore it depends on how
much you pay me and he says oh we'll work it out this time like

we always have we'll come to a friendly agreement, and he dismisses me grandly after putting the two ten-thousand-lire notes in my hand so I can buy a little present for my signora he says, but naturally I am far from buying little presents with all the bills there are to pay not to mention the varicose-veins victim who has been waiting for her pay for several days, and anyway who would dare buy anything for my wife after the unfortunate results of the *marrons glacés*, however I see a glum-looking woman selling violets outside Doney's trying to keep under the cornice as much as she can, she gets two hundred lire for a little bunch of violets worth twenty-five the slob but you have to bear in mind that this is the Via Veneto and it's raining like hell, I wonder if my daughter by any chance has come into the world along with another Deluge, anyhow the violets are a really good idea my wife is all pleased and wants to be kissed and says forgive me for last night but you see giving birth makes a woman nervous and those *marrons* really were awful, and I say you're right you forgive me for not getting them at Moriondo's, and she says it doesn't matter now they're going to bring in Michaela and you can see how she eats, and I say remember that Michaela isn't named Michaela but Augusta, and she smiles and says all right but there's no law against our calling her Michaela even if she's registered as Augusta, even your mother though it's not very nice is called Augusta when she has another name, but for God's sake let's not fight again and really my wife has a curiously fertile talent for creating the right atmosphere for a fight, anyway a nurse comes in with the newly born Augusta in her arms and my wife unbuttons her nightgown especially designed for this job and attaches the baby to her breast and the baby sucks with her eyes shut, the little monster with those long fingers, and she's already a little less purple than the evening she was born, moreover my wife tells me that Sister Innocente told her they've never seen such a beautiful baby in this clinic, and I say well maybe, risking an immediate fight because my wife says that if I say well maybe it means I don't love my daughter, and I assure her that I'm crazy about her and for me she's the most important thing in the world which besides is also the opinion of the Commendatore who was supposed to give me two hundred thousand lire and instead gave me twenty, and my wife says how dumb can you get and I say that between the two of us it isn't clear which is the dumb one because I'm willing to bet that Sister Innocente tells every new mother that her daughter or son as may be is the most beautiful she's ever seen because it's customary for the mother when she leaves the clinic to make an offering for the chapel and naturally the contribution is bigger if the baby is the most beautiful ever seen, and my wife says I'm sarcastic and she says just look at her and see if she isn't the most beautiful baby in the world and I say of course for us she's the most beautiful because she's our daughter, but my wife obviously isn't convinced that this is how it is she watches the baby sucking and her expression is the same as when she looks at me and wants to make love, women are funny I say to myself, and later when they bring her meal first she makes me shut the door tight and then she makes me sit in the easy chair and also makes me take off my shoes and socks because heaven only knows how soaked I must be, and she makes me slip my feet under the covers to get them warm, and she gives me a bit of overcooked spaghetti to eat and some meat with mashed potatoes and she peels the apple and we divide it in half, and while she does these things she still has that expression like she wants to make love and while I'm eating I wonder how long we have to go without doing it and I ask her if we have to go without doing it for forty days, and she says I'm crazy she wants to do it again already but we have to behave ourselves for three weeks or at least two she corrects herself, and I tell her that maybe I have to go Paris with the Commendatore who wants me to go with him at all costs since we have to work together, of all the producers I know the Commendatore is the one who has the highest opinion of me I say, and my wife says of course because he's also the one who manages to pay you least however this time you're not going to make a move if he first doesn't give you every penny of what he owes you plus an advance on the new job the way all others do, and I answer her with a gesture as if to say that

she doesn't have to tell me these things and in fact I'm thinking
that in any case the Commendatore will have to give me the money
since I have to pay the clinic, and with this thought in mind I
ask my wife if by any chance she is thinking of coming home one
of these days seeing that the clinic must cost plenty, and naturally
this subject immediately dispels the erotic-sentimental atmosphere
of a moment before also because my wife with a firmness that is
perhaps excessive answers that here in the clinic she is comfortable whereas at home without heat it would be a crime for the
baby who's so delicate and requires so much attention, however
I inform her that thanks to the continued state of low pressure
presumably responsible for the fact that here in Rome we're
having a November such as they don't have even in Siberia at
least not with as much rain, our fellow tenants have agreed to
start the furnace next Saturday that is day after tomorrow, and
my wife says if that's so then I can come home it's perfectly obvious the idea of coming home doesn't appeal to her at all but
she's got to come back sooner or later, and in fact as soon as the
Commendatore gives me a hundred and seventy thousand lire on
the two hundred and eighty due me I pay the clinic resolutely
neglecting the claims advanced by Miss Varicose Veins, as it
turns out the money is barely enough for the clinic or rather it
wouldn't be enough if providentially at the moment she was
brought in they hadn't made me leave an advance or deposit of
a hundred and twenty thousand and so for better or worse I
manage to leave that place with wife and daughter and take them
home in the car during a pause in the constant cloudburst, and
as soon as she's there my wife feels a bit depressed because of the
empty house and this gets on my nerves obviously or rather her
way of making heavy weather of the fact that I dragged her from
the clinic by brute force, she knew as well as I how bare the house
is unless she was thinking that while she was spending more than
two hundred and thirty thousand lire to bring a daughter into
the world with a normal easy delivery I was going to spend at
least the same amount to adorn the house festively, anyhow thank
God tomorrow I'm off to Paris if this damned Commendatore gives

me at least fifty thousand lire to leave at home, actually he only
gives me forty plus the promise of a hundred and fifty if we work
well in Paris, which means I am to work under his guidance on
the ultraterrestrial story while he has to line up some co-produc-
tions and look at the night clubs because he has a terrific idea for
a picture all about night clubs so the hicks in the provinces poor
things will also have a chance to admire Abbe Lane and the finest
acts in the world, this idea seems stupid to me however it's his
business, and in the end I leave my wife the forty thousand and
I swear to her three times in a row on the head of our innocent
daughter that I will not under any circumstances fornicate with
Parisian women, then I join my benefactor at the Excelsior and
from there we take a taxi to the station in good time to catch
the all-sleeper fast train the *RP* and we settle into his drawing
room me with my typewriter on my lap and without even waiting
for the train to pull out he begins to tell me for I believe the
hundredth time the beginning of the picture, in the midst of the
war in the desert with every imaginable confusion of guns going
off, bombs and dust, in the greatest battle ever created on the
screen which however won't cost much productionwise since you
won't see much thanks to the dust raised by the grenades and
the tanks, it so happens that in the midst of all this great confusion
of the battle six poor human beings terrified and trying to save
their lives dive in a hole, and they are an Englishman, a Frenchman, a German, an American Negro, a Sicilian and of course a
Neapolitan, and this Neapolitan's name is Gennarino Esposito
and he doesn't even know who his mother and father were, it then
happens that while all around them rages the battle which can't
be seen but can be heard perfectly these six poor devils discover
that making war is a big mistake and so they fall into one another's arms and display photographs of their mothers except of
course for Gennarino who is all sad over in one corner, and then
when this splendid human manifestation is at its peak that is
when everybody in the audience has tears in his eyes a grenade
makes a direct hit on the hole sending its six occupants to their
Creator, and this is where the good part begins because there's

a cut and from the confusion of battle we cut to a huge valley where there's a road all zigzagging and not a sound is heard absolute silence while a convoy of maybe ten thousand trucks crammed with men climbs up the road, but since it's a dark night and there's also a fog you can only see about ten of these trucks and you have to imagine the rest, and in one of these ten thousand trucks are our six heroes who stare straight ahead because they are dead, and then we see these ten thousand trucks in the driving rain reach a kind of open space where a huge shed stands and where the dead men rush in to avoid getting wet, and inside the immense shed in the background there are three doors each with a different sign and the three signs are Hell Purgatory and Heaven, so now everybody has caught on that we're in Limbo that is to say the vestibule of the next world, and if by chance somebody hasn't caught on there are these sages with long white beards who judge the men and send them to one side or the other according to the sins they committed in this life, and when Gennarino's turn comes they don't let the foundling past any of the three doors because it is written that he for whom no one weeps on earth cannot enter the Kingdom of Heaven and it seems not even the Kingdom of Hell, and here the narration breaks off because as usual the Commendatore opens a discussion of the basic religious question I mean he wants me to dig up in the Gospels or some sacred text or other this article of faith whereby a person that has nobody to weep for him on earth cannot enter the Kingdom of Heaven, and for the hundredth time I explain to him that such an article of faith doesn't exist because it isn't in accord with the ethical principles of our religion, nor of any other religion in the world I'm sure, however I believe he needn't worry about this since it's a film he's making and not a theological treatise, and since the gimmick involving Gennarino is poetically valid according to me he can proceed freely without any articles of faith, but since I have used pretty obscure words like ethical principles and theology and poetically valid he looks at me like I'm trying to put something over on him and for the hundredth time he repeats that he's no **fool** and isn't going to risk hundreds of millions on a film that

the Vatican then may have confiscated, and as we pass the Civitavecchia station at a hundred and twenty kilometers per hour he
says let's go eat and while we eat in the dining car he also tells
the rest of the film which for that matter I almost know by heart,
and namely he tells how the head man there in the immense shed
takes pity on poor Gennarino the head man being Saint Peter in
person who makes an exception to the rules and sends Gennarino
back to earth for five days to see if he can't find somebody to
shed this damn tear without which he can't go any farther, and
then the German, the Englishman, the Frenchman, the Negro
and the Sicilian ask this poor Gennarino to go to their homes
maybe to say hello to their mother or wife or girl friend, and here
come the five international episodes with Gennarino after the
war going to visit the family of each of the others and from the
five episodes as a whole we must get the message that anybody
who got killed in the war was screwed, this is the new and profound message of the picture, until on the last night of his special
leave on earth poor Gennarino is wandering tired and depressed
along a picturesque beach in the environs of Naples and guess who
he meets there, he meets a whore but instead of going to bed with
her as is the custom he talks to her in a funny way nobody has
ever talked to her before, talking to her for example about the
stars and this is precisely the poetic dialogue I've got to write, and
after this dialogue they fall asleep on the sand in each other's
arms like brother and sister, and then she wakes up at dawn with
the birds singing and she's alone, she sees Gennarino walking
off along the beach toward a rock and at first she doesn't move
because maybe she thinks he's going behind the rock to relieve
himself but then she has a kind of presentiment and she jumps
up calling desperately Gennarino Gennarino, but as if he couldn't
hear her he goes on walking behind the rock and the whore still
calling Gennarino Gennarino runs desperately and reaches the
rock and here she stops and there's music and we see that at a
certain point Gennarino's footprints on the sand stop, there aren't
any and so the whore understands that Gennarino was a heavenly
being who has gone back to heaven, so she sinks to her knees and

weeping desperately she calls Gennarino Gennarino, and thus
through the tears shed by a whore Gennarino can finally enter
heaven, however when he gets to the shed he finds the Sicilian,
the German, the Frenchman, the American Negro and the white
Englishman who have waited for him to bring them news from
their families and rather than disappoint them instead of telling
the truth Gennarino makes up a pack of lies so they'll believe they
died for some reason, and they go off happily toward their destiny
and Gennarino also heads for the door to the next world however
there is Saint Peter facing him who says now what are we going
to do about all these lies, you can't expect to go to heaven after
making up stories like those, but then he shuts an eye and slips
Gennarino through with an affectionate pat while from on high
we hear a rumble of thunder with words we can't understand
although it doesn't take much to guess it's a big chewing out addressed to Saint Peter, but he raises his head towards the sky
and says O Eternal Father what would you have done in my place,
and apparently the Almighty absolves him because Saint Peter
smiles, and this is the end of this beautiful story which anybody in
the dining car who knows Italian has enjoyed to the full since
my patron tells it in a loud voice, and since he often supplements
his grammatical deficiencies with eloquent facial expressions and
lively mimicry I believe the story has been enjoyed also by the
foreign tourists and the others who don't know much Neapolitan,
and after this public unburdening the Commendatore seems to
forget about the whole thing and after dinner nobody mentions
it and not even that night, then we get a good sleep and the following morning we're in Paris staying at the famous Georges V
because these producers may have debts on all sides but they
insist on a hotel with prestige which is only right after all since
their job is primarily based on appearances, and I'm not shocked
about is especially since my wife for example holds that my work
is also based on the wool I can pull over other people's eyes and
in fact I'm sure it would go better if instead of that little broken
down Fiat I bought myself a convertible Appia or better still an
MG, I don't say Jaguar because only producers and big opera-

tors can have Jaguars, and also well-known directors obviously whereas as far as I know there aren't any script-writers with Jaguars yet, but I answer her how can I buy a new car when I never have a spare cent, and my wife says dope see how other people buy things on time and signing notes, then I try once again to explain to her how I can't sign notes or make any other kind of debt because my father doesn't want me to, however she flies into a tantrum when I talk like this she knows my father has been dead for ages and so what does he have to do with things, then I reply firmly I may be a dope but I don't go into debt for luxuries, and she shrugs and with good reason predicts that we will live all our life in dire financial straits, and it may turn out as she foresees but at least I have a clear conscience, and anyhow when I travel with producers I cut a fine figure myself, lower berth in first class and Georges V and breakfast at the Berkeley, and then in the evening we go to the Lido only the first evening obviously because then we find a young and idle script-writer from Rome who latches on to my benefactor since he is without a cent in his pocket at present, and he takes us to the clubs that are worth seeing that is to say the ones where presumably there aren't any American tourists, and there my employer starts talking still in Neapolitan with beautiful girls because he came to Paris especially to set up a film about night clubs and then maybe these beautiful girls show up the next day at the Georges V and there they can't know how broke and unimportant I am, with a minimum of deceit I could lead them to believe their future is in my hands at least to some small degree, and they wouldn't split hairs another man more or less is the same to them and God knows how often they've been taken in this way since the age of fourteen or thereabouts, however with the oaths I swore to my wife how could I make any of these attractive girls, she even brought the head of my innocent daughter into it, and then to be sincere inside me I have a whole compendium of the principal duties of the citizen husband and father, in my spirit are indelibly impressed the two words loyalty and honor concepts which originally referred to King and Country but which can also be extended to other fields especially now that we haven't any King and not much Country, so I skip the beautiful girls and try to write the poetic dialogue between Gennarino and the whore on the beach, his words must have a magic dimension which one assumes the words of somebody who comes from the other world always have, and she has to talk like a poor wretch who after so much shame and persecution has finally found Jesus Christ on earth, but just you try and write these things in Paris with all the comings and goings in the suite of my lord and master, because to give you an idea how dumb I am I not only worry about the money I spend myself but even the money producers spend, so on the second day I say to my patron why spend money on my room I can fix myself up in the antechamber of his suite where there's a daybed, and this in fact happens and now I'm there the slave of the comings and goings of girls and envoys and French movie Commendatores to whom my benefactor makes interminable speeches in Neapolitan a kind of export version of the dialect so to speak, and naturally I can't work also because I am constantly being called in to confirm that this or that film of my master took in so many hundreds of millions or billions at the box office which is all the same to me, and to confirm that this other film made a mint of money, no thanks to the director but to my master who really directed it but didn't sign his name because glory means nothing to him he leaves that to the others, to confirm that we really ran away from Rome because my master was being persecuted by the Paramount people or the Metro people who wanted to force him to make a film with at least a five million budget on the ancient king Divo by whom he means queen Dido, and I confirm all of this without any problems of conscience over his lies which I guarantee with nods and *oui oui*, I know perfectly well that the men listening don't believe him and moreover are spinning out equally big stories of their own which my master doesn't believe, until paradoxically and without any plausible reason it happens that one of these lies is swallowed on one side or the other and then they set up a film in co-production, so this is the precarious world in which I earn my daily bread and to tell

the truth since I've been here in Paris also my daily oysters and
even champagne in the evening, and now four days have gone by
since I left and I still haven't telephoned home for reasons of
economy although obviously the call goes on the bill of the person
who brought me here, anyhow after four days a new father has
a right to telephone and I do and the maid with the varicose veins
answers and says the signora isn't home and I'm annoyed naturally, aha I say to myself I'm sure that if I'd let her stay in the
clinic she'd have stayed there even two months without moving
and now before I've turned the corner of the building she lights
out too, and my daughter Augusta is left in the hands of God only
knows who, some wife I've picked for myself, in short I have a
lot of angry ideas that keep me company until five in the afternoon
when I decide to telephone again I'm not paying for it after all,
and the varicose-veins girl with an undisturbed manner as if I
was calling from the druggist's downstairs says the signora is
out, then I lose my temper and start yelling out where goddammit
this is the second time I've called from Paris and I want to talk
with my wife, and at this point the maid's mind starts clicking
and she tells me the signora is out because she's gone back to
the clinic with the baby and a fever, and I shout would you mind
telling me who has the fever the baby or the signora and that
fool maybe because she's scared now says she doesn't know and I
can't get another word out of her because she's stupid, and for
that matter if she weren't stupid she certainly wouldn't be working for us since we pay her next to nothing and are generally late,
and now I'm more upset than ever and I tell myself who gives a
damn about the bill I'm going to call the clinic right now and I
do and I hear a couple of operators saying Paris Rome on the
line Rome this is Paris calling Rome here, and finally I hear my
wife's voice overjoyed because she's being called from Paris and
she tells me not to worry it's nothing just a little mastitis almost
over by now, still I think she has misinterpreted my mood I'm
not at all worried about her but about the expense, and I tell her
she must be crazy to go back to that clinic with what it costs and
she promptly answers you're a monster and at the very least I

ought to be unfaithful to you that's what you deserve never a
thought about me with this high fever and not even for your help-
less baby poor thing what a father, and she explains that she's
gone back to the clinic to save money because if she had stayed
at home she would have had to pay a doctor for penicillin every
four hours and a nurse and a special nurse for the baby because
naturally she would never leave her daughter in the care of just
a servant, and then she says her temperature was a hundred and
three and terrible pains especially when feeding the baby because
her nipples became chapped but she's going to go on nursing her
daughter even if she dies of the pain, and then she says that if
by chance the thing isn't cleared up with antibiotics they'll have to
amputate her left breast but she doesn't want to live with her left
breast cut off so she'll go to Sweden for plastic surgery, and in
this way she overwhelms me with a series of dangerous plans
and frightening information and she says are you happy now
that you've made me cry and in fact she sobs a couple of times
into the phone and this is the fitting conclusion of the long Paris-
Rome telephone conversation, at times a man is led to think that
technological achievements like the telephone and other things
make a very small contribution indeed to human happiness. Anyhow this stay in Paris also comes to an end and has broadened
my knowledge in the field of night clubs and variety shows and
has given me a certain nonchalance in places on the Berkeley and
Georges V level, however to tell the truth it isn't as if I had felt
any great need of these things and it's not likely I'll have frequent
opportunity to profit by this knowledge, and what's more it seems
that the information I have acquired in Paris isn't of good quality
for example among all the things I saw I don't know which I
liked best the belly dancer or a Spanish pansy with castanets, but
my lord and master to whom I confide all this as the *PR* is speeding towards Rome says that as a consultant for his night-club
film I'm not worth shit, and when we reach Civitavecchia or
rather when we're passing through that station since the *PR*
doesn't stop there he says let's have a look at this dialogue for
Gennarino and naturally he does this on purpose because he has

seen how in Paris especially through his own fault I haven't
been able to work well, this fine gentleman really wants to put
me on the spot and find an excuse not to pay me a cent for the
ten days he's made me waste, and sure enough this is how it is
I go up to his suite at the Excelsior and when he says thanks
a lot now run along home your wife will be worried I say worried
my ass what about these ten days I've wasted, and he says what
do you mean how about it where's the dialogue for Gennarino
just thank God I'm not charging you for traveling expenses and
your hotel in Paris, and I who am docile by nature and tempera-
ment when dealing with Commendatores I say at least give me the
hundred and ten thousand you still owe me for *Monte Cristo*,
however he insists he's sure he paid me down to the last cent and
so before granting my request he would have to check over his
receipts and consult his accountant, in short he tells me all his
favorite fairy tales for occasions when he doesn't want to pay
however since I pull an ugly face in the end he sighs to underline
the big sacrifice he's making and gives me forty thousand lire and
tells me that'll have to do for the moment, but I say Commendatore
have you forgotten I've just had a baby girl and he says oh yes
and goes and opens a fairly important drawer where he keeps
precious documents and sometimes money, and I say to myself
what if he now pulls out a big pack of ten-thousand-lire notes and
gives it to me maybe as an advance on something and instead
he comes back with a cheap little rosary in his hands and he
kisses it devoutly before he gives it to me and he says it comes from
the shrine of Pompeii and the Madonna will shower blessings
on my daughter if I put this around her neck, and I realize that
with a giant like this any struggle is lost before it's begun so I
head home in a taxi and the only fine thing about Rome is that
it's stopped raining, all the rest is black especially considering the
dilemma that I don't have the money to get my wife out of the clinic
and at the same time if she doesn't get out the bill goes up higher
and higher, in short I risk discovering something very close to
perpetual motion although in an entirely different field, but
luckily my wife has come home without paying the clinic using

the excuse that her husband is in Paris and what's more this time the bill isn't so big, it seems to be less than eighty thousand lire even and I don't know how my wife manages to say the words eighty thousand with that charming casual air, I however am full of concern because I don't have the eighty thousand and I have to get to work and put the sum together, and I succeed in the end though in a secondhand way that is I accept a subcontract from an important writer to revise *Clelia and the Virgins of Rome*, and in fact while I'm doing a job of this sort which allows you time to think also of other things one day I realize that it's been quite a while since the five lumbars had a temperature sensibly higher than the other vertebrae near them, nor do I think of heart disease any more or leukemia or other diseases hard to cure, and I haven't had any more of those terrifying attacks which plunged me into fear and desperation, why I say to myself just think those doctors were right they said that exhaustion is a thing that comes on you unexpectedly and leaves the same way, a time comes when you feel cured and that's it, it's just the way they all said and the universe all of a sudden is beautiful more beautiful perhaps than it ever has been though it's still a bit frightening to think about, and as far as my special situation of being a fatherless orphan is concerned oh well I bet a majority of the men of my age have lost their fathers and quite a few have lost their mothers too, and for the rest I take advantage of these improved general conditions to perform what you might call a *rapprochement* or armistice with the deceased, and this becomes possible especially thanks to the discoveries I am making through my daughter Augusta in the field of those ties of affection which bind fathers to children and also but not necessarily vice versa, actually the question of whether my father loved me or not is one I had never investigated deeply enough since from my point of view it wasn't the least bit interesting, and as for the opposite process or rather whether I loved him this is a question I simply eliminated altogether thinking that my father had been first an omnipotent and remote deity and later a poor bastard who gave me a pain with his demands, and frankly if you exclude the period of early infancy when in

effect you understand too little the period when I gave him most
affection was the one when I was animated by extraordinary religious ardors and tried to put into practice all the commandments
of the Mosaic law including the fourth which in fact goes honor
thy father and thy mother although it seemed a bit exaggerated
to me to put this kind of thing up there among the commandments
when after all there were only ten of them, anyhow I then hadn't
developed any critical faculty as far as the commandments were
concerned so I accepted the fourth the same as the fifth or whatever, not to mention the ninth which to my mind was a completely superfluous extra, and as to paternal love I didn't go beyond the commandments any further than reading with all due
emotion Pascoli's poem O dapple-gray horse, however even in the
poem filial devotion was only a part of it since the verses were
all aimed at that final neigh that reveals at last who had done
in the exemplary father, in other words it was a kind of detective
poem with the fault that in the end the only ones who knew
the murderer's name were the widow and an animal, in any case
the fact remains that I had gone through life without love for
my father it seemed and therefore without paying much attention
to the possible existence of a father's love for me and now it
turns out that if my daughter insists on sticking her fingers in
my eyes to hold them open or if I bounce her on my knees singing like an idiot Ride a cock horse to Banbury cross or if she
asks me for kisses as she frequently does filling me with happiness, all of a sudden from the depths of the forty years that have
gone by in the meanwhile re-emerges a father never perceived
before into whose eyes I stick my little fingers and who bounces
me on his knees and sings Ride a cock horse, my God I had even
the same tone of voice, and the cadence too if I remember right,
and so even overlooking the power of the funeral photographs
for the moment inert and buried in God knows what drawer how
enormously I resemble my father, this is what I am discovering
through my daughter Augusta as she gradually grows up, and I
wonder if he loved me as I love her I mean immensely, and now
I'm sorry I didn't understand him when he was still alive and at

least in part I could have returned his love, however in this regret
there is fortunately nothing unhealthy it is only a perfectly normal
regret such as even Saint Francis of Assisi or Adolf Hitler to
name two extremes might have felt under similar circumstances,
and for the rest always with my daughter's collaboration I begin
to penetrate more deeply into the nature of the relationship between fathers and children, I discover that the children needn't
do anything in return for the fathers' love since their only duty
is to exist if possible in good health, for when I see my daughter
healthy I feel an enormous joy and so it's obvious she makes me
happy without doing anything at all, that is pursuing her own
good if not her own convenience too, in conclusion a father's love
is a *motus animi* which in itself contains every possible recom-
pense, or you might also say that it is a one-way street along which
the generations follow one another, and you could even find in
it a concrete analogy with life itself which doesn't allow for
any turning back, and therefore having lived myself in fairly
good health up to a certain age I may have given my father
plenty of satisfaction who can ever know, although it was only
rarely that he looked satisfied in fact we can even say that very
often he looked annoyed with me for an infinite number of reasons,
but then to tell the truth these reasons were infinite because of
his difficult character more than anything else, and at least in that
habitual grumbling and that constant dissatisfaction I hope I
didn't resemble him too much although according to my wife I'm
a pedant and a bore just like my father if not worse, however a
person would have to know my wife the way I know her before
deciding whether to pay any attention to her, it may even be true
that in the past when I wasn't very well I did grumble a bit
in certain circumstances when I could just as easily not have
grumbled but since I've been feeling better my household grumbling doesn't go beyond the rightful norm, everything is normal
when you're healthy and vice versa apparently, certainly if I
remember how much I suffered during that agonizing illness I
believe it's better to be normally idiotic rather than suffer, and
on the other hand the fact that I have recovered my health doesn't

signify that I've lost my sensitivity and what you might call my artistic capacities, I would say the contrary if anything, I mean after so many years of misfortunes I feel mature in a way I never felt before, so it's a real calamity to have to work on these movie scripts which as a rule don't give a writer the chance to fulfill himself day after day and season after season the years go by and nothing is achieved, on the other hand if I don't work I don't eat and a writer who doesn't eat also has a hard time fulfilling himself, all told the best thing is to work hard as hard as I can with the movies and at the same time save up a bit of money, six months' worth let's say and then go off to a lonely spot and then I'll be bound to write the masterpiece that will bring me glory, I already have it all in my head so to speak however my wife would have to help me at least a little bit in this difficult task of saving up the money for my glory, and instead either because she doesn't have sufficient faith in my glory or because her only pleasure in life is spending money she collaborates very little and we are always broke and scrambling after the next penny, and since I'm afraid I don't have too long to live I decide to divide my working day into two parts the first devoted to these films I'm stuck with I mean sex and violence and the second part instead will be all mine devoted to a story I already have in my head well not entirely, I would be telling a lie if I said I had it all in my head but I know how it begins pretty clearly, and I also know that generally speaking it's a love story between two young people and in addition there isn't any action or almost none as far as I can see because I'm fed up with the movies which are nothing but action, and besides let's face it the days of neorealism are over I mean when a writer believed with every book he was going to start a revolution that would bring justice to the common man especially in the Southern provinces, in this country no matter how much you write there aren't any revolutions apparently so it's much better for each writer to resume his personal freedom and without looking to left or right aim straight ahead at glory as best he can, by God this is what I'll do and indeed it seems that the right story for the goal I have in mind is the story I've been thinking about for some time, the love story of two young people by God, that is a boy and a girl to be precise though I'm aware that the almost constant heterosexuality of the various works I dream of writing will not bring me success, but it isn't success I'm aiming at it's glory which is quite another thing, although those who enjoy success wouldn't agree, despite the examples furnished by the past.

So as far as possible
I divide myself in two and during the hours towards evening which
for me after all are the best also because mother and daughter go
off to see the puppets in the Borghese Gardens, I begin to write
the first chapter and since you can't really start without any
action at all I put in a scene with the two seeing each other and
then thinking about it for all the rest of the chapter, and besides
this is really what happens in life or ought to happen if life was
a bit less lousy than it actually is at the present time, and then in
the second chapter these two young people meet thanks to his
taking the initiative and going up to her and they begin to talk
but they don't talk much to tell you the truth, mostly they think
and think however that doesn't mean that a writer can't reach glory
along this line, everything depends on the beauty and originality
of the thoughts going through the heads of the couple, and like
all true artists for that matter at moments I'm sure the thoughts I
attribute to them are valid and at other moments I'm not so sure,
but I grit my teeth and overcoming any hesitation at least for
the present I start in on the third chapter where what happens is
that the two young people at the beginning exchange some kisses
which arouse in them pages and pages of thoughts, and in this

way at least theoretically you achieve endless psychological pro-
fundities however anybody can see how the material is getting
progressively more intractable, in fact it is harder and harder for
me to pursue this story with only half of myself so I concoct a
plan which in theory at least seems pretty good to me, namely to
work now as hard as I can on scripts and all that muck whereas
with the glory novel I will now break off work and content myself
at odd moments with polishing tirelessly what I've already written because it's widely known that works meant to last have to be
revised and polished, I think Horace felt this way and God only
knows how many other writers before him not to mention after,
and meanwhile by writing all the muck I will no doubt manage to
save up a bit of money even at the risk of fighting every day with
my wife and then when July comes I'll send mother and daughter
to the mountains, or to the sea whichever they prefer, however if
it's the sea they might go to Fregene so they would be on my back
all the same on the telephone night and day no doubt, better the
Alps which thank God rise at some distance from the capital, and
believe it or not everything seems to be turning out right for me,
producers give me work and pay for it, my wife in the course of
a heated discussion during which I order her to go to the sea and
specifically to Fregene in order to be near me answers that she
wouldn't go to Fregene if her life depended on it with the snobs
that go there she wants to go to Cortina unless I prefer Saint
Moritz, and Cortina would be fine for me except for the prices
there however at the last moment I mean a couple of months before when you have to make the reservations and after my wife
makes several dozen phone calls per day to inform a vast circle
of acquaintances that this year she's going to Cortina, she finds
instead a girl friend she had completely forgotten about in the
last thirty-six months but now they're great friends again since
they manage to talk on the phone for two hours and forty-five
minutes without any interruption, and this girl friend isn't going
to Cortina she's going to Siusi which for the children is much
better she insists because of the air or the position or I don't know
what, and in this way my wife decides to go to Siusi sacrificing

herself for the good of the child and oddly enough no obstacle occurs in the months of May and June except that my wife and I argue a bit because I want them to travel in the daytime to enjoy the landscape of half of Italy which is very beautiful, instead on this subject she says I'm stingy and capable of making my wife and daughter suffer the awful heat just to save the price of a sleeping car, she wants a sleeper and if she had thought about it before she would certainly never have married a tightwad like me, tormenting her with economies when I'm working well and earning good money, and if I were a real man now that it's summer and they're half price I'd buy her a fur coat not mink of course which is too *nouveau riche* but beaver which is simple and youthful, in short we have a fairly long argument with infinite variations more or less on the same theme until one fine evening I manage to load her on to a sleeping car of the night train toward Austria the Brenner Express properly called, and from the window she says good-bye with many tears because at heart she's happy and I should think so too, she says when are you coming up darling even if we do argue all the time we two love each other nobody is more in love than we are, and I agree of course and assure her that I'll come to see her very soon maybe even next week, but this lie as I thought it was comes out as the train is already moving so maybe she doesn't hear it or at least I can remain with this doubt, because of these innocent little fibs of mine my wife is always saying it's obvious I was educated by priests and maybe she's right anyhow the train vanishes with mother and daughter waving handkerchiefs from the window weeping with emotion I can easily imagine, and then I promptly turn and think how beautiful it would be to run home and sit right down at the typewriter for chapter four because a month goes by in no time and the road to glory is long and arduous according to all reports of those who have traveled along it or at least attempted it, however it occurs to me that I may not be in the right condition of mind and spirit to resume a task of such great importance, sending off wife and daughter apart from every other consideration has been real work, better to face the new chapter with my mind fresh and my body rested, so now to get the disturbing thought of those two in the train out of my head I look in at the Via Veneto, I go for a bit of fresh air and at most one beer, I even find some pleasant friends to drink the beer with, friends with girls obviously, a likeable company all in all so it's three thirty-five when I go back to the house which is empty not only because of the absence of wife and daughter but also because there is still a scarcity of furniture, anyhow instead of thinking of the two absentees I am thinking that only an idiot wastes his time the way I've wasted mine tonight in the Via Veneto, but starting tomorrow a new life by God glory doesn't wait for the lazy you might say, and I'm so convinced of this motto that it keeps me awake and at a certain moment I see the light of the new day through the crack of the blind which doesn't shut properly, at this hour the train is somewhere between Bologna and Verona or Verona and Trento and I wonder if those two are sleeping, my wife surely not because you never sleep in trains and anybody who takes a sleeper is throwing good money away, and this thought is enough to make me mad all over again at her stubbornness in taking the sleeper as if when she arrived she had to work or had business engagements when in fact she doesn't have a damn thing to do and could sleep for a whole month as far as I'm concerned, in the end I fall asleep after six and in spiritual conditions which don't favor a refreshing repose and so I wake up at two in the afternoon that is eight hours later with my head heavy and a vague sense of discontent at having wasted the whole morning, thank God I can wander around the house naked since the maid who naturally is no longer the one with varicose veins but another who however resembles her greatly at least in her capacity to depress anyone looking at her, and I think besides that my wife being jealous and possessive and also aristocratic isn't likely to grant me a less depressing one, this new woman in short has also been sent on vacation poor thing so I can now walk around stark naked in the darkened house, and this is something that gives me a great satisfaction although the motives aren't clear, according to me it isn't exhibitionism since there's nobody looking and maybe not even narcissism since there isn't any pool for me to gaze at myself in I mean no mirror with a surface more than a foot square like the one where I shave, and meanwhile since I really feel picked up I wander naked from one room to the other especially in the hall and living room where usually you don't go naked and I have to think of a return to the origins of the species when men didn't have clothes and were much stronger and braver than now, maybe this is the right idea in fact my present most pressing need is an absolutely elementary one namely the desire to eat, and so I eat what I find in the house in other words two eggs a piece of cheese and some cherries, and after I have eaten these things though I practically just woke up I feel sleepy, in fact at this time of day in summer I usually take a little nap and even in winter I do it but now we're in summer and with the heat this need for a siesta is felt more strongly, and it seems to be felt fairly strongly today too despite the long recent sleep so I lie down still naked in the double bed stretching out diagonally to my full length and breadth, and this too is a satisfaction a man can have only when he has shipped his wife off to the mountains, in short I have another fine sleep and when I wake up towards evening I'm a bit dazed obviously when you sleep too long this happens, and sitting down at the typewriter I don't feel so much in form as I should be to undertake the beginning of the fourth chapter which is crucial and in fact in it the boy who is poor goes to her house and she is rich and he has to ask for her hand and needless to say things go pretty badly for him, now this of course isn't a new situation as far as I know but for this very reason it's all the harder to write about in such a way as not to preclude a certain immortality, so for today also to get myself back into the right atmosphere the best thing is for me to reread the preceding chapters which by now are thoroughly polished, however in works like this one must never tire of perfecting and embellishing and so it happens in fact that I spend a couple of not unpleasant hours on the three polished chapters, then I go out because there's nothing left to eat in the house and in the restaurant I find some friends in a good humor because after all summer in Rome is marvelous and inspires jovial and corroborative sentiments since in the daytime you don't do anything because it's too hot and in the evening when it cools off you go out to eat in restaurants with tables set out in squares and courtyards, and then you linger until late in the cafés in the Piazza del Popolo or the Piazza Navona or the Via Veneto although at present this Via Veneto with the influx of the movie world has lost some of its tone if you except of course a short stretch where the better men of the liberal party gather those who have become radicals and also the liberals who are still liberals but left wing, however it isn't very easy to find a seat in this little stretch so I for example prefer the Piazza Navona or the Piazza del Popolo, still I'm surely not going to stay out as late tonight as I did last night and in fact a little after one I'm already home almost tempted to go straight to the typewriter and begin the famous chapter four however on sober reflection better not face it now but tomorrow morning when my mind has rested, so I go to bed and on purpose I choose a book to read by a writer who writes pithily that is his every sentence is fertile the source of many thoughts that can be of use to me, and moreover he writes fairly badly so he isn't one of those writers who discourages a beginner which after all is what I am, a beginner at my age I happen to think perhaps my father wasn't entirely wrong when he used to say I'd never achieve anything worthwhile, but now I'll show him whether or not I'm worthy of all those sacrifices he made to give me an education, tomorrow morning I'll get up at nine on the dot I'll even call the telephone alarm service to make sure and then at nine forty-five or ten at the latest I'll be at the typewriter not of course tied to my chair like Vittorio Alfieri since I've always considered gestures like that frivolous, and besides unlike the proud Piedmontese I am at present without servants who could tie me up, however even without bonds I won't leave the machine until I've written at least three pages of this fourth chapter whose light and bitter tone finally comes completely clear to me, actually when I'm about to go to sleep I happen to see everything completely clear not to mention while I'm actually sleeping and I dream of writing marvelous short stories and novels and after

writing them I dream of lecturing on them before great crowds
with a subtly self-congratulatory manner, like Carlo Levi for
example, and also plenty of others besides him of course however
these others don't have any reason for congratulating themselves
whereas Carlo Levi does in my opinion, maybe this is why in my
dreams I dream of being him although I realize that it would be
pretty difficult for me to become like him at least as far as the optimism concerning himself in his speeches is concerned and his bizarre dress which attracts people's attention, but dreams are made
on purpose so we can enjoy the things we have no opportunity of
enjoying when we're awake or rather we don't have the opportunity at present because nobody knows the future and anyhow
it's a bad idea to deprive dreams of their somewhat prophetic
power, and so amid these basically comforting fantasies I fall
asleep after three a.m. and at nine when the phone rings I'd like to
go on sleeping for another week straight however the alarm call
is the trumpet of glory today, so I leap out of bed naked and
dazed as I go to the bathroom thinking that they say six hours
sleep for a middle-aged person is more than enough, but maybe
despite my almost forty-five years I am not yet middle-aged probably because the ten years I spent in the army aren't to be counted
at least not in connection with the senile tendency to sleep very
little, however in this case what about my father who was in
uniform for twenty years at the least and all the same when he
was my age as I recall he got up at dawn because of the garden,
I follow this line of reasoning while I shave in front of the little
mirror and at the same time I am secretly trying to give myself a
bit of courage, the truth is I always need courage when like this
morning it's a question of performing one of man's most important
duties that is to say expelling fecal matter, there you are I had
hoped to avoid this subject in fact I had avoided it up till now with
the best of intentions but my God at this stage of the narrative
I'm afraid it can't be overlooked, we all know that in this world
there exist coprophiles and even coprophagists however the latter
are considered crazy so we can skip them, whereas coprophiles
are mentally sane people who take a sympathetic interest in excre-

ment mostly telling little jokes based either on the act of defecating or on the faeces themselves, and we can gauge how numerous these coprophiles are from the almost infinite number of smelly jokes some of which are fairly funny, anyhow I'm convinced the true characteristic of coprophiles isn't so much their jokes as their great satisfaction in defecating, according to their own frequent statements, well I can in no way be numbered among the ranks of the coprophiles and in fact to perform every other day this duty once so praised by the Salerno school of medicine and then by hygiene specialists in general I have to bring to bear great moral force especially since as is well known my colon has taken its place among my greatest worries, and in addition from time to time I try to cheat with myself and do it every third day although subsequently one pays for these tricks dearly, anyhow this morning on which it is probable that I am to take a decisive step forward on the road to glory I feel the question of defecation is imperative as if to free myself from all visceral heaviness and from the foul matter were necessary before facing the wholly spiritual labors of literary composition, so once it's been established that the operation is ineluctable I prepare myself sitting on the toilet with a cigarette in my mouth and a bunch of magazines in my hand because in order not to dramatize this evacuation I have recourse to frivolous and absorbing distractions like tobacco and magazines generally, as I smoke I leaf through one and the other and I look at the illustrations which are generally of kings and rulers most of them deposed because undeposed ones are few by now and then I look at pictures of former Fascist bigwigs and the Duce's mistress and then scenes of various murders which are never lacking since if by any chance we don't have any here we import them from France, I can also skip through the articles on Sophia Loren and Claudia Cardinale provided they aren't written as sometimes happens by important novelists from whom you can always learn something, and finally I reach the arts page or something of the sort where the literary critic generally speaks well of the books he has to speak well of and badly of the books he mustn't speak well of, in short there's a great variety of articles and situations and

I don't remember what I happened to be reading that morning certainly not stories about suicides because to tell the truth I carefully avoided them after that bad experience in the past, finally I am reading God knows what and smoking and then suddenly from my damned guts and also somehow from the five lumbars that warm current starts and in a flash it's climbed all the way up my spine towards the top reaching the cerebellum and I'm overwhelmed with terror, in the least propitious conditions for facing a catastrophe like this whose first requirement is that I rush out of the house and yell help help, anyhow trembling and stammering my God here it comes again here it comes again my God with the help of Divine Providence I manage to wipe myself and put on my robe and now assailed by waves of anguish from all sides I reach the door and call help help attracting in no time a dozen neighbors who still haven't gone off for their vacation, and now that they've come I'd like to send them away because I'm afraid of them I want a doctor and mine naturally isn't here at the height of the season with all the money to be earned in Chianciano, for God's sake call me a doctor call one right away, and then two or three charitable souls run out to look for a doctor in the street or in the nearby buildings while trembling and overwhelmed I stand still for a moment with my head in my hands and then pace up and down looking at those horrible tiles on the floor with the frightful designs that aren't straight my God why aren't they straight and now I see clearly that the floor itself isn't level it slopes all off to one side and off to the other, so the straight line no longer exists in any direction help why doesn't this doctor come isn't there anybody to help me poor me, my God my wife so far away and my daughter far away, oh my child my child young as you are you won't remember your father you'll never know what your father was like unless you look at some photographs where I'm not really myself, oh help me help me save myself from this terror and despair, and then at last a doctor arrives a stranger perforce and I have to overcome my repulsion and consider him my rescuer my savior, good heavens he can't be much of a doctor if he's staying here instead of going on vacation or to some place like Chianciano or Montecatini, anyhow he does the same things they all do to me pulse heart blood pressure, and he pulls the skin under my eyes down a little to see if I'm anemic, finally he seems satisfied because except for the overexcited state due to the circumstances all the rest is in order considering my age, so it's only a bit of nervous exhaustion caused in all probability by the heat and by overwork if it's true as I say that recently I've been working hard to save up some money, of course it's true but that isn't the trouble for God's sake there are other things besides work weighing on me, and I realize that a doctor can't do anything for me nobody can do anything so I tell him I'll go to the mountains as soon as possible for a change of air, and I pay him on the spot since there's no use in his coming back, it's over now after all it was only a slight nervous attack but now please go away everybody go away now, and finally all these charitable fellow tenants go out and I throw myself on the bed and cry and cry begging forgiveness, I let my fear go out of me with my humiliation and my tears but inside me my despair remains fairly permanently established, and I know full well I'll never be cured never in my whole life if this terrible disease can come on me like this by surprise whenever it chooses, there are infinite and obscure sins to expiate and so even my ridiculous attempt to achieve glory has been interrupted forever, *Domine non sum dignus* and nobody can say a word to heal my soul, now I want to look myself in the face I want to see on my face this boundless ruin so I go back to the bathroom and with the little mirror I penetrate to the depths of my eyes to discover the fear there and the nothingness, there I am this is me on the brink of madness or of suicide, it may come any moment but come it will, how often have we seen close to us death by disease or violence but it wasn't death like this not ending up like this, this is something more perverse which goes beyond the end it's the bewilderment of eternity perhaps the hell beyond life, but since the sins against my father are not enough to warrant such a desperate collapse, they can't be enough, there are others God knows how many others a whole jungle of guilty actions behind me, defiant blasphemies and solitary ejaculations, challenges to God and hell bartered for a

moment of solitary pleasure, my knowledge of the tree that stands
in the center of the garden and now everything must be paid for,
I must crawl on my belly I accursed among all animals, every sin
has to be paid for obviously but now just now it wouldn't be fair
now when with good intentions and humility I was about to begin
the fourth chapter of my best achievement, and why father why
when I wouldn't have sought glory just for myself, remember how
pleased you were with every success of mine although admittedly
they were successes of quite a different nature from the success
that can be achieved with the story of two young people who fall
in love and make mistakes, this must be the error since true glory
belongs to the man who sacrifices himself for the Fatherland,
maybe on a hill in Abyssinia or on the stones of Libya I should
have given the full measure of my blood to square up this comic
bookkeeping of life, I can imagine your pride in front of the
monument to the fallen with the name of your first-born carved
in marble, but you see it isn't that I didn't want to it just never
happened to me that's all, and I think that's enough now although
I might also mention my reluctance on the subject of steady
government jobs, your father gave his life you used to say to let
you study and you turn down the job at the high school, remember
your father's words you said because you'll be sorry, and so help
me God in Heaven here I am sorry, how much better it would
have been with a regular salary and a paid vacation and in the
end a respectable pension, I confess this to atone for my arrogance
because it's now clear that I wanted glory only to show you you
were wrong, as if that were possible you so wise and so prudent,
this was my stupidity but now I renounce all glory so don't continue to be pitiless with me, you see I'm nobody I'm a failure
going from one room to the other of this empty house, my hands
are still shaking after the attack and my mouth is dry and I can't
smoke I'll never be able to smoke again after this terrible illness
that struck me while I had a cigarette in my mouth, or defecate
either my God it'll be harder than ever to defecate, when will I
touch the bottom of my abjection, I feel only pity and shame for
myself, I won't go naked around the house any more because

like Adam I am ashamed of my nakedness, after sin comes shame, and what can crawling on your belly mean except a bestial destiny now that the fourth chapter is in my mind and will never get onto paper, not even now when I had saved up the money to write like a free man, and here I start crying again over my failure and despair, and over my solitude at the brink of the void, I am alone and I can't stay alone without anybody to help me without the presence of her love cleansed of all unlovingness, but she is far away now my child bride, I want to hear her voice at least over the telephone before it's too late, I can't even remember the name of the hotel where she's gone, I know it's a German name however I can't remember it remembering things or reasoning even in the most elementary way is always hard for me after one of these attacks, and this time seems worse than the others my God what is that name surely this attack can't be worse than the ones I had before, in that case it means I'm going to get progressively worse from now on it's clear I'm getting worse and worse and if another attack came it would mean death, or damnation in the next world which is worse than death eternal fear, ah now I remember Hotel Milchwasser that's the name all right, and I say operator I would like the Hotel Milchwasser in Siusi, but I can't make the call urgent because that costs more and I mustn't waste money, my God I'm going to need so much money now that I have this obscure disease again, you see there was a meaning in my stinginess, the money I had saved up for the fourth fifth and sixth chapters, maybe I would have got to the end if this disease hadn't come upon me again and now everything I possess will go for doctors and medicines and all in vain, and when I finally die I won't have anything to leave my wife and daughter, if I could at least die quickly to save expense then young as she is she could marry again and somebody would provide for her in my place and work and keep them both, and if my daughter doesn't remember her father so much the better since I'm not a father worth remembering with a crumb of pride, how could she be proud of a father whose whole life was a mistake and who never achieved wealth or glory and who dies without leaving her anything, good God I mustn't think of this loss of myself in my daughter because this is perhaps the cruelest thought of all and maybe it will bring on another attack of the disease, God don't let me be sick now and make her be at the hotel let me hear her voice soon now I'll try to hurry up the call I'll make it urgent, so many sins my God how many sins, I'll never see the end of them but why don't others have to expiate theirs, this is what I'd like to know why the others don't have to pay, I really would like to know if I am the greatest of all sinners on earth or if there is something that isn't working in this deformed machinery of justice something specifically directed against me, assuming that there is justice and not merely chance and chaos, where are we going to find the metaphysical reasons I'd like to know, where can there be a God of such mistaken justice since there are surely other people who hate and grind the faces of the poor more than me and have barren hearts, so it can't be possible that there's a transcendental mechanism not even connected with my father, the gods have a remote imperturbability Lucretius teaches us, and the deceased as far as we can make out are even worse, so now I can think only in terms of hard luck and organicism, there may be in me certain nervous fibers that no other living being possesses which malevolently connect my lumbars to the colon and the muscles of respiration, they surely haven't discovered all the diseases especially since to judge by my experience doctors are jackasses, the more illustrious they are the more they're jackassess, and all things considered I could speak fairly well only of one but how can you speak well of somebody who in the summer goes off to make money with widows and old maids and ladies generally of advanced age who have swollen livers, although on the other hand I don't know how he could go on treating me if he didn't go and make money somewhere else, I'd almost telephone him too if it didn't cost so much, but then apart from the cost he isn't exactly what I need, what could he do he doesn't believe in my father or in my exceptional nervous fibers, I could perhaps hunt up the acupuncture man but since my wife told me he stuck needles so long into me I'm afraid of him too, however let's suppose it's true that a man with this acupuncture cured a cancer he might very well also cure this disease of mine which perhaps isn't as desperate as a cancer, but the fact is I can't even remember the name of this acupuncture man, I know the street however and I may go there after all, but now thank God this telephone rings and she is there yes there she is really from far away with her happy voice and I don't have the courage to speak I let her talk if you only knew how cool it is up here and Augusta keeps looking for you and she's always asking where's Papa why don't you come up we both love you so much, then with a lump in my throat I desperately hunt for a way not to ruin this distant happiness of hers, but how can I help ruining it when I have such a huge need for her compassion, and so I say to her you know that disease has come back that disease the awful one has taken me worse than all the other times, and she is silent for a long while and with my heart stopping I have time to think now she'll tell me to go screw myself and then I'll jump out of the window and end it all, I want to end it all but from afar she finally says darling tell me what can I do for you do you want me to come down I can leave the baby here with my girl friend and I'll take the first train, and then I cry into the phone with relief that I'm no longer alone in the world I'm not embarrassed for her to hear me crying from so far off, I say if I have to crawl on my belly we'll crawl together won't we crawl together, but the words come out all broken and twisted and she doesn't understand she says don't cry like that you're breaking my heart tell me quietly what you want, and I manage to say together say together, and she says yes yes together we'll always be together don't be afraid I'll take the first train maybe I'll be home before midnight, and I say no don't leave the baby I'll come up to you tomorrow or the next day as soon as I can but not with the train trains scare me I'll come by car I hope I can make it, and then she says there's the husband of a girl friend of hers who has to come up and we could make the trip together she'll take care of everything and organize it and I mustn't worry just stay at home and remember it's the heat that frightens me so she insists I mustn't go out in the day-time, and I say I won't go out day or night but please don't leave the hotel I want to know that I can reach you at any moment if I have another attack, and she says don't worry darling and I would like to go on talking for a long time and hearing her console me but how much does it cost from here to Siusi it's been nine minutes already, so I say to her don't tell the baby about my being sick don't say anything to her please and then I cut short the good-byes before we start another three minutes, there I've finished talking and I feel half drained but I'm not so afraid as I was before, now I look at the corners of the room and maybe they aren't crooked, not crooked enough to be frightening anyway, my God make me believe I've only had an isolated attack of this disease and it's over, oh if all of a sudden I felt sure it isn't going to come back and I could telephone her and say darling I feel fine really fine as if I had never been sick with that awful disease, it's not true that I'm afraid of going crazy you know I'm so sure of myself and you'll see I'll write the fourth chapter immediately and then the fifth and the sixth, I think if I can do the sixth then afterwards I can go straight on to the end, then I'll have to polish of course but the important thing is to get to the end because I can always find time to do the polishing, but I wouldn't want to be misjudged for this I mean for my longing to write since it isn't mere vanity to want to leave behind some memory of yourself especially when you consider that a man's wife should be proud of him if he writes a lasting book, and his daughter even more so obviously because his glory may not come right at first but afterwards it can't fail to come, now I really try to get up and sit at the typewriter, now I have the impression that I really feel fine, after all this disease isn't like cancer for which there is no cure or like consumption which maybe can be cured but only with injections and treatments, this is kind of a *sui generis* disease that might even suddenly disappear if it chose, naturally I can't expect to start writing the fourth chapter today with my mind whipped my thoughts almost dissolve before they're formed, my head is always confused for two or three days after these attacks, so in two or three days' time maybe I'll resume the hard part of the job but in the meanwhile I could reread the first chapters which are polished and seem to read pretty well so I derive some comfort just reading them, we'll see I may have my share of glory yet, with my bare strength I'll win it not with intrigues and friendships and nastiness the way everybody else does, he said the important thing was never to need anybody, mark my words he said, but a man can surely need his wife after all even he needed his wife without her he couldn't have done a thing, not even run his shop or go to the markets before they were too old, anyhow I'll try to sit at the desk now maybe making notes on a few ideas so the day won't be completely lost, but then I stand up and the corners aren't straight and the floor isn't as level as it seemed, my God I have to lie down on the bed again right away to keep from being overcome by this sense of instability and catastrophe, you see you mustn't ever think you're well in too much of a hurry, luckily here on the bedside table I have everything I need I mean the telephone and water and Valerian and the new tranquillizers that they've invented now, and the door of the apartment is ajar so if the disease comes back I can scream help or telephone and people can come without my having to go and let them in, and so I wait forcing myself not to despair and toward evening she calls from Siusi to find out how I am and to tell me that her girl friend's husband will telephone me and he can come up the day after tomorrow, but in the meanwhile she would be glad to come for me now making the trip without the baby she wouldn't need a sleeper and she could even go second class which doesn't cost much, and I summon up my courage and tell her not to move it isn't necessary, I feel all right just a little weak as usual after these attacks as she knows better than I but otherwise I feel fine and it makes me happier to know she is up in the cool mountains with the baby only I ask her to stay in the hotel so I can find her right away if I need her, and she says we love you so much you know and I say I know but now hang up or the phone bill will be too high and she doesn't get mad or say how stingy I am, she's good when I'm sick however I can't stay sick all the time just to make her good, she ought to understand this and be good and help me economize even when I'm well again, however I have to be very careful in saying this or else she'll get

mad and we'll fight, according to her in fact the member of the
family who spends money is me and the accounts go badly because I don't leave everything in her hands, and when she suggests
I turn all the money over to her I answer that she's sick in the head,
I even hate her when I realize that in one week we have spent a
hundred and twenty thousand lire without knowing how, and she
hates me in those moments she says she's never free to do anything I'm always there checking up on her even peeking into her
purse to see if she's spent the ten thousand lire I gave her in the
morning, and when a person behaves the way I do she feels like
spending money on purpose just for spite and making debts and
signing promissory notes, this is how my wife is but when I'm
sick she's good and comforts me and then I don't know if a wife
with a well-balanced and responsible sense of domestic economy
would be of any help to me when I'm sick, maybe she wouldn't
even try, instead my wife does try and she's able to help me and
so I decide from now on to grumble less when she spends money,
who knows I might even try this experiment she wants and turn
the accounts over to her, I would really be so happy to say to her
here this is all we have you handle it I don't want to hear any more
about it I place myself in your hands, however to do this I would
like to have some hope that she has a sense of responsibility and
she doesn't have any at all, I can see this when she goes to the ten-
cent store or the supermarket she starts roaming around madly
from one department to another buying all sorts of things we don't
need, once just to give you an example she bought five hundred
lire's worth of needles for sewing machines but of course we don't
have a sewing machine and I got mad that time and she said to
me aren't you ashamed of being such a pinchpenny look at this
pretty box they come in and what's five hundred lire, so for some
time now I haven't gone with her any more to the ten-cent store or
the supermarket and she gets mad when I don't go with her, this
is really what my wife is like however when I say help me this
horrible disease is coming over me she is always ready to help
me, young as she is compared with me and so full of the desire to
live happily, and I am so little inclined to be happy my God be-

cause I have so little happiness, however I resolve to keep quiet from now on, and I'll also let her get a driver's license so she can drive the car the way her girl friends do, and I know full well that afterwards when I need the car I won't be able to have it except at the price of terrible fights but it doesn't matter I'll buy myself a bicycle, there was even one of those faddist doctors I went to during a certain stage of the disease who in fact wanted me to buy a bicycle, and I didn't pay any attention to him at the time but now I'll buy it, I mean when I come back cured from Siusi, maybe it really was the heat that made me feel sick and naturally a little stay in the mountains will soon fix me up, this was also the opinion of the doctor who examined me this morning and especially the view of the lady who lives opposite us and the lady on the fourth floor who now come separately each bringing me a bowl of soup, and I say thanks to them both but I don't need anything only I'll sleep with the door ajar since when I'm sick everything frightens me even being alone in the house with the door shut because if I have an attack they can't come from outside to help me, anyhow I'm almost sure I won't have an attack after all I now tend to believe it was a heat spell as they say, that doctor this morning was exaggerating when he talked about exhaustion, maybe a person doesn't digest something too well and then all it takes is a little shortness of breath from the heat and he feels faint, however the thing needn't come back again in fact it won't come back for sure, although as a simple precaution it's best to leave the door open a crack so they can come in if I need them. Later on my wife's girl friend's husband calls the one who has to go to Siusi and he says we'll leave day after tomorrow morning early, however while I was thinking he would come with me in my car he was thinking that I would go in his car with him, and since he has a Giulietta sports model because he is a contractor whereas all I have is an old small Fiat obviously it would be logical for us both to go in the Giulietta, however at this point there is the catch that I can't be left without a car which is the only means of transportation I can still use because I'm the one driving it whereas I'm not the one driving a train or an airplane, but this gentleman I'm talking to is evidently unacquainted with states of nervous exhaustion and has a hard time understanding, or else thanks to my mental confusion I can't make myself clear, in any case he cuts the discussion short saying we'll work it all out on the spot as if he were buying a load of building stone, and the spot is to be the filling station on the new bridge at five thirty day after tomorrow morning, and after this telephone call which is frankly not too satisfactory because of our reciprocal incomprehension I swallow a couple of tranquilizers preparing to get through this dangerous night as best I can all alone in the house, however I have the telephone beside me and in case of need a man doesn't count the cost and it's obvious that if I say it's a special and urgent call and pay three times the normal rate the national telephone system works wonderfully, so my wife is here with me you might say, and in fact I tell her my thoughts which thanks to my weariness and confusion are shall we say elementary, in reality all I keep saying is what a calamity eh what a calamity oh yes a real calamity and saying this little by little I fall asleep after this fatal day, and the next morning at the moment when I wake up I am perfectly well it frequently happens that I feel completely sound at that particular moment and I know that to make the moment last I would have to remain completely immobile not even thinking, but while I think this I am performing the act of thinking and then it all blows up and I'm already sick in the intestine or the lumbars or the heart area or somewhere so when you think about it the thing for me to do would be to take the sleep cure, honestly I don't know why I haven't taken it before or rather I do know and the reason is lack of money however at present I have the money to sleep for a couple of weeks maybe in a local clinic instead of a Swiss or a Swedish one, but to spend the money would mean bidding farewell perhaps forever to the fourth and following chapters and frankly today I don't feel sick enough to do that, in fact though I still feel slightly stunned and have little warning pains here and there I can safely say the attack is passed, indeed I phone the good news at once to my wife and though it's an ordinary call and what's more strictly limited to the three minutes I am strengthened by it, so much so that I go straight into the bathroom but only for number one and to brush my teeth and I would also like to glance into the study just to look at the table and the typewriter however I feel the straight lines even today are still not eminently stable, so all things considered it's best for me to go back to bed where I devote myself to what is my almost incessant occupation in these cases that is to thinking of the disease in its various manifestations and concatenations, and now the new fact to clear up if possible with the greatest calm is that this was a relapse I mean a real disaster when you think about it, because I was cured or at least I thought I was and instead this disease has attacked me from behind taken me by surprise and now I believe that nothing will ever be able to free me from the fear that it may come back again by surprise whenever it wants to through no fault of mine, no recent fault I mean that is, without any plausible cause-and-effect relationship unless there are supernatural revenge phenomena in the air, but when the worst is past as a rule I tend to hunt for physical causes like deteriorating nerves in the cells or maybe the time when they operated on me when they put my intestine back they didn't put it in exactly the right place so some days it's all stirring around inside whereas on other days like today it seems blocked in a perpetual stasis, but today to tell the truth it may be the fear of defecating that makes the stimulus disappear this is logical after yesterday's blow, anyhow when I'm in Siusi everything will be fine again I'm sure, unless I am the victim of an exceptional disease that the doctors have never encountered, or better still an exceptional combination of diseases, a bit of diabetes for example or on the contrary a bit of hypoglycemia put together with the spastic colitis on top of the duodenal ulcer and lumbar arthrosis which can't be questioned since they were found in the X rays, according to me these combinations of diseases however remote they may be from one another have not yet been sufficiently studied in relation to that other field of infinite complications namely chemistry, not to mention radioactivity which I am always very reluctant to think of, besides the doctors are so far behind in their knowledge of ordinary diseases that it would be asking too much of them to have any knowledge of or even sympathy for the diseases that I term fairly correctly I believe combined diseases, this then is just a hasty example of the thoughts that keep me company all through the day when I am left alone if you except the brief appearances of neighbor ladies with tea or soups, and then it is night again and I tell myself to stop this thinking about the disease also because tomorrow morning at five thirty I have to be at the filling station on the new bridge, it's already past midnight and I've placed an alarm call for four thirty so I ought to sleep, and to tell the truth gradually I do fall asleep almost without realizing it only annoyed by a troublesome falling sensation especially in a backward direction, but also toward the right or towards the left, then I have to wake up completely to remind myself I'm lying in bed which means I'm in a position of stability if not absolute stability at least about as close as you can get to it in this world, and moreover the room certainly has straight lines and everything is in order I could easily check this by turning on the light but I'm too lazy or tired or perhaps prudent to do that, there once again I'm heading for sleep penetrating into a concave and even slippery immensity in which it would be hard to remain free from that unpleasant sinking sensation, anyhow at a certain moment without even realizing it I go beyond or more simply I fall asleep but not perfectly, it's as if one half of me were there watching the other half sleeping and obviously this kind of rest is hardly refreshing however you have to take what you can get because in these attacks my sleep also becomes difficult and sketchy, in any case finally even if I can't establish the precise moment the fusion of my two halves that is to say real sleep comes over me and this presumably occurs not long before a gentleman informs me over the phone that it's four thirty, and I immediately find myself faced with the familiar job of preserving as long as possible through immobility and non-thought the unstable condition of life without suffering or with only a reasonable amount of suffering, but it would be absurd to expect too much and substantially it's a matter of facing with due caution these first thoughts and movements which seem to have a determining influence on the day's destiny, as luck would have it however the first movements for that matter completely involuntary occur in the intestine thanks to contractions or shiftings of air bubbles and in consequence my thoughts also are channeled in that direction that is towards colon and death and physical or chemical currents perhaps obscure ones from the various parts of the body to the brain and vice versa, so it's now all too obvious that I can win only at the price of torments each day of my life for myself till my death always hoping that death is a fixed point at least as far as suffering is concerned, and I really wouldn't even complain about any of this if I could aspire to literary glory but I can't and there I am stuck in the third chapter thanks to the aggression of God knows what demon or of this father of mine who defined glory in an entirely different way, anyhow I don't have to think about working or sacrifices today but of the trip a long trip with a radiant goal wife and daughter against a background of woods and fresh air, it wouldn't be surprising if I were to be cured the minute I get there and in fact I'll take the three polished chapters with me and I'll write the fourth and the fifth and so on up to the end in clearings in the woods with that trembling of pine needles which at every gust of wind sounds like a storm, in my infancy this was the vast sound of two or three fir trees in a garden near our house and I could dream of conquests and far-off places and inexplicable ambitions, oh God all I have to do is get there and I'll find all this again and I'll be healthy and industrious, when you come right down to it I'm only asking for my health in order to work and all right I want to work for glory whereas I ought to be praying *Non nobis Domine non nobis* however there are some people in this world who are healthy and work and even cheat to make money or have women or acquire power to use against their neighbor whom they hate, whereas I love my neighbor as Jesus commands with a few exceptions naturally, and for that matter even our Saviour at a certain moment seized a knotted rope and lashed out on all sides, something that truthfully I haven't yet done not having ever had the courage to attack even verbally a famous homosexual or an entrenched radical of limited importance, but you have to take

into consideration that I'm sick, give me a bit of health and you'll
see what I can do, and meanwhile for a start I'll write the fourth
and fifth chapters in the mountains by God if I had only thought
of it before I could have avoided this attack which surely came with
the heat, however it's no use dramatizing it now since I'm well
in fact I couldn't be better both as to present condition and as to
hopes for the future while I go to the meeting on the new bridge
with the three perfectly polished chapters in my suitcase, and here
comes the character with the Giulietta sports car all full of vitality
and optimism except for a few thoughts regarding my car, by
God I bet he has defecated without any pain or problems this
morning and hasn't thought of eternal life for at least twenty
years so you might say we have completely different attitudes and
destinies, in any case he has to have a coffee and fill his tank and
I who can't drink coffee and have already filled my tank say I'll
go on ahead because I feel fine, so I turn the car on to the Via
Flaminia so clean in the cool morning really a person should
always get up early in the morning to look at the world and
mankind with purity and then he wouldn't ever get sick although
speaking for myself the few times I've tried it I have felt sick
the same as always, but today no not today when I'm rushing
toward the Alpine forests and the people dearest to my heart I
feel pretty well only I'm a little worried about the heat which may
come and indeed will surely come since these are the dog days,
and meanwhile this benefactor in the Giulietta has caught up with
me just after Prima Porta where the road runs alongside that long
cemetery in which according to my sound principles I will be
buried at small expense, they say that there aren't any names or
stones on the graves just numbers and this is all right with me no
matter what the great poet Ugo Foscolo may have written, besides
it seems to me that I have a right to differ with him on the subject
of the amount of publicity to be given corpses when all I have to
do is drive past the wall of a cemetery to feel the deleterious influence of death, my God I wonder how many dead people there
are in the terraqueous globe and the funny thing is that they are
increasing all the time, every moment that passes the number of

corpses in this decomposed planet increases the time will surely come when we feed on the deceased and breathe the deceased, we're already well on the way I think and surely when you imagine them all together several billion accumulated dead from the *Pithecanthropus robustus* on down it's quite a sight, in a sense you ought to be consoled by the thought that you will end up in such a large company, but with me it doesn't work that way at all thanks partly to the irremediable contradictions I feel about the value of life that is to say whether it is a good or an evil, and on this score I make a fundamental distinction between non-life and death which generally isn't accepted whereas it's clear that non-life is so to speak a life that has had no beginning I mean it's nothing compared with which life is a positive evil, whereas death is a life that has had a beginning and then ends generally with sufferings and fear which above all have a capacity for making themselves felt far ahead of the final event proper and so obviously compared with this horrible event which is death life can also be considered a good, and in fact even I so overloaded with misfortunes am pleased to be alive although only in the sense that by living I don't die, in short I believe that all told life is a fine mess at least for sensitive spirits while the others normally don't give a damn especially those with healthy bodies and minds like this character escorting me with the Giulietta who surely doesn't give much thought to life and death but is thinking of his millions lucky man and maybe also thinking with less bliss about the enormous nuisance of following me, I can easily imagine him huffing and swearing at the wheel of his car which can go a hundred and sixty kilometers an hour if not more whereas mine only in favorable conditions and downhill manages to hit a hundred, however as soon as we stop in Foligno for more gas I say to him thanks a lot you can go on ahead if you like I'll manage all right by myself, and in reality the character was waiting only for the word to go flying off in his sports car while I struggle along as best I can up and down hills and around curves worried about my solitude but also happy not to have that idiot driving impatiently behind me, especially since for the moment I don't feel

bad at all in fact I would almost say I feel good, the countryside is
green and yellow and I see it green and yellow, there are crickets
singing and I hear crickets singing, there is this reassuring contact
between me and the real world, only I mustn't be afraid I must be
sure that my relapse the day before yesterday was only passing
and accidental, I mustn't be afraid otherwise this joy in the world
dissolves and I see only inert and twisted and threatening things,
and this is how the world outside me can all of a sudden become
hostile, my God don't let me have an attack right here among these
mountains nobody could save me nobody, for example I don't even
know where the nearest insane asylum is, please my God I better
start singing but not the first thing that comes into my head which
is Come with me sweet flower of May, not that good God I don't
want that I want to sing instead Like the moon I'm a vagabond
which is also a song of many years ago but one which has absolutely nothing to do with my father, my child wife wasn't even
born when I used to sing this song of great grief O at night I sing
in the streets of the world, it really is a moving song and sometimes
when we go out in the car just the two of us or even with Augusta
who is so little and is a part of each of us, she likes for me to
sing O my false and carefree smile hides my grief but a little while
a little while, she wasn't even alive and I was already singing
these desperate words on the great plain where I was born and if
the moon rose while I was singing tears would come into my eyes
when I thought how I would go through the streets of the world
weeping with love, and now too I'm crying but not with happy
unhappiness as when I was a boy but with just plain unhappiness
because I'm sick, there's no more youth now nor exalting sentiments but only this obscure disease that can take me by surprise
and deprive me of that little bit of joy I might still have along with
the hope and ability to go beyond the third chapter, and thank God
I'm crying now since as a rule when I cry I never have really bad
attacks with the terror of ending up eternally mad, when I cry I
feel simply dejection and compassion for myself and this suffering
is sweet compared with the terror, a bitter sweetness that accom-
panies me in my race down the Apennines, then at Fano I stop

and decide to eat something in order to telephone my wife in the meanwhile, however the call hasn't come through after I've eaten so I start speeding on again maybe I could reach Siusi before midnight, but how can you speed along the Adriatic where people have come to the beaches from all over and the roads are packed with cars and it's so hot, I stop in some town and open the roof of the car and I buy a big straw hat the kind peasant women wear around here when they go to work in the fields in the summertime, and now with this hat and the roof open things seem a little better though I still have to be very careful about the pressure of the hat on my head because not being used to it it makes me feel odd at times, in other words I wouldn't want at the present moment to have to deal with the dear departed since the buying of a hat has perforce recalled him to mind, as a precaution it's better for me to think of some physical factor as for example though this is a somewhat forced idea to attribute currents of spiritual uneasiness to the slight weight of a straw hat, however suppose we combine this slight weight with any sort of chemical factor deriving for example from the food I ate in Fano, specifically boiled rice and boiled sole which are bland foods since when I'm sick I have to be very careful about what I eat, anyhow let's suppose that the already digested sole doesn't combine well with the nervous flux which from the colon and from the lumbars can rise to the cerebellum where you see there is the unfamiliar weight of the hat, and so obviously from one moment to the next an enormous disaster could take place which nobody would understand anything about since as you can plainly see it's difficult to clear a plausible path through the tangle of hypotheses and suppositions, this or any other path naturally since it isn't as if I wanted to force anybody to my interpretation which for that matter is purely conditional, let's pray God conditional I mean that nothing happens and everything is reduced to a skein of thoughts even if filled with fear while I proceed along this road past Italian beaches at an average speed of under thirty so I have the impression of being farther from my destination now than I was this morning in Rome, it's no use my getting the notion I'm going to make Siusi in one lap I'll have to

sleep in some hotel along the way, my God sleeping alone in a
hotel I must make sure to pick one in a city that also has an asylum,
Ferrara for example since if they had an asylum in the time of
Tasso there must surely be one now, however now that I think
about it I'm not so sure that Tasso was in the asylum in Ferrara, he
was in Rome of course there on the Janiculum but as far as Ferrara
is concerned now that I think about it further I am sure he was
confined there in the Hospital of Sant'Anna, hospital I remember
well and not asylum, and it's logical to presume that in those days
Ferrara didn't have asylums properly speaking and God only
knows if between then and now there has been any progress in this
field, it would be best for me to ask the clerk of the hotel before
settling on the room, however when at ten minutes to nine I finally
make my entrance into the lobby of the Hotel Touring I don't
have the nerve to ask for such information since I suddenly realize
I have forgotten about the straw hat on my head, my God first it
was pressing on me and now I forget all about it and naturally I
hasten to take it off but all the same I haven't the courage to ask
for information about the asylum because I realize it wouldn't
make a good impression a guest who as soon as he comes into a
fairly smart hotel with air conditioning asks about the local
asylum trying to conceal as best he can a huge Romagnola-
peasant-woman straw hat and moreover looking around with those
slightly pop eyes which I generally get after attacks, so in the end
I prefer to ask quickly for a room on the second or third floor but
not higher with a telephone and bath in case of defecation im-
probable as that is, and I go up to this room immediately still
thinking about Tasso for whom I am gradually developing an
affection since I have to acknowledge that his glory large or small
he won at the price of terrible suffering if it's true that in the
Hospital of Sant'Anna where he was confined as a madman they
kept him chained to the wall, my God just think of a man chained
in a cell when he has claustrophobia the way I have, I'd die for
sure but Tasso didn't die and in fact he found a way to poetize
even in there so it's understandable that a man like that should
achieve glory, but I give up if it has to cost me that much, though

at heart once the fear is past I'm prepared also to put up with a reasonable amount of suffering in order to work, here for example are these three chapters I've taken out of the suitcase and put on the bedside table while I'm waiting for the call to Siusi to come through they certainly cost me pain and toil but I don't complain about it if as I believe they are three excellent chapters, not even critics of radical tendencies could find much to criticize in them I imagine, too bad they are only three chapters and not thirty which would be right but I will write thirty one of these days if I have any luck, I mean if I'm in good health since that's all I ask, and to tell the truth at present I don't have much to complain about if I can stay here alone in a hotel room with Valerian and tranquilizers of course however without knowing the number and exact location of mental hospitals and rest homes in the province of Ferrara, although at the right moment that is when I'm attacked by my currents of terror I don't split hairs and I've already demonstrated that I can also turn to the municipal police so long as I can entrust to someone besides myself the responsibility for me, in any case now what are you thinking about I say to myself just take it easy and nothing will happen, if you keep calm this night will pass without incident and tomorrow you'll be in the cool air of the mountains with your wife and your daughter Augusta, there will be a bit of wind and a sound like a storm in the branches of the fir trees and you will be protected by happy memories and the love of your dear ones and finally you will write also the fourth chapter, my God why didn't I think of this before I'm no longer the man for adventures like staying all alone in the city in the month of July, I need protection and love around me to keep well I'm the family type basically like my father was, and then at last comes the longed-for telephone call she tries to tell me suddenly a number of things in order to economize on time but all I understand is that she loves me and this is naturally a great thing however we also have to arrange about tomorrow, then she says more calmly that she was worried all day and now at last she hears my voice, her girl friend's husband with the Giulietta got in at five thirty but with my old car I naturally couldn't do the same and I

was right to stop over in Ferrara tomorrow morning she'll come
to meet me in Verona, well if I don't want Verona at least as far
as Bolzano, but I don't even want Bolzano I prefer for her to come
on foot with the baby a bit outside the town so I'll see them among
the woods, there are surely woods around there if I remember
rightly and she says of course there are however we have to decide
whether we want the woods toward Castelrotto or the woods toward Fié because there's a new road that maybe isn't marked on
my map because it was just opened and it's asphalt and almost all
good and it goes through Fié and you have to take it making a
right turn eight or nine kilometers out of Bolzano on the Brenner
road, remember don't take the Ponte Gardena road or otherwise
we won't meet since she is going to come along the Fié road, anyhow we'll talk again on the phone to work it out better and
naturally she will stay in the hotel to wait for any phone calls from
me, for the last couple of days she has been living next to the
telephone booth since she of course doesn't have a phone in her
room, she is in a simple second-class hotel she isn't like me who
need the Georges V and air conditioning, but obviously she is
joking when she says this and I answer also joking that I never go
anywhere except out of necessity whereas she would like to do
nothing but travel, and then the series of good-byes begins a
kiss from me and a kiss from you so in the end it's twelve minutes
this time according to the courteous information of the porter or
telephone operator or whoever it is, however the money is well
spent since I feel better after the call, I feel so good that to avoid
wasting time I start rereading the three chapters while I wait
for sleep, however this isn't an entirely happy idea since the three
chapters which I just leaf through here and there don't seem all
that good to me, not that they're bad of course however usually
they make a better impression on me and this may come from my
tiredness in fact it must surely come from that since I've driven
more than five hundred kilometers and besides in an hour or
thereabouts I've swallowed about three tranquilizers, I am a bit
sleepy in fact and I fall asleep almost at once after I've turned off
the light at about ten twenty, then at three I'm awake it's only

natural and strange to say I'm not a bit sick not even after thoughts and movements of both hips although I find myself a bit tense listening to the silence and the sounds of this unfamiliar place thinking what a disaster it would be if I got sick here, and naturally when I begin to think like this I'm simply setting in motion the obscure mechanism which can rapidly bring me to the brink of an attack so it's best for me to take a tranquilizer right away, not that I'm hoping for miracles from these tranquilizers but if they've been so successful all over the world they must have some beneficent effect, and sure enough here I am calm again thinking both of the silence and the noises without dramatizing them at all that is without losing that trusting relationship so to speak that exists between a healthy man and the things that surround him, whereas I for example would be capable of hearing in the distant sound of a train which still remains the distant sound of a train the imminent presage of the end of the world, and also in the absence of the sound of the train I am capable of hearing the end of the world, these things are far from simple as you can easily see however the tranquilizers help me not to give them too much weight and in fact I am thinking that since it's now three thirty-five in a half hour or a little more it will be dawn and maybe it would be best to get up and leave this unfamiliar place, but though this seems an excellent idea to me I still lie there thinking and I see the three chapters on the table and I feel like glancing at them resolving to get up in half an hour if in the meanwhile I haven't fallen asleep and to leave in the cool dawn, so I start on the first chapter which gets off to a brisk start *con brio* or rather *andante con moto* you would say in musical terms something very similar to a good concerto of Vivaldi just to give you the idea, and so very soon I feel sleepy and although this sleepiness could result from the tranquilizer or the hour certainly unsuited to reading it isn't nice that I should feel like sleeping while I read the first chapter which of the three is the most polished and let's hope also the most interesting as to content though there's nothing but thoughts in it, however who can say that above a certain artistic level thoughts are less interesting than actions, anyhow I turn off the light and

then it takes me a long time to fall asleep, there is the uneasiness
about the disease not alarming but subterranean as is only natural
after a big attack like the one the other day, in any case what
matters is not to have any more relapses and to be able to go back
to work in a week let's say, in reality it would be a big disaster
from many points of view to lose more than a week, but why
should I have a relapse after all, and on this indirect and basically
rhetorical question I fall asleep while others in the hotel are already getting up, and then I wake up and it's late past nine and
while I wash and dress dismissing with various sophisms the
defecation problem I ask for the Milchwasser Hotel in Siusi on
the phone so she won't be worried if I don't call from Bolzano at
lunchtime as I told her I would, I surely won't reach Bolzano for
lunch and maybe not even Trento anyhow it's best not to fix a
schedule, and she feels the same way when the call finally comes
through and we conclude it with a few greetings and kisses so I
won't have to pay too high a bill since now more than ever we have
to economize, and I finally manage to leave I go over the summer
roads of the great plain where I was born in a little car with its
top open and a big peasant-woman straw hat on my head, a
modern and perhaps a bit bizarre tourist you would say on seeing
me but not certainly a sick man anxiously hurrying to his wife he
can't do without because he's afraid of being alone, but it may also
be that there's a slight exaggeration not to say self-gratification in
this description of me sick and running to my wife, today I'm fine
in fact why not admit it I'm almost as good as I was before the
fatal relapse of the other day, and anyhow I mustn't get discour-
aged, take for example my father the hatseller if I think of him I
can clearly see how far I've come as to social position and everything else, and the progress has been made thanks to my abilities
and my work but I also have to admit thanks to a series of fortunate circumstances therefore reasoning objectively I can even
conclude that in general I am a fortunate man, and if good fortune
has assisted me until today there is no reason why it should abandon me just now when I have three chapters ready and a desire
to write another twenty-seven, if I had the money to live for a

year or even for six months without having to scratch around to earn my daily bread I would show a certain defunct person that I'm capable of writing twenty-seven chapters, unfortunately I can't go on for more than a couple of months with the money I have but still in two months if I fall to with a will I can get ten or even twelve chapters down on paper one way or another and then in the winter I can polish them, while I'm doing scripts or ass-kissing some of these film producers who have the great idea of making movies like *Nude and Lewd* or *Red Hot Sex* I can easily polish a dozen chapters, and with three plus twelve chapters in order the job is half done and when a writer is halfway home nothing can stop him, so without great difficulty I can imagine this crowning work of mine, aha they will all have to say this man though son of a humble hatseller is the artist who interprets our time for posterity thanks to him future generations will understand how we think and live, after all this is what I ask not necessarily wealth or fleeting if profitable fame, my goal is glory which can also come to me after I'm dead however I'll know even when I'm alive if glory is going to come to me after death, maybe only me and a few others will know and all I need is thirty chapters on the level of the three I've already written, even if yesterday evening or last night reading the first of the three I didn't find it the chapter of a masterpiece not completely at least, but maybe that came from my tiredness or my peculiar spiritual state, I bet that if I read them now when I'm not at all depressed they would make a more favorable and proper impression on me, and in fact since I know a lot of these three chapters by heart I recite long extracts to myself as I go up this valley which is the valley of the Adige and in general they make a good impression on me, even an excellent one I'd say, to begin with my prose is fluent and doesn't betray the enormous effort it cost however it isn't as if it flowed along idly no not that since behind the apparent lightness of the *andante con moto* there is to say the least a whole moral world, this is the ultimate result of art I mean the harmonious fusion of form and content, and by God I realize clearly that when I reason like this I am reasoning like plenty of others including the intellectuals of radical tendency whom on the contrary I should eliminate from my reasoning if I want to retain this thin margin of faith in my health and in my work, so to hell with the radicals and their homosexual friends and social climbers in literary salons we're on quite a different plane ladies and gentlemen, *Odi profanum vulgus et arceo* just to show you that my papers are all in order too, and for this very reason I aim at simplicity both in style and thought however in my case simplicity doesn't mean facility quite the opposite, I well know the cost of the three chapters I have in my suitcase but these are three masterpiece chapters that they are beyond any doubt, if they weren't at the next curve instead of turning to left or right according to how the road goes I might just as well plow straight ahead into a plane tree or some other tree to end it all in this valley which has a very picturesque appearance and in fact from the milestones I see that we are near Bolzano which in these parts is also called Bozen, just as the Upper Adige is also called the South Tyrol which according to me isn't completely mistaken since here the houses and churches and a good part of the people around really have an Ostrogoth look, and as if this weren't enough it's hot as hell in this valley which makes me all the more sour because I've been very afraid of the heat ever since one time when I almost went crazy in the Piazza Barberini, anyhow here is Bolzano with its fine display of bilingual signs and ads, I have the impression of great weakness or hunger or whatever but I stop only for a glass of milk and a call to the Hotel Milchwasser in Siusi, and she is right there by the phone as she had promised and she says her heart is pounding like the first times when we used to meet as lovers, she'll leave the hotel at once to come and meet me on the Fié road and she tells me to make sure to take the new road eight or nine kilometers out of Bolzano on the right, that if I don't we certainly won't meet if I take the wrong road and go through Castelrotto, I must pay attention to the arrow and to remember that Siusi in German is called Seis pronounced Say-ease, anyway on the sign there's Siusi-Seis and that's the road I'm to take but to go slow because it's bad, or rather it's nice and new but there are cliffs, please darling she says don't make me worry about you, and in fact I go fairly slowly on this new road which climbs up and my God on the left there's a drop all right that makes your blood run cold luckily it's on the left so sticking to the right as a good driver's duty requires I can keep as far as possible from it, but just to make sure I also recite the Litanies of the Blessed Virgin so I keep my mind occupied in some way, and finally with a nasty rocky pass this climb ends and I find myself on a kind of plateau, here this is what you usually dream of when you think of the mountains a green high plain with firs and the wind, I see the wind moving a little the branches of the firs and if I stopped I could also hear the sound, the fabulous hurricane sound that can stimulate the spirit and give health to the body although I also have the impression that you have to be a bit careful with these easy enthusiasms, in any case I don't stop because I have first to meet a girl with a child dressed in Tyrolean style whereas the girl has on beige velvet slacks and a sweater with horizontal stripes pale green and a dull grey, that's what she said over the phone however I must tell her I don't like dressing the baby in Tyrolean style, not today however today it's best not to open any discussion of dress, there they are in the distance coming forward in the wind in the middle of the road the child of my life and the woman of my life *cumulus passionum* and also *portus naufragantium*, they've recognized me and they're shouting something and waving their arms and I stop the car right in front of them and jump out and all three of us are hugging together and she asks me partly in words and partly in signs if it was bad and speaking in a way the baby can't understand I answer that it was really bad I was afraid I would never see them again, even along the road I was trying to think of an infinity of things anything but the disease but inside I never stopped being afraid I wouldn't make it here, and then since the baby wants to pick wild flowers in a meadow we sit at the edge of the road and I watch my daughter who has an immense sky over her with white clouds, and I am a bit consoled because she is beautiful and healthy and happy but I am even more dismayed by a sense of not belonging as if she had already some time ago set out on her own road turning back ever more rarely to wave, and it is right this way and it is fitting this way, and my wife takes me by the hand gently asking me what I'm thinking and I meditate before answering and then I tell her that I am more and more afraid of going crazy, but she smiles at these words of mine she says that now she knows everything about my disease because fortunately while playing canasta with some friends she met a man who's the assistant to a big psychiatrist in Milan, and this youth with a bright future told her that according to him and judging by what she said about the phenomena and all the rest I'm a neurotic pure and simple, my exhaustion is properly called neurosis and that's what we should always call it also to avoid looking silly among people who are in the know on these things, well this boy says neurosis has nothing to do with psychosis which is what we laymen call madness, they are two separate compartments with no possible communication between them and therefore I can be sure of at least one thing namely that I'm not going to go crazy, and besides it seems that for neurosis there are recently discovered medicines which are downright miraculous and the budding psychiatrist is convinced that in two or three years chemistry will defeat all nervous and mental diseases, and so you see she says but without any bitterness you keep making the mistake of not putting yourself in the hands of specialists as was proved also in the case of the kidney stone when instead of going to a urologist you got into all those troubles which then caused the exhaustion I mean the neurosis, anyhow this evening if I feel like it we can call on these friends of hers at a hotel much better than the Milchwasser and that's where the young psychiatrist is or else if I'm too tired this evening tomorrow at the Alp which is where her friends go every day since even in Siusi it's a bit hot but although her friends invited her these last few days she hasn't gone so she could stay by the telephone, and I listen to her a bit absently thinking though in a vague fashion of the many things that seem to have importance for her whereas for me they haven't any at all, and meanwhile I put back on my head the straw hat which in the sentimental fullness of our meeting had remained unutilized in my hands, and suddenly forgetting her canasta friends she says where did you get that hat you must be crazy, and she immediately apologizes for having said crazy she really didn't mean to and I have a feeling that her recent talk about neurosis and psychosis which are mutually exclusive doesn't merit much faith, maybe she only said that to encourage me at the suggestion of the young psychiatrist however I don't feel any fear at this moment only a great sadness for my daughter who is going off on her own and this wife who in a couple of days if you consider that she has spent the last two by the telephone has managed to create a whole circle of friends where she feels at home without me while for that matter I naturally have no desire to follow her in these canasta games, I wonder I say to myself not without bitterness whether I haven't made this whole trip for nothing and I'll be alone here worse than in Rome, however she holds my hand and says what are you thinking I love you so much and then I smile at her and say it seems a century that I've been away from her when really it's only five days in fact not yet five, and with her eyes and her smile she says yes and waits for me to say something else so I tell her that considering how those last days in Rome we were always fighting over the sleeping car it must now be eight or nine days since we made love, and she says yes and in her face I can see that she wants very much to make love however she tells me that in the sleeper she didn't close her eyes but she had never traveled in a sleeper until then whereas I had gone to Paris and who knows what other places before I met her, anyhow now I'm going to change she says I'll do everything you want and we won't fight any more, and then she says if the baby wasn't here it would be beautiful to make love on the grass in the midst of the woods and I say it would be beautiful all right, to tell the truth I want to make love too although I'm not sure whether I feel desire most or fear however I am also afraid of eating or not eating and moving or not moving not to mention evacuating and so many other inevitable things, anyhow we call the baby and we go to the hotel where we leave her playing in the garden while we go toward the entrance and then toward the steps which lead to the rooms and

of course many guests at the hotel look at us and understand that
I'm the husband who has just arrived and she shows me off as if
I were God knows who and in fact I am somebody who however
marginally works in the movies and I have met Silvana Mangano
personally and Anna Maria Ferrero and I are on first name basis
when we happen to run into each other, in short all I do is tell the
people who ask me that down in Rome it's roasting hot and the old
Fiat is a fantastic car the best the company ever turned out and
that's why we haven't traded it in, after which my wife hastens
to say I'm going upstairs to freshen up a bit after the trip and
naturally everybody in this little hotel with its family atmosphere
gets a wise look imagining that we're going upstairs to do precisely what we're planning to do, and I am hugely irritated by this
curiosity of theirs or this lack of discretion whereas my wife
doesn't give a damn and with the ladies whose husbands are down
in the city she assumes an attitude of open superiority, I really
don't understand how women are made when in general before
they get married they think twice before they let anybody see
them so much as kissing their fiancé and then once they have
the gold band on their finger and the marriage certificate they
would make love right at the church door so to speak, anyhow
here in a somewhat old-fashioned bed with all sorts of quilts we
make love however on my side it's only so-so since I'm secretly
still a bit afraid, and then I pretend to sleep until my wife does
fall asleep and instead I lie there thinking how my behavior is to
say the least foolish if you consider I came here rather miraculously to save myself with the help of God from an incredible
catastrophe and as soon as I arrive I succumb to the call of the
senses I mean I squander an enormous amount of energy right
now when I have to struggle against the disease, I really feel it
upon me this incessant illness even at the present moment, of
course not to such a degree that I can't see straight however
beyond a shadow of doubt I feel uneasy and insecure even though
I'm here with my wife, even the wind in the fir trees after all isn't
the fabulous thing I thought and I don't give a good goddam
about the birds twittering and I almost say the same or worse

about the cries of the children playing in the garden only my daughter is among them so the cries are joyous and the children are happy and the happiest of all is my daughter, this is what I want to believe even though I know that by imagining her happy I am trying to evade the guilt of having brought her into the world, finally I could go mad despite the contrary opinion of my wife and her questionable adviser and if I went crazy what a terrible thing that would be for my daughter the day she finds out her father died crazy or worse is still alive in some asylum, my God at this point how insecure I feel, all the fault of these bad thoughts, I better take a tranquilizer before it's too late, in fact I do take one and after a while it works thank heaven and I leave the bad thoughts behind however all of a sudden something new makes me jump up in bed that is they begin right outside our door to bang on a percussion instrument of Chinese origin known as a gong, and my wife wakes up in a grand humor saying this gong is the signal that dinner is ready and although when you think about it I haven't had a proper meal since noon yesterday I don't much want to go downstairs and I would be satisfied if she brought me up some bread and ham if possible and a glass of milk, but she insists also for the child's sake better not to cause her unnecessary worry so we go down to the dining room when all the others are already on the second course and my wife says hello left and right, and she whispers to me say hello to this one and don't say hello to that one according to a private social scale of her own, and she says sit up straight, and I also see she's a bit strict with the baby whom she has taught in these few days how little English girls sit at the table she says, in short I notice all the efforts my wife makes to put on a good show in front of this community of vacationers who for the most part come from the fertile valley of the Po, however despite my wife's efforts and the efforts of various other guests the hotel seems more and more crummy to me with a watery broth for first course and the ugly South Tyrolean or Upper Adigean waitresses running back and forth to and from the kitchen breathless as slaves each of them serving twenty-two people, and I'm aware that in a few weeks the

vacationers will go away and the poor waitresses will be able to
sleep for ten months in a row so the heavy work is all here and now
however this heavy work annoys me as do these cheap-skate vacationers, all in all I can't feel too pleased at having come to the
mountains nor even very happy to be forced to eat a lousy peach
with knife and fork so that my wife won't lose face whereas at
home I peel it with just the knife and no fork which is right especially given this kind of miserable peach with a damn peel that
won't come away from the inside, now I am really in a bad humor
so I say I'm tired and I go to bed and instead my wife is equally
in a bad humor because she says it's no good making scenes when
you can't even eat a peach properly so she goes into the lobby to
watch TV with the baby, and after some effort I get warm under
the feather beds and think I've come all the way up here to suffer
the cold in the middle of July and finally I fall asleep before the
two of them come upstairs and I wake up in the middle of the
night while they are asleep she beside me in the monumental bed
and the baby on a somewhat improvised couch however we've had
to make do like this because my arrival wasn't planned, and as
sometimes happens when I start thinking in the middle of the
night I am surprised at the relationship that binds me to these
two creatures what am I doing here I ask myself, and then I ask
myself also if I love them enough and whereas for the daughter
the answer is unconditional, for the other there are always doubts
that come and go so I often imagine that if I had been able to
foresee the future on that day when I met her at the fountain I
surely wouldn't have gone to the Piazza del Popolo, but obviously
ideas of this sort only come to me when I'm a bit angry with her
as at present, and moreover these are reflections of no practical
value and in fact nobody can go back however convenient it would
be at times, anyhow I now have this wife and out of love or duty
I have to keep her so I might as well concentrate on some more
relaxing subject as for example my future glory, if I listen to the
wind a bit of my childish exultation returns to my spirit ill though
it is and then everything seems possible, in the last analysis a person who has real talent can overcome obstacles even greater than

mine, it ought to be possible to work even in this hotel seeing that
there is a good table in the room and naturally I have brought my
typewriter which however I haven't so far managed to set on the
table since it's cluttered with an extraordinary number of sweaters
and slipovers and skirts and slacks and many other garments belonging both to my wife and to the baby, and in addition there are
pocketbooks and purses and various toilet objects and cosmetics
especially creams to foster suntan, I hadn't realized they had left
with so much stuff but they really did bring it all with them, anyhow let's face it the main difficulty isn't space on the table which
with a bit of effort can always be found it's the intestine which has
been in a blocked state ever since the terror broke out however I
can't expect to go on like this till infinity, I will have to get this
weight off my guts at some moment even if the hotel doesn't offer
sufficiently inviting facilities, to tell the truth last night before
retiring to the room I made a tour of inspection and I discovered
that there's a bath or to be more precise a W.C. on every floor
whereas on the fourth floor there is a proper bathroom with a
tub and a stool of such proportions that one can easily imagine the
Emperor Franz Josef sitting on it, so on sober considerations
when the time comes I'll go up to the fourth floor unless I decide
in favor of *plein air* which isn't such a bad idea considering the
discreet wooded landscapes all around, and with my mind full of
these images which after all are among the most serene I've had for
a week now I fall asleep again, and then in the morning my wife
wakes me up to say the breakfast they give you in this hotel is excellent, they give you hot chocolate or tea or coffee and bread and
butter and jam all things that she never managed to eat at home
whereas here she eats them with a will, even the baby eats them
whereas in Rome in the morning she was nourished almost exclusively on cold pizza, here everything works better it seems and
heaven be praised for it however even if the breakfast here is
exceptional I am thinking my own thoughts, namely about my
health and my work, I might even exhume the three chapters from
the bottom of the suitcase where I've hidden them and reread
them once again since every time I reread them I find something to

revise, but my wife has decided that today a trip to the Alp will do me good this is where her friends go including the aspiring young psychiatrist, and in fact we set off in the car up a rather bad road on which I embark without the slightest suspicion as if this were an innocent excursion and only when we're several kilometers into it do I realize the kind of road this is, narrow and rocky and with breath-taking precipices on the right compared to which the ones yesterday were little Arcadian dells, my God I'm forced to go on because it turns out that in the ugly places you can't go into reverse or still less make the so-called U turn that is turn tail and go home, and then once the difficulty is overcome there is a less nasty bit and you think well if we've got this far we'll manage the rest especially since my wife says the worst is now over, and so we go forward toward deeper abysses and greater fears I am all rigid gripping the wheel because I feel in this disease nobody knows a damn thing about the important thing is to hang on, if you give way even a little complete collapse can follow, and so with great strength of will I manage to reach the plateau where I ask myself why in the world people come here in such numbers since it's a mangy windy place where of course you can see mountains, show me a place in the mountains where you don't see other mountains, well to tell the truth such places do exist near Rome, at Campo Catino or Terminillo for example where you don't see any moun- tains around for the simple reason that there's only one and you're on it, but in the Alps the most common thing is to see mountains everywhere because there are plenty of them, anyhow I begin by asking my wife if we really have to come all the way up to such an ugly place to see mountains and in fact she explains this isn't the nice part, the nice part is farther on at a little hotel called God knows what and we go there on foot naturally because the road ends here, in a quarter of an hour or a few minutes more you're there and so we start out arguing all the way because I don't care about getting tan in fact I'm afraid of the sun in the mountain altitudes and I've put on the big straw hat and I don't want to take it off not giving a damn if people look at me curiously even though they are wearing sporty caps on their heads or worse still Tyro-

lean hats which are certainly no less ridiculous than my big straw
one, the Germans whom we encounter in big groups start laughing all overjoyed and say *sombrero*, as if I wanted to start worrying about the Germans now and besides *sombrero* isn't a bad
word, and I think what a little while the idyll with my wife has
lasted that is from our meeting on the Fié road to the satisfying
of the senses, and I also begin to think that the road to this lovely
little hotel is rather long, in reality when my wife wants to coax
me into doing something she can say it's only a quarter of an
hour when it's really an hour and a half, anyhow this time in a
little over half an hour we make it however we haven't arrived
at the hotel but at the station of the chair lift which goes straight
to the hotel a bit higher up, but when I finally catch on to my wife's
plan I tell her she's got another think coming if she thinks I'm
going in that chair lift, for years I have been avoiding various
means of transportation like trains and even buses not to mention
ships and planes and now she wants me to get onto this contraption from which a person if he wants to can throw himself down
at any point and maybe break his neck, and she answers that if I
don't make an effort I'll never get well, and I tell her she can go
where she pleases and with anybody she pleases but as for me I'm
going back to Siusi and who knows maybe even back to Rome
again, in short after quite a quarrel we start walking again toward
the hotel which they swear isn't more than half an hour farther
on our daughter goes ahead of us along the path picking flowers
here and there and we follow her side by side as cross as can be,
to tell the truth I am already past the quarrel stage and at present
am pursuing a much more important line of thought which is that
I am getting myself into a trap on this damn mountain, my God
why didn't I think of this before I left Rome the enormous trap
I was falling into, Lord in heaven of all people I who need straight
lines I rush and rush to get here where no matter how hard you
look there isn't one line that's straight either vertically or hori-
zontally, and I also have to keep quiet and act as if it were nothing
because my wife isn't receptive at the moment and my daughter
comes back every now and then to show us a flower and she

mustn't see her father distraught, there I say to myself there is
your daughter the being you love most of all on the earth in front
of you in a green and varicolored meadow picking flowers happily and you feel no joy at all because you're clinging desperately
to cohesive power, try to let yourself go of all the doctors you've
consulted in the last five years there must surely be one who told
you to let yourself go, so let yourself go then, but it's not that easy
if I do let myself go I'll stay here forever on this damn mountain,
what a fool I was to listen to my wife who thinks of nothing but
excursions and amusing company, so it serves her right that when
we get to the little hotel the others have already left because
naturally they go and come in the chair lift, so we sit down all
alone and grumpier than ever in a fairly icy breeze to look at the
panorama which actually is better than the earlier one however
what do I care about the panorama, here I am clinging to myself
with every crumb of strength to hold myself together, and as if
this weren't enough I have to argue about trivia with my wife
and for example now she wants me to order something because
this is a hotel and you can't sit here without ordering something,
but I can't eat or drink anything when I'm in this upset state
for fear of chemical reactions, in reality who can prove to me for
example that Coca Cola mixed with God knows what amount of
bile surely corroding my stomach won't produce poisons that de-
range the brain, and yet she is stubbornly determined that I must
have at least a Coca Cola but thank God they're all out of it so I
order mineral water, I ask if a man has to come all the way up
here on this mountain to drink mineral water which on top of
everything else contains carbonic anhydride and you never know,
so it's all nonsense what they say about cool pure water of the
Alps, these crooked mountains can't even provide decent water,
and now I think I feel a warmth around the five lumbars, good
God the warmth is there all right and this means that I want to
kill myself for fear of some disaster that might be shaping up
before me, certainly I don't know what the disaster can be but I'm
wildly afraid of it, for the moment it's localized in the five vertebrae and I pray Lord Lord don't let this warmth rise to the cere-

bellum think what a catastrophe it would be here on the Siusi Alp
where there surely aren't any asylums, Lord O Lord I am not
worthy but help me all the same even against my father's will
Lord you ask him what he wants, and meanwhile my wife looks
at me and understands, if she's alert she always understands when
I'm beginning to feel sick, she sees it from the way my eyes go
blank or how I distort my mouth and gasp for breath or even from
how I move my fingers, in short there are many signs when I'm
afraid of being sick and if she watches out she notices them so she
sends the child away on a pretext giving her the purse and telling
her to go in and pay the bill, and after the baby has gone off she
says are you sick and I nod my head yes looking at her in despair,
and she says don't be afraid I'm here with you and I say yes with
my head, my mouth is dry and I'm afraid to speak my God what'll
I do if I'm sick here, my wife's here I know but it would be horrible all the same if I got sick, and my wife takes my hand and pats
it and says I love you so much, and I would like to say to her why
do you love me when you also know I'm going to go crazy my Lord
it wouldn't take much for me to be lost for good in this terror of
mine, and then why should she love me this girl who's so much
younger than me better for her to go away and take the baby with
her toward a happier life, and as I think of saying these things to
her I start crying of course, I feel the tears in my eyes about to
come down and then I get up to look for a bathroom to hide in, and
my wife wants to come with me but I say to her no no for heaven's
sake watch out for the baby she might get hurt, but she comes
with me all the same as I was secretly hoping and we both lock
ourselves in the bathroom and I sit down on the stool since there
isn't any other place to sit down and I start crying thank God
because when I cry so desperately I don't get such bad fears only
I feel sorry for myself because I'm a failure and this is bearable,
so I cry and I tell my wife she must leave me she can't ruin her
life with a failure who on top of everything else runs the risk of
going crazy she'd better find herself a rich man because I'm poor
I'll never manage to become rich and not even famous, I say all
this while I'm crying and my wife says she'll never leave me be-

cause I'm her whole life and she doesn't care if I'll never be rich but I mustn't think I'm a failure because I'm going to write the most beautiful book in the world, and she also cries as she says these things so I take her on my lap and we cry together gently now and even with a touch of humor because I can't help thinking with one part of my mind how funny these two people are locked in a toilet on the mountain and crying over the stool, anyway we cry liberatingly and after I've swallowed a couple of tranquilizers we go out and with the baby we walk toward the distant clearing where the car is and I try to keep myself weepy with some thought or other to save myself from more serious ills or so I believe, and in any case one sure thing is that I won't set foot on this miserable mountain again for the rest of my present life, I don't know about the future life because since I deserve hell they may even put me right here with all my sins, in any case patiently first on foot and then in the car down the fearful descent we reach our hotel and in view of my wife's state of acquiescence I consider risking the suggestion of leaving as soon as possible maybe even tomorrow since I always feel cockeyed with these mountains on my head in this absence of straight lines, but my wife doesn't know this and I don't really believe I can say it just like that, I wouldn't want her to be upset at this new phase that's come over me thanks to which I can't feel level even on floors that are honestly straight, inside myself I'm always tilting to one side or the other, there if I think about it I feel the floor of the room is crooked and to remedy this ailment I would need vast seaside horizons or flatlands, and instead here in the mountains thanks to the abnormal conformation of the terrain there is a scarcity of straight lines or a total lack of them so I am almost always thinking I tilt to left or right and in this way I am constantly exposed to attacks so I think I could hardly have landed in a worse place than this, and besides to get away I have to face that ugly descent in one direction or an even uglier one in the other I mean the Castelrotto road, there aren't any other roads if you except that infernal one that climbs up the Alp and ends, and then here another mania starts working the so-called claustrophobia thanks to which I feel a prisoner any-

place where there isn't an immediate possibility of escape, and
since this claustrophobia is an old story I can discuss it freely with
my wife and in reality I bring it up in support of my thesis that
it would be a good idea to get out of this Alpine locale right now,
however my wife dissents gently but firmly among other things a
guest who just got in this afternoon said that down below the heat
is literally killing, and in fact I know myself that everybody who
comes up especially husbands who come to visit wives and children insist that down below the heat is killing, however it may
well be that in this particular case it's true I mean the temperature
may have risen a lot since yesterday, and since as is only too
natural I am very afraid of the heat also when I think about it this
becomes a strengthening component of my claustrophobia, now
I'll have to see which is stronger the heat phobia or the phobia of
the mountain as prison and as almost total absence of straight
lines, moreover I try to remind myself that after all millions of
people have remained in cities like Milan and Naples and Rome
and even Palermo and Catania and except for some unusual cases
of sunstroke they manage to live decently despite the heat, however millions of people also are in the Alps and live there even
better according to them, and also according to my wife, and in
the long run the comparison between the conditions of those who
are up here and those who are down there isn't much help to me
in getting out of the dilemma in which I find myself, but it helps
my wife who decides that in the mountains I'll be better if I just
get it into my head to have myself treated properly, and since up
here there is this new psychiatrist friend of hers or aspiring psychiatrist why don't I take advantage of this at least for a visit or a
chat, and in fact the next day we go to see him in his hotel which
is much better than ours and I discover a boy I would call fairly
likeable if he didn't establish immediately an atmosphere of reciprocal distrust namely the feeling let's see now which of us is going
to screw the other, now of course this isn't anything surprising to
me inasmuch as I often have similar sensations at the first encounter with new doctors, and they aren't too harmful in fact in
the present instance they help me to recognize a doctor in this

youth with his pipe and yellow sweater and so just to give him an example of my upper-middle state of tension I tell him the sufferings undergone only yesterday on the Alp where my wife took me I would say by force, but he says at once that the signora was quite right to take me up there where the air is cool and fresh and I understand that this one for better or worse is always going to agree with my wife because she appeals to him shall we say and therefore I would be wise to cut it short with thanks a lot we'll meet some other time, but still it may be that this desire to agree with my wife is part of a system of treatment and in effect it would help to strengthen my faith in my wife which is something I need very much, so giving him the benefit of the doubt I continue conversing with him and he is affable and nonchalant although perhaps only apparently so since I can guess he is busy overcoming his worry at taking me on as a patient in this mountain area where presumably he is the only one who knows anything about psychiatry and therefore the responsibility is very big and might lead him to be over-prudent, on the other hand however he might also be driven to greater boldness at the thought that a doctor at the outset of his career rarely gets a chance like this, I can read all these thoughts in his mind while I talk to him of the defecation problem which is dramatic for me but he pays no attention to me because he is in the grip of larger problems, and it seems to me that at the end of this complicated inner struggle he makes up his mind that he better get down to business and not miss this experience which can be valuable for him, and in fact he illustrates to me a fairly meticulous plan of treatment with a new drug which in the psychiatric clinics has worked wonders in the sense that it has solved or almost solved cases which till now were insoluble, in a few words this is a treatment which in some ways replaces electroshock and is carried out according to a pre-established schedule with subcutaneous injections and with tiny pink pills to be swallowed with water first in increasing doses then decreasing, in short a business that is not without its fascination which moreover is in agreement with my old idea that the key to these nervous muddles is chemistry after all, and so I tell him yes with the tacit reservation that before I take any risky steps I will read that valuable literature enclosed with every drug in the form of generally encouraging explanatory folders, but as luck would have it when I read the folders inside both boxes the injections and the pills I can't understand a word, now you might say I have a fair experience of this literature and yet here I don't understand anything, they act on the reticulum but how they act on it isn't explained and besides I don't know what the reticulum is, I ask somebody who's going down to Bolzano to look it up in the encyclopedia in the library and he brings me a written answer to the effect that it is a delicate fibrous business like a cobweb that appeared in the cephalorachidian fluid in the course of tubercular meningitis, well we're doing fine if I'm not mistaken, on the other hand I've bought these brand-new medicines now and the store won't take them back especially since there isn't a pharmacy or *apotheke* as they're called locally so I had to send to Bolzano for the stuff, and thus I begin this interesting cure which lasts for three weeks I think including increasing phase acme and decrease, and these are three calamitous weeks in which I don't have one good day so that at a certain point I don't have much hope in this medicine which I fearlessly continue to introduce into my body both orally and through a Pravaz syringe used by a bona fide doctor now that I no longer trust local nurses to give me injections or those mature and helpful ladies who are to be found in every second-class hotel, now I insist that if anybody is going to stick a needle into my behind it must be a doctor with a degree and if possible a specialist since you never can tell with these chemical products and the theory of combinations, however this insistence costs good money and for this reason too I think it would be better to stop the cure which apparently only makes me feel worse, but my wife who is on the side of the young psychiatrist as much as he is on hers says I can't absolutely affirm that it makes me worse since I don't know how bad I would be without the cure, and this is a line of reasoning that adds up surprisingly well especially since my wife is somewhat backward in the field of logic and I imagine the same young doctor has inspired her here, the fact remains that also to avoid opposing her in her sentiments of friendship I complete the new cure amid anguish of every kind connected with a mountain called Sciliar which is apparently so beautiful that it deserves inclusion in almost all the picture post cards of Siusi, so it seems to be a kind of local pride but for me this Sciliar with its crooked looming mass has procured only mortal sufferings and to tell the truth when by some lucky chance I managed for a moment to forget I was sick this omnipresent Sciliar immediately reminded me and to escape its malign influence my only defense was to walk with my head down, however this was only a provisional solution and basically also dangerous just try walking for a quarter of an hour with your head down all the time and see if when you raise it you don't have a sensation of confusion, and since I already felt confused inside I never raised my head not even when I could be sure I wouldn't see Sciliar, in the dining room for example where however in the absence of the fatal mountain its depressing effect was still achieved by any number of people both vacationers and South Tyrolean waitresses, and to make a long story short I was in a state where I didn't look anybody in the face any more and I was constantly swaying between grim desperation which among other things was something that the new medicine had promised to cure and slightly less grim desperation when in the rare moments of calm I reminded myself that one of these days I was bound to go down that disastrous mountain and back to Rome where I would immediately feel better and in three or four hours of work daily or maybe even at night I would soon break the barrier of that fourth chapter, however when the moment of calm passed I quickly realized that these were impossible fantasies and in reality I had never been so sick as I was in that period, two or three times I had even come close to big attacks of terror walking up and down along a hall with a pine flooring with all those lines that aren't exactly straight the way pine wood's grain goes, and obviously what with the really crooked lines and the ones I imagined crooked I ran the risk of losing my bearings and in fact I began to feel my head swimming and cardioplegic numbness but above all a warmth around the lumbars, and since at the

end of the corridor there was a balcony with a big view I often
said to myself that with a little jump I would probably solve my
every earthly problem, and sometimes I even went out on the balcony to calculate if the jump would be sufficient to cause death
however it was a mistake for me to go outside where there was
an incalculable quantity of crooked lines ready to attack me culminating in the baleful Sciliar, so in the final analysis that stay in
the Alps which I had placed so much hope in was an outright
disaster also because the defecation problem persisted not of
course in the sense that after three whole weeks I hadn't yet had
what is with obvious exaggeration also called relief, however I
believe that the expulsion of excrement especially if laborious
presents difficulties for anybody in a second-class hotel and especially on the fourth floor where Franz Josef's stool seems the
toilet preferred by all since you barely have time to sit down when
immediately a procession of people in a hurry come and rattle the
doorknob and maybe even grumble or knock when they find the
door shut, and I had become reduced to doing that painful duty
at night every five or six days using the baby's suppositories and
with a handkerchief stuffed in my mouth to stifle the groans which
otherwise would have waked up the whole hotel, and with my wife
outside the door in her bathrobe asking me for news at brief intervals to make sure I hadn't fainted, and in short this period of
what you might call holidays was really disastrous from almost
every point of view, but what could I do if my wife said that going
back to Rome would be a disaster not only for me but also for the
baby who in a couple of years would start school and therefore
had to build herself up, and besides every fool who arrived there
said you're so lucky the heat down below is sheer murder, it was
September and the few people who came up by then kept on saying the same things, already the town had assumed its autumnal
aspect which for neurotics if not for others is even less favorable
than its summer look, the future psychiatrist too had gone off to
his beloved studies, but my wife wouldn't give in she said that for
anybody who really loves the mountains September is the most
beautiful month, however I didn't love the mountains my God my

wife didn't seem prepared to grant me this right not to love the
mountains, so after various quarrels I resolved to go off by myself,
and then as I could easily have predicted my wife at the last moment seeing that I wasn't going to leave her more than twenty
thousand lire anyway decided that we all had to stay together and
she kept me waiting for a couple of hours while she prepared the
enormous quantity of packages and bundles and sacks and suit-
cases which almost completely filled the car to the extent that my
daughter had to travel part of the way on her mother's lap and
part of the way squeezed in the back under the roof which had to
remain up because it was cold, even down below it was cold by
now, and the next day we reached Rome and our house bare but
roomy and with a bathroom almost entirely at my disposal, and
maybe also for this reason I seemed to feel well often I caught
myself singing Like the moon I'm a vagabond or else Come with
me sweet flower of May while I shaved, I bet I'm cured I said to
myself, it was all the mountains' fault I should have guessed it
but now I am really well and I'll start chasing producers and
directors and famous script-writers to see if I can't snatch some
crumb from this shaky banquet table of the Italian cinema, by
now the nest egg I had set aside for my glory had almost all gone
in mountain idleness and injections and medicines however thank
God it wasn't as I had feared money poured down the drain if it's
true that I'm pretty well and now in the daytime I'll work to make
my daily bread but in the evening instead of going to see idiotic
movies or playing canasta with people removed from all spiritual
interests I'll sit down at the typewriter and it only takes a couple
of pages per evening in a year that makes some seven hundred odd
pages, I believe that not many masterpieces are more than seven
hundred pages long and in any case in two years they will be one
thousand four hundred and I imagine not even *War and Peace* is
that long, so summing things up I feel regenerated and obviously
that new medicine in the long run has done me good, and the
stay in the mountains too, if nothing else it has trained me to resist
bad influences, or so I think abandoning myself trustingly to an
unusual optimism, and a week goes by during which I more and

more fervidly imagine that I have begun a new life, *Incipit vita nova* I say to myself frequently also to link myself ideally to a person that I respect quite a bit, and then bang one Monday morning that obscure and diabolical mechanism snaps treacherously and before I can say My God my God I am swept away by anguish and fears, and currents of cold and warmth all mixed up and overlapping, and frightful twistings of the guts but without pain this time as if they were the guts of another person only I feel them moving around my belly with a dragon's ponderous steps, and on the contrary the testicular glands hurt terribly mysteriously stirring, and the five vertebrae also hurt and burn of course, in short I had never felt anything so terrifying not even the first two times which began the catastrophes had been so fearsome, and in this way I achieve a new record in these sufferings for the splitting is no longer arcane or abstract as at other times but visual or at least hallucinatory, that is to say I manage to see my brain outside my body with all the bloody spirals that brains generally have and somehow very similar in appearance to the cancer extracted from the viscera of my father, only this exposed brain of mine isn't death and cancer it is fear of the abyss and darkness beyond death, so quite rightly it seems to me I start saying ah I'm crazy there it is my crazy brain, my wife is present and she doesn't see it of course, to tell the truth she doesn't even look where I tell her the brain is and yet it is there I see it very clearly, and she starts crying poor thing she doesn't know what to do, this time she doesn't know what to do because I don't pay any attention to her and I say I'm crazy and my brain's already removed from me, and she cries and cries saying don't be like this darling don't don't, and I would like not to be however I don't feel anything for her nothing at all there's just me and my fugitive brain and the active memory of that carcinoma that's what I am, my wife doesn't exist no woman exists not even my daughter except for a residue of desire not to have begotten her, Oh had she never been born, and this woman here weeps and implores me and says tell me what I can do tell me, and I want to go to the asylum I say take me to the asylum, and she weeps still more and says no if you go to the

asylum I'll never see you again look at me at least, and I look at
her with some effort but even above her I see my mad brain and
I think what does it take for a person to die what does it take, tell
me father see how I'm in agony sweating blood and with the
trembling of death and not even death's liberation, Oh I can't go
on I want to go crazy really crazy if I have my wife here kneeling
in front of me and crying and beseeching me, and here thank God
I begin to feel a bit of pity for her, and also for myself of course,
my hopes are over my work is over, I'll kill myself let me kill
myself but don't say anything to the baby, swear she will never
know you can tell her I'm dead but not dead like this, and now
I finally start to cry, this fearful knot of terror begins to dissolve
into tears, it's a relief to cry and to let myself be shaken by sobs
after such anguish and tension, to weep and to say I don't know
anything and to say I want to die let me die, and to hear her weeping and to be united like this in despair and suffering as in love,
my wife my consolation, I tremble and I weep in her arms saying
how awful it was I never suffered anything that awful before,
my God if it happens to me again what can I do tell me what can I
do, and she says sorrowfully it won't happen I'm here it won't
happen, and I hug her and kiss her with gratitude and love, and
little by little also with desire, and as I hold her she is yielding
in her body and in her spirit, and I think you want to bet that after
such a terrible disaster now we make love, but why not what does
the rest matter, and she says no no darling maybe it's better not
to standing there with her mouth open and her spirit which is
warmth and desire spreading through every part of her body, and
when we've reached this point we certainly can't put up any resistance to such a need to make love although I feel that the act of
carnal love has a great sense of sin still attached to it from the first
time it happened they say in the garden of paradise, and naturally
if there is sin there will also be penance that's one axiom you can't
escape so as I fulfill this now inevitable operation of possession
and together we feel the pleasure that unites me to her and her
to me I hold so to speak in reserve a nasty presentiment of proportionate future calamities, or rather I advance along two tracks

one of which is pleasure and the other is all bitter prophecies and as I thrust this love towards its rapid conclusion I am mentally bartering my sufferings and my non-glory and disease, until when the climax is reached I also barter death for it, and so then beyond the orgasm solitude remains and the waiting for divine punishment, and much commiseration for the glory that will never come and the disease that will remain forever.

Then a rather mixed-up and feverish period begins as far as my health is concerned, to say nothing of money since we have already reached the point of making debts despite the aversion of the person who gave me life for such forms of liability, and meanwhile when I'm able to I go around looking for work and especially for advances and so I come to meet some new producers, for example one who sits at his desk with behind him on the wall a large portrait in bright oils depicting himself dressed as an ancient Roman emperor with haughty mien and triumphal laurel crown on his head, so I logically foresee that he'll give me something to do in the line of Sodomites or rebel slaves to put together with a lot of scantily clad dancing girls because these producers know that the ancient Romans most of the time were having orgies, and instead he digs me out a story entitled if I remember rightly *Bigbreast* which takes place in our own time presumably in a depressed area in the South, and Bigbreast is the nickname of a poor prostitute who aspires to redemption but the rich bad men prevent her and in the end set fire to her, and while I listen to this beautiful story I can only think of my wife who is always saying to me get smart, and for that matter if you look at the plots of the stories of Shake-

speare or Tolstoy or any other really great writer you can see that
they're the same as any soap opera, it's all in the way they develop
stories like *Resurrection* or *Macbeth*, meanwhile however the ancient Roman emperor is explaining to me the profound message
of his story *Bigbreast* and he says I mustn't make any changes
but only develop it in an up-to-date way with plenty of sex and violence and sociology like the *nouvelle vague* if I follow him, however no pornography because otherwise there's trouble getting
credit from the Banca del Lavoro, anyhow seeing that the story
after all ends up with a great purifying burning at the stake like
Joan of Arc's I have to figure out without lessening the spectacular
side a way to keep the picture from being banned to those under
sixteen, and while we're on the subject if I have any good friends
at the Catholic Film Center it might be a good idea for me to contact them, and I say to myself get smart and I tell him that I have
several good friends at the Catholic Film Center so he needn't
worry, moreover this story which is so full of suffering and psychology is right in line with my talents as a writer and I have
always dreamed of writing something really important for the
movies and until now I'd never had the opportunity but now
thanks to him here is my chance, so if he'll give me a million in
advance I'll start work right away since by a lucky break I don't
have any other jobs on at the moment, and in fact I dropped that
figure with great nonchalance as if I weren't accustomed to considering sums with less than six zeroes, but the emperor looks at
me really alarmed and says frankly that he isn't prepared for such
a heavy sum since the over-all budget of the picture has to be kept
low, immediately after this picture he's going to make another
with a budget of at least a billion and then he will of course give
me a million in advance or even two if I prefer but for this picture
where the story is already blocked out and all I have to do is make
a few adjustments of slight importance he was thinking that a
hundred and fifty would be enough, and at this point it's all very
well for me to say to myself get smart think of your wife but in
the present situation who knows what getting smart consists in, I
mean if it's taking this hundred and fifty thousand an insulting

but after all necessary sum or insisting on a million or even half
a million at the risk of losing the whole job, anyhow I say why
Commendatore for a hundred and fifty I'd go and write for TV,
and my heart aches because the truth is that with the TV I don't
make any hundred and fifty in fact I don't make anything at all
because I don't have any guardian angel there who'll give me
work, however the angels in heaven who haven't helped me with
the TV now are moved to give me a hand with this ancient emperor who at the end of laborious *pourparlers* lasting a couple of
days finally gives me a check for three hundred thousand which
on being taken straight to the bank turns out to be covered, and
now here I come to grips with the preliminary script of this *Bigbreast* which from what I can tell is not in the ranks of those films
that finally come off because the ancient Roman producer before
giving me any more money is going to wait for the distributors
who on the basis of the magnificent script that I'm to write he expects to shell out let's say a hundred million or so as a minimum
guarantee but I'm not such a fool as to give him a whole script for
three hundred thousand so in a short while the deal will run
aground as it has already done I would bet at least twenty times
before it arrived by chance in my hands, in any case one thing is
sure namely that whatever happens I will never see a lira more
than the three hundred thousand already received and so I set
to work with what I would call inadequate enthusiasm following
pretty much the story and the ideas furnished me, therefore I begin the story with a fine village procession band leading and landowners and dignitaries and all the population but they don't want
the prostitute and it's the dignitaries who drive her away also
offending her deep religious feeling, and then that evening these
same men whom we saw so devout and pious are now drunk and
they go to the hovel where she lives with all her starving little
brothers and they force her to dance half naked and then to lie in
sin on the cot before the tearful eyes of the children, I really think
that at a later date we'll have to cut out the little brothers because
of the Catholic Film Center however with her half-naked dance
and the rest any good director can create a magnificent sequence

it's all in the way he shoots it, anyhow in the meanwhile it's best for me to go on sniffing around for other jobs and I pick up an advance of two hundred thousand with a story that still has to be worked out about our war amid the sands of North Africa, but the basic idea is there already and it's about this prostitute from Benghazi who flees on a camel from the city occupied by the English and reaches our lines where she disguises herself as a soldier and fights gloriously and other things until she dies offering her heroic breast to the enemy's bullets, and then I open a discussion with a third producer and here I have to be very careful not to make a misstep because this is a very big producer who makes at least five or six pictures a year some of them even in co-production with America, in short if I can get into his good graces I'm all set therefore I don't even ask him for an advance so he won't think I'm hard up for cash, and besides he asks me to do a treatment on a high level very serious although here too as luck would have it there's a prostitute of the fields whose name is Mila di Codro, sure enough it's the deservedly famous melodrama by Gabriele D'Annunzio entitled *The Daughter of Jorio* and I'm sincerely rather pleased that a producer should think of making a film of *The Daughter of Jorio* whose author though at present disliked by the radicals is nevertheless a poet, so I set to work with a dedication that I might call excessive and in two weeks I have a really substantial outline practically speaking a half treatment with all the sequence of events in order and the psychological development and the rest of it, and then I tell myself it's time to get smart and therefore I ask for an audience with the big producer to show him the fifty-odd pages I've written and to ask him for an advance, and after having compiled my little request form to be received the way you do in ministries I wait for a whole afternoon sitting in a corridor where actresses and actors and directors of international repute go by, and in the end when he manages to receive me the producer is very tired or rather first he asks me what I want and when I tell him I came for an advance then he tells me he is very tired and he won't even manage to kiss his children before they go to bed and haven't I seen all the comings and goings all day long, and I certainly have seen comings and goings however I would be happy if he gave me an advance not that I need money of course but as a sign of his satisfaction with my work, and he is a big producer with all sorts of deals in his head so he doesn't even remember what this work is, and I say why *The Daughter of Jorio* by D'Annunzio don't you remember saying that if the script turns out well you're going to give the picture to De Sica or to a big American director like John Huston, and he says oh yes how silly of me I'd forgotten and then he says I have to forgive him but he finished school a long time ago and of course he knows quite well what this *Daughter of Jorio* is but maybe I'd better just give him a quick run-down on it since he's so tired, and trying to infuse a genuine warmth into my words and leafing through the fifty-page outline which I hold under his nose as closely as possible so he can see how much I've worked I tell him the whole story from beginning to end including the changes and embellishments I'm suggesting, and in the end he looks at me stunned and says where is Jorio and I say to him what do you mean where is Jorio and he insists on knowing more about this Jorio but what can I tell him except that he's her father, this Jorio doesn't appear in the play at all, and then he says I must be crazy if I think he's going to make a picture called *The Daughter of Jorio* without any Jorio and he is really angry with me about this oversight which if anything is D'Annunzio's, so angry or rather indignant that he dismisses me rudely without giving me a lira naturally, and this was a real screwing after two weeks of almost serious work and in a period when it certainly wasn't easy for me after that big attack had left me exhausted in body and spirit, and other attacks however slight had followed and had gradually driven me from one abstraction to another to the fear of fear, psychopathological phase I would call intermediate and to my mind not entirely negative since as long as one suffers from fear of a cancer or a heart attack or some other physical ill it is just considered a disease, whereas the fear of fear is metaphysical, I mean not associated with ailments not even unusual ones like extraordinary nervous fibers reserved for me alone which start materially from the lumbars or the second curve of the colon and end up at the heart or the cerebellum, a hypothesis whose correctness can only be established after my death if anybody cares, anyhow this pure fear which becomes disease excluding cancers and heart attacks and so on is in the long run a big step forward although not from every point of view to tell the truth, and in reality with a heart attack or a cancer you can also foresee the end imminent or otherwise as many examples show or else with tests and careful examinations doctors can establish if only temporarily that the disease doesn't exist but the fear of fear is mysterious and omnipresent, it eludes X rays and histological examinations so no outside person can understand if it's there or not until it explodes in all too evident manifestations such as pallor or tachycardia or diarrhea and then even the stupidest doctor manages to understand that there's something wrong, but unfortunately this fear doesn't always take the obvious route and often it remains in the form of abstract fear or it ends up in the lumbar warmth or testicular commotion and in these cases it's easy to find doctors who say that the warmth is just an impression of mine and that everybody's testicles move about some, and thus you remain alone to meditate on your private misfortunes trying to figure them out somehow and this is what comforts you in the end, the persistence of this demand for clarification, I mean all is not lost with me if the desire to see things clearly survives which is in a sense a will to be cured or at least not a total abandonment to the disease, for in this case it would be dementia whose peculiar characteristic as everyone knows is incurability, whereas a cure for my troubles is still possible it seems though costly, and in reality this desire to see things clearly is translated into an almost incessant search for new doctors all specialists naturally, because now both my wife and I are oriented towards the specialists who cost ten thousand a visit at the very least, which isn't an outrageous price when you consider the fame of these luminaries, and their authority maybe even internationally and finally when you consider the time they spend on the examinations because you have to concede that these are very long processes whether they adopt the knee-tapping system or what you might call the physiological approach or whether on the contrary they adopt the entirely interior system of examination since in this final case I start in with the story of my troubles and obviously I don't stop in a hurry.

Anyhow this is pretty much a period of travail and confusion that I'm going through, in this constant focusing on the disease and the resultant change of doctors, and to tell the truth there is a greater psychological value than you would think in the process of shifting your trust from a doctor who no longer deserves it to another who still hasn't demonstrated that he doesn't deserve it, so the approach to the new doctor willy-nilly always has some benefit I mean for a couple of days if not longer I think that very soon I'll start in on the fourth chapter which meanwhile is ripening inside me, and then I feel that the beautiful things of the world are reaching me with their enlivening force whether they are sunsets or the warm cloudy wind in winter when the sirocco comes or girls especially in the spring or the green of the countryside when the sun is low or even the Piazza Navona and the view from the Pincio of the Eternal City, and then I tell myself maybe I've hit on the right doctor and I'll regain the joy of living and the ability to work, however the fact is that these benefits are always precarious in the sense that for one reason or another the new doctor soon loses his professional authority and thaumaturgical power, and this happens inevitably either because he does and says exactly the same things the other doctors have done and said with no positive results, or else because he is a person completely without true prestige and at times even without intelligence, or because it is obvious beyond the shadow of a doubt that this person's sole aim is to drag things out, or because he is so full of ambition and self-satisfaction that he thinks only of himself and of telling himself how smart he is and then I am constantly forced to start the whole story over again from the beginning and I become depressed when I perceive how things I've already explained at length during the preceding visit arouse in the luminary the same amount of polite wonder that they aroused before, in short the fact is that my doctors during this period undergo a rapid turnover so much so that I could even avoid paying them if I were smart, however I'm not smart my God not even this progressive clarification and spiritualization of my disease succeed in making me smart, rather you could say that they make me more and dumb I mean more attached to the petty bourgeois concept of honesty inherited directly from my father so that it becomes a positive spiritual joy to give thirty or forty thousand lire to a quack who doesn't deserve it, anyhow as things go on like this the rapid turnover finally stops producing any effect and then little by little I'm reconverted to an idea that first came to me a year and a half ago, which is that I mustn't go to any doctor at all except for the neighborhood doctor who when I tell him what certain of his colleagues have said or done to me generally sighs and shakes his head or laughs indifferently, it's all too clear he isn't very much in favor of psychiatry above a certain level of specialization instead he is for simple and concrete things like a good intravenous course of calciophosphates, he is always wanting to give me these intravenous injections as if I paid him for them, and instead I tell him that if he wants my opinion these intravenous injections still have to be perfected their immediacy already made me suspicious when I was well not to mention now when my exhaustion or neurosis has brought me to this acute repugnance for possible chemical combinations with the result that I eat nothing but vegetable broth, chopped spinach, fresh cheese and a number of cooked apples, I remain strictly faithful to this kind of nourishment which I might define as bland however the trouble is that I can eat what I like but if I have sins to expiate nothing is going to save me from expiating them, and I have committed plently of sins all too many especially against the sixth commandment, at times thinking as I sinned of defying the demons or even God directly since in the act of pleasure maybe even solitary pleasure as happens in youth a man is as powerful as God since he is enjoying the fruit of the tree that stands in the middle of the garden, truthfully speaking in the moment of pleasure man makes himself immortal destroying the value of the future, instead pleasure passes and the future remains more and more compromised by the burden of these ethical debts which it is then difficult to pay, and in fact now these pleasures many of them downright provocatory have fallen due like so many accumulated promissory notes, and this is really how this obscure disease has grown in me and now I am watching out to see where it will strike me to make me expiate my sins, I even reach the point where I say to it strike me here or there according to my momentary preferences, since it has also turned out that the vagueness and spiritualization of the disease have run their course, I'm tired of fighting fancies and abstractions, now I want this disease if it exists to become concrete in plausible forms, and so a bit each day I manage to localize a nice cancer of the stomach which however might also conveniently be located a little lower down namely in the second large curve of the colon although at the moment the pains turn up chiefly in the stomach, in any case with a gastric or visceral cancer whichever it is there isn't much to rejoice about and in fact I am very sad and I don't work any more not even on scripts about rebel slaves and prostitutes who aren't redeemed because of our unhealthy society, now I stay in bed all day long with my hands over my belly feeling my cancer gnawing away and if by any chance I get up and go out I scare people with my wild eyes only a bit softened by the knowledge that I am going off in the most unfair way imaginable, and anyway what would be the use of my going out when now I can't even go to Ciampino any more to see the jets that fly off about the world because Ciampino is far away and if by any chance the disease suddenly took a turn back toward those abstract terrors I wouldn't have a doctor handy, to tell the truth I've established a fine network of aspiring young psychiatrists in training or assistants to this or that luminary who have remained friends even after my rupture in many cases clamorous with their chief and at times for this very reason, and now when I go out I always carry in my pocket the list of their names and addresses and telephone numbers so that if I can't find one I can surely find another, however I haven't been able to find one who lives at

Ciampino or in that neighborhood and so now my diversion of
watching the jets coming and going is impossible the jets from
New York or Tokyo or Johannesburg where I certainly can't go
but it's enough for me to see them land or take off, and if you except Ciampino I don't have any other place where I enjoy going
and for that matter just tell me what's the fun in walking along the
Corso or the Via Tritone with the fine thought that you could
drop dead or at least go crazy at every step, so I prefer to stay
home in bed with a stomach-ache and the various suppositions
connected with it, however this fact doesn't make a good impression and everybody is worried at my increasing surrender to the
disease, and more than anybody else my wife seems concerned
by now she knows better than me that I can't face this thing
alone this cancer and fear, so a way out has to be found that
is somebody who can help me or better who can take my place
and assume responsibility, and you can be sure I'm not opposed
to this principle and in fact it must not be forgotten that once
when I wasn't so far gone I was caught off guard and I threw
myself on the mercies of a traffic cop who when you think about
it isn't even a carabiniere, and so my wife and our young psychiatrist friends begin to discuss various solutions which however since everything was on a serious level insofar as possible
in this field boiled down to two i.e. go into the hospital for a
nice series of electroshock treatments which sometimes succeed
in fixing up misfortunes like mine at least temporarily unless of
course it's cancer, or else follow that cure which to tell the truth
is a bit long and drawn out which many people are talking about
now especially ladies who have been in America or have seen
American movies dealing with the subject quite superficially in
reality as for that matter certain of our novelists have dealt with
it for them the psychoanalytical touch is given by the fact that
Antonio as a little boy pulled the cat's tail and this explains why
when he was big he became perverse and a Fascist, so there is
this psychoanalysis cure which holds an undeniable fascination
and moreover it seems to do you good if you follow it seriously,
or so our friends say the ones who are in favor of psychoanalysis,

and naturally the decision about these two treatments in a sense opposed to each other is up to me, however clearly it's up to me only insofar as I am capable of making such an important decision in my present state, and in fact from the way my wife talks with our psychiatrist friends in whispers but at the same time without any prudence and giving me glances sideways the way they used to do in silent movies or on the stage of La Scala before Luchino Visconti started directing operas there I realize that this decision about the cure I'm to take is a decision they're going to try to make behind my back and frankly speaking I don't give a damn, how can a man who has a cancer in his guts give a damn whether they put him through electroshock or psychoanalysis, however, there can be some moments during a day especially after I've taken some belladonna when the cancer doesn't hurt so much and then I can pretend I don't have it and cry softly over my definitive inability to go beyond the third chapter, or else with the help of some angel in heaven I can feel less pessimistic and think one of these days I'll write that damn chapter, and at such moments of intellectual aggressiveness though they are rare I realize I can write the famous chapter only with my brain which therefore becomes an organ requiring maximum attention and which I can't let them slam around empirically with electric current running the risk of putting it out of commission whereas it seems that psychoanalysis doesn't damage an artist's creative capacities in fact you might say it enhances them as is proved *ad abundantiam* by the case of Italo Svevo whom it would be my ambition to resemble if it weren't for the detail that I'm afraid of smoking whereas he based all of his problems of conscience on the last cigarette which was never then the last one, however it may be that if I'm cured I'll take up smoking again, I'll take up smoking and writing together I say, so all things considered and with the future in mind it's better for me to decide on psychoanalysis and not electroshock.

Now rather strangely I'd say it happens that my wife and our young psychiatrist friends and also the neighborhood doctor obviously have reached the same conclusion namely that in my case psychoanalysis if preferable, and I'm willing to bet that the merit of this basically respectful decision can be attributed largely to my wife who must have said to herself we better be careful with that brain of his because who knows one of these days he may manage to write this masterpiece he's always yammering about, and to tell the truth I am thinking that for a girl like her not insensitive to spiritual values it would be a real swindle to have united herself matrimonially with a character without money or health and moreover incapable of winning for himself and his loved ones any sort of celebrity or fame, anyhow once this psychoanalytical decision is made it is only the first step because immediately thereafter other more detailed decisions are required, namely whether we want a Jungian analyst with a complex psychology or a Freudian who tends more to pansexualism, and in the latter case whether a member of the Viennese school or the Swiss or the English is preferred since in our country it seems the American school isn't much considered, and on all these problems there are arguments sometimes quite animated ones which to me buried in my pains and huddled in bed seem like arguments over the funeral arrangements outside the dying man's door, and in reality I've only converted myself to this psychoanalysis business to avoid a worse fate so I'm without any profound conviction also because all I know about the subject is the little I've learned through Svevo and if I understand rightly the therapeutic result of the business is depicted as very slight in the amusing novel that tells about Zeno, and starting with this inadequate cultural preparation obviously I don't give a damn about schools and tendencies the only thing I insist on is a man who is upright and honest by God, it seems necessary to find a man with these qualities which we all know are rare nowadays whereas in my father's time perhaps they weren't so rare, anyhow when this wish of mine is known which is also a *sine qua non* condition the young psychiatrist friends begin to talk to me about a man who seems to possess the qualities I demand, and moreover is a specialist in the field since he goes to all the international congresses the Freudian ones of course since he belongs to the traditional branch of the science, and they swear that in Rome at least if not in all Italy there isn't a better man than this one, in short since I can now no longer get out of bed not even in my best hours I tell them to make an appointment with this exceptional psychoanalyst, and I go and I find myself facing a little old man rather short and all things considered somewhat scrawny as to physique who looks at me of course in an open and friendly way however I'm not exactly a novice who can be taken in by such tricks which many doctors before him have tried at first meeting, and besides this one just in saying please have a seat displays a strong Southern accent my God a hick I say to myself and I wasn't prepared for this, what I was expecting I don't know or rather I know perfectly well now but at that time only my unconscious knew and required that this old man not at all tall and something of a disappointment to look at should at least have a mythic voice, or to be frank the voice my father had in my remote infantile recollections, and since the doctor's voice was nothing of the sort there I was full of discontent and even distrust and instead of returning his open gaze I sit there staring at the top of the desk and in addition I wring my hands and obviously don't know what to say to him, but then with sudden grumpiness and an abrupt wish to bring things right out into the open I confess to him that since my father first of all seems to have bequeathed me a pleasure in being honest I feel it's my duty to tell him I don't believe much in psychoanalysis, no more than Svevo believed in his time in any case, and that if I'm here in his office it's more out of desperation than conviction, a kind of surrender no doubt, but the least dangerous one possible in view of the masterpiece I still had to write, however in my present condition it was not only hard for me to write but even to live so he might as well go ahead, and this was in fact why I had come giving him complete freedom, in other words I didn't even demand too much concern about any possible psychical and intellectual transformations since the masterpiece to be sincere was a kind of hide-and-seek game between me and my misfortune, I mean I had managed for better or worse to write three chapters and maybe they weren't even too bad but then the thing had got stuck there and it was quite improbable that it would go any farther since I needed hope to go on as well as my health and all things considered the two were the same thing, but I didn't have much of either, anyhow these matters were a bit too tangled up to explain then and there and for me the important thing was to inform him of my serious worry about the cost of this psychoanalysis, they had already told me that the treatments was going to last a couple of years at least however I wasn't at all sure I would get to the end, or rather I would go on with it as long as I had money to spend and then that would be that, since my father didn't allow me to incur debts even though he had been dead now for some years, and besides I knew very well it was not customary to incur debts with psychoanalysts this had been told me for certain, anyhow if he succeeded in straightening me out a bit I would start working again here and there since the movie industry contrary to every reasonable forecast had not collapsed, and when I was working of course I would have the money to pay him and therefore to continue the treatment, in short it was a kind of chain like so many other things in this world maybe everything, anyhow he shouldn't misunderstand me or believe that I thought straightening me out was a simple affair, especially since I wasn't at all sure of the kind of disease that had attacked me, that is from a certain point of view it was unquestionably an exhaustion or rather a neurosis but from another viewpoint one could very well believe that since I had this awful pain in my stomach it was a big cancer and this latter misfortune seemed very probable to me since my father had had one exactly like it which had brought him to his grave, and in this case I certainly didn't ask him to cure me but I wanted him some way or other to spare me suffering, and in fact it would be best to eliminate this suffering or at least attenuate it in the event that it wasn't a cancer but colitis as many previously consulted doctors thought, and he who had listened to me till then without saying a word now calmly said that I was to get the idea of cancer out of my head, I didn't have cancer and not even colitis as an organic disease, I wasn't sick

in the colon but in my psyche and in other words it was neurosis
that gave me a stomach-ache and not vice versa as I might think,
and if by any chance I did have colitis I could also treat it taking
aspirin if the pain was too great and avoiding the wrong sort of
food which was milk cheeses fruit and green vegetables, and so
I learned that in recent times I had been nourishing myself entirely with the wrong things with all the doctors I had around me
and now this little old man was telling me I'd be better off if I
ate like everybody else, for instance I could even eat spaghetti
all' amatriciana if I liked it, and then I left his office and started
home with my wife who had come to pick me up and who kept
saying tell me tell me what he said and I kept my mouth shut and
she said he must have told you something you were in there
for an hour and I said he didn't say anything, but I was fairly
pleased and I was thinking of spaghetti *all' amatriciana* and was
saying to myself tonight I'll go out to dinner and eat a double
portion, so I was again charged with vital energy after this first
psychoanalytical encounter and in a sense I felt that if I overcame the test of the spaghetti maybe I would overcome other
even more serious ones, and in the meanwhile my wife was saying you must have said bad things about me to him you always
say bad things about me to everybody, and then I told her I had
forgotten to mention her to him or rather the opportunity hadn't
come up, and I realized that for her this psychoanalyst was already
irrevocably condemned but on the other hand I couldn't tell her
things that weren't true or even true things which it seemed
best to keep from her, and so to let her share at least partially
in that conversation she was so curious about I told her he had
said I could eat whatever I liked except for milk cheeses fruits and
green vegetables which I was to make up for with vitamin pills,
and that night we would eat out spaghetti *all' amatriciana*, but
when she made a face because she really doesn't like spaghetti
much I said all right we'll go to Riano and I'll eat noodles with
meat sauce and you can have the chicken *alla diavola*, and I mentioned Riano on purpose because it's a few miles outside Rome
maybe fifteen or even less, and I said to myself if you have the

courage to eat noodles with meat sauce you'll also have the courage to go to Riano, but as it turned out toward evening my
courage failed me and we had to make three or four phone calls
before we found one of those young assistant psychiatrists who
was willing to go to Riano to dinner, and while we were at table
I naturally had to tell what I had said to the psychoanalyst and
what the psychoanalyst had said to me, although when you think
about it there wasn't much to tell and in fact between the two of
us nothing worth reporting had happened except of course my
impressions, however on sober reflection it was best for me to keep
these to myself since they were feelings which if exposed might
even seem ridiculous, namely my expectation that the little man
who might have been born anywhere even in the country below
Rome should speak with a Veneto accent and that he should
be at least two feet taller than he was simply because my father
when he was alive had been a couple of feet taller than the doctor,
all of this when you think about it had nothing to do with the
analysis as such nor with a fair evaluation of the person to whom
unless other factors intervened to change my mood I planned to
show reverence and obedience in all seriousness as I was already
showing by eating a big dish of homemade noodles with a sauce
of chicken livers, but then the next day I had a terrible pain in
the stomach and almost went out of my mind with suffering and
the drama of interminable defecations, my God Oh father I said
I'll never eat noodles with meat sauce again and naturally I planned
having a clear discussion on the subject with my little old man
whose prestige was already seriously undermined by the dubious
success of his dietary suggestions, and in fact when I went back
to him I told him with great firmness about my terrible stomach-
ache and my fear of losing my mind over it, however he calmly
observed that it was better to have an attack of colitis for what
we might call mechanical causes than for psychical causes, and
anyhow I wasn't to fear anything because I wasn't in any danger
except naturally of an anxiety attack, and I said to him you say
an anxiety attack is nothing but if I have another one I'm afraid
I'm going to go crazy for good, and without changing his sage's

attitude though his accent was still Southern he answered that
he well knew how frightening attacks of anxiety were, he even
agreed that in all likelihood there was no worse suffering in the
world however if it was madness I was afraid of there was one
thing he could guarantee me which was that I wouldn't go mad
because I couldn't, but even though his words were inviting and
moreover pronounced in a tone of benevolent persuasion I listened
to them with the suspicion you feel when you think somebody
might be telling you stories thinking to help you go mad without
making a fuss about it, to tell the truth after having just been
burned in the matter of the noodles I wasn't all that disposed to
believe in him, anyhow since I was there and I certainly couldn't
go on and on about my stomach-ache I began to tell him generically the history of my misfortunes taking as point of departure
the hematuria and continuing with the books under the legs of
the bed and the famous colic that brought me into the hands of
those doctors who had cut me up for nothing though not gratis,
and every so often he made little sounds of displeasure with his
mouth but more often he had a look as if he were subtly amused at
so many extraordinary coincidences which without exaggeration
could be ascribed to the evil eye, and I bet that secretly he was
more than a little amused also by the colossal blunders made by
his colleagues the doctors of the body whereas he a doctor of the
soul wouldn't make any blunders I could see this clearly in his
honest face, and naturally I wasn't very much amused myself that
is I admitted there might be a certain humorous aspect to my mis-
adventures and if they hadn't been mine I would have been the
first to smile at them but since unfortunately they were mine I
didn't derive any great fun from them, however as often happens
a person always takes some satisfaction in finding himself in the
center of adventures even if they aren't nice, and then the next
time I told him about my father's death and the lousy thing I had
done leaving him alone at the moment of his dying and naturally
I tried to tell all this to the doctor with a certain casualness as far
as possible so as not to display any cheap sentimentalism in front
of him, but then when I reached the moment of the death almost

abruptly I start crying, I'm ashamed of crying in front of this old man who after all doesn't know me very well but this story of my father dying abandoned by his son is certainly a tearful story, and surely no son ever behaved toward a father with worse ingratitude and so all the spectacular misfortunes that have rained down on me so far and the even bigger ones that are bound to befall me are no more than I deserve, and it would be much more honest if I gave up trying to cure myself it's all the same anyhow even if I'm cured and in the final analysis the only thing I'm sorry about is a book I would have liked to write properly and in fact had already started as far as the third chapter and it stopped there and hasn't progressed farther, in short I was making with this old man one of those scenes you might call disgraceful that I generally made when I was alone or at most in my wife's company, and this thing obviously annoyed me however when I had finished he acted as if nothing had happened and started to explain to me calmly that psychoanalysis is an effective treatment for some diseases and ineffectual for others, and moreover it generally doesn't work miracles but limits itself to seeking the causes usually remote of our anxieties and fears and makes us aware of them so that we aren't afraid any more or are less afraid than we were, so I mustn't expect from analysis what analysis can't give and must bear in mind that to achieve worthwhile results takes diligence and perseverance both on the part of the analyst and on that of the analyzee or patient, and in short if I felt up to facing the business seriously he thought that in a fairly short time therapy could give me the will and the strength to work and in a much longer time also health and the joy of living, however he was wondering if in my case it might not be a good idea for the analysis to be done by a woman, and I must say this was quite an unexpected suggestion as far as I was concerned, heaven knows I prefer women to men in almost every field but not here in fact I had never considered the fact that there are also women analysts, of course the notion wasn't entirely new to me but I had never thought about it before that moment, and in any case I had come to the decision to go through with this psychoanalysis only after long hesitation also about the person to whom I would entrust myself, and if I had chosen him it was because everybody assured me he was an honest and upright person and honesty and uprightness were virtues I held essential in the person who was to analyze me and God knows why but to my way of thinking these were male virtues so to speak, rather I knew the reason why full well but it would be impossible to explain it to him in a hurry since it was connected with my father and his distant career as a carabiniere culminating in the certificate of loyalty and honor, in conclusion I said that if he tried to turn me over to a woman I would give up the whole thing, it was him or nothing, and maybe he realized how profoundly even if perhaps unconsciously I was looking for my father or maybe even a better father than the one fate had allotted me, so after sufficient reflection he said all right he would analyze me himself, and so the next visit without wasting time he points to the Freudian cot or couch which I haven't yet used, and I find myself totally unprepared for the first dilemma of my analysis namely whether or not to take off my shoes before lying down, and I stand there thinking that if I take them off it might be disrespectful to show my stocking feet especially when you think of all the jokes they make in barracks about smelly feet and indeed many people's feet do smell terribly and I remember how certain men in the army were unbearable precisely because of the way their feet stank, for this reason therefore I consider it rather impolite to take off my shoes in front of somebody I mean to respect although in my personal case I can be sure my feet don't smell otherwise God only knows how many times my wife would have thrown the fact in my face, on the other hand however putting your shoes on couches isn't nice either, at least that's what I think and though at home we don't have any couches there is my day bed in the study where I go and sleep after we've had a fight and it's fixed up like a couch with a striped cotton cover, nothing special of course given the regime of strict economy we live in but when my wife lies there with her shoes on it annoys me terribly, at times we start fighting because of her shoes on the day bed also because when she lies there with her shoes on it's a sign she wants to start a fight since she knows perfectly well I take this attitude of hers as a proof of her lack of respect for my money and therefore also for my more noble aspirations, in short I believe it's clear how I attach great importance to shoes on couches perhaps excessive importance so I argue within myself whether to take my shoes off or not, and of course I could ask him if I'm to take them off or not however it doesn't seem right to me to begin the analysis proper with a question of this sort especially since I have trouble becoming intimate with people, even with my father there was no intimacy, and in conclusion since hesitating any longer could also look insulting to him while he waits and perhaps doesn't understand I resolutely take off my shoes and lie down my eyes then fixed on my feet sheathed in socks which luckily are without holes since for some years now they have been making better quality socks than when I was little and always wore socks with holes in them, now the socks are perfect thank heaven and so they look all right but still I have a nagging suspicion that maybe you're not supposed to take off your shoes in order to be psychoanalyzed, in general I always get these things and other similar things all wrong, and in fact I've got this wrong too as I learn later upon inquiry, however when I discuss it with the old man after transference has taken place and consequently greater confidence has been established between us he tells me it doesn't make any difference about the shoes on or off, the important thing is for the person lying on the couch to feel completely at ease which shouldn't be difficult since the piece of furniture was designed on purpose, anyhow as I believe I mentioned before I find myself lying there from the very first time with the burning in my lumbars and my insides all screwed up and the necessity of giving a logical order to the thoughts I express, which is a big mistake they say because for analysis you have to be as free as possible from intellectual superstructures and other conventional things, but strange to say it's easier for me to be unnatural in this sense than to be natural so in a way I'm all set insofar as I can be in this business which after all is a bit out of the ordinary, and therefore with a few inevitable mishaps I begin the long journey towards my unconscious to discover the obscure roots of my present ills, and though at the moment I don't have any great faith in the final results of this endeavor which you mustn't forget is also a big expense I willingly and even scrupulously prepare to do it well, and I must say at once that this is another big mistake and far more serious than the shoes which was basically only an error in procedure whereas this is a mistake in substance since in analysis there shouldn't be any preoccupations or excessive scruples, the patient should say in complete freedom everything that comes into his head without mediation or intervention of his critical faculties but here I am really afraid I can't manage it and in fact the first resistance that the old man tries to overcome is what you might call the resistance to exposition, and to encourage me to speak frankly from the start he says that if at a certain point in my talking I felt the necessity or I happened to have to mention for example the male sexual organ I should name it in the way that comes to me first that is with the word I generally use to think of or to define it, but I answer at once that I can't really do this because whether out of bourgeois propriety or some other hereditary ailment from my father at least as far as the grammar and syntax are concerned I always adapt my speech to the person I'm addressing, and indeed maybe a lot of people do this and to my knowledge there are very different ways of talking depending on whether you're addressing a cardinal or a colonel or a streetwalker, and so with him I feel obliged to produce a lucid and correct exposition of my thoughts, and I would never refer to the cock as cock for example because I consider him a highly respected man of science, and with men of science I always refer to that thing as the penis or the male member and so on, sometimes even more metaphorically. Now in analysis one of the most important and I would even say indispensable things is to have dreams and remember them so you can tell them to the doctor who through the description of the things dreamed and the free associations that the patient makes as he discusses them manages to figure out things buried in the patient and to stimulate

very remote memories which the patient thought he had completely forgotten although they had only been laid aside that is
stored in the unconscious where for that matter they don't just
lie idly but determine actions and conditions and unhealthy states
which the thinking part of the individual doesn't understand
anything about not until he discovers the concealed truth, so that's
the importance of dreams which somebody defined as windows
opening on to the unconscious, but unhappily when it comes to
dreams I have rather tough going either I don't dream at all or
else I can keep dreaming the same thing over and over again,
for example that I get up in a hall or even a stadium crowded
with people who ought to be Venetians but instead are radicals
even though there aren't enough radicals in the world to fill a
stadium, and generally with a stentorian voice I say interesting
things brilliantly and everybody indicates assent and in the end
they applaud, and this one according to me is all too easy to
interpret since I have a hard time speaking distinctly if there are
more than two people listening to me, and to tell the truth three
or four times especially when I was young I tried first memorizing
the things I had to say, however it then happened that when I was
in front of the audience my memory jammed or to be more precise it found a way of condensing into a few words almost all
of them monosyllables the intricate and complicated thoughts
that others would have used to make two or even three whole
lectures, therefore the insistent dream according to me meant
that I have an inferiority complex and maybe a complex of envy
toward lecturers and in general towards people who can stand
up and talk on any subject in front of any audience, moreover
it means that I long to have success among those people who
bestow it only rarely and generally unfairly like the radicals,
and the fact that I dream of success with speeches or lectures
might also be connected with the little detail that for some time
I have had in a drawer three marvelous chapters of a masterpiece
I can't get on with and so in view of my inability to write I fall
back on oratorical success which is more within reach, however
when you think about it even in the dream I don't forget my ambi-

tion to win literary celebrity and in fact I am almost always speaking about my works and I speak fairly well of them obviously consoled by the agreement of my enemies, it turns out however that while I am making these basically courageous associations which after all are a naked revelation of my vanity not to say my fatuousness the doctor is toying with his keys or with his lighter which is a sign he isn't satisfied at all and in fact he tells me to make a greater effort and tell him something else, some episode of my early childhood for example, and I lie there racking my brain with all the will in the world until I suddenly remember the Venezia café with its counter and the white and gold shelves in neoclassic style and the big Murano chandelier and as far as I know it's the most beautiful room in the world not to mention the fact that there are cakes and candy and chocolate, and there is my sister the one nearest me who while everybody listens to her recites her poem Holy infant meek and mild and she is terrific she really is, and she has a big silk ribbon on her head, I don't know the color but it's beautiful, and after she's finished reciting the poem everybody congratulates her and a gentleman gives her a cake which she devours on the spot enjoying it along with her triumph, and then my mother takes me with my pageboy blond curls and my sailor's cap and wants to thrust me in front of the people so I can recite a poem too and maybe earn myself a cake, but I wouldn't be caught dead reciting poetry in front of people I turn all red and won't budge and am about to cry and then Mamma who is a little angry says I'm a dunce and I am terribly unhappy at all this, I mean that Mamma loves my sister but doesn't love me because I'm a dunce and don't know how to earn the cake and can't make people tell me how clever I am, however when I'm big I'll show them all whether or not I'm clever a lot more clever than my younger sister, everybody will have to admire me and applaud me, and here you can clearly see how even the matter of the three chapters has its roots in my early childhood, it's a part of my excessive and insolent desire for glory as Leopardi rightly put it, and there is no doubt that one of its chief manifestations is that whenever I'm with anybody who speaks elegantly and successfully in front of people I feel inferior, that is, not me but my unconscious, so in reality I have the impression I don't give a damn about making speeches and when I can I don't even listen to other people's. There is then a solid sense of reality and of the present rooted in me which this analysis bangs up against right at the start, and naturally I'm not trying to deny that regressions toward early childhood can reveal good clues as in the above-mentioned envy of my smarter sister, however I keep asking myself so what or rather I say it'll take more than this to explain my terrible fears of going crazy, so all told I wish the doctor instead of obstinately rummaging in my past would give me as persuasively as he can some practical advice on what to eat namely noodles and spaghetti if I want them, and every time I manage to eat a big dish of these fairly heavy things without suffering God's own stomach-ache I feel I've made a big step toward health, except that the next time maybe I have an attack of colitis which on top of everything else brings me to the brink or even past the brink right into an anxiety attack, in any case with some patience we have managed to establish and for my part I am convinced though not constantly that I don't have any cancer, I simply have this neurosis which causes the stomach-ache, or to my way of thinking the stomach-ache which causes terrible nervous attacks, or to make everybody happy both neurosis and colitis exist each on its own though they influence each other harmfully that is they are interdependent which is probably the proper description, anyhow the first positive step toward a basic clarification is made, we make it together, he does everything he can to convince me and I do everything I can to believe that my disease isn't mysterious with unique nervous fibers which maybe connect the prostate to the ears or the notorious lumbars directly to the coronary arteries, it seems that there are fundamental constitutional rules for all human beings except for a few specimens that are locked up in a special and famous institution at Cottolengo, and it's true that when I feel things are taking a bad turn for me I instinctively aggravate matters imagining an internal conformation against all the rules of anatomy that is to say something worthy of the Science Museum, however this is an unhealthy tendency to exceptionality which must be fought, and I really have to get it into my head that my body inside is made like all other bodies and it's healthy even though badly affected especially in the colon by a neurosis which however is just an ordinary neurosis like so many others it seems, in fact it is less serious than many others only it does have to be treated and the old man's opinion is that it was wise and fortunate on my part to undertake this psychoanalysis, since psychoanalysis gets right at the origin of this disease and often cures it or at least produces such improvement that in the end for better or worse the patient manages to resume his productive place in society and even enjoy life reasonably of course, this really is the aim of psychoanalysis to restore to society happy and productive individuals productive according to their inclinations naturally and in my case productivity might well mean writing that thing which means so much to me, however I ought to collaborate with a bit more alacrity in remembering my dreams, at times to tell the truth it happens that I wake up in the middle of the night after having had a wonderful meaty dream and I have it all in my head with events and meanings and developments so I think lazily why should I bother to make notes it's so clear in my head and then I fall asleep again and in the morning I can't remember it for love or money not even a shred of what I dreamed so I feel guilty for not having overcome my laziness and not making notes on a sheet of paper I set every evening on the table by my bed so far in vain, however I mustn't dramatize this venial negligence either, I must believe I will unquestionably be cured and I must be optimistic even in what concerns my strictly artistic activity, however I don't mean that this little old man has me spellbound with his talk I am still pretty much on my guard against him and against psychoanalysis per se, and the slight improvement that has come about so far I can easily attribute to the novelty of the cure and the novelty of the doctor, other times I have fallen into the trap of false hopes, however to be fair the old man has one good thing which is that he always remembers everything I've told him since the first session, I won't say he doesn't take notes behind my back while I talk to him but still I have the impression he keeps in his head everything anybody tells him, and this fact makes a good impression on the patient who believes he's dealing not only with a doctor who possesses exceptional mnemonic gifts which would be nothing but with a man who brings diligence and love to his profession and especially in the case he is treating at this moment, and it's obvious that proceeding along this line of reasoning a person can feel downright flattered, and moreover the old man has another good quality which is that he doesn't talk foolishness from the standpoint of common sense which anybody even a person who knows nothing of psychoanalysis might possess as without presumption I can say of myself, generally I must say that many things about this old man seem to confirm both his honesty and his uprightness which are substantially the same virtue, however I also must admit that I retain a good residue of distrust not only as a more than justified precaution after my preceding experiences but also because to tell the truth the greatest result of this psychoanalysis so far is that it's reawakened a bit of aggressiveness in me and therefore the fights with my wife have become more frequent and rowdier thanks partly to the fact that she has turned from a fervent supporter of psychoanalysis to a relentless opponent of it in consequence I believe of my policy of telling her absolutely nothing about my conversations with the old man and this makes her furious of course, that there should be a part of me that eludes her completely and passes to another person, therefore to keep her from suffering too much sometimes I confide little marginal matters to her like for example that it's too bad for this therapy that I dream so little and what's more that I forget almost everything I do dream, and she says I'm stupid to forget everything all the time she never forgets a thing and least of all her dreams, and in fact she tells me one which she considers highly interesting and she would like me to go and tell it to the old man perhaps without saying it's my wife's just to know what the dream means, and then I tell her that a psychiatrist is a man of science and not some-

body who gives you the numbers to bet on in the lottery, and so
we have another good fight and she says why do I keep going
to this psychoanalyst seeing that since I've been going to him I've
got much worse as she has clearly noticed and so has her mother
who is worried about the baby, and obviously I pay no attention
to her indeed I affirm the exact opposite of what she and her
mother are affirming, however the fact remains that we are conditioned by a great number of events many of them very stupid
among which you could rightfully classify my wife's chatter and
fights and even the secondhand opinions of my mother-in-law,
and so I can't deny that my instinctively defensive attitude toward
the old man is strenghtened by my home atmosphere, aha I say
to myself you watch out sooner or later it's going to be the same
old swindle, but then one day talking of this and that I happen
to mention to him my great fear of going outside Rome without
an escort of young assistant psychiatrists who now have become
friends of the family but are also providential now that the neighborhood doctor as always when the hounds of summer are on
spring's traces has gone off to line his pockets through the bad
livers of elderly ladies, and since I'm reluctant to travel we had
come to an agreement with one of these assistants a girl in fact
who is always the first one I call when I'm afraid of an attack
or anything because she is sweet and patient and I need this especially in these days of increased tension with my wife, as I was
saying we had made this agreement with her to attempt a real
trip at last that is as far as Spoleto for the closing of the cutural
rite known as the Festival of Two Worlds since there will be an
open air concert namely a Mass in I don't know what key by
Frescobaldi with a very handsome Mexican conductor who appeals however mistakenly to women including my wife, and so
we had decided with this young lady psychiatrist that we would
all go together and instead she had later told us that next Sunday
she had something else to do, and without her I wouldn't venture
to Spoleto however regretfully because of the Mass and also the
sight of the splendid cathedral square with the swallows wheeling
around like crazy squawking among the solos and the choruses

and the orchestral music while night falls over the world whereas thanks to the spotlights the Duomo stands there steadfast with the faith that raised it intact and the music though disturbed by the cries of swallows and the babies crying is complemented with beauty and mystery, in short I believe that in spite of everything it's lovely to go to Spoleto and it's a shame this friend has backed out, and the old man who until then had let me talk now said that if the knowledge that he was also going to Spoleto for that concert was any comfort to me then I should be comforted and should risk the trip nothing bad could happen to me anyway, so on Sunday in all the heat we get into the car my wife and I and we head for Spoleto, to tell the truth I don't feel too self-confident at times even more confused I bet than one of those sailors who sailed with Christopher Columbus on the three caravels maybe without having given the matter enough thought, and gradually as I drove along the Via Flaminia in the roasting heat on top of everything else my alarm mounted even though from time to time I swallowed one of the new little capsules my doctor had suggested which are known as psychoplegics and which were excellent like all the medicines in this world for that matter when you believe in them and these were still too new not to believe in them, however they couldn't work miracles no not that so I was thinking it might be wiser to go back to Rome before it was too late, however my wife wasn't of this opinion she said I had to stir myself sooner or later or else I'd never be cured and from her point of view she wasn't wrong since she really wanted to have a look at the Mexican conductor, in short also because of her encouragement I manage to get to Spoleto which like all the cities of that period is built on a hill which means it's a bit sprawling and rather lacking in straight lines in any direction, so I go around half dazed trying somehow to keep myself perpendicular at least ideally according to the force of gravity and making an effort to keep myself together psychically, and I succeed I won't say I don't but with enormous trouble and with the lurking presentiment that I've got myself in a big mess because the doctor said he too would be in Spoleto all right, however in

all these crooked streets and squares there is such a collection of
people homosexuals and otherwise that if by chance after all this
tending toward an attack I really should bring one on now maybe
seeing my brain outside my head like the other time just tell me
who's going to find in the midst of all this confusion my little
old man who is so short of stature and even at the risk of monotony
I am thinking that all in all it would be better to give up the Mass
and the square with the swallows and the fascinating Mexican
conductor also because it seems that he is arrested in the Oedipal
situation as far as the heterosexual erotic object is concerned,
however I know that my wife wants to admire him all the same
so it would be wasting my breath to insist on going straight back
to Rome where there is a downright abundance of psychiatric
clinics, my wife at this moment I bet wouldn't give up Frescobaldi
for anything in the world and in these circumstances as in others
as well for that matter she is the stronger, and so I swallow another psychoplegic and let myself be dragged along without putting up any resistance you might say, and we enter the midst of
a teeming crowd shut in the square where to say the least there
must be three or four thousand people all or almost all of them
milling around to hunt for their seats or to change the seats they've
already found, and I who am naturally not without a little caprice
known as agoraphobia say to myself right away well here is just
the place to go crazy in and I look around anxiously hunting amid
this mountain of people for my little old man without any hope
of course, and instead there he is on tiptoe I bet looking around
no less anxiously for me you would say, and there's no need to
say what lost sheep this good shepherd of mine is going after,
I suddenly feel comforted and warm with gratitude for him who
seems to take my well-being so to heart even outside the paid
hour of our psychoanalytic session, and it doesn't matter that I
also feel shame and a sense of guilt at having retained for such a
long time that residue of mistrust toward him, now I'm ready for
utter faith and I'm sure I will go on to the end of this cure because
even though I don't believe enough in psychoanalysis I have un-
bounded belief in this man more honest and upright than any

other, that's right father, and in reality without my being technically aware of it at that moment the first fruit of my analysis has ripened namely transference, which means redirecting to the person of the analyst the sentiments and emotions which in the distant past were directed toward a certain person I needn't name, or perhaps you can even say that the impulsive need for love which in my infancy I had been able to satisfy with great difficulty I can now satisfy easily in loving this man, who despite his less than average height and his Southern accent was already my father even if I still didn't really know it.

So with this transference now in working order psychoanalytical things proceed a bit better from the standpoint of affections although not in the sense that there are any particular effusions between me and the old man when we meet, in fact superficially everything goes on as before if not even more prudently, that is to say he waits for me at the door of the office almost always with a nice smile on his lips and he extends his hand, then I shut the door while he goes to his place behind the desk and I go over to him and he looks at me with attention and intensity without letting it show too much trying to understand from my appearance how I am, and at times he even says that to look at me he'd say I'm well and he hardly ever guesses right because I'm really not well in this period though of course I'm not as bad as I was when I began the analysis several months ago, anyhow often he doesn't say anything except come in and after I have respectfully waited for him to be seated I lie down on the couch taking off my shoes even though from information collected from the young psychiatrists I now know for sure that shoes are not taken off and according to what they say I am apparently the only case of a patient who is analyzed without his shoes on, but what can I do about it now I've started out by taking them off and I think I would have to offer some explanation if all of a sudden I didn't take them off any more, so I take them off although then in the course of the session I am disturbed by the sight of my stocking feet and so as not to see them I often shut my eyes and keep them shut even for a long time, therefore all things considered this shoe problem ought to be resolved also to assist the success of the cure but since the holidays are near I've decided that I'll shift to lying down with my shoes on after our summer break and thus it will pass almost unobserved I hope, so I lie down on the couch and as I lie there I feel behind me the affectionate and vigilant presence of this old man who wants me to be cured, there I think the advantage of transference is chiefly this namely the perception of this affection and the certitude that our relationship has moved to a plane that is no longer the merely professional one, and this obviously increases also my responsibility toward him I mean that now I am sorrier if as often happens I don't have any dreams to tell him or worse still have forgotten the ones I had, anyhow now that we are so to speak intimate I can always find something to tell him for example I talk to him about the fights with my wife it seems to me we get along fine in everything except our domestic economy, to tell the truth while the majority of couples of our acquaintance are tormented by sexual problems of infidelity we fight over matters of character and in general finance, and maybe I'm too strict with my wife seeing that I can't handle my own money and yet I demand of her a virtue I myself don't possess, however the fights concern not so much or rather not only the quantity of the money spent but above all the way in which she spends it, namely that when I was running things I spent a lot of money and grieved over it, my wife doesn't grieve in the slightest on the contrary she enjoys herself madly, her pleasure in spending is second only I would say to that of sex, and on this score there must be something a bit unhealthy in her in fact I believe that through particularly useless expenditure she is displaying a kind of desire for power or something else equally diabolical which to my mind could even make her comparable to Stalin, however it so happens that this talk about my wife doesn't interest the old man too much, if dreams fail he prefers for us to get together and plumb the depths of my remote childhood examining as critically as possible my father that merchant and ex-carabiniere who surely wasn't a good father, I wouldn't even dream of asserting that by now however I would say you have to be a bit careful with these negative opinions and in fact I believe my father didn't mean any harm, and intention is the first characteristic of wickedness, he was doing his best poor man and I know this especially now because with my daughter I have been able to live again however empirically through many sensations of my childhood when he bounced me on his knees singing Ride a cock horse or when strong as he was he permitted me to rumple the scanty hair on his bald head and he didn't protest if I stuck my fingers in his eyes, now it's in the light of these truths it seems to me we have to judge my behavior toward my dying father and then the story is simple, too simple I'd say since it was precisely the abandoning of my father on his deathbed that must have sparked the moral conflict which has brought me to psychoneurosis, and this is the horrible reality which I am trying to escape by remaining in my illness, this the guilt that sums up all the others of my life and I have to expiate it by punishing myself to the point of torment with anguish and madness and not writing the fourth chapter and continuing toward my glory, quite a different glory was the one desired by my ineffable sergeant-quartermaster ah we know this much already, and so a stab in the back is no more than I deserve every time I try to raise my head again, and I welcome it because I have to remain in my nothingness and disease to go on expiating and expiating, however the little old man when he hears me talking like this doesn't agree chiefly I think because it's a matter of principle and professional dignity since if the science of psychoanalysis were to be reduced to these elementary little games of normal reactions to mistaken presuppositions then humanity certainly wouldn't have had to wait till Freud and the end of the nineteenth century to discover it, but life as I see it is only a negligible portion of real life the most important part takes place in the unconscious where it has all accumulated in the very first years of our lives and maybe even before we came into the world, and therefore we have to fish it out of the unconscious and bring it up to the conscious level so it can't harm us or frighten us any more, and while I as a thinking and reasoning being allow myself to be dragged along by several thousand millennia of bad habits and to everything I can to construct a honeyed and false image of my father my unconscious knows perfectly well that this father was a son of a bitch who stole my mother from me every day just when I was at the height of my Oedipal phase that is when I was dying for love of my mother, an omnipotent son of a bitch against whom little as I was I had no defense except hate, a disproportionate hate characteristic of children who have no limits to their loving or their hating so any number of times I killed this father in my thoughts and wishes or to put it differently in my unconscious I'm a parricide many times over, and maybe all this is true I don't know, if these explorers of the unconscious say so they must have good reasons, and therefore I now have the impression that the job to be done is to rid myself as far as possible of the remorse for these numerous parricides and this can be accomplished by my fishing from my unconscious the facts and occasions that justified my desire to kill, and now it is night, a winter evening on our muddy road with the electricity poles marking a distance that seems insuperable to my little-boy weariness, he stayed playing cards till late and now we are going home from the shop along the road full of mud which will never end and I'm tired and I'm cold and I'm sleepy and I don't want to walk, I want him to pick me up he's so big and strong, I love him boundlessly this father of mine since there is nobody bigger and stronger in the whole world, but he doesn't want to carry me and then my mother is willing to carry me though she is small and weak, and I would let her carry me even though I know she isn't strong, I'm too tired really and also attracted by the sweetness of being carried by her but my father won't have it, he is walking on the other side and my mother is in the middle and he doesn't want her to pick me up, he says I'm too big his voice is hard and he says it's shameful at my age to be carried, he says I have to walk and be strong and I'm not strong and I can't recite the poem at the café in front of people and when I run a little my spleen hurts and so I'm not supposed to run, I'm not strong but I have the strength of my pride so I clench my teeth and walk on and of course at this moment I hate my father, and if it's true that all children on certain occasions hate their fathers to

the point of wishing for them to disappear and die well then I
must have done this too, however I also have to put myself in my
father's place he could easily think I'm just being spoiled and am
only pretending to be tired so he'll carry me, or he might even
believe in my tiredness but maybe he thinks that if I force myself
to walk even when I'm tired I'll become strong both in body and
character and when I'm grown up I can even be a carabiniere
captain, or else maybe he's edgy because he's lost at cards and
then he's gruff with his son it happens to me sometimes when I'm
annoyed with producers and directors or only disgusted with
myself I'm unfair with my daughter, and sometimes when she's
tired and wants me to carry her I say no, and then my daughter
even though I love her more than anything in the world might at
certain moments want me to die and be out of the way, she can
hate me to this unreasonable degree, and it seems that all children
have these sanguinary impulses and since they're impossible to
enact they are rejected or repressed properly speaking, that is
they are stored up in the unconscious where at the same time they
retain a vitality of their own a malefic vitality let's call it which
comes out when the occasion arises, maybe at the least opportune
moment when a person says to the surgeon who's going to operate
on his father if you find a cancer kill him, let him die, and I wanted
him to die as fast as possible even after the operation when the
tumor was exposed and everything was arranged for the artificial
anus, I thought that in his place I would have wanted to die and
this was why I wanted him to die not because of the stink he had
though in my annoyance at that stink I pretended to believe the
surgeon and ran away from all his misery and pain leaving my
father without me at the moment of his death although he may
have loved me more than my sisters and he certainly made sacrifices for me that he didn't make for any of them, he gave me an
education spending piles of money even if he didn't take the
bread from his mouth as he said no doubt speaking figuratively,
and I knew that the letters I had sent him when I was fighting
the war in Abyssinia and the clipping from the *Gazzettino* where
it said I had fought with honor and won a medal were kept in a

drawer all tied up with a tricolor ribbon, this was his way of loving me and though this way was remote from my habits you couldn't say it wasn't love, and yet all I could think about was making him die as fast as possible and when he didn't hurry it up I left him there in his miserable hospital room, so how can a person possibly evade the punishment he deserves when he desired the death of his father the death of the one who loves us more than anybody else on earth, well according to this little man who is sitting behind me and who in a sense is now also speaking on behalf of the deceased my line of reasoning is ingenuous not to say bombastic, on the level of *Heart* to give you the idea, whereas insisting on the reality of the facts namely that a stink is a stink even if it comes from your own father I haven't done anything that deserves to be punished, I have behaved in the most normal manner under the circumstances, even too well if you consider as is only right that my father though out of mere ignorance wasn't by any means a good father, however I suppose that in saying this to me the little old man is exaggerating a bit for my own good of course, but if by chance I hint at this supposition he might resent it because if I suggest that he wants to force my convictions to the point of making me think my father was a shit I am reducing psychoanalysis to a simple-minded and also slightly dirty game, and instead I should get certain truths into my head even though they're a bit complicated concerning everybody's psychic formation according to which we are composed of three parts one of which is called the Id a Latin word that means It and this is a rather lousy tangle of instincts which lies diffusely in our being and would drive us to perform immodest and criminal actions or asocial or antisocial ones anyway and despite this the Id is a valuable reservoir of impulses and energies, and then comes the second part which is called the Ego and is constituted if I've got it right by a kind of compromise between the afore-mentioned Id and the real world, in short the Ego is what you do and what you think the most apparent portion of our soul the part that gives us a sense of existing in relation to events and problems, and then finally there is the third part to which I must draw especial attention since this is the very part that screwed me up, and this part is called the Superego and I have no trouble at all believing in this one because some time ago however crudely I had discovered the existence of something of the sort, namely a part of myself that stands over me and watches me and normally takes pleasure in mocking me when I do something serious, when I decide to go beyond the third chapter for example and much more often of course when I'm making love, and thus once the sexual act is exhausted after those effusions and writhings which seen from outside are certainly not without their humorous aspect I have to deal with this sort of other self that has observed my exploits without a scrap of humor and to try to shake it off I come out with some joking remark like for example well another day's work done or else you can't teach an old dog new tricks eh, which as a rule makes a bad impression on the women who lie with me by which I mean my wife since to my misfortune I am strictly monogamous and it not infrequently happens that after making love we have a big row, and this is the real difference between man and woman namely that the male as soon as his seminal reservoir is drained starts thinking of other things whereas the female still in the grip of residual sentimentality wants more kissing and tenderness than before, anyhow to get back on the track I must say that this Superego of my invention does not coincide with the Superego invented and introduced into psychoanalysis by Freud though the two have some points of contact, just as Freud's Superego has some points of contact with the conscience as it is commonly conceived namely with that thing that makes us feel remorse after we have committed evil, however the Superego seems also to differ from the conscience in the sense that it is much more active in blocking the path to evil and much more severe in censuring it when it hasn't managed to keep evil away, but above all it is different because whereas the origin of the conscience isn't explained or is given some metaphysical provenance, the origin of the Superego is quite clear and it can be said to be the result of a progressive intromission of the privations imposed by reality and especially by educators, or to explain myself better

I could say that when we're born we don't give a damn about anything or anybody, our only thought is to satisfy ourselves sexually passing through the oral phase and the anal phase and in short though it seems impossible to me as far as I personally am concerned the very first period of our life is utterly determined by pleasure, indeed by those murky pleasures that stem from the filth of the Id, and we would go on merrily like this for all our lives if we didn't bump up against reality and particularly our educators chief among whom obviously is the number one pain in the ass of our life namely our father who does nothing but say you mustn't do this and you mustn't do that, and little by little all these prohibitions and intimidations enter into us and form that part of our soul which in fact is the Superego, and the best of it is that all these intromissions aren't by any means forced on us, strange as it may seem there are also some voluntary ones in the Superego in the sense that we children don't always want our father to die or to go away, the tie that binds us to him is ambivalent as they say namely an alternating sentiment or even a simultaneous feeling of hate and love so while on the one hand we would even kill our father if we could on the other hand we would like to resemble him be strong like him big like him and even a pain in the ass like him maybe, and all these mistaken ambitions to be like our father honest and upright and Faithful through the Centuries contribute to our Superego making it strong as a carabiniere, and now this superior part of my soul is always there watching what I do and in general disapproving, it stands guard against all those hedonistic impulses pressing from the Id and says to them go back to your muck, and they go back sometimes but then sometimes they don't, sometimes to tell the truth the Ego manages to ignore the inhibitive and intimidating vetoes of the Superego and to enjoy itself a little, but then my God how that Superego policeman makes me pay for it, how it massacres me under tons of guilt feelings, how it punishes me by getting into the middle of my road to glory and saying you aren't worthy you aren't capable you will never win the applause of the radicals, and when the Ego manages to stand up to him and tell him I am worthy and I am

capable and I don't give a good goddamn about the radicals and
their applause which is only right, and also I don't give a damn
about the producers since I've saved up the money to write the
fourth and fifth and sixth and who knows maybe also the seventh
chapter of my masterpiece, in short when I seem to have grabbed
this Superego defunct father father memory father inheritance of
duty and honor, when I've grabbed it and have it with its back to
the wall, at a moment when I'm not looking it rummages in my
unconscious and brings up long-forgotten sins and griefs and
throws them at me by way of the colon or the lumbars, and it un-
leashes on me its anxiety attacks to bury me in my terror and in my
finally admitted incapacity.

Now from this frankly somewhat mechanical distribution of
the parts you can begin to understand something about the terrible
conflicts that take place in my psyche with tormenting and paralyz-
ing effects, however these aren't the only conflicts of course, in
fact there are many others which will be investigated a bit at a
time at leisure, all the same from what has emerged so far the
figure who more than any other superintends my misfortunes is
my father, though not in the quasi-ghostly form I used to think
he was haunting me in but through the scientific process of trans-
ferring his worst qualities to my Superego which in consequence
has had an abnormal development both in severity and in over-all
activity, so as a general preference we discuss my father, but influenced precisely by the Superego who wants order and discipline
and obviously justice before everything else, as I lie on the
Freudian cot I have to say what seems only fair to me in favor of
my old father so that this new father won't get too unfavorable an
idea of him, I explain for example that it wasn't so much my
father who took away my mother as my mother who ran after him
whenever she could, and of course this was a fine thing namely
that he an ex-quartermaster-sergeant and bald into the bargain
should have such fascination that my mother left us with the
maid in order to go with him to the shop and the markets, so he
wasn't the one who did all the harm to me and besides there were
concomitant circumstances in which he was only involved up to

a point and surely not voluntarily, we can take for example the honorable discharge which was in the deep drawer of the dresser along with the gold watch I later broke and the ring with the red stone that I later sold and the Etruria cologne that my father never used because he didn't like perfumes except naturally those incorporated in hair lotions, the honorable discharge as I was saying had at the top the picture of a lady almost as beautiful as Mamma and maybe taller if she had been standing up but she was sitting down with the flag and this lady was our Fatherland or Italy which is the same thing with a crown on her head the like of which I'd never seen with the towers of her cities and I didn't know what our Fatherland or Italy was and I couldn't figure it out for myself so all I understood was that it was something like God, but then I didn't know very well what God was either but I knew he saw everything even if you couldn't see him and he was big even bigger than my father and all the fathers of the world put together though it wasn't easy to believe this, and the Fatherland and Italy were also big and powerful even more than my father, and there on the honorable discharge there were printed words and other words written in ink and these words written in ink were my father's name whereas the printed ones said that he had served the Fatherland with loyalty and honor in the Carabinieri Corps Faithful through the Centuries, and I knew what carabinieri were but not loyalty and honor, and my father explained that loyalty and honor meant being an obedient boy and doing what your parents told you and not crying when you had to go to Sister Carmela's kindergarten where the soup was so bad, and in fact it was made with carrots and cabbage and not much rice and they brought it in a cart drawn by a horse from the insane asylum where the nuns cooked it, and it took them an hour I think to get from the asylum to the kindergarten with those big cauldrons and when it got there it was a revolting paste and anyway I didn't like carrots and cabbage but I had to eat it because my father had served the Fatherland with loyalty and honor, and I also had to wear my striped smock and learn to be a good citizen and respect the laws and the authorities and a fine soldier of the King who had won the war, and I'm afraid that all these things for better or worse became a part of my Superego which took advantage of them later to screw me on several patriotic occasions, but of course it wasn't my father's fault that on his honorable discharge, as on the honorable discharge of any one of the King's carabinieri I think, they had printed the words loyalty and honor, nor was it his fault that the paper fascinated me because of the picture of Italy sitting there in her towered crown, and then finally when Mamma read the poem of Fusinato with the knight who went off to die for the fair lady I knew who the fair lady was it was the Fatherland and one fine day I would do the same thing, and as it turned out I came pretty close to doing just that. In short according to the little old doctor's way of thinking and he understood as much of all this as anybody could, in this kind of trial we were having the chief defendant was not me but my father, or rather my Superego into which however either through intimidation or through identification my carabiniere and honest and upright citizen father had been completely fused creating a Superego that was stern and demanding and at the same time strangely receptive that is prepared to welcome also my later educational influences especially those that came to me from the grade school and the boarding school where just to give you an example the potassium chlorate they gave you in the infirmary was considered a treat and therefore many boys went to have some during recreation on the pretext of a sore throat also because in the infirmary there was the orderly who was an elderly lay brother who always stank of wine and he was very generous about giving away the chlorate because he marked the medicines down on a sheet of paper and then the parents paid for them along with the tuition, so thinking of all the sacrifices my father was making to give me an education I never went to have any chlorate but one day I did go because I really had a sore throat or at least I thought I did and then I went to the old orderly who stank of wine and told him to give me the chlorate, and he took the hand of the little boy of nine or ten I then was and led him in the next room which was all deserted and made the boy sit on his knees and said open your mouth so I can see if you really have a sore throat and I was a little afraid to open it because by then I wasn't so sure any more that I had a sore throat or rather I had one all right but maybe it wasn't so bad you could see it, anyhow I finally opened my mouth and he looked close and suddenly he did something disgusting namely he put his tongue inside my mouth and began to suck, and paralyzed with fear and disgust I let him do it and thank God that old drunk must have been impotent otherwise he could have taken advantage of me like a sodomite, instead he just gave me a revolting kiss and let me go off with the yellow box of potassium chlorate, well I never told a living soul the filthy thing that had been done to me because that idiotic Superego which was already in operation began saying to me what have you done you wretch aren't you ashamed of yourself mind you nobody must ever know, it would be better for you to die sooner than have anybody know, and in fact I buried this episode deep inside me until I had forgotten it, but of course it remained in my unconscious as a source of shame and guilt, and I remembered it only many years later seeing my daughter one day sucking a little potassium chlorate pill and I ordered her God only knows how unfairly to spit out that muck and to take others medicines for her throat maybe less efficacious and more expensive but not that, however on thinking it over I believe that it was anyhow a lucky thing the filthy episode was suppressed and stored away in the unconscious otherwise who knows if I would ever have managed later to kiss a girl without feeling disgust and revulsion, although I also have to suppose that even buried in the unconscious the foul deed retained a deleterious vitality since it was only much later and very rarely that I succeeded in fusing the two kinds of love into one, I mean spiritual and carnal love, in my error however strongly supported also by an imposing collection of wrongheaded educational impulses which go from the principles of Catholic morality to the propaganda of whole generations of poets beginning with the greatest of all father Dante who was particularly good at angelifying on the one hand and having on the other a sexual life presumably energetic and normal which seems a big blunder but maybe only at first sight, because on second examination the thought arises that this might be a very valuable rule of life in the sense that dissociating the senses from the sentiments a person maybe loses the satisfaction of going to bed with the one whom he loves also spiritually, however nobody knows the troubles he's saving himself except the man who has in fact gone to bed with the woman he also loves spiritually, since women certainly don't miss this chance to extract endless advantages generally economic from such a situation. Anyhow that disgusting old pig who attempted to seduce me in the sodomist sense in addition to everything else also picked the wrong moment, namely he happened along in a period when my Superego which needless to say is also a perfectionist had driven me toward mystical exaltations in which from the generic wish to become a priest in order to please Mamma who wanted to live with me in the rectory and have capon broth every day, from this vague desire I had gone on to direct conversation with the Divinity based above all on an ardor we might call destructive praying in front of the chapel's sanctuary lamp which indicated the divine presence of Our Lord Jesus Christ in the Sacrament, Jesus abstract essence of divinity, Jesus mysteriously present body and life in the Host and also non-body and non-life and symbol like His divine Father, and I prayed to Him Jesus let me die at once let me join myself to You my God, annihilate me in your intangible embrace Holy Spirit, Single God, and Trinity receive me without delay into your spiritual and unchanging eternity, and in short while my Ego was aiming straight as an arrow toward self-destruction and indeed since I had only my life to offer to my God I offered it to Him incessantly at every minute of the day and only secondarily that is if God didn't grant me the perfection of death I might have accepted the mortification of the flesh on top of a column in the desert like the ancient stylites, and so while the adolescent was all abstract and angelic passions who knows what the Supergo was fixing up for him, that is while it's all too clear that on the one hand in his mysticism he was trying to placate feelings of guilt and enjoy the voluptuousness of expiation buried in the unconscious, on the other hand he achieved however involuntarily a result of great importance for the future in the sense that his earthly father and the chief component of the Superego was himself relegated to a position inferior to the Eternal Father's, a hierarchy of duties to the one and the other was formed and although the duties to the earthly father also combined the duties to the Fatherland and Society and People of Importance in general in which according to my father who must have known something about criminals the concepts of honesty and order were embodied, the duties to the Celestial Father were of a category not only more refined but also superior both from a spiritual and moral point of view, so in the end this implacable Superego of mine was screwing itself because thanks to a deathly inspiration of a mystical quality luckily destined not to last long it was freeing itself at least in part from the tremendous compulsory force exercised by the perfect paternal discipline, and in other words in all this business about wanting to die for God I was making the first important step in my struggle with my father since if I aspired to identification with God Eternity Death there wasn't much room left for my previous identification with the Father Loyalty and Honor who was demoted, as is only natural, to a lower rung.

So in that period I was only a hair's breadth from becoming a saint especially following the footsteps of the Servant of God Domenico Savio who to his other perfections had added that of dying fairly prematurely, but then with the approach of puberty my natural sexual instincts which after the really infantile curiosity about little girls with no underpants had been dozing God knows where but I suppose in the unconscious suddenly and violently broke out again seizing the opportunity of certain elucidations providentially furnished by a classmate during recreation walking up and down the yard where our Salesian priest-teachers were strolling with an entourage of pupils hanging upon their lips and to tell the truth I myself was often there hanging upon a teacher's lips for my edification and instruction and to be honest also using this subsidiary means to obtain more credits which then directly or indirectly contributed to my final standing which obviously had an excessive importance for my father who was overjoyed if I was the first in the class instead of the second, or the second instead of the third or the third instead of the fourth but no lower, I mustn't go lower than third because there were only three merit medals namely a gilt medal for the first, a silver or rather silver-plated medal for the

second, and a bronze medal for the third, and I absolutely had to
win one of these three if I wanted in some way however inadequate
to repay my father and mother and sisters for the terrible sacrifices
they made to keep me in school, and so thanks to all these things
in those years I could sing with every right our school song Work
and Pray it was the holy banner that led Don Bosco on his arduous
path, and I was on the arduous path myself and I naturally didn't
overlook the opportunity to acquire supplementary learning in
addition to the benevolence of the teachers when I followed them
in their instructive and edifying strolls around the yard during
recreation hour, but on that particular day God knows why I
happened to be chatting privately with a classmate, I can't remember why perhaps discussing some ordinary matter he asked me if
by any chance I knew the difference between a man and a woman
and suddenly two things happened to me, the first was that I
found this subject much more interesting than the virtuous peri-
patetic harangues of the teachers and the second was that I saw
again the little girls without underpants up in the figtrees and the
following attempts at fornication unsuccessful despite the sincere
efforts of Dirty Lucia, all this stuff which somebody I don't know
who but probably the Superego had suppressed and hidden in the
unconscious and which now burst out with its enormous vital
energy while my classmate was telling me about certain houses
where you could go and inside there were women sitting around
and you paid and you could pick out whichever one you wanted and
go into a room with her and do all sorts of dirty things which were
fun, and I listened knowing that listening to him was a mortal sin
which would irreparably stain my immortal soul until now white
as snow but all the same I felt a pleasure deep down inside my guts
and my bones and my brain and my blood, my God maybe this was
how Adam fell into sin with this frightful pleasure, and meanwhile
I was trying to picture the scene he was telling me about and I
asked him how those women sitting around were dressed and he
said they were dressed like priests that is with cassocks buttoned
up from head to toe but underneath they were naked and naturally
the buttons weren't the kind with buttonholes like the priests' but

with snaps so that they could be unbuttoned with one tug, and since I was a bit puzzled by the thought of these fallen women dressed like priests he swore that he had seen them once when he had sneaked inside secretly because you can't really go in till you're eighteen and this was too bad since by now my immortal soul was already stained and I was thinking I would go there during the holidays but unfortunately I would have to wait another six years before I could experience those pleasures, and then my classmate explained that you didn't have to wait all that long because you could do it by yourself in such and such a way and if I wanted to try all I had to do was go to the bathroom and shut myself in, and naturally I did this right away because there was all that chaos of the Id that was trying to overwhelm me and in fact the pleasure I felt in these solitary manipulations was such that it completely overcame my fragile ethical structure, a person began at the most impure and sinful part of the body and was exalted to the threshold of Paradise but then plunged down again with his conscience devastated by sin and shame, how could you then go into church and show yourself to God although God was there watching even in the bathroom or at night in bed when they turned out the big light in the dormitory and the master retired behind his curtain in the corner, or in any other place where you committed a sin or talked about it or thought about it with pleasure, God was omnipresent and a stern judge and I no longer dared raise my eyes to the tabernacle on the main altar or even to the little lamp that indicated the divine presence of Jesus in the Sacrament unless I had first confessed my horrendous sins, luckily there existed Confession to cleanse the soul and luckily also you could choose between two confessors one of them obviously senile, when you told him you had committed impure acts he only asked if you had committed them by yourself or with others, and if it was by yourself he made you promise rather casually not to do it again and sent you away with a few Our Fathers and Hail Marys as penance, really nothing when you think about it and in fact it wasn't as if you could always square his absolution with your conscience and still less with what the preachers said especially

the ones during Spiritual Exercises who felt that committing impure acts gave you a ninety-nine per cent probability of eternal
damnation since a boy who began committing impure acts then
had a hard time finding the moral strength to stop as I well knew,
and so by constantly committing impure acts you were constantly
in a state of mortal sin and if you happened to die suddenly you
ended up right in the clutches of Satan, and naturally I agreed with
the preachers and I prayed to Saint Joseph and Saint Anthony to
strengthen me in my good intentions but then the vital impulses
that is to say the Id and its chaos of filth turned up again with
overpowering force insisting on my desire being satisfied maybe
in a hurry, and afterwards there was the abyss of guilt and
repentance and the longing for punishment because obviously the
senile confessor's four Our Fathers and four Hail Marys weren't
enough to square things especially since in addition to our Eternal
Father there was also the Superego snooping around in these dirty
matters, anyhow the one that bothered me most at the moment
was the Eternal Father and naturally I had to give up any idea of
emulating the Servant of God Domenico Savio with my conscience
shot full of holes now or patched up rather shakily, nor could I
aspire to death and identification with the eternal God since apart
from the fact that I had the impression I loved life a lot more than
I used to if I were to die now I would go straight down to roast
in the flames of Hell, and only in the most optimistic of hypotheses
namely if divine mercy had permitted me at least a moment to say
My Jesus have mercy I might have got off with a huge number of
years in Purgatory where the flames as our preachers made
eminently clear are just as tormenting as the flames of Hell only
they don't last for all eternity which is something at least, however at a certain point I begin to wonder how is it that my Eternal
Father allows me to commit such horrible and frequent sins in his
place I surely wouldn't allow it, I know he is all patience and
infinite goodness however there's a limit to everything otherwise
I'd like to know who would ever go to Hell, and what if there isn't
any Eternal Father after all, in fact the classmate who introduced
me to the solitary pleasures of the locked bathroom says that if you

ask him it's the priests who've invented the Eternal Father, we discuss this problem at length walking up and down by ourselves in the yard and he is calmly convinced that the priests invented Him but it's not all that easy for me, I have to go into the church and ask Him straight out if He exists or not, I kneel down as if to pray and I say if you exist you've got to destroy me go ahead destroy me if you dare, strike me down like Saul on the road to Damascus and save me or else send me right to Hell whatever you want but do something because I'm blaspheming, I'm here in your house to blaspheme against you and you don't do a thing, and in short after reasoning in this vein a bit I liberate myself of the annoying presence of God so now I'm not afraid of Hell any more or of hurting Our Lord who is standing between me and my pleasures, I am free but there's still the Superego though naturally I don't know it, or rather there is remorse for the bad action I've performed, the bitterness of satiety, anger at the weakness of the flesh, anxiety about punishment, and obviously after such important and finally laborious inner revolutions at the end of the year I'm excluded from the list of medal-winners, I'm eighteenth or nineteenth in the class with an unsatisfactory report and apparently it's only by a miracle and because of my good record in the past that they don't fail me and make me take my exams over again in October, and my father who has come to the end-of-the-year ceremony looks like an unpaid creditor, with all the sacrifices he has made to raise my tuition every quarter I don't even bring home a bronze medal, I even risk failing which would mean spending extra money for tutoring, and if things go on like this I'll end up in jail he says and I let him talk because since I've liberated myself from my Eternal Father I'm obviously not prepared to pay any attention to this pain in the ass who does he think he is, a sergeant that's what he is, when I was little I thought a sergeant was somewhere above a general like Diaz and Cadorna who had won the war, and instead he was nothing and now I went and hid myself in shame when he attended the patriotic ceremonies with the flag of the Association and the troop of retired sergeants and corporals the eternal petitioners for increased pensions, but what was the use of their writing when my father who wrote out the petitions for all of them made one spelling mistake after another, not to mention grammar with his conditionals and subjunctives all wrong in those endless sentences, in short for better or worse I managed to finish the *ginnasio* and at the same time my father made a great downward plunge in my esteem while my Ego asserted itself with extraordinary independence breaking free of all slavery human and divine, oh how I could intoxicate myself in my sinful liberty, but instead there's the Superego which is observing my errors and storing them up accumulating precious material for my future neurosis, and besides what do I mean by freedom, when I see a girl I like the first thing I want to do is to die for her and I imagine her absolutely without any sexual apparatus even without any intestine or urinary tract, for me a maiden to be loved consists chiefly in a soft gaze and long hair and I know this because I am really in love now, she is a classmate's sister and two or three times in the visitor's parlor I have seen her shy beauty, I would have liked to be a poet for her and handsome and rich but since I couldn't be what I wasn't then I wanted her to be poor at least, but no she was rich and arrived at the school in an automobile and then I wanted her to be consumptive and you couldn't tell about this because in fact she was rather thin and pale, in other words I fell in love and now during the holidays when I can manage to borrow a bike from somebody or take my father's I dash over to where she lives and ride up and down in front of the house hoping to see her and trembling at the very thought that she might see me, I wouldn't want her to see me but I'd like to die for her, so now Fusinato's poem has found its proper application and for this maiden I would like to die as for the Fatherland, we might even put the two together and I could die for them both, I can do anything for this maiden who makes me tremble when I think how much I love her, I can fuse her with the figure on the honorable discharge idealizing her any way I like although there is a problem of proportion since the Fatherland on the discharge was rather on the massive side, and this girl all things considered is more easily pictured as an angel, I don't know

anything yet about the *Dolce Stil Novo* but I seem to have reached
it on my own, she is a desexed creature like the sweet mother I
loved as a child who had a melodious voice when she read the
poem about the knight who went off to die in the wars for his
lady fair, then this lady fair was Mamma and later the Fatherland
and now this chaste and wondrous maiden, however in a strange
way each of these concepts mingles with the others and perhaps
basically Mamma is still on top, and then one day during this
vacation somebody tells me that my father does the same filthy
things to my mother that I would do if I were eighteen with the
sinful women in those houses all naked under their priests' cassocks, however I would never do these filthy things not for anything in the world with the maiden I love whereas my father does
them with my mother, if he didn't do them I certainly wouldn't
have been born nor my sisters either, so it must be true and I could
have figured this out for myself if I had thought about it but instead I was still miles away, there must have been some opposition
in me to genetic knowledge, maybe it was what they call idealism,
in fact I was an idealist in certain things but in psychoanalytic
language this didn't mean a thing I suppose since it wasn't self-
explained, and to tell the truth in my remote infancy something
must have happened to inhibit me as far as sexual knowledge is
concerned, now I can't find this naturally no matter how hard I try
but it must have happened when I was sleeping in my parents'
bedroom, I slept there for at least three or four years until a couple
of sisters came along to kick me out, and I must surely have happened to hear my parents fooling around, maybe with the lights
out excluding me from their lives, evading my curiosity with
vague phrases or even with threats, shut up or else I'll tend to you
my father may have said, and my mother may have said go to sleep
or else the old witch will come or the bogeyman, and she may have
said this with a harsh irritated voice like when I did something
naughty whereas then I wasn't doing anything naughty I was
only staying awake and listening and anxious to share in their
lives, oh yes she said this at times I'm sure now and in her voice
there wasn't just harshness but something else so close to my

father and so far from me, and at that moment even more than my father perhaps she was the one who wanted to exclude me from that part of herself I could only sense, and this meant plummeting to new depths of solitude and alarm and humiliation, so episodes like this if they did happen were repressed as we say, and also repressed was the desire for knowledge of sexual matters connected with beloved persons, and as a result my father and my mother and the maiden I love are like angels, or rather as far as my father and mother are concerned it isn't that I think of them as angels I just don't direct my thoughts to their sexual functions that's all, so when a boy tells me my father does dirty things with my mother I stand there like a dope making the other boys who are also there discussing these interesting problems burst out laughing, and I immediately have to recover myself and pretend I was joking but inside me one of the mainstays of my universe is collapsing, I feel anger and grief and dismay and nothing can console me not even the thought that everybody is made like that and everybody is born from such acts even kings and princes and the Pope, it's horrible that it should happen in this way God shouldn't allow it if He existed, and anyhow my father and my mother shouldn't have done it, I don't want to accept this original sin of conception and birth, I don't want to crawl on my belly and eat dust all the days of my life, and when it comes to wretchedness and loneliness this is worse than anything else that has happened to me till now, now I understand how filthy the world is and how necessary the ways of sex are, however when I manage to drag myself bruised and battered out of this turmoil I am more of a man, and my Ego has stopped letting itself be shunted around like a fool between the Id and the Superego now it has a personality of its own and also its own pride and firmness, now my father has really stopped dominating me and so have the passions or impulses of the Id finished dominating unopposed or almost, I have to believe in myself and in my own strength, there is no masturbation for a whole year, I've had far too many humiliations to let myself in for the ones that always come after the solitary pleasures, I am proud of my integrity and intelligence and perseverance and at the end of the year I win the gilt medal, the first in my class to be called up onto the platform and this is sweet revenge for having come into the world *inter feces et urinam*, and amid the crowd of parents invited to the prize-giving ceremony there is my father radiant with satisfaction and I believe this year he will give me a bicycle, for years he's been promising me one provided I am promoted with honors and this year he won't mind the sacrifice since I am the very first in the class, but I didn't do it for the bicycle obviously nor for my father, I did it for myself by applying myself to my studies and resolving to resist temptation, however since I've made it and I've won the gilt medal I would be pleased if he bought me the bicycle, and in fact when we come out of the school the first thing my father does is to take me to the window of the bicycle shop and ask me which one do you like, this is a great day for me but not without its problems, my eye ranges from one model to another of the ones on display, and naturally it lights on the racing bike with the low handle-bars and the slender wooden wheels and the back-pedaling brake, it would be wonderful if I had the nerve to ask for the Girardengo model even if it does cost too much money and anyway my father surely doesn't approve of racing bikes since they aren't serious, maybe to ask for an ordinary bike would be better after the sacrifices my father has made to keep me in boarding school however I've made sacrifices too, I've studied with all my strength without committing any impure acts to dedicate myself completely to my studies and now I say I want a racing bike, and my father is a bit hurt maybe he would have been pleased if I had chosen an ordinary bike like his namely a Zardo which isn't a famous make but it's made with the same parts as all the big names and so you don't pay for the name but otherwise it's just like the Bianchi or the Legnano if not better, besides while we're on the subject of buying a bicycle my father says we'll have to talk it over with my mother to see if she agrees, and that's not all because before coming to a final decision we have to wait till Saturday to see how sales go in the store, and then finally when Saturday has gone by they bring home my bicycle-reward but it's a girl's bike with a net over the rear wheel to keep their skirts from getting tangled in the spokes, and they tell me that after thinking it over they've bought this girl's bike because in this way my sisters can use it too after all I only ride it during the three summer months and for the rest of the year I'm away at school, and in any case they'll give me a bicycle all my own maybe even a racing bike if I want it when I've passed my final exams namely in a couple of years, and I say all right though it's very painful to go around on a girl's bike with the other students of the town not to mention the Venetians who come for the summer and have big-name bicycles and also toys I can never have like the number five Meccano which has more pieces than any other set or else an electric train with sixty feet of track and switches and a station that lights up, and then they go off on excursions together the boys and girls from Venice and this year I'm in love with all these girls from Venice who have come up for the holidays they have pretty sweaters and plaid skirts and shining hair, but of course they don't notice me the son of the village hatseller from whom no Venetian would ever buy a hat or an umbrella since it's all peasants' stuff, and I would be satisfied even with the least pretty of these Venetian girls but how can I manage when I'm never well dressed and wear old shoes and ride a girl's bike, and my hair never has time to grow out because in boarding school they crop my head right up to the last month, and so I plunge into my loneliness and my humiliation thinking one day I'll show them all of these Venetians who I really am, but in the meanwhile I'm a boy with a girl's bike, always off to one side waiting to be called to join in their games or their excursions or to be invited to their houses where there are beautiful gardens with wicker chairs and maids in white uniforms who serve lemonade and a gramophone to dance to, however they rarely make up their minds to ask me only when they need an extra boy to have an even number, and anyway I don't know how to dance and I never accept the lemonade because I wouldn't know how to take the glass from the tray and where to put it after I've drunk, and then I can hardly move when I think how badly dressed I am compared with them, so I almost always say no

when they do remember to invite me, and I ask why did you bring
me into the world, why I ask of everything with desperation, and
I go back to committing impure acts not seeking the pleasure
but the frightful repentance and expiations, so that no girl will ever
fall in love with me ever, and already trapped in my future
diseases I read immense books by Tolstoy and Dostoyevsky and
I seek my damnation after the pleasure, and I steal money from
my father's pockets, I wait until he goes to wash his face after his
afternoon nap maybe singing Come with me sweet flower of May
if the nap has been refreshing, my God he goes down in his under-
wear to wash at the sink and he leaves his pants in the bedroom
and I quickly hunt in his pockets for his purse and I take one or
two silver five-lire pieces, depending on how many there are I take
one or two, then I buy cigarettes for myself and chocolates to offer
the Venetian girls if they happen to stop in the square after going
out riding on their bikes and they accept the chocolates but seem
to forget about them immediately afterwards, anyhow this isn't
why I steal, certainly not just for cigarettes and chocolates and
other things but to prove that my father doesn't even notice it
when they take five or ten lire away from him, so why did you try
to make me believe in those sacrifices father, causing me to suffer
for every lira I forced you to spend, the nasty school bread and
the foul school soup and the books and the Italian and Latin dictionaries which are so expensive and the anthologies and the shoes,
the shoes that every so often had to be bought, my God how I
suffered over that money I made you spend, and now if I steal five
or ten lire you don't even notice it, and you bought me a girl's bike
and I always have to fight with my sisters to use it, but with the
money I've stolen from you so far I could have bought myself even
two racing bikes, and it's wrong I know, it's wrong to steal and
you're wrong too, because why did you bring me into the world
then why, to deceive me and make me suffer, I didn't ask you to
I didn't want to, I keep looking around for some purpose in my
life and I can't find any and only when I read do I seem to live,
reading marvelous stories that could never happen to me, I live
the lives of others without finding my own, where is my Natasha

life or my Sonya life, where are the Nerina and the Silvia of my
regrets, I think and think and I have nobody and I cry often in
complete unhappiness when I ride off alone along the country
paths on my girl's bike and the moon rises over the endless plain,
the moon big against the dark poplars and the plane trees and the
willows, and crickets all around and a nightingale here and there
but as if everywhere, and with my soul in upheaval I say so we'll
go no more a-roving, my God I'm not fourteen yet and already I
have such a great longing to die, what am I doing in this world
what am I doing, I love love love so wretchedly and immensely
that I don't have the courage to decide on an object for my love,
and then mine is love in bitterness love in renunciation, now
houses and human beings are far away and I can sing without
anybody hearing me Lovely liar beauty of an hour your lips are
like a poisoned flower, and this also makes me cry like when Leopardi says the bitter memory and a song disappearing along the
paths and dying little by little, that's how I am, that's how my
heart was aching, and now autumn has come, the Venetians have
gone away, in the countryside there is the smell of must and a bit
of low fog, tomorrow I'll be going back to school tomorrow morning, and I am so starved for affection that I can't decide whether
going back to school is good or bad whether I'll suffer more or less,
apparently there is suffering everywhere and who can tell where
there's less and where more, and besides what do I care there is
a long highway with great plane trees going to Mestre and lights
burning in the distance at the crossroads or in front of a tavern,
I pedal fast to warm myself up and at the top of my lungs I sing
Why don't you leave me alone with my woe why do you follow
wherever I go, this love business must be real suffering for plenty
of people besides me, but lover without you no peace can I find
says this song that I like so much, in fact I start it again at the
beginning Like the moon I'm a vagabond at night through the
streets I shall sing my song, besides what do I know about love,
I could die of love for one of these Venetians named Luciana or
Liliana or Resy and none of them would ever give me anything in
return, Your lips are like a poisoned flower, tomorrow morning

I go back to school but tonight I'm free and I'm going to Mestre to the St. Michael's Day fair, the last Sunday of the festivities, there are lots of people in the square and band music, festoons of colored lights, the big platform where the tombola was held in the afternoon, I wonder who won the thousand-lire prize lucky bastard, now however the raffle is in progress with the bedroom suite as first prize and a kitchen stove and bicycles of course, a girl's and a man's and a Wolsitt special, and I think I really would like to win that racing Wolsitt just to show my father I can have one without him bothering to buy it for me, tonight's the last night so they're bound to put the good chances in the bowl, I want to try my luck and so I slip in among the people milling around one of the booths which I have carefully picked out because among the ticketsellers there's a classmate of mine from boarding school, maybe his father is on the committee and that's why they've got him selling tickets and maybe he knows more or less where the good tickets are which side of the bowl and naturally when he sees me he will try to get me one of the good tickets, in fact I hold out a lira to him and say four tickets and he gives me the four tickets and also gives me nine lire change as if I had given him ten lire instead of only one, I look up to point this out to him and he winks at he, I immediately turn redder than a rooster's comb of course, here's a highly complicated problem to be solved in an instant, I could say to him look you made a mistake in fact I ought to say this to him according to what my Superego promptly suggests, don't let yourself be drawn into dishonest actions because you'll have to pay later the Superego warns me, however it's also nice to receive nine lire like manna from heaven, so the Superego is rapidly silenced under the favoring circumstance that this is a period when my carabiniere father has lost much of his authority, and now I don't give a damn when the four tickets the friend has given me prove to be three blanks and one worth a candy, now so as to be inconspicuous I go and buy four more and another four and still another in different booths and all I get are blanks and candies and a cheap comb, so I am rightfully a bit contemptuous of such a dishonest raffle, you see I say

to my Superego you don't want me to cheat them but just look at
the way they're cheating me, and this is a comforting thought and
at the same time a dynamic one I mean it gives me the nerve to
go back to my friend again with a lire in my hand, and again he
gives me four tickets and nine lire change, and three more times I
repeat the same trick though not so light-heartedly of course and
in fact the fourth time it seems to me that instead of just ordinary
people around me there are all these carabinieri and policemen
maybe in plain clothes, the Superego can't find more moral forms
of intimidation but anyhow in my case the device works and in
fact I leave the square as fast as I can determined never to go back
there, in my pocket I have a lot of candy thirteen clothespins and
two combs, and I have twenty-three lire and I can honestly say I
have never been so rich in my life, the feeling of wealth is en-
hanced by the fact that I am in a sense obligated to spend these
ill-gotten gains within the evening since tomorrow morning I
have to go off to school, so I go into the Luna Park like a person
who knows what he wants out of life whereas the fact is I don't
know what I want at all, I mean the shooting gallery is stupid I
can't see the fun in smashing clay pipes or hitting the rabbit that
if you hit it in the center of the belly it falls down and some gun-
powder explodes, target-shooting is downright silly and in fact
there aren't many people shooting except for one stand where
there's a redhead with big boobs and a glistening laughing mouth,
there are lots of older boys there shooting also with the automatic
American-style rifle and she laughs at them, but I certainly can't
go over and join those older boys and court her even though if
she knew how much money I have in my pocket maybe she would
leave them for me, I believe that in the back of the stand she has
a place where she does dirty things and if she let me do them with
her I'd even give her twenty lire, however how can I let her know
I have twenty-three lire on me she doesn't even look at me and anyway if she did look at me I surely wouldn't have the nerve to
motion to her or anything, my heart is already pounding just because I'm thinking these things, and I would be satisfied merely to
look at her for a while from the distance trying to imagine what

dirty things I could do with her, and then I get fed up standing there like a dope and I start to go on the rides first on the roller coaster and then on the swings, and of course it's fun to go on these rides but by myself without a friend it's not all that amusing in fact after a while it upsets your stomach a bit and so when I come down from the swings I find her in front of me looking at me, maybe she's not very beautiful at first sight like this because she has a long nose, but her hair is pretty with bangs and her eyes are strange and she's thin, with a heavy sweater that comes down almost to her knees so her skirt seems very short, and three or four boys are buzzing around her saying God only knows what to her and she contemptuously doesn't answer and she looks at me maybe only to spite them, but anyhow she does look at me that's the important thing and I feel all atingle at the enormous responsibility of this occasion, now I have to say something to her I tell myself in excitement and panic mixed, luckily I remember I still have almost twenty lire in my pocket and with twenty lire you can behave like a man, so I get my nerve up and I say signorina would you like to come for a ride on the swings with me, and now she looks at me as if when she looked at me before she hadn't really seen me and then she answers yes with a nod I won't say contemptuously but haughtily anyhow, so we sit down obviously she is in the seat in front of mine, and the kids who were pestering her before now laugh and yell hey blondie next time it's our turn and she glances at them with superhuman scorn and tells me not to pay attention to them they're just silly kids, meanwhile the swings begin to move and we're holding on to each other and when they're moving fast she says give me a push, and I say to myself now I'll give her a push and I'll lose her, but I have to push her and I do with all my might but with my arms only, I can't push with my foot since these swings are the kind vulgarly called the kick-in-the-ass and I mustn't remind her of certain words by pushing her with my foot, but even with my arms I manage to push her pretty hard and she flies into the air whereas I conversely sink down, and then she sinks down while I rise in the air, and

then comes the difficult moment because if the push is hard
enough the two seats come close together and we can grab each
other again, but if the push by any chance was weak we can't
manage to grab each other again and then we have to make a
whole turn separated and looking at each other like a couple of
idiots, or rather me like an idiot since the fault would be only
mine, but she holds her hand back as far as she can and pushing
myself forward I manage to grab it, and now we are united again
flying through the air and she says what's your name and then
she says give me a push with your foot it works better, and she
says this sweetly without making me think of kicks in the ass so
I push her and she flies happily into the air with her bangs
flapping this way and that depending on which way she turns
holding back her hand to be caught again, and already her nose
isn't so long and when she smiles her eyes shine and her mouth is
beautiful, my God here I am already thinking that it would be
wonderful to go off to the wars to die for her and this means that
I'm on the verge of falling in love if I haven't already fallen, and in
fact I'm annoyed that those kids who were pestering her before
are now standing down below to look at her legs, but she doesn't
pay any attention to them she's so caught up in the joy of flying
aloft and she wants to go higher and higher, and we take four
turns in a row on the swings and then three or four on the roller
coaster, and when the moment comes when you go hurtling down
the big descent she lets out a cry and holds on to me tight and
when we get to the bottom she laughs delightedly, and then we go
on the little cars and she always drives bumping into the others
and then laughing, and she bumps into the other cars on purpose
so that our car is crosswise and the others pile up one after the
other and then they have to stop and untangle us, and she laughs
so happily and is more and more beautiful and every now and then
she asks me do you still have any money and I say yes so we keep
on going around, but at a certain point she says that's enough because maybe it's almost midnight and this time when she goes
home she's sure to get a beating, but she says this gaily with a

shrug and she even asks me if I'll see her home since she lives in Via Piave not far away, and I would go with her to the end of the world I'm so in love, ah I think this is the girl for me because she's sweet and pretty and doesn't put on airs, we buy roast chestnuts and peanuts before leaving the Luna Park and we go towards the Via Piave walking along in no hurry though it is surely past midnight, and I tell her that tomorrow I'm going off to school and I won't see her for nine months but she can send me a postcard or two if she feels like it to let me know she's thinking of me only she has to sign it your loving cousin Germana and not just Germana otherwise the prefect will understand and throw the card away, and she keeps saying yes and eating the chestnuts as long as they last and then the peanuts, she says she's glad she met me because she's had such a nice time, she's never had such a nice time at the fair she says because the other boys aren't polite like me and I'm a student and educated, and then she suddenly asks tell me do you like me and I am immediately half confused by the difficulty of this kind of dialogue and also overcome with emotion naturally, can't you understand that by yourself I manage to say and she says she understands it but she also wants to hear me say it, and getting my nerve up I say I like you so much I want to die and she starts to laugh saying why die I'd rather live, and then she looks at me seriously not eating any more not even the peanuts because she's finished them and she says I like you too, and naturally by then I knew she liked me but it was incredible to hear her say it, and right after that she stops under the arcade in the Via Piave in front of a doorway and says this is where I live, there are people going past under the arcades and she looks at them nervously and tensely and suspiciously because they might be people who know her and if her father finds out she stops and talks with boys in the street he'll beat her black and blue, but all the same she stands by the door of the building while we hold hands and when there's nobody going by we are looking at each other gulping with emotion and every now and then she says I have to go now, and I say yes nodding my head in despair but then I say to her not yet and she stays because she really likes me to be there with her, I know she feels something for me too and for the first time I understand the value of my person which can make somebody else happy, I didn't understand this with my father and my mother since they had to make all those sacrifices and so basically if I hadn't existed it might have been better for them, but this little girl Germana whom I've only just met says that in her heart she will always remember me even if I have to stay in school for nine months in a row, she says that she's lucky to have met me but unlucky too because now she's very fond of me and when you love a person for one reason or another you always have to suffer, she sighs and says once again I have to go now and she opens the door of the building and really is about to go away, but then she gives a quick look around and seeing that nobody can see us she takes my hand and says come in, and I go with her into a narrow hallway there are the stairs going up and she is tiptoeing towards the back also looking up to see if by chance anybody can see her and still holding me by the hand she leads me to a place where you go downstairs and we go down a flight of steps together, there it's almost dark and there's a slight smell of garbage and she suddenly takes my face in her two hands and we look at each other for just a moment and I'm thinking now now it's going to happen, it's going to happen and I don't know what and then she kisses me putting her tongue into my mouth, this is what was to happen and I'm afraid God God why am I afraid, and then all of a sudden I stop being afraid even when I feel her whole body sticking to me even with her stomach against my stomach beyond all sin or shame, and I don't understand anything now I'm all filled with a new pleasure that runs through my body and in my blood like when I dream, it's an endless pleasure that contains every kind of thrill and delight, like when I was afraid as a baby and Mamma protected me, and when I was shuddering in front of the holy tabernacle asking God to let me die in Him, and when I was trembling with pride as I went up onto the platform to receive my medal, and when I was in torment at my solitary pleasures, it all seems contained in this kiss in addition to all my dreams of sexless love and dreams of poetry, now an immense fusion is fulfilled in this extraordinary and very sweet thing, and now it ends but I also know that it can never end, she says wait for me here a moment if I can I'll come down again, I see her go off waving her hand and then I hear her footsteps on the stairs higher and higher mingling with other sounds, and then no sounds, and the sound perhaps of a door shutting, and I am there waiting filled most of all with bewilderment trying to connect the cellar smelling of mold and garbage with love for her still composed of heart-pounding and tenderness, and the mystery of my sex related to another sex perceiving how the two can be two and also one thing at the same time, and I wonder if all men know what I now know perhaps they know, men have a common condition and common experiences and after all what I have done is kiss a girl, however what I have discovered in doing this is mine and may be different from what the others discover and feel, this must be true otherwise there wouldn't have been any Tolstoy or Leopardi or Dostoyevsky and I couldn't be different from other people the way I want to be, now I know I was born for something great, before I used to think of this only out of spite to show those who scorned me how wrong they were to scorn me but now my greatness is within me already achieved with a new measure of my strength, I'll be somebody in life yes I'll be somebody, but in the meanwhile she doesn't come down and I have to go and get my bike otherwise the watchman will go away, at one o'clock he leaves and I'm afraid it's already past one, if she hasn't come down by now she isn't coming maybe they've locked her in her room and maybe she's crying and suffering because she can't come down, anyhow I'll make a dash now and get my bike and come back, I do come right back there though there's no hope she can come down by now all the same I wait after putting my bike against the wall of the house opposite so if by chance she should come down she won't see that after the airs I gave myself with that money in my pocket I have a girl's bike and not even a famous make, I wait till after two o'clock walking up and down because it's cold and obviously I'm not expecting her any more but tomorrow I go off to school and I feel

I have to linger just a little more near this place where in a sense the veil of my mystery has been rent, now my mind is opened to all the great problems of life birth and love and death and fate, all things that until now I've read about in books and vaguely perceived through poetry and believed they belonged only to others except for wretchedness and grief, and now instead there is also this share of joy that is mine, maybe this is the meaning of life not solitude and desperation but some force that is not only an evasion of evil, life also means having thoughts of joy you can escape to when you want, and now with all my being in turmoil I head for home along the great road with the plane trees shedding their leaves, it is autumn a new season and year and weather, and this can't hurt me the cold and the fog because my blood has never coursed so triumphantly through my veins and arteries, I am energy itself and fate, there are stars above the fog and worlds without end and I am here watching and feeling and sharing in it all, and in the heart of the night a song that was heard along the paths dying little by little once before had gripped my heart, and now my heart is gripped again at Leopardi's words but in a different way from before, it's filled with consolation which brings solitude and love together or rather solitude no more with two people, and so life that was evil may not be all evil now that there is strength and sweetness and the desire to be somewhere not out of despair but love, and then I reach home and my mother is leaning out of her window on the upper floor, she says where have you been all night you no-good you won't be satisfied till you've killed your poor mother, and I am not even touched by her suffering by the hours she has suffered waiting for her fourteen-year-old son who went out on his bike at eight in the evening and hadn't come home at one in the morning and two in the morning and two thirty, and unspeakable thoughts of accidents have upset her for all these hours of the night her heart racked by thoughts of death and I pay no attention, I can even imagine she did feel all this and I don't care, I have a fullness that cannot be touched and indeed there is no room for the annoying presence of a mother, and my

father isn't to be seen he must surely be in bed and I hear his voice
say harshly don't bother with him I tell you he's going to end up
in jail anyhow mark my words he says, and behind the closed windows of the other rooms I can picture my sisters listening smugly,
who am I who must be given everything only to cause suffering,
oh God if only they didn't exist if nobody existed, and instead my
father is there and from his bed he continues prophesying that
I'm going to end up in jail, and why do I have to have this father
and this house, certainly today I can imagine myself waiting for
my daughter until three in the morning and she doesn't come and
it kills me, I wouldn't exist for her and my father didn't exist for
me when he said in a harsh voice from his bed mark my words
and my mother didn't exist at the window saying don't you have
anything to say for yourself you young scoundrel you're going to
kill me, and I have nothing to say to her no words come to me, I
realize this is another break after the one when I learned that she
and my father did those things, maybe I don't have any bitterness
toward them and it isn't that I don't answer her because of any
whim or to make her angry, I just don't know what to say or how
to answer the question where have I been and what have I been
doing till three in the morning, I couldn't talk to them of love or
of kisses or of all the thoughts I had while I was pedaling towards
home, these are events and feelings that have become a part of me
and have made me different and more remote than ever from my
mother and father, now I belong to a woman to my friends to the
world to anybody with whom I can speak of myself but not to
them, and therefore while I wearily fall asleep thinking of the
marvelous experience and also keeping in mind that tomorrow
morning they will wake me at seven to take me off to school I'm
not sorry to go to school, I would go anywhere to get away from
the oppressive presence of father and mother and sisters whom
I have now left behind me with no regret, I really have nothing
more to do with them, the hatseller who with two or three retired
sergeants or corporals piles up misspellings on unlined paper in
petitions sent to General Headquarters to Ministries to His Ex-
cellency the Chief of State Duce of Fascism Benito Mussolini,

eternal requests of people who have served the Fatherland with
loyalty and honor for so many years and are now faithful and most
humble servants of the Excellencies whom they take the liberty of
addressing, now I can go off to school even with relief, and then
I am bearing within me this mysterious and shy treasure which
morever is supposed to last a considerable number of months
except it actually lasts a very short time because the boy from
Mestre who gave me such generous change for those one-lire
pieces when I ask him if he knows such and such a girl who lives
at a certain address in the Via Piave he says she's a little whore
who will do anything with anybody who gives her two or three
lire, she even did this to him and that to him he affirms, and naturally I also tell how she did this and that because of course I had
caught on right away the kind of girl she was and that you could
even take her out in the fields and go the whole way, and I say
these things with a grief that burns through my body and with
shame at my cowardice but also after he has explained that she's
just a little two-or-three-lire whore I'm no longer capable of loving her very much not even in the secret depths of my heart, but
on the other hand I can't tell myself that when the school year ends
in nine months I'll go and see her and do dirty things in the fields,
inside me there is a painful confusion on the subject of this girl
and to tell the truth although she was the one even in a cellar
smelling of refuse who gave me an idea of the universal orgone
energy or in other words sex I tend to place her as much as I can
in the spiritual sphere, and I succeed at least halfway in the sense
that I would like her to kiss me again that way and hold me tight
however I wouldn't want to do with her the things I would do if
I could with the women dressed like priests who live in brothels, I
say to myself how can it be that she goes with all the boys she
has honey-colored hair and a sweet smile and kindly eyes, she who
can say with such sweetness and simplicity I like you, true there
were those kids who yelled hey blondie next time it's our turn and
maybe they were referring to dirty things to be done thereabouts
perhaps behind one of the stands however I mustn't forget Katyu-
sha or Sonya whom I had so often accompanied across the end-

less steppes towards Siberia, and so I ask myself if I wouldn't marry her anyway provided she never did anything with anybody afterwards maybe not even with me, and I come to the conclusion that maybe I would marry her especially to redeem her, but after less than a week I get a postcard with affectionately yours xxx your cousin Germana, and she has succeeded in making five spelling mistakes counting one in the address and what's more the handwriting is awful nothing but hen tracks as they say, and so for general literary reasons in which if you like you can see a sign of the future my first love goes up in smoke, and I can rightfully call it first love because what I had previously felt for Venetian girls and sisters of classmates wasn't love mostly I dreamed of dying, but this time not only my soul but also my senses were gratified, and I could swear that they were never again to be gratified as surprisingly as they were that time.

Now this episode's importance I say is not so much the sexuality though sexuality was certainly in question revealed for the first time at least as a focusing of the libido, the important thing was the effect produced in the sphere of family emotions, and at this point I should note that there are some discrepancies between me and my little old man who tends rightly enough to talk always about sexuality as if the roots of my disease had to be found there perforce, whereas I as a rule tend in the other direction that is I insist on the strictly anti-erotic relationship with my father who with every step I make along the inevitable path of life loses ground, and it isn't simply the fact that I'm now running around with girls or to be more accurate I would run around with them if I had the opportunity since I have at least learned what kissing is, no I think the profound reason for my detachment from my father isn't in these events with women which everybody goes through without necessarily becoming neurotic over them, it must be sought especially in my abnormal student status, seen both as a social evolution which brings me into contact with people of higher standing like the Venetians who when they run into my father simply pretend not to know who he is, and as cultural

gain and here I can truly and legitimately begin to wonder how
a man who can't get a subjunctive right if his life depends on
it can think of being my guide through life, and here mind you
it's not just snootiness although speaking objectively it isn't any
fun to have a father who balls up the subjunctive but the fact
is that he is driven to publish abroad his weaknesses in the subjunctive and other equally complex means of expression because
he is a graphomane, I mean he writes endless letters and petitions
both for himself and for others who are even worse off than he,
and when he writes on his own account he usually puts at the
bottom of the page, sometimes a long sheet other times note size,
a big rubber-stamped signature with ornaments and his last name
and first name and his denomination Merchant, and on this point
alone one can remark that educated persons sign with their first
names first and their last names last which is exactly the opposite
of what he does, and as far as the title of Merchant is concerned
even overlooking what Cicero writes I feel quite correctly on this
score namely that a man's profession is a title of honor only if it is
exercised on a grand scale, it must also be said that my father to
my way of thinking adorned his signature with the word arbi-
trarily in the sense that the shop's business was going from bad
to worse, but I ask myself how it could have gone any better since
apart from all the rest he didn't know how to buy or how to sell,
that is to say he bought the wrong things stuff not even the peasants wanted unless a smart salesman could unload it on them
which was not my father's case, and despite this even if he wrote
to the bishop of the diocese or to my Latin professor he obstinately
used that rubber stamp with the title of Merchant and underneath his signature with seven linking swirls to underline the
importance of his last name and first name in that order, however
the big trouble wasn't so much in the signature as in what preceded it I mean the body of the letter, and yet I must confess that
up to a certain point in the story my interest in his writings must
have had a voluptuary aspect since I went snooping on the sly in
a big ledger where he kept a copy of every letter he sent off not

because there was any practical reason for him to have a copy but I believe in order to renew whenever he liked the satisfaction of having written them, except that one fine day after I had brilliantly passed my final examinations my father almost as if to signify that I was now a man submitted to me of his own accord a very laborious memorandum with an incredible quantity of erasures and variations, quite understandable since it was a letter addressed to the Most Illustrious and Excellent Procurator General of Taxes, four closely written pages arranged I must say with some logic since first there was an exposition of the facts, then a proportionate number of complaints, and then an abundant list of even the most far-fetched merits of the Most Illustrious and Excellent Procurator, and finally the petition aimed at a tax exemption since business was really very bad, however if you overlook the all too carefully worked out arguments there was nothing else that could be praised and in fact I could only make some sense out of it because by now I was secretly accustomed to my father's prose and moreover on the days when he was distilling his missives it was his habit to go over the arguments amply to himself but aloud and in the presence of his family, he talked about them at table asserting his reasons and preventing the others from interrupting, so I already knew the communication's contents but the Procurator General who didn't know them would have had a hard time understanding a thing since my father's prose might indeed be called exuberant but never clear, and anyhow the question here wasn't so much the letter per se as the relationship between father and son in the sense that when he urged me to read the document and therefore I suppose to express an opinion we both knew that we were at an important turning point in our life together, in fact he wasn't altogether able to conceal his uneasiness although tactically he was reserved maybe so he could afterwards say he had let me read the thing to show me how to write a petition, and I was no less uneasy than he was since as I proceeded through the four laborious and long sheets I realized that paradoxically his prose was sustained only by virtue of a total upheaval of syntax, namely that it was all a prodigious and fantastic construction of nonsense and if you touched even a single subjunctive the whole thing would collapse irreparably, so I was already thinking perhaps cynically of saying that according to me it was just fine anyhow I didn't much feel like rewriting letters to Procurators, but my Superego though it was going through a rather listless phase was ready and waiting to reproach me if I made a misstep, and here I didn't have much choice anybody can understand that whatever I did I would be making a mistake whether I said black or whether I said white, so I chose the path of greater satisfaction for my conscience and said that if he asked me the whole thing had to be rewritten, and at that moment my father must have realized his colossal error in sending me to school, to tell the truth I had realized this myself some time before but he hadn't as yet, now we both knew but we didn't feel any better for the knowledge, in fact he didn't say a word he painfully folded up the pages he had sweated over and put them in a drawer and since at that time I had a taste for disastrous finales I said a man should maintain his dignity also in matters of taxes and it was wrong to have recourse to oily phrases of the kind this letter was full of beginning with bombastic superlatives like Most Illustrious and Excellent which were out of fashion by now, and he asked if by chance I was trying to teach him how to get along in this world, and after this episode there was a new awareness of separation between us so that we even avoided occasions to speak to each other directly, for example in the old days when I came home late at night and obviously the next day woke up so late that when I came downstairs the whole family was already eating my father would look at me though without much amiability asking me what sort of no-good bum I have been out with till four in the morning, or he might say to me without any preamble I tell you you'll end up in jail mark my words, well now he didn't look at me any more not even glumly but stared in the other direction and tried to attract as much as possible my sisters' attention saying with a certain solemnity mark my words somebody in this family is going to end up in jail, and there was no doubt about the identity of that somebody however I acted as if nothing had happened and ate with good appetite since at that time I enjoyed excellent health, and I never bothered to investigate whether his persistent prophecy came from genuine conviction or from the circumstance that, since my father had been a carabiniere for so many years, the idea of jail as the final destination for an idler like me must come into his mind almost without his wanting it to.

Anyhow this rupture
of direct relations between me and my father and the resultant
shift of our struggle to what you might call a superior plane of
allusions and nuances is what suits me best at the present moment,
namely when with great heedlessness I am entering the first year
of the *liceo*, out of boarding school at last and in a Royal Liceo
and Ginnasio where there are also six or seven girls sitting on the
front benches, but I don't fall in love with any of them and instead
God only knows why I fall in love with our mathematics mistress
who is at the very least twice my age, but how can I help it at times
I sit there spellbound staring at her and when she notices me she
goes all red which could be a sign she's not entirely indifferent
to me either, but frankly it's a completely profitless love which
doesn't even lure me into studying mathematics in fact at the end
of the year I find myself failing in this fairly disagreeable subject
and forced to take the October make-up exam, however I have to
thank God that it's the only bad subject I have and that I wasn't
flunked outright as my father, for that matter, had predicted and
who went on frequently saying to my sisters at table just listen to
me before long a certain member of this family will have to go
off and learn a trade, however it must be borne in mind that for me

this was shall we say an overwhelming year with the sudden
responsibility of being completely free after boarding school, and
my first real experiences with women since by using ink eradicator
on my identity card for better or worse it turns out that I'm eighteen already and so I can go to the houses and the first time I go
with an older classmate who's repeating the first year of *liceo* and
who really is eighteen and widely experienced in these things, and
since we don't have any extra money to throw around we go to a
five-lire house which is fairly crummy to tell the truth, and naturally for some time now I've known that the women in there
aren't dressed like priests but in transparent evening dresses however all things considered it would be better if they were dressed
like priests because a woman's breasts and sex aren't things a
greenhorn can look at without a cerain squeamishness, and in any
case here there wasn't anything joyous to be seen especially for
me who was still so spiritualized that I turned up my nose at
Titian's Venus, so I tried to ignore the body as much as I could
and stare at the faces though I was only going from bad to worse,
perhaps I was lacking common sense because in my heart of
hearts I was no doubt expecting to find well maybe not Beatrice
but at least Nausicaa instead of those four women in filmy dresses
with sequins four real crocks who aroused thoughts that were
Lenten if not actually funereal, maybe if I had waited and saved
up more money to go to a ten-lire house it would have been better
but now I was there and I certainly couldn't show I lacked the
nerve to go upstairs, so when one of these women I don't even
dare to look at comes over and caresses me here and there and
says come on upstairs with me handsome and I'll show you a good
time personally I would gladly say no, but instead I get up and
follow her up the steps trying not to see that enormous behind
which perhaps not accidentally she is waggling before my eyes,
and here the guilt mechanism starts working in advance because
my chief thought is I bet they catch you with the faked identity
card and put you in jail, and obviously this is all it takes to
make me also think of my father which is just the right thought
to block any sexual arousal before it starts if it were going to

start, but one way or another we get to the room where I linger
a moment and look at the bed with the counterpane all rumpled
and the bidet and the absorbent cotton and the bottle of perman-
ganate on the shelf over the washbasin, my God the clap now I
suddenly have to start thinking about the clap too, the clap in relation to my father namely how would I manage if I caught it and
had to ask him for money to treat it, and naturally this is another
kind of thought that doesn't favor erective potency so along with
my other fears there is the new fear of not proving myself a man,
and maybe beneath all this the fear of castration which I must
have had since they say everybody has it, and for that matter if
you except the largely mistaken information given me by the
schoolmate who told me the women in these houses are dressed
like priests my education both recently and in the past even
ancestrally so to speak was all directed at forming a splendid
shackled nature capable of blocking the course of my sexual excitement even in front of Marlene Dietrich if I had chanced upon
her, anyhow this woman here surely doesn't understand any of
my moral tempests and all of a sudden she says well handsome
what are we here for you want to pay overtime and I show her
my five lire saying this is all I have and she says hurry up then
since she's already stretched out on the bed all naked with her
abundant flesh in a pose which should arouse desire and I won't
deny I've imagined time and again in my solitary erotic fantasies
a woman lying just like this if not worse however in this absolute
lack of any emotional contact the pose seems a mistake to me considering its aim, in any case since she's told me to hurry up I
imagine I will have to lie down beside her and the first thing I do
is bend over to untie my shoes and when a man tries to untie his
shoes while he has immense moral problems he never manages
and she says what the hell are you doing now you really are dumb,
and she tells me that shoes are not taken off and obviously this
error over the shoes which for that matter seems a recurrent
problem in my life doesn't favor the release of orgone energy,
nevertheless I lie down beside her and remain motionless and she
says I suppose I have to do it all myself and with this she un-

buttons my pants, but I stop her at once finally displaying a bit of courage and I tell her I don't want anything and she looks at me almost irritated and says well what did you come up here for and then no longer irritated she asks me if this is the first time and I tell her it is and I feel she is looking at me for a moment with a human expression and I feel that one of those things might happen whereby I could later dream of going to Siberia with her to atone for our evils, but she obviously doesn't want to go to Siberia and she simply shrugs and says you have to pay anyhow you know, and I nod and then I hide my face against her naked side and lie there torn between shame and a sense of mystery with a terrible need for tenderness, I would come here of all places to look for tenderness but here I am and with all my strength I press my face against her flesh and her body and animal depth or warmth thinking that it isn't her, not that I want it to be another woman I just don't want it to be her, who knows maybe I am attempting of course unconsciously to reconstruct the Oedipal situation and I am in revolt because all this is ugly it's so ugly, there I say to myself we're hunting for a conflict that can explain my neurosis and why couldn't this conflict be my inability to accept the flesh, our sick and dirty and ugly flesh, ah now I see a game I used to play when I was little you rubbed the palms of your hands hard together till they felt hot and painful and then you rapidly raised your palms to your nose to smell the smell and I used to say this is the smell of death, our flesh is an instrument of death, and it's true that later thanks especially to foreign widows I gradually adapted myself to combining the senses with the higher feelings or to put it differently the presentiment of death with physical pleasure so that now having reached what we could call a belated maturity on that side everything is sailing along smoothly it seems, and I say seems because in reality it isn't that all conflicts take place in the light of reason, some in fact the most important ones take place in the unconscious and so while I believe I am enjoying to the full these pleasures that the flesh still grants me nevertheless disgust and remote rebellions and fears survive in my unconscious, mystic terror survives and anxiety about mortal punishment for the wretched sins against the sixth commandment for the impure acts committed in the secrecy of stinking bathrooms, and even though my little old man preaches that it's all healthy I almost always approach the sexual act with the profound conviction that this pleasure or sin whichever it is will have to be paid for in some way, I'll have to pay for it with weakness and sickness, and also with anguish very probably, and in fact when my attacks of anxiety come on me I always do some calculating to see if it can possibly be connected with the sexual act, and these calculations certainly aren't simple or probative in any absolute sense because you have to consider not only the period and the frequency but also the intensity of the orgasm which obviously can't be measured in yards or pounds, and I also tell myself to watch out because one of these days if I think about it it'll be like it was with smoking ever since the time I had an attack while I was smoking I haven't been able to put a cigarette in my mouth, and there are various things I can't do any more like ride on trains or in planes or on boats, or go to the mountains like at Siusi of course, or to football games or to the top floors of buildings or to church or to concerts if by any chance there are a lot of people, or the theater or often even the movies unless it's a comedy or farce, and I can't go to the barber to get my hair cut unless my wife forces me to by arguing with me and then by going along too, and I feel sick in the downtown streets when you can't go forward or backward with the car in heavy traffic, and once I felt funny even in front of the Naval Ministry at two o'clock in the afternoon when all the sailors and civilian employees were coming out and now I normally take fairly circuitous routes to avoid the Naval Ministry around two o'clock, and then also I've taken a dislike to policemen I can't stand even officers or Ph.D's or commendatori, and I dislike night watchmen too, but not the carabinieri it's rare for me to get into an argument with anyone belonging to the Faithful through the Centuries Service, still even if I don't quarrel with carabinieri I have enough manias I should think so all I would need now is to get a phobia about the sexual act too which is one of the few good things I

have left along with spaghetti *all' amatriciana* the rare times I
have the courage to eat it, but I know full well that this other
phobia is lying in wait inside me and my doctor knows it too and
every time I tell him I've made love he says good good for you
like you say to babies when they do their number two in the potty,
but then he's displeased when I tell him that after making love
I kept thinking intensely now I'm going to have a heart attack,
though I used to have the fear of heart attack at the beginning
of my analysis and now it's almost disappeared and has been
replaced by other things like pins and needles in the lower limbs
or a strange weight on the brain or a usually lateral shift of the
center of gravity, and above all of course by vague intestinal
sensations which in some completely indeterminate cases reach
the intensity of depersonalization, that is at a certain moment I
have the impression of no longer having a belly and this occurs
without any pain with absolutely none at all, and I should be overjoyed at this fact since normally my belly hurts me and instead
I start thinking Oh God I don't have any belly for God's sake
what's happening to me now I'm without any belly, and naturally
it isn't that I really think I'm deprived of viscera, that is I touch
my belly and my fingers feel that my abdomen externally exists
and even internally there must be everything that's required, however at the same time and as if contradicting direct experience I
know that as far as inner sensation goes my belly doesn't exist
any more, to give you a more comprehensible notion let's say
it seems paralyzed, that it's lost all sensitivity, in such an eventuality mine would be an extraordinary disease which nobody has
ever had before, and it had to happen to me of all people, and in
this vein I can go on reasoning or unreasoning if you like gradually
working up to a nice anxiety attack which would then be the
proper counterweight to the pleasure felt at the conclusion of the
sexual act, so I have to take a psychoplegic fast or maybe two
before it's too late and sometimes I even get up and start walking
around, provided when I get up I don't notice that the straight
lines are out of whack in which case I have to get right back into
bed and sometimes even wake up my wife so she can help me as

best she can to keep from being overcome with anxiety, and though
recently she tires easily and gets understandably mad if anybody
wakes her up she huffs a bit and says take it easy everybody says
you're not going to go crazy because you keep worrying about
it otherwise what's the use of psychoanalysis, anyhow if there is
any danger that she also might associate my attacks with the
sexual act it's best for me not to wake her at all because she might
take it wrong as she already has on occasion and this isn't too
clear I mean I can't figure out whether she won't let me talk
about it for fear of being influenced by me and therefore spoil-
ing her own pleasure or whether she thinks this is just another of
my manias that's not worth wasting time over, and I believe the
latter is the correct hypothesis namely that for my wife there
is no connection between the above-mentioned act and the subsequent punishment, she even has a hard time believing what is
completely established for me and also for my analyst namely
that it isn't Our Heavenly Father who punished me but my Superego which for reasons of its own not too hard to discover either
has decided against following the Ego in its admittedly belated
sexual evolution and has remained bound to certain anti-erotic
prejudices or has had to remove God only knows what monstrous
Oedipal desires, anyhow it's certain that this Superego which
moreover began to function by absorbing an entire carabiniere
sergeant is chock-full of prejudices, however why it started punishing sexual acts in this special way I don't know, mine is a
Superego that censors even the grumbling of my guts, and this
certainly isn't anything it can have directly absorbed from the
Sergeant I really don't think that, but I must have idealized this
father of mine so much in my very earliest childhood especially
when he was a pure symbol of excellence in the line of creature
comforts in the military chest while he was far away guarding
D'Annunzio, well I had so idealized him that I had constructed
him for myself entirely without sex or intestine, and in its craving
for identification the Superego would want me also to be without
sex or intestine, and since it can't deprive me of these two vital
functions then it tries to screw me with depersonalization or with

serious suffering every time I make use either of my sex or my intestine, which is a big pain especially as regards the intestine, since whereas both by education and maybe by heredity I seem disposed to connect the sexual act with linked concepts of guilt-punishment agreeing on this score also with the Bible not to mention the most authoritative Church Fathers, as far as the anal evacuatory processes are concerned on the other hand I can't find any sense of guilt possible in the conscious sphere, although defecation can very well be linked in the unconscious with the guilt-punishment process if by any chance the parents have been too brusque or severe in interrupting the pleasures of the anal phase, that remote period in our life when it is said we enjoy having bowel movements. Now these regressions toward earliest childhood which psychoanalysis in various ways encourages might first of all be said to aim at what we could call statistical results in the sense that on the basis of experience and studies categories and subcategories of neurotics have been formed and I can't exactly refuse to belong to them even though I put up as is natural no small resistance, and to continue on this subject though I am more than anything else incredulous concerning the pleasures of bowel movements and indeed as I regress toward my earliest childhood I can't seem to find anything better than a bellyache, still when you reach a certain point your conscious memories stop and after that I have to limit myself to what other people tell me, I mean if they tell me for example that between my sixth and twelfth month I went through the anal phase even though I'm fairly unconvinced I don't have any arguments to rebut with, but for this very reason namely to compensate for this virtually unconditional surrender to the other people's ideas my intestine having reached its present disastrous state I remain so to speak stuck with my familiar prejudices like the terrible impression made on me by my father's cancer exposed on his dying belly or the idea of this posthumous revenge for my bad behavior at the moment of his decease, and therefore nothing could be easier for the late lamented even under the guise of the Superego or whatever to come and strike the very area of the colon where he himself was screwed, however as I can figure out by myself if I insist on believing this then psychoanalysis can go hang, or rather I can't expect to have supernatural or even pyschical adventures as unpleasant as you please but exceptional at least, and in other words I have to stop clinging perhaps out of pride elsewhere frustrated to the singularity of my situation, as if since I couldn't manage to write a work of art in any other way I had said to myself well anyhow I have a disease nobody else in the world has, ah no I have to hang my head and admit that in reality intestinal troubles are the most common thing a neurotic can have, and in fact there is some doctor who without having to disturb any dead fathers has managed to distinguish three types of influence exercised on the stomach and the intestines by psychical conflict, and he says that there is the gastric type of neurotics with troubles localized in the stomach, the colitic type who naturally has colitis, and the constipated type who logically enough suffers from constipation, and though I have meditated at length on these classifications which I discovered in a once fairly well known popularizing book I haven't been able to fit myself completely into any one of the three categories, to my deep disappointment I must confess since in general I like things to be clear and neat or if I don't my Superego does which is still worse, anyhow thanks to my duodenal ulcer I would seem to approach the gastric type which displays tendencies to absorption that is to keeping everything in itself especially aggressive impulses, and my wife naturally says no no as far as she can see and of course I don't agree with her although I have to admit that with my psychonanalysis a certain increase of aggressiveness has been noted limited only to traffic cops and other policemen, and this I suppose for the reason that ever since the Fascist dictatorship fell without unfortunately any active participation on my part I have become a zealous defender of democracy, as for that matter my father was despite the fact that on his honorable discharge the phrase or motto Faithful through the Centuries stood out prominently I think it means faithful to yourself because they surely can't be said to have remained faithful to the king and how rightly only the king himself could know I

imagine, so since I've been converted into a paladin of the democratic process I have perforce to argue with those who through
ignorance or self-interest don't understand much about democracy
and especially traffic cops who give you tickets and policemen even
of high rank who seem to favor the psychological crushing of the
individual citizen for the benefit of whatever regime, and in fact
if they find a citizen of a democratic disposition who for example
refuses to reveal his father's name as the law requires they
promptly think he's some kind of crook and they employ every
artifice to lock him up on the spot so it's probable that one of these
days I'll prove my father right by ending up in jail even though
for a highly honorable reason, anyhow despite the fact that I
do have a duodenal ulcer and aggressive impulses which are not
always buried I rather favor my inclusion in the colitic type since
my colon always hurts when I think about it and naturally I think
about it constantly, and the colitic's typical expression is diarrhoea,
however to tell the truth I am capable of alternating periods of
diarrhea with others of constipation, and moreover I am sick even
in the rare eventuality of my faeces having a normal aspect and
consistency, and to sum up I must say that there really is a bit of
confusion at least with regard to the external aspects of the question, whereas if you consider primarily the psychical reactions
I believe I can't help but belong to the colitic type who is usually
a generous giver but at the same time is rather demanding which
is only fair, and in fact as far as generous giving is concerned I
consider myself absolutely in order because even if everything I
have given for example to the Fatherland in the time of my youth
which happened also to be the Fascist period was completely
wasted as everyone knows I still have the knowledge of having
done my duty with serious personal risk and suffering, and within
the limits of this abstraction we might define as symbolic namely
duty moreover coinciding with the motto Faithful through the
Centuries I feel inferior to none, and as far as the following period
is concerned I believe I just said what a generous paladin of
democracy I am, and in addition I still have those three chapters
which when I go on with them will surely constitute a monument

more lasting than bronze to the glory not only of myself but also my country and why not also of the whole human race, so there can be no doubt that I've given plenty and therefore I have a right to demand plenty, except that no matter how ardently I do demand nobody gives me anything and so of course a few hostile impulses arise directed against society especially the literary part of it, and such impulses are manifested it seems by defecating since the unconscious significance of excrement is an offensive weapon, except that thanks to a process which must not be very common I turn these offensive weapons against myself, not in the banal sense of fouling my pants although this too has happened but in the slightly more elevated sense that my dramatic defecations are sadomasochistic manifestations, a combination which reveals in me a sadistic impulse satisfied through acts of cruelty committed by me and at the same time a masochistic impulse satisfied by cruelty committed against me, and since I do all this on my own I can be properly defined as a sadomasochist, and there is certainly nothing to rejoice over because my sadomasochism isn't confined to the colitic field where instead of using my excrement as an offensive weapon against the radicals for instance or the police I use it against myself causing terrible bellyaches, but it spreads into the strictly sexual field with pleasures ruined by anxieties, and even to the intellectual field as can easily be understood from the circumstances of the famous attack which took place halfway through defecation just as I was preparing to break the barrier of the fourth chapter and this was an act of cruelty toward the noblest part of myself to prevent me from proceeding to the conquest of glory, but at this point we're back where we started because I begin to ask myself what sins I have to atone for that make me hurt myself continually and I can't find any, or rather my doctor can't as he tries to help me whereas I can find plenty if I recall for example how clearly I had in mind the principle that no punishment could ever be adequate to the monstrosity of masturbation, and yet I went right ahead with a will even challenging fate or Our Heavenly Father to strike me dead on the spot in punishment and instead they didn't strike me

dead at all however they made a note of my attitude and now
the bill I have to pay is handed to me years later and is enormous,
too enormous for my frightened soul, and so if I think about it
I have the impression that no matter how many troubles befall
me now I'll never finish paying these sinful debts, however the
old doctor naturally doesn't agree, according to him my tendency
to fabricate misfortunes for myself goes back as usual to my
father the chief artificer of a Superego that we can call plethoric
and that's understating it which has developed to a surely abnormal degree my sense of duty to which the sense of guilt is always
linked, and consequently if the sense of duty exploits the absolute
concept of duty per se as my father worked hard to inculcate it in
me then there's never any hope of being in the right, and the
few times that a person more by chance than anything else does
happen to be in the right we can be sure that some event will inter-
fere and switch the cards as in fact happened to me with the
Fatherland which naturally was one of our chief ethical creditors
according to the Sergeant, so off I went to fight wars as best
I could to pay up this debt and then at the end I find myself
with a Fatherland that was no longer the former one, and the
great old screwing I took in the patriotic department was clear
to me only when I came home from the last war and found the
Sergeant with his followers in the local chapter more than ever
Faithful through the Centuries already reorganized and sending
letters and petitions to the new rulers, whereas I had a hard
time working out a new concept of the Fatherland and in reality
I feel I still haven't succeeded, and maybe this is precisely why
my insatiable sense of duty has turned to the concept of democracy
which is international and we all hope universal, although there
are those hoping on the one side and those hoping on the other
for differing not to say opposed democratic ideas, so I have had to
restrict the democratic idea to respect for the citizen as an individual and I have devoted myself to this ideal with all my old
ardor always far from accepting any compromises especially as
I said before with traffic cops and other policemen, and to tell
the truth when I am reasoning lucidly I realize I am inevitably

heading for trouble that will get me locked up by some policeman or by some minor official perhaps and this is also slightly because of the attraction of the well-known paternal prophecies, and also because of a psychical process typical of the man hounded by misfortune who usually seems to be one whose unconscious is full of a sense of guilt so that it gets all involved in anxiety and to re-establish his proper psychical balance the poor bastard can't do anything but behave in such a way that he is inviting constant kicks in the pants, and the kicks have the liberating effect of an expiation of the unconscious guilt, at least in theory because in practice I will know this only when they have shut me up in a cell maybe in the Catanzaro jail with all my claustrophobia.

Generically therefore as the motive of my psychical conflict I can point to this inadaptability to reality since my father made me very strict like the carabinieri and I have remained strict while others change of course and even the world changes you can hardly expect it to stand still, but I stand still always belated always in conflict, in addition to being a tremendous bore and nuisance as my wife maintains, on the other hand despite outside opinion I feel rather proud of the way I am that is of my upright character, however I would like some recognition also from others which isn't forthcoming except from my daughter and only in the period when she hasn't reached the age of reason, a period which if you think about it coincides with the Oedipal phase and that explains everything, anyhow except for my daughter I find no consideration in anyone and I am the first to admit all my many defects although I am also aware of having some notable good qualities and why hasn't anybody else noticed them I often complain to myself, and it seems this kind of question and the lamenting tone I use don't please my wife much and according to her she understands the world better than I and she says I'm an idiot if I expect other people to notice the good qualities which she agrees I may even possess though certainly not to the extent I believe, in short to her way of thinking I am a mediocre person though no worse than plenty of others who

enjoy successful careers even as novelists but I'm crazy if I expect
others to bow before my genius with no effort on my part, and
fundamentally I don't disagree with her since I know all too well
that we live in a time when everything proceeds through friendships and reciprocal recommendations and prodigious social
climbing and belonging to cliques of various kinds anyhow my
wife observes that since I can't speak well of myself I can't expect
others to speak well of me, and she's right I would be glad to speak
well of myself maybe even too well and at times I try but always
with miserable results because I have this strict Superego which
censors me on all sides showing me how fatuous are the achievements of those who receive applause and notoriety and women
and of course a pile of money, none of this counts says the Superego
and of course I agree I'm prepared to give up applause and cheap
notoriety and wealth in exchange for a single masterpiece, maybe
not even a long one let's say a total of fifteen chapters, but here
I am stuck at chapter three because of this frightening illness
which has blocked my creative energy and deprived me of the
taste for smoking and the bliss of emptying my bowel without
anguish, but also because of this perfectionist Superego which
demands God knows what of me, I feel like a child again with
my father wanting me to be a model son however I didn't know
what model meant apart from obedience which was the only
thing the Sergeant explained to me, so now this Superego wants a
masterpiece without helping me understand what a masterpiece
created by me should consist in, I mean it says to me this book's
a masterpiece and that one's a masterpiece referring perhaps to
Svevo and to Musil just to cite two suffering examples that by and
large would suit me fine, however the books of Svevo and Musil
are masterpieces which already exist and which obviously can't
be done over again so something else is required, well my Superego doesn't explain to me what this something else is but demands
excellence per se as a kind of compensation for obedience per se,
and maybe my doctor's right when he says I should try to make
myself write works that are a little less excellent, for the moment
of course just to get around the resistance to work that blocks me

because I am always aiming at the absolute work of art, whereas
if I set out to write something not quite such a masterpiece
chances are I could achieve something, the fact is that when
scripts come along I can write them now that with my analysis
or with the passing of time there is a bit of general improvement,
but I believe it's the analysis because in this period I am thinking
psychoanalysis is an excellent discovery and it isn't just money
down the drain as my wife argues when we have a fight and I take
advantage of the situation to tell her that the doctor wouldn't
disapprove of an occasional spot of marital infidelity which it
seems would do me good and also do her good in the sense that
if I committed some really guilty act toward her as for example
a trifling escapade with one of these starlets who are of course
cute and even young but for the rest nothing, well if I felt in the
wrong I would automatically be less demanding less of a bore,
however my wife belonging to the possessive type or only to
spite me or perhaps even to hinder my complete cure since we are
not in one of our better phases flies into a rage at the very mention
of escapades and certainly doesn't bury her hostility toward the old
man who according to her is far too broad-minded and it wouldn't
be a bad thing for the police to begin sticking their nose into the
doings of these doctors who think about sex too much, for that
matter she maintains she isn't the least upset by the fact that I'm
demanding or rather she feels perfect the way she is and can't
understand how I could want her any different, and to tell the
truth she always manages to bring up a half dozen wives of
friends of ours who perhaps in some isolated area are worse
than she, instead of me you'd be happy to have that fat one would
you she asks me or that other one who signs promissory notes
with her husband's name or that other one who doesn't wash too
often, and I have to admit I prefer her to all of these women she's
citing however all the same I wish she were a little less nagging
and didn't spend so thoughtlessly the money I earn with such
effort and at the price of many humiliations, and here my little
doctor says I'm in the wrong or rather he says I'm right to complain however its' no use getting mad and insisting my wife

become a good manager since it would be like asking as much of the cat who obviously can't go out and do the shopping, so there are weeks when I go and do the marketing and I keep the accounts and it turns out we've spent the same as when my wife was managing if not more, and in other words we just don't know where this money is going however I believe that the responsibility for the family's bookkeeping belongs to wives and not to husbands and my wife also supports this principle although she then demonstrates that she's incapable of managing anything at all, in short nearly all our arguments in this period are of an economic nature and when she's in a good humor my wife says I can thank God I don't have more serious grounds for quarrels, but if on the other hand she's in a bad humor she raises such hell that if I were a normal person I would already have freed myself from any sense of guilt thanks to this matrimonial punishment, but I am not a normal person I am a neurotic who is always seeking new punishments in the most various fields especially in those which lead to intellectual and professional frustration, and when I am all nicely frustrated and comparable to a worm or a disgusting louse I feel like saying there you must be content now father although not with the same intentions I had before I began my analysis, now I say it with a new spirit a bit aggressively to tell the truth with expressions like look at this model son you made for yourself, always dissatisfied with what I did and throwing everything in my face, and you said that if your father had been able to pay for your education like you paid for mine you would have become God only knows what, Chief of State like Mussolini, whereas I didn't amount to anything once I got out of boarding school, and so there to spite you I've gone on not amounting to anything for the rest of my life, or rather I've done some things but all of them or almost all were mistakes, and so I'll never be anybody but so much the better, if you were hoping to make your name as father of a famous son you made a big mistake yourself, I even missed my chance to be killed in the war which all in all was the best chance I had, however even if things have proceeded in a stupid way I don't have any debts toward you, understand, the one of us who was most wrong wasn't me it was you for bringing me into the world, but if it were only that then what the hell, the trouble is that my early childhood I'm told must have been a tormented period through your fault, and truly as I go digging into it in this belated regression searching for conflicts mostly it all saddens me, just think of my sense of abandonment and solitude renewed every day or maybe twice a day when you took my mother away from me, God all that abandonment and solitude in my infancy and you didn't even suspect it or else you thought I'd become a carabiniere captain through my sufferings, and instead look what happened, and what's more you stubbornly go on persecuting me even now from your grave or through this Superego which obviously from the very beginning has been blessed with a robust constitution refractory to any adjustments I'd say if after so many years it's still there telling me that I have to be a model that I mustn't compromise that if a person wants to write then he has to write a masterpiece or nothing, and then when I'm there all prepared to set this damned masterpiece down on paper then the Superego hurls a disaster at me that freezes me *per omnia saecula saeculorum* on the threshold of the fourth chapter.

And so as anyone can easily see I had plenty of psychic conflicts and this doesn't mean there weren't a number of others still buried in the unconscious which we hadn't yet been able to put our hands on but we would catch up with them eventually thanks to the high degree of perfection reached by the psychoanalytical technique, and who knows but that with all this digging around maybe the big flaw would turn up the one able to cast a final and resolving light on the whole tangle of my disease, however there was the impression that finding this flaw was a bit like hitting the daily double in short a rather rare happening to tell the truth, and probably even the old man was of this opinion since we went forward with a prudential tactic based chiefly on little conquests and perhaps more on psychotherapy than psychoanalysis properly speaking, and we did make progress no denying that, still it seemed more substantial results were being blocked by my general attitude toward the disease in the sense that I made an arbitrary and above all mistaken choice of the reasons for which I wanted to be cured, that is while on the one hand I cared nothing or almost nothing about my phobias and easily assumed a renunciatory position toward football games and upper stories and theaters and journeys that couldn't be made by car, on the other hand I was inflexible about the masterpiece, in short I concentrated all my will to be cured on the one thing that I had to get out of my head if I really was to be cured, and instead I stayed there with my three chapters which I didn't even reread any more they were so perfect and I caressed them from outside in their blue folder where I kept them thinking when I'm cured I'll go on, but in my unconscious there was something that said so you think you can write masterpieces why at the Venezia Bar you couldn't even recite a simple poem, remember how tongue-tied you were, and in fact in my more reasonable moments I was very much afraid I wasn't suited to writing masterpieces however I couldn't admit it just like that, I had to find an excuse perforce and it seems to me there was no better excuse than the disease, and this was the simple mechanism through which the ambition to write a master-piece fed the disease, and until I could really manage to stifle that longing for glory even posthumous glory it was highly im-probable that I could achieve an even average spiritual condition which for me would have meant health or better still the reconsti-tution of a reasonable Ego connected with the Id on the one hand and a more permissive Superego on the other, and in fact one of the principal aims of the analysis which from a certain viewpoint was a re-education at the hands of a better father than my first one would have been to reach a balanced evaluation of the reality principle with the least possible reduction of pleasure, and in other words all I had to do was to take my place productively in society and enjoy life, but I don't know how I could take my place in society until I had got rid of the notion that my final purpose even socially speaking was to write at least one masterpiece, and as far as enjoying life was concerned this expectation was downright absurd in my condition when a plate of spaghetti was enough to drive me to the brink of disintegration, and then if I indulged in what are called the pleasures of the flesh things went from bad to worse in the sense that I added to the usual concept of sin-punishment the thought that these were energies stolen from the masterpiece, or rather I should have sublimated at least in part my sexual impulses as they say directing them toward fine writing if this was my destiny and instead I didn't sublimate a damn thing and all I did was sharpen the sense of sin and punishment, and the punishment consisted chiefly in my grief at not managing to write the work of art, and often I could find no other way to console myself for this grief than by making love conjugal of course after which I started in again with my remorse at having stolen energies from the masterpiece, and obviously at this rate I could go on and on developing an erotic activity that was even surprising for my age, to sum up I could have enjoyed life perfectly well if that thorn of the work of art hadn't remained stuck in my side, and so let's take a look and try to see where this thorn came from and to tell the truth there were so many components it was enough to make your head swim, however the nub of the matter perhaps was whether I wanted glory to please or to spite my father, per-haps to spite him since he didn't want to carry me when I was little and then he always said I'd end up in jail and then he wanted me to be a government employee instead of wandering around like a bum, but we mustn't forget that for him glory was quite a different thing from any literary work of art, the truth of the matter is that I never talked about these things with my father just as we never discussed a number of other things but I'm sure that for him the poet-patriot Antonio Sciesa with his On to the Gallows was worth more than Shakespeare and Cervantes put together, especially since in the field of literature if you exclude Arnaldo Fusinato who besides had been a great patriot my father had no other predilections, and then I wonder why I never man-aged to reject my aspiration to write works of art and replace it with more modest undertakings as in fact the new father I had found in the doctor kept advising me, and then the Superego turned up again with the story of the sacrifices and the ambition the ex-Sergeant cherished to see me climb up onto the platform

and receive the gilt medal, my God he was so proud to see me
first in the whole class and according to him this was the right
path toward becoming a captain of the Royal Carabinieri but I
began to be lazy anyhow and he poor man couldn't figure any
of it out, in reality he didn't understand much also because he
didn't know much about studies and for example he thought a
young man in my condition had come into the world especially
to go through the *liceo* with great honor, and since this event did
not then take place and moreover since because the hats he sold
were downright embarrassing to wear I went and bought one in
Venice he overlooked no opportunity to prophesy disasters for me,
and then he preached that it was a scandal that a boy whose father
made great sacrifices to pay for his education didn't manage to
keep up an average of eighty which would completely exempt him
from paying tuition but only a seventy average which involved
merely a partial exemption, and then he said he couldn't go on any
longer because business was bad and in fact the famous American
crash of 'twenty-nine as it spread all through the world had even
reached the little hat shop where it took my father completely
by surprise though he had had plenty of time to foresee it, so
suddenly he found himself on the verge of failure, or rather when
he found himself on the verge he had already failed, and though
he had wisely put the shop in his wife's name he felt threatened
with dishonor after his past as a sergeant of the carabinieri, so instead of just failing and letting it go at that he tried to come to
an agreement with his creditors to pay off at fifty per cent, however
he didn't have the money even to pay the fifty per cent and then
he had the bright idea of mortgaging the house and borrowing
eleven thousand lire from the bank without realizing that he was
getting himself into an endless mess, and in fact I was the one
who got him out of it several years later but obviously neither he
nor I could sensibly have foreseen that I of all people would be
the one to save him, so with a rather scant sense of justice really he
laid on me a great deal of the blame for his ill humor and his
bitterness, and even when the quarterly grades or the principal's
reports spread in the family the news of my lack of advancement

I obstinately used to answer back one of these days you'll see who I am, and for me obviously this day was vaguely remote whereas the catastrophes foreseen by my father according to him were going to take place much earlier starting with the next series of final exams toward which in fact I was heading with insufficient preparation inasmuch as the awakening of my senses had caught up with the legal age and now with full rights and full pleasure I was a frequent visitor to the local brothels, and in addition I had become a very active billiard player and good at a card game known as rummy, and so I approached these terrible exams with a preparation I could call inadequate especially in the scientific subjects because when it came to the literary subjects I could get by somehow on what I had learned in boarding school, and yet when my father solemnly said that somebody in this family was shortly going to end up in jail or would go off to be a barber or practice some similar trade I used to produce a little laugh of defiance which meant you'll see what I can do and instead the terrible exams arrive after I have studied for them furiously for about three weeks in all and I take the first series the literary ones which are so-so but not really bad generally and coming out of the hall where they're giving the literary subjects I feel a curiosity to glance into the hall where the scientific exams are in progress and as luck would have it there was sitting a certain Marinini namely the first in the class so I stop to ask how he's getting on hoping in my heart he's getting on badly since for at least three years now those who are first in the class have been getting on my nerves especially because of my father who does nothing but throw them in my face as examples, and this Marinini who was especially good in Greek isn't getting along exactly splendidly and the wretched lady professor of science who is questioning him encourages him every now and then suggesting certain properties of iron he has forgotten or certain details of photosynthesis or the names of the veins or arteries that go to the heart, and moreover this lady to show off I suppose also mentions a lot of things that aren't in our textbook and that therefore even the first in the class has a right not to know, well exactly a week later it's my turn to present myself for the science exam and I sit there in front of the wretched lady professor being practically ignorant of everything about chemistry and botany and the human body, and then I have a stroke of luck the first thing she asks me is a question on valencies and since she asked the same thing to the first of the class a week before I promptly answer everything Marinini said plus what she had herself suggested and I promptly leave her dumbfounded, and then she asks me the second question about iron and again I fire off one property after another, and then she asks about photosynthesis, and in other words the fool had written out the questions by groups and through the grace of God I had the same group that the first of the class had drawn and since it never occurred to her to ask me a question that wasn't on her list it turned out I knew more about science than almost anyone else my age in the world, and so thanks to science I manage to get a six even in mathematics where I don't know a damn thing and a six in philosophy where I know a little bit more, and to make a long story short surprising friends and enemies alike I pass the exams and even get a nine in science, and I believe that anybody after a stroke of luck like that would be oriented toward optimism for the rest of his life but instead I suppose even then I was thinking these are things you pay for oh yes you pay for them all right, but in any case for the moment my passing gives me a sense of well-being and power especially towards the Sergeant to whom I say nothing about the grades already posted in the corridor of the Royal Liceo Ginnasio Antonio Canova and I let him read the news for himself in the *Gazzettino* where the next day they publish the complete list of our bright promoted students, and then I glance at him all day long without letting on and thinking let's see how he swallows this one, and he swallows it with a glum look as if my promotion had insulted him, and the truth is this father of mine would let them split his head open before he would admit to being wrong in his three-year prophecies of jail or trades like cobbler and barber, how wrongly he was wrong only I know however the fact remains he was wrong, and instead of admitting it and saying well let's stop all

this wrangling between the two of us he sits there gloomily like
when the older of my sisters who is now grown up teases him
because he was a carabiniere since in our part of the country
there's a general idea that a man who's a carabiniere is stupid
and indeed there are some rather picturesque expressions on the
subject, well though I'm in almost constant opposition to my
father I'm hurt when my sister teases him, really I never tease
him not even about his past as commander of the Station of
Occhiobello or Perarolo although ever since I was born he's been
telling the very same stories which on top of everything else are
silly, whereas when he starts out by saying when I was in com-
mand of the Occhiobello Station the listener expects some marvelous tales of thieves and murderers, and instead he tells how one
time the richest man in the town sent him a turkey to the barracks
as a present but he sent it back, or else he tells as if it had happened to him about that carabiniere in the Great War who was
on guard in the rear and cried halt to His Majesty in person and
wouldn't let him by because His Majesty didn't know the pass-
word and instead of punishing him His Majesty rewarded him at
once with a special leave because guard duty takes precedence
even over the King himself, in short he produces for the most
part edifying stories like this one which give my oldest sister a
chance to tease him whereas I remain serious and maybe pretend
this is the first time I've heard the story, however on the occasion
of this unexpected promotion I decide to tease him a little too
and toward evening seeing him glummer than ever I say well
what do you think about the way I passed my exams, and he answers I think I won't spend another cent on your education since
you're grown up now and can fend for yourself, and he cites
several examples of local boys who pay for their university tuition
by giving lessons or doing temporary clerical work at the town
hall, but most of them are boys formerly headed for an ecclesiastic
career who then lost their vocation along the way but not entirely
so that they still have a clerical look to them, and also a cleric's
mentality I say so they aren't examples to be followed completely,
anyhow I hope this is just a passing attitude on my father's part

since he kept me while I went through the *liceo* he could also
keep me while I go to the University which anyway costs less,
but he is really obstinate about denying me any further aid and he
even deprives me of the weekly five lire he gave me for cigarettes
and other pleasures, and in addition he must have caught on that
I've been stealing money from his wallet and so he's careful not
to leave his pants unguarded, in short he tries to humiliate me in
every possible way and reduce me to starvation, and so when he
announces that he's found a job for me I don't have the courage
to say no to him, and it turns out to be a temporary job in a
lunatic asylum where they have to recatalogue completely all the
furniture and other materials they have been issued, and in this
way I find myself involved in an experience so unpleasant that
despite the fact that I'm eighteen and have a fairly sturdy Ego
I've had to repress the experience to a large extent or in other
words hide it in the depths of the unconscious from which it
emerged like new in the course of the analysis, and in fact as I was
telling him certain details of this experience my little doctor
must have been fairly pleased because my father cuts what I would
call a very sorry figure at getting me a job in the asylum because
he was annoyed I hadn't flunked my exams as he had so constantly
predicted I would, however I may also think this but I'm not
certain about it I mean I'm not certain that for him making a
complete inventory of the furnishings of a madhouse might not
be considered a position of responsibility and trust, and I believe
nobody can honestly maintain that in some ways it isn't, moreover
he was surely convinced that being in a madhouse wouldn't affect
me one way or the other and oddly enough I felt the same thing
since I couldn't foresee that many years later I would get these
terrible fears of going crazy too, in short I can't really condemn
my father now because he sent me off to work in an asylum instead
of at the town hall or the pepper factory, especially since neither
the town hall nor the pepper factory needed a white-collar worker
whereas by chance the asylum did, and for that matter I would
have felt the same amount of disgust at any kind of work and
not just for the job in the asylum in fact it promised to be a

fairly interesting experience since I had to see every bit of the asylum including the special wards because there were objects to be catalogued everywhere, however to tell the truth at times it was actually revolting because of the smells and the rest, especially the mentally deficient children some of whom were much more deficient and ugly than a snail might be, so when I looked at them I had the suspicion that our Heavenly Father really hadn't meant to give them a soul otherwise you couldn't see why he had failed so miserably, anyhow not all the asylum was as repellent as the simple-minded children and for example there were some of the madmen who wrote poems generally very long ones, and others who painted or rather made drawings with colored pencils, and many had a tendency toward philosophical discussions some of them apparently meaningless and others apparently full of meaning, and then there were the ordinary conversationalists who in a very urbane manner would talk about themselves saying for example that their mothers were noblewomen or that they had enjoyed the favors of Queen Margherita, and obviously you had to take these things with a certain amount of skepticism, on the other hand not all of them were so megalomaniac and in fact the majority spoke of their families as one of us might speak of his own, even with much more affection I would say, and naturally though they weren't all that uncomfortable in the asylum their chief wish was to go home, and some of them really seemed quite close to this longed-for event and they confided in me that next week people were coming to take them away, and when I heard a story of this kind I was overjoyed but then the nun told me this man had been saying for about twenty-nine years how next week they were coming for him and instead nobody had ever come to see him or written him since the day they shut him up, in any case the most interesting ones were the madmen in cages not to mention the madwomen in cages some of whom were mad in a special way, namely when they saw a man such as me for example they went wild and since they couldn't pull up their tunics with their hands which were bound, with great cunning they crouched down and caught the hem of the tunic in their teeth and pulled

it up to display their sex, dancing at the same time with savage
cries so that the nuns quickly pushed me out to avoid any occasion of sin, and in short this job in the asylum also had its
picturesque side although for the most part it was boring since
it consisted of going from one ward to another with two children
from the orphanage annex for whom coming along with me was
like a holiday so it's not hard to imagine the lousy life they
usually led, and one of these children had a little pot of paint and
a brush while the other had the stencils with the numbers, and I
had the ledger with the old inventory and a lot of paper to take
note of variations and new additions, and so the three of us went
wandering around everywhere and I looked into the various rooms
to see if the present furniture was marked in the old ledger and
if by chance it wasn't there I had to make a note on the paper and
give the furnishings new numbers and also the old furniture's
numbers were changed according to a new order, and naturally
it happened that some of the furnishings or objects indicated in
the old inventory no longer existed and then they were canceled
out only later maybe they came to light four or five rooms farther
on and then they had to be restored to the list, and in short as
anyone can plainly see this was a highly complicated job in view
of the vast expanse of the asylum, and though it was strictly
speaking a work requiring thought it could nevertheless offer
very few spiritual satisfactions, so after a week I was utterly fed
up with it and then after much thought about how to escape from
such a calamity I got the idea of joining the army, my God it
seemed funny I hadn't had the idea before since it was unquestionably a brilliant one because with my *liceo* diploma I could be
an officer and according to what everybody said officers enjoyed
great luck with women especially married ones, and then I could
see them for myself strolling up and down under the arcades of
the Calmaggiore which is the elegant street of our nearest city
and I said to myself what a fine life they lead and naturally I
couldn't imagine the enormous annoyances they had to go through
before their strolls along the Calmaggiore, and so without thinking twice I went off to the local recruiting office to enlist and

there they tell me I can choose among the cities of Turin, Spoleto, Avellino, and Palermo, and I apply for Palermo thinking in this way I am going as far away as possible from my father, and instead it now emerges that by selecting Palermo in all likelihood I was obeying unconscious forces driving me I would almost say fondly to follow the footsteps of the carabiniere who so many years before had lifted his hand and picked golden oranges from the boughs that hung over the walls of the gardens, anyhow while my application makes its bureaucratic round I have to go on with my job at the asylum, that is I pass from one ward to the next and from room to room carefully observing tables, night stands, beds, stools with porcelain pots in them, spittoons with tops that don't work, wooden crucifixes, and giving each object a number which when possible is stenciled onto it by the two unhappy orphans, and at the same time I make fairly garbled variations and additions on the old ledger, and no less garbled annotations on the sheets of paper with honest intentions of clearing it all up and making a clean copy in a new ledger when the work is finished, anyhow I am hoping to God that my summons to arms will arrive before the end of my long tour of the asylum, and so it does and I suppose that unless some other white-collar worker began the inventory all over again from the beginning they are still there trying to figure out my numbers and notes, anyhow I go off with a magnificent gift of five thousand lire that the Sergeant God knows why perhaps to follow his own father's example of so many years before gives me at the moment of our parting, and in short I make this long trip with the conviction that something is really changing in my life, namely that I am eluding at last my father's obtuse and burdensome control initiating the second phase of our struggle which generally speaking is the phase of my supremacy, however if you exclude this I receive no other advantage from my military experience to which I arrive luckily already prepared by my period in the asylum, in any case not everything is bad even in a barracks since I come into contact with people from a well-to-do station in life and even aristocrats Sicilian barons for example and sons of big lawyers and even of small industrialists, in short I broaden my horizons so to speak even though here too I am ill at ease since I don't have the money to buy kid shoes and so even when I go strolling in our two free hours in the evening I have to wear the Royal Army's solid hobnailed boots which make you risk breaking your neck by slipping on the lava slabs that pave the city of Palermo's streets, and as if the hobnailed shoes weren't enough to show the sons of barons and well-to-do people of half of Italy how humble my origins are now the sergeant begins to get at me from afar sending me at least every three weeks not money orders or checks but postcards adorned of course with his rubber-stamped last name and first name and his title of merchant, and then there is the written text which is one long exhortation to prove myself honorably in the army with any number of errors of grammar and spelling scattered here and there in the labyrinth of his prose which is generally bedecked with verbs tending all to the subjunctive even the past or perfect subjunctive just to make everything less clear, and I think now he has to take out his graphomania on me as if he didn't have any more ministries and ministers and high commands to address petitions and memoranda to, however I also have to consider his satisfaction in writing the address to the Officer Candidate so and so of course with the last name first, and in other words I believe he writes me so often because when he writes the two words Officer Candidate in the address he is savoring already the delight of having an officer for a son he who was only a non-com, and in fact almost without realizing it after seven months of insane efforts and intricate details I am named to second lieutenant, and now I too can stroll up and down the Calmaggiore with a flashy new tailored uniform and soft boots and the girls look at me of course since after all I'm not too bad, and I look at them as best I can mostly blushing and feeling more or less paralyzed, and I think now I have everything required to win over the ladies namely a furnished room with a private entrance and a double bed and enough money in my pocket to invite them to an *apéritif* and maybe even to dinner if they insist, but despite these unquestionably propitious circumstances and the sexual impulses fiercely pressing from the Id I can't con-

quer even one woman, until then one evening at the great Officers'
Club Ball during a foxtrot I find myself with no particular intentions in the arms of a buxom girl who among other things looks
five or six years older than me, and this sainted creature does it
all namely she takes me for a walk in the country, and there she
arranges things so that I have to kiss her and embrace her enough
for a girl of a good family to be able to abandon herself with a
show of decency, and I don't know how much she enjoyed it but I
certainly enjoyed it very little because my head was swimming
with two or three ideas each more unpleasant than the other,
namely my God now what can I do to keep from making her pregnant, and then what sort of fool will I look if I soil her or I don't
behave like the others, and then my uniform is going to be a mess
after all this grass, the fact is that when it's over I heave a sigh of
relief since one way or another I have managed to conquer my first
unpaid woman, unless she is expecting to be paid but I think not,
and I am supported in this supposition by the fact that the following day she shows up at my room with a great bouquet of red
carnations since I had hinted to her that we would be more comfortable on my double bed, however the next day I am out of commission thanks to a raging fever I've got maybe because of the
dampness in the country or my emotion since even then though
without knowing it I must have been fairly neurotic if my first
experience of love brought on a feverish delirium, and that poor
girl who had come with a bunch of carnations presumably to
improve upon the mediocre experience of the preceding evening
must have been dismayed, and in fact she came another time
or two to see if I had survived our little adventure and then she
never showed up again as was only right, and I hope that her lucky
star later helped her find somebody more efficient, as for myself
once I was over the fever I found another girl about my own age
who without having to be coaxed came to my room took off her
dress and got under the covers of the double bed in her slip and
all the rest of course and there was no way to persuade her to take
off any important garment like her panties or brassiere, she said
that she loved me and all she wanted was to be beside me and as

you can well imagine I lacked the strength to use force against
such a debated virtue, we lay in bed embracing like a pair of
angels you might say and then she went away and I saw her
several years later and on this second occasion there took place in
a fairly unamusing way the thing that hadn't happened the first
time when there was no amusement at all, and in the meanwhile
the period of my military service was almost over and a little
later I was placed in the reserve and suddenly afraid I had to think
what am I going to do with my life, and I couldn't find an answer
even if from the social-bureaucratic point of view so to speak I
was all set because I had saved up a bit of money from my salary
and had managed to enroll at the University in the Faculty of
Literature to be exact which was the cheapest of all, and so I find
myself enrolled in courses I don't give much of a damn about
and I live at home naturally with my father without our speaking
to each other hardly ever, I don't speak to anybody and during the
day I am always shut in my room sleeping or thinking or hunting
through the works of the great Leopardi for misfortunes comparable to mine, and at night I go out in the country and especially
when there is a big moon rising over the frozen plain or beyond
the rows of poplars summer seizes me like an anxiety of total
catastrophe, now the moon is precisely a distant world and a useless one too if you except the expressions of poets and lovers, and
I am neither poet nor lover, my God not to be in love at twenty
nor a poet and all the same to be brimming over with a boundless
fever to make the world mine or die and preferably to die, and I
said O moon in Heaven what are you doing tell me, but rather
than find an answer to Leopardi's interrogation of the moon I
would have liked to know what I myself was doing in this world,
and there was no convincing answer and again I felt the desire to
die, however at other times if the moon was really great I had God
knows why the impression I too would become great, I would
still leave some mark on the earth to show that I had passed there,
and I rode on my now dilapidated girl's bike along the paths
collecting cobwebs on my face, and I yelled like a madman in
the countryside the verses of this Leopardi who seemed congenial

now even in the rare spurts of euphoria, or else I sang No no
Nanù, for me you're no longer you, and for this Nanù who was
actually completely unknown to me my eyes would fill with tears
all the same and I let the tears come down freely it seemed to me
that to cry was one of the few good things left to me on the earth,
and then sometimes late at night I would run into Manza going
home and Manza was a girl who went with all the boys and then
they were all ashamed of her but not I, even when the people were
coming out of the last Mass on Sunday if I saw Manza I stopped to
speak with her and I might even offer her a drink at the Venezia
Café to show the people of the town how little I cared about them,
and she was fond of me for this and when we met at night she was
happy if I went with her a way toward home, sometimes she was
mad and she would curse and say those sons of bitches I hope
they all drop dead and you too you son of a bitch and in general
this happened when four or five had gone with her at once in the
fields behind the church and then had run off without paying her,
but at other times she might perhaps have two or three hundred
lire in her purse and she wanted me to take a hundred because in
those days I often didn't have money even for cigarettes, and at
other times she was full of tenderness and sad because I didn't
want to make love with her, I told her I didn't make love with
anybody because I didn't like making love but she didn't believe
it and said that I had done it with the druggist's niece and the
young schoolteacher and I swore to her it wasn't true and she
meanwhile would take my hand and put it on her breast which
was firm and fresh because she was young and she said I want to
make love with you for nothing and you don't want to, and I would
have taken her there on the grass but I knew her blood was dis-
eased the doctor told me she had syphilis and hadn't treated it
properly, at times I thought it would be right to take her all the
same and catch syphilis and go to Hell completely, to make an
end of this life without charity, but then my courage failed me and
I swore to her I didn't like making love because I wasn't able to
and she wanted to feel and she said why do you tell me lies you
damned son of a bitch if they were all like you ha, and I told her

that I wasn't impotent but I couldn't manage to go with women, and she would cry and say it was a shame that I had gone wrong because I was the only boy in the town she would like making love with, let's just try once she said really crying and caressed me and caressed me with anger and sweetness both until she caused the orgasm which I submitted to with shame and despair, and then I said to her furiously get out get out and I stayed there almost hugging the trunk of a willow or a poplar or whatever tree was close at hand, there with my certitude that I will never more fill the world with my glory, with the desolation of having scattered my seed on the ground with no joy for anyone, with the loneliness that comes from this action and the bitter sense of cowardice, and everything seemed to me preferable to this mood even syphilis or the abjection of guilt, anything was preferable to this nothing that I was with my seed scattered on the ground and the girl who went off sadly without having understood anything of my unhappiness and of my love for her as for all creatures, and I thought Oh why can't I be like Jesus of Nazareth, oh why aren't these the roads of Galilee so I could say Woman go thy sins are forgiven thee, and maybe also work a kind of miracle to free her blood of its disease, oh night and prayer without faith, and then I head with my sadness towards home with the idea of my father now fixed in my mind, aware of his frightening distance from everything I might do and think and suffer, my God why did he want me to be so different from himself and at the same time so similar, why has he ruined me in his ambition to have a son who was a bookkeeper or a schoolmaster or a lawyer it was all the same to him because what counted was a sound middle-class standing where he himself was but not so firmly to tell the truth because of his inability to keep his hat business afloat and his even greater inability to handle petitions and letters with decent grammar, oh the hatred I felt for him then or maybe compassion I don't know, maybe more compassion than hatred since by now I dominated him from the loftiness of my hopes and my despair, and obviously the despair was much vaster and deeper than any hope, but at that same time the war in Abyssinia breaks out and here I see an excellent chance to get far away from home and see the world and earn good pay, and in fact I don't let this chance escape me and I leave almost at once thinking of death naturally, in fact this was a great opportunity to achieve along with everything else also death and glory except that when I arrive despite my genuine impulses toward heroism they set me to counting sacks of barley and oats and flour and cans of meat, mountains of the stuff scattered over the Adigrat plains, the others covered themselves with glory on the battlefields and there I was seeing how many people were earning money with army supplies, but I drew overseas pay all the same, three thousand lire a month or even more if I remember rightly, and so in about four months' time I have ten thousand five hundred lire saved up, namely the amount the Sergeant needs to pay off that mortgage he crucified himself with to avoid the shame of bankruptcy, and he was always saying how the bank drained his life's blood but the debt stayed what it was, so to make a long story short I send him a money order for ten thousand five hundred lire and I receive in exchange a letter with his rubber stamp and his errors of course in which the Sergeant from the fullness of his heart and with the usual police-report phraseology tells me he will never forget my noble and generous gesture and what's more he urges me to serve the Fatherland with loyalty and honor, and in fact I've had all I can take of counting sacks and cases of food and almost every day I hand my direct superior the quartermaster captain an application to be transferred to a combat unit indicating between the lines my contempt for the supply corps, and for a while he calls me a dope and then one fine day he gets fed up and sends on my application with his approval, so after a short time there I am commanding a platoon of valorous Eritrean natives and in this fortunate condition I cover myself with glory in so far as possible and win medals for bravery under fire and the citation is also published in due course in the *Gazzettino* and wins me the most glowing letters I've ever had from my father to whom in the meanwhile I have sent more money orders suggesting he install on the upper floor a nice bathroom with colored tiles and hot and cold running water since he hadn't thought of this at all when he had built the house, and apparently for him this wasn't a necessity whereas it was for me or perhaps for my unconscious in which the episode of my entering the shed when he was taking a bath in the washtub had caused the bathroom to become the very center of the house, so I send him the money for this use and the months go by and I have no thought of going home because down there in the Empire policing operations continue since the higher commands with their nonsense have managed to make half of Abyssinia if not all arise in revolt, so life is really interesting often one of us dies but those who don't die accumulate an enormous quantity of sexual experience with the Abyssinian girls, when you see one you like you only have to say to the batman bring her around and he brings her because down there thank God they are civilized people and pay no attention to these things you just have to pay a few thalers, and two or three years go by during which every now and then I ask myself what am I doing here however more often I don't ask myself anything, anyhow at a certain moment I say to myself now I'm going to save up at least ten thousand lire and then I'll go home but obviously in my unconscious I don't want to because once I've saved up more than ten thousand I squander it all in a single night playing baccarat in the *ghebì* of Debra Tabor where we are shut up because by now the rebels are shooting at us from all sides, and after I've lost this ten thousand lire or more I say to myself I'm all screwed up because I don't even enjoy playing baccarat I enjoy playing bridge where at most I lose twenty or thirty lire, anyhow since I hadn't had any experience of the unconscious in those days I imagined merely that I was a dope whereas now I can also believe that unwittingly I didn't want to go back and get involved with my father, in any case the problem now is to start saving up again, and in fact being careful not to play baccarat and spending only money for mess fees and girls and maybe a flask of wine to get drunk now and then in a few months' time I have eleven thousand lire saved up and I immediately make a repatriation application and since I've been down there for almost four years they grant it fairly quickly, and I begin the long journey first toward Mas-

saua and then on the ship to Naples, and I was thinking I would
have all sorts of adventures on the ship where it seems behavior
is somewhat relaxed and instead there wasn't a single woman
aboard worth touching and it was a real shame since with the
great sexual experience acquired in the meanwhile I would have
known how to manage, the truth of the matter was that it would
be a great pity to waste such experience and as I ponder how to put
it to profitable use I think of sending a cable to Manza to come
to Naples to meet me but unfortunately I don't know Manza's full
name and maybe Manza itself is only a nickname, and besides she
has syphilis though the experience acquired in Abyssinia has
taught me not to fear syphilis so much in the sense that if I haven't
caught it there it's unlikely I'll catch it anywhere else, anyhow I
start thinking about a woman with whom I can pleasantly and
without any great responsibility exploit my sexual energies and
knowledge, and I think the right girl would be that one who came
to bed with me inhibited by God knows what so she wouldn't
take off her bra or anything but I'd like to see her get out of it now
with the technique I've picked up, and since in the first months of
my stay in Africa we had exchanged a few letters mostly on
patriotic themes as was the custom of the time with war pen-pals
I now send her a cable to come and meet me in Naples, and a few
days later I get an affirmative reply, and so when the ship docks
at the Beverello pier among the people waiting there is also a
girl for me though I don't know which of the three or four present
she is also because in these four years I've been away fashions
have changed and now the girls look funny to me, anyhow when
I come down the gangplank a girl comes to me and after a
moment's hesitation we exchange an embrace still half patriotic
and then I look at her, she's wearing a big ridiculous hat of course
and she's neither beautiful nor ugly however she's more than good
enough for my purposes since we aren't going to spend our lives
together but will have a fine honeymoon as they say for a week or
ten days and then each will go his own way and no hard feelings,
and to confirm these good intentions we take a double room in the
hotel though she makes a bit of a fuss, and then we go to eat and

while we eat I talk about nothing but sexual matters to let her know
I now have plenty of experience and she listens to me saying
nothing or almost nothing, and then in the hotel she locks herself
in the bathroom and fiddles around for half an hour and in the
meanwhile I get all worked up in my imagination and then I
see her come out dressed like the other time in her slip and all
whereas I was thinking she would appear before me almost naked,
certainly the prospect isn't too easy with this kind of woman who
generally waits for the menopause before relaxing though how
belatedly I don't have to say, anyhow I'm not the fool I was at
twenty and you might say that in making war I've learned how
to conquer women and in fact after a few attempts at frontal attack since she stiffens in defense I try a flanking strategy namely
I begin to talk about human unhappiness in general and my own
in particular and how I need to feel a person near me not for those
things of course which aren't basically as important as they might
seem but to share my thoughts and my sufferings and for example
I would like her to feel more in communion with me and if she
has some secret sorrow she should drag it out because I'm ready
to offer her every consolation and comfort, in short I make this
lovely speech probably a lot better than I can reconstruct it now
and little by little she breaks down and begins to sob with emotion
and then in fits and starts she tells me the story of a boy a classmate of hers at the commercial high school who one day took her
for a walk in the fields and taking advantage of the fact that she
was completely inexperienced and maybe not even fourteen he had
as they say given it to her, and she could never forget this she
still flushed with shame when she thought of it and felt she was
unworthy to belong to another man, and while she was crying
and talking I drew her to me to console her and managed to oc-
cupy some of the key positions of her body and little by little she
gives way until finally she says do whatever you want with me
however adding that she granted me this liberty because she loved
me with her whole heart and soul, and naturally I also say I love
her with no less abandon, and so toward one in the morning we do
it and she likes it fairly well I think whereas I like it a bit less

than I expected since during the operation I happened often to think how much better the native girls are especially when she insisted on knowing to what extent I loved her and such things, and even more especially when she wanted to hear me say that despite the unfortunate incident with the classmate she wasn't unworthy of being loved, in any case we make love several times during the night and always in the dark because it isn't as if she has lost her modesty along with that basic inhibition, and in the morning I get up first and go into the bathroom and after a while she calls me and she seems quite upset, and still thinking how much better the native girls are I prepare myself to listen to some new drama and in fact there is a new drama and a far from small one if you can see it from her point of view, namely she has realized that her old schoolmate hadn't really deflowered her God knows what he had done but he really hadn't deflowered her, so she had lost her virginity with me around one at night and in fact she had felt pain then but she had clenched her teeth so as not to spoil things for me, for which I might also thank her however now she seemed to want to give events an abrupt new turn and a rather tendentious one on the whole and that was since it was all too clear that I had had her virginity and since we loved each other and since the only obstacle to our lasting union she had thought was the fact that she had previously belonged to another, but now seeing as how this wasn't so we were almost unexpectedly you might say in the ideal spiritual and emotional condition for matrimony, and as far as our economic condition was concerned it went without saying that she would continue working so she wouldn't be a burden to me, and as I listen to her I keep thinking I would have been a lot better off if I had stayed in Abyssinia however I don't reveal this thought to her and I simply urge her not to dramatize things because I really wasn't so opposed to marriage although on the other hand I wasn't in favor of it either if only because when you thought about it I was a mere university student on extended leave who hadn't yet passed a single exam, and she comes right back with the observation that I could easily be a government employee in category B or an elementary schoolteacher if I liked,

and I think what fun teaching in an elementary school with this
girl here on my back as well however to her I say this matrimony
question is something we can examine later with due calm but
now the important thing is to enjoy our honeymoon without any
cares, however easier said than done I keep thinking about this
marriage question so much that I don't feel like making love any
more, and she thinks about it as much of course but with I would
say an opposite view namely speaking often of the house we will
furnish thus and so and the babies we're going to have a boy and
a girl to be precise, and with this fine assortment of complications
I make my pleasure trip from Naples to Rome and from Rome to
Florence and from Florence to Venice along the well-established
honeymoon route, and when I'm in Venice I finally take the opportunity to tell her I don't have the slightest desire to get married
and as far as I'm concerned she can jump in the lake, and once this
misunderstanding is cleared up I leave her on a rumpled bed tear-
ing up the patriotic letters and the snapshots I had sent her from
Abyssinia until three years before, and after abandoning her half
raving with anger and disappointment in the hotel bed I must immediately face another far from slight nuisance, namely my return to my family home which for that matter is only a hop skip
and jump away, and the family as soon as they see me start crying
with relief except my father naturally although his eyes too are
on the brink of squeezing out tears since I have covered myself
with glory, however he hasn't built me the bathroom upstairs, he's
done a lot of work enlarging the house because my sisters have
grown up and they can't sleep three or four in a room so no bath,
and he says it's also because he couldn't take on the responsibility
since these are delicate matters and have to satisfy my taste since
for poor ignorant people like them anything is good enough, however he doesn't mention money and I imagine that he's used it all
up enlarging the house for my sisters and moreover it seems things
at the shop aren't doing too well also because since he and my
mother are old now they don't go off to the markets any more
and you earn money at the markets whereas you hardly take in a
cent at the shop, but I think how can you expect to make anything

in that shop with the broken mirror and a musty smell and those corporals writing petitions and those hats dating back to 1913 thanks to which I'll go bareheaded since I can't repeat the insult of going and buying a hat on the Mercerie in Venice, as for the bathroom however he's crazy if he thinks I'm going to spend the money to build it now I'll go to the public baths when I need one, and besides to be perfectly frank I have no intention of staying at home, and in fact using my studies as an excuse I go to Padua where I find that my old idea of enrolling in the Faculty of Literature wasn't all that mistaken since the department is full of girls most of them ugly and religious but there are some who are a little less ugly and not at all religious, and besides in this department there isn't much competition because males are rare and mostly priests or others who ought to have joined the priesthood, and besides I possess a sexual experience which nobody at least not in the faculty of literature can boast, and with the money in my pocket I lead a fairly entertaining life though these silly girls in my classes are influenced by the provincial atmosphere and let me do everything except the thing I like best, in any case I adapt my acquired sexual experience to the circumstances and amuse myself as much as I can and also take a couple of exams which aren't many and in fact I calculate that if I keep on at this rate I'll get my degree when I'm thirty-six or thirty-seven, but then at a certain moment Hitler starts making war and I think that pretty soon we'll be in it too striking a couple of blows at perfidious Albion and so I should hurry up with the exams and in fact I take several without any serious difficulties since having fought in Abyssinia with valor and scorning danger as is written in the citation with my medals I'm certainly not afraid now to take an exam, and when you're not afraid of an exam that's already enough to keep you from flunking at least in the literature department where the girls get scared over nothing and even the boys who for that matter all look like *castrati*, in short between October and February I manage to get through about ten exams, so when Mussolini decides it's a good time to get into the war I make a final little effort and take the exams that are left and then I show up to discuss my thesis

in my uniform and decorations saying to myself I'd like to see
them have the nerve to flunk me, and in fact they haven't the
slightest desire to do anything of the kind and since I'm not too
well prepared on the thesis subject we talk about other things,
and then there I am with a nice degree in literature that I don't
know what to do with except to offer it up to the middle-class
vanity of my father before immolating myself on the battlefield
for the greatness of the Fatherland, and in fact I send off an urgent
request to volunteer specifying my long colonial experience so that
if possible they may send me back to Abyssinia or as second choice
North Africa where we are advancing victoriously as we are
everywhere else for that matter, but it seems the Fatherland
doesn't much need her brave son for the moment, and when
autumn comes I find myself without a cent and with my university
degree to which I would gladly set fire and instead all I can use it
for is to make an application to work as a substitute teacher and
needless to say they immediately give me the job as a much-
decorated Africa veteran, something which has very little to do
with teaching or if anything has a negative connection as I soon
realize since I have to start studying everything all over again if
I want to give a modicum of instruction to my students who are
all girls around sixteen to eighteen since by God's grace I have
ended up in a girls' school, however in a year's time my recall to
arms arrives but they want to send me off on an advanced course
and I haven't any desire to go so I say my stomach hurts and in
fact they find the ulcer with which I take six months' con-
valescence, and after the first six months I take another six, but
in the meanwhile I am running the risk that they'll win this war
without my personal participation so I address myself to the
Voluntary Militia for National Security keeping quiet about the
ulcer of course, and the Militia can hardly believe its eyes at
the sight of a sincere volunteer these days since though I am unaware of it the war isn't going as well as I am accustomed to think,
and so with the thought that God only knows I might change my
mind they treat me with great respect and send me to North Africa
as I wanted and had requested, and soon after I arrive there we

begin to fall back farther and farther with the English coming forward, and all those who have some experience of war in Africa say that pretty soon the English will stop on their own because of the desert but they don't stop and as if the English weren't enough now from the other part of the world come the Americans, so now I realize things here are going to end badly and I bring up the old ulcer for which they send me to the hospital in Tunis and they make X rays a couple of times without finding anything, in fact they explain to me that ulcers are like this here today and gone tomorrow and at the moment it isn't here the son of a bitch I think, in any case all I can do is resign myself to my fate my cruel fate we may as well call it and rather than capture and imprisonment I am thinking of a glorious death on the field of battle but first I collect all the money I have on hand and I send a money order to my father and in a letter under separate cover I try to explain to him that with the twenty-eight thousand lire I'm sending him he must absolutely buy something maybe even shoe buttons or gondola prows but something in any case, and naturally I can't explain to him the basic reasons of political economy behind this advice since the letters are censored and I wouldn't want to pass for a defeatist, and after having given these instructions like a last will at least in part I face my destiny which means I am taken prisoner and shunted here and there around the world and then sent home again when thanks to the Almighty everything has ended some while ago, and I come home dead broke and find everybody very happy because you can make a fortune dealing in cloth or grain or automobile tires to say nothing of cigarettes or gasoline, I even find my father in high spirits thanks particularly to the satisfactions the shop has given him during the war when heedless of the bombing of the railroads my sisters went to Padua and Milan and Novara and Alessandria and God only knows where buying hats and umbrellas from the factories and as soon as they came back they sold like hot cakes, people came from Mestre and even from Venice to buy hats and umbrellas in my father's shop, and it was a real shame that toward the end of the war the prices of everything went up so much at the factories that a person couldn't keep up with them, my father least of all, and so when the war ended the shop was empty except for a few odds and ends left over from the First World War and the money wasn't enough to buy anything, this was plain hard luck he said certainly things would soon be flourishing again, and as for the twenty-eight thousand lire I had sent him *in extremis* from Tunis he had got the money all right and he had even received the letter luckily though the postal service in those last days of the African war was terrible, however after thinking it over he had decided to deposit the money in the savings bank where with compound interest the sum in the meanwhile had increased almost to twenty-nine thousand lire with which he could buy me a beer or two if I happened to like beer, in any case after some hemming and hawing the government gives me a bit of money in return for my sacrifices and suffering for the fatherland, and with this money I start working with a mason and a plumber and I build a spectacular bathroom with concealed pipes and pink mosaic tile on the walls as high as the hand can reach and a shower with a proper drain, only the basin the bidet and the toilet aren't right as to style but in these days it's hard to find bathroom fixtures all the same style, anyhow I create this extraordinary bathroom an act which I bet in my unconscious corresponds to the payment of an ethical debt, and in fact my father's eyes glisten when he sees it finished since it's the most beautiful bathroom that he a merchant and ex-sergeant of carabinieri has ever seen, anyhow when the bathroom is finished I try to talk to him fairly seriously about my future but as if nothing had happened in the past few years he keeps on saying just you listen to me, you have your university degree and you're a veteran and decorated and they have to give you a job even if you did fight the war with the Fascist Militia, just think about it you have a steady salary and a pension at the end, and I don't much feel like thinking about the end when I haven't yet begun, and then to tell the truth I felt sorry for him with his court of corporals and noncoms sending one petition after another because with the devaluation of the lira they can't keep body and soul together, they were so busy with all this that they hardly noticed the King was going away to make room for the Republic and the motto Faithful through the Centuries was changing its objective, or rather it wasn't clear what Royal Carabinieri meant any more and in fact they weren't called royal any more but just plain carabinieri though it had a funny ring to it, for that matter the pensioners had little to do with this change and for them as long as there were offices and ministries and higher commands to forward petitions to they were all right and thank God there was no lack of these institutions so they were in their own way content, but I was thinking look at the state these poor wretches are in and my father still thinks he can give me advice when you come right down to it the best thing I can do is the opposite of what he tells me, and so I go off to seek my fortune with my intellectual baggage and a suit from before the war and some reddish flannel shirts and no necktie since I think I'm pretty much to the left, and at the same time I say to myself you went and spent a pile of money to make a beautiful bathroom in the house where you were born and now you're going off to seek something and you yourself don't know what, and I really don't know however one thing is sure that is I have this father who keeps saying from morning to night just listen to me and mark my words when he hasn't done anything right for the last twenty-five years at least since I am able to remember events with any critical faculty, and I don't want to live with such a father on my back, this is what I'm thinking as I go to Milan crammed into a cattle car with other vagrant humans as travel demanded in those days, and after various experiences in Milan I go on to Rome where there is the reborn Italian cinema and I rarely write home since as soon as I communicate an address to them my father swamps me with letters and cards with his rubber-stamped last name and first name and the title merchant although he isn't one any longer since he has sold the shop making according to him a fine deal, and these letters and post cards from my father all say more or less the same thing namely you're in Rome and with your degree you surely must know some big shots so find out why this or that ministry or headquarters hasn't done anything about the petition of the retired sergeant Maccatrozzo Luigi or the retired corporal Fontanella Erminio, and then there are the letters from my sisters who insist they are writing also in the name of my old mother and they inform me that with the sale of his shop my father has let himself be swindled like an idiot and what's more the little money he received he has deposited in the bank in a blocked account so if I can send them something please I have to do it quickly because they have only his miserable pension to live on and the little assistance they get luckily from the two married sisters and of course I'm the oldest and the only son and I shouldn't evade my duty of helping the family in its present distress, and then there are the benedictions and the warnings not to get into trouble which my mother usually adds at the bottom of the letter also saying nobody will ever love me like my own Mamma, and I haven't the slightest doubt of this but at the moment it doesn't matter much to me since in the final analysis the best thing I can do is change my address and put off as long as possible writing them the new one even if I do send a bit of money home all the same, and in this fashion we go on without remarkable variations in our family affections until that disaster of the intestinal obstruction occurs and all the other abundant and extraordinary troubles that have brought me to my nervous exhaustion or to be more specific my psychoneurosis, but in this case it must be said that the disease was already lurking in me caused by some conflict of a sexual nature dating back to God only knows when in my earliest childhood, and the family troubles were only the occasion through which it clamorously exploded, with manifestations which cause it to be classified beyond the shadow of a doubt as an anxiety neurosis.

And so I myself begin to reason in psychoanalytical terms abandoning that passion for realistic rationalism with which I insisted on seeing life and the misfortunes that constitute it as a mechanism of causes and effects strictly linked together in the light of day, or conversely buried in the darkness of magic and the mysterious relations between the dead and the living, now I manage in fact to travel I would say at my ease among the hypotheses of the unconscious and the haggling between the Ego the Id and the Superego, I know that when I imagine my father is persecuting me from his tomb where he lies I suppose decomposed by now I am producing a poetic figuration because if anything he is persecuting me through all the nonsense he transmitted into my Superego when it was first being formed, anyhow in these two years of psychoanalysis we have managed to fix up my plethoric Superego more or less that is we have reduced its tormenting activity as much as can be hoped and in any case we know it exists in a given way and for given reasons, and moreover it is clear that of the three libido types devised by Freud I belong to the compulsive type dominated by the Superego which detaching itself from the Ego creates in the individual a high degree of tension and a tendency not to give a damn about the outside world but with marked inner dependence and fear of his own conscience which is certainly exact also according to my own way of thinking, and in addition a fact that seems particularly important in its reference to my unremitting aspirations, the compulsive type unlike the erotic type where the Id prevails or the narcissistic type where obviously the Ego prevails so that both these types the lucky bastards are inclined for opposite reasons to mind their own business pleasantly, the compulsive type as I was saying not infrequently becomes a supporter and custodian of culture and unquestionably here the term culture must be taken also to cover creative activity specifically speaking not excluding therefore the writing of works of art which by and large could be my case, and to sum up belonging to the compulsive type would be for me as for anybody else a lucky break, except that when you look at the thing from another point of view you can't help observing that the presence of an overefficient and dominating Superego checks one's ambition with a sense of the ridiculous and perfectionism, so that the whole business turns out as usual to be considerably complex and confused, and as if this weren't enough you also have to bear in mind the connections with the murky Id in the sense that the libido or orgone energy as others call it can also be sublimated that is directed towards non-sexual goals, and I believe this does happen in me that is a good part of the libido is sublimated in my artistic tendencies or at least it aspires to be sublimated, and this obviously is very fine however it creates new problems increasing one's sense of responsibility and so on and also an impression of irremediable unhappiness since however the person behaves he can't help making mistakes in one direction or the other, and in fact every time I manage thank heaven to make love in addition to the various repentances already described there is the new one namely the thought there a libidinous impulse has followed its own course instead of being sublimated and now who's going to write that fourth chapter for me, and I think that at this point I would even make a pact with the devil for my masterpiece that is if he will let me write it I'll give him my virility in exchange, however this is a temptation that comes to me only in special circumstances and

it's pretty risky so much so in fact that I've never mentioned it for
example to the doctor, but I believe he knows about it even if I've
never said a word and in fact when we talk about my work and
my unfortunate artistic ambitions he always encourages me to
undertake if only for the present works that are a bit less perfect
than the ones I generally dream about otherwise I am simply
seeking my own misfortunes, that is while I'm inclined to think
childishly that destiny or the late Sergeant is loading me down with
an unfairly large pile of troubles, in reality I'm procuring them
for myself through my ambition to undertake tasks let's not say
beyond my capacities but excessive in proportion to my present
psychic conditions, and it then happens that just when I feel ready
to write a masterpiece and maybe two or three in a row my unconscious on the other hand is terrified or pretends to be for reasons
of its own and prepares for me to escape into illness as it's called,
and if it isn't real illness it's those long periods of timorousness
and psychic stasis which could also be mistaken for laziness by an
ignorant and unkind observer, and even if they were laziness they
would still have every right and reason to exist since as it happens
when I'm doing nothing I can regress to the happiness you feel in
the womb when you enjoy the uninterrupted flow of warmth and
nourishment without in fact doing anything at all, and anyone can
easily see how in my case it would be useful to cultivate such a
type of regression, except that while I'm there in blissful idleness
I'm assailed as a rule by a collection of remorseful notions about
the time wasted or we can even say stolen from my works of art,
and then I'm off again worrying myself with lofty thoughts of
action which in addition would allow me to take my productive
place in society assuming that the society I happen to live in needs
masterpieces, anyhow it needs film scripts this is beyond doubt
and for my doctor it would be a good sign if I would take on the
film scripts without too much disgust and postpone the masterpiece to a more favorable moment, and I say yes though with the
bitter thought that more favorable moment is a euphemism to
indicate the period post mortem that is a state in which masterpieces are notoriously not produced any longer, in any case I

can't go on forever with this masterpiece-no-masterpiece conflict because it seems I have all too many conflicts conscious or unconscious, and thank God from the critical reconnaissance of the past carried out by analysis my Ego has emerged considerably reactivated and reinforced against the Superego which as I said before has had its dimensions a bit reduced in its conditional defects which are especially its perfectionism and its cruelty, but unfortunately it turns out to be strengthened in its structural defects namely in the recognition of the very process of its formation, and in fact when for example it was a matter of overcoming the Oedipal situation and that is when my boundless love for my mother and the consequent hatred for my abhorred rival my father ended, like all other human beings it seems I went from one extreme to the other that is for a limited time anyway I started loving my father as much as I had formerly hated him, taking him even for an ideal receptacle of every perfection in which I could mirror myself and better still identify myself, and it was precisely in this period that my Superego assumed what we might call its structure taking into itself a great part of my father, so you can imagine the conflict that broke out later on when I realized I had absorbed almost a whole carabiniere sergeant taking him as an ideal receptacle of perfections, and this in all likelihood is the true nucleus of my disease although we can't naturally underestimate the coadjuvant power of my too many sufferings and misfortunes and disappointments and renunciations and humiliations to which if you like you can add the suspicious behavior of the radicals, anyhow if I have a Superego made like this I also have an Ego which for better or worse has managed to hang on to itself and to reality if we except a few brief periods of confusion, and in fact even when for example I happen to see everything crooked I believe I am mistaken and not the world otherwise I would belong to the category of the insane to which somewhat to my surprise I do not belong, anyhow the supremely positive factor is that I put up no more resistance to the knowledge of myself, and my three psychical provinces may not be arranged in complete harmony and I won't say that the Superego for example is pleased with the Ego or that the Id transmits impulses that can be satisfied simply without any fear of having to atone at once maybe with a heart attack or a long phase of idiocy, still they manage to live together somehow and at times it even happens that the Ego and the Superego pretend not to know each other as it were and while this lasts I remain in naked and affectionate communion with my ancient and less ancient sins, and finally through all these reflections and this new awareness I modify my psyche slightly and become so much stronger that the old man begins to tell me I can consider myself cured to the extent that psychoanalysis can cure anybody of course, and when he touches on this subject I rebel inwardly a bit since I don't feel that much cured, however it's also natural that it should be hard for me to leave this doctor with whom I have achieved an exceptional transference changing him into a proper father, and it seems that now this is my most active form of resistance to cure since for the moment I don't think about the masterpiece as exclusively as I used to, an unmistakable sign of health however there are also plenty of others and in fact if I recall the state in which I came to him the first time I can testify to the great progress made both in undertaking journeys though not yet by plane or ship nor even in trains and in going to football games and concerts and even to the theater if it's worth going to, and in thinking with some confidence about future work so long as it's film scripts or something of that kind, and also in encountering traffic cops and policemen who don't give much of a damn about democracy and I can not give a damn about them too, and also in my relationship with the radicals when by chance I go past the tables at Rosati's, all of this adds up to marvelous progress and as far as the anxiety itself is concerned I have to admit that for the past seven or eight months I haven't had any bad attacks, I do have little attacks but I start thinking what the doctor has advised namely that they aren't the end of the world that they'll pass and that if I don't feel so hot today I'll feel better tomorrow, and when I tell myself these things naturally I have a terrible fear that they won't work and in fact I don't really believe in them but maybe they achieve their effect in the unconscious, and moreover there are some pills or little capsules to take and on this score it seems chemistry is making giant steps towards inventing the ideal drug that will make us all idiots with no anxiety or vaulting ambition out of proportion to the capacities or strength of our Ego, anyhow the fact remains that I can now consider myself generally cured and for the rest I have to have confidence that time will help me, and I hope this is so because I'm still afraid whenever I feel that something isn't working properly in my psyche and this happens frequently, however frankly speaking my greatest sorrow and even danger at the moment is in leaving this sort of acquired father who unlike the preceding one teaches me that the ethical makeup of an all too upright and honest carabiniere sergeant isn't the ideal one for the harmonious passing of the days I still have left to live, and moreover contrary to the teachings I may have had since early childhood in boarding school and elsewhere he tells me that making love isn't harmful or a sin and I could even do it extramaritally if a nice opportunity should arise however I must be careful not to give my wife a chance to torment me or my Superego a chance to attack me with any excess sense of guilt, I really should convince this Superego of mine that making love anyhow is one of the most beautiful things in the world and one of the least harmful too, I really should explain if it keeps on with the business of the masterpiece that even Dante Alighieri to name one counts for little if you start thinking about a galaxy or the *Parapithecus* or better still nuclear warfare, in short the important thing is to achieve a serene evaluation of oneself in relation to reality, something that is however easier said than done since we change very swiftly and also or contemporaneously reality changes inasmuch as it consists of an infinity of things in constant mutation not to mention several millions or billions of individuals each rapidly being transformed and engaged himself in chasing this changing reality, so this world would be a great big crazy Catherine wheel if it weren't for the art of compromise which is after all the renunciation of the notion of doing perfect things which as is well known are not of this world and in all likelihood not of the next either, so I only have to extend the area of compromise in the sense that I mustn't demand too much of myself or of others, and as for the masterpiece I'll postpone it as I said to a more favorable moment continuing at present my activity as a screen writer and if the opportunity arises also TV writer, and so the day has come for me to leave this doctor of my soul and naturally I don't speak to him of my grief and turmoil at leaving him but he knows it and in fact he says that even if the treatment is finished we can still remain friends and see each other now and then, which isn't exactly true I think since this emotionally charged bond which moreover has been expressed in so far as possible while I was lying on a cot or couch and he sitting behind me without my being able to see him is not the kind of relationship that can continue outside the atmosphere in which it was born, in any case I have to be firm with my Ego in this difficult situation which slightly resembles a second birth, as if the first weren't enough I happen to think, anyhow I pay the bill for the last sessions and I go off on my bicycle through the somewhat suburban streets and then I cross the Borghese gardens bearing within me my condition as a cured man and the consequent duty of a normal relationship with reality namely trees and automobiles and ladies with dogs and streets that are never perfectly flat in the city of Rome which as everyone knows stands on seven or more hills, in short this reality consists in a number of things that could also be dangerous if relationship with them is set as a condition for proper psychic functioning, not to mention the fact that from simple questions like what day is today or I wonder which way I should turn down there it is easy to spill over into concepts of time and space and in other words into the sea of the infinite so dear to anyone who like Leopardi tends toward shipwreck, so all in all it's better if I limit myself to more concrete problems which besides concern me more directly, namely in the first place what are my relations as a cured man going to be with my wife and my daughter who after all are also a part of reality, that is will our relations be as they were before or will they be somehow changed, in fact no doubt instigated by the Superego I picture myself as I make a speech informing them that now we all have to put ourselves on a sound basis especially my wife as far as the family bookkeeping is concerned and also respect for the head of the family which in recent times has been somewhat in decline, it occurs to me I could also use the word discipline if it weren't harmfully ambiguous for a person whose Superego is largely composed of a carabiniere father, still it remains established that my attitude will be sufficiently firm and this surely doesn't contradict the old man's recommendations since I have clearly been using the art of compromise all too freely up till now with my wife, I may be a bore however she's the one who has always had her way in our family, and very ill-mannerly she has been about it these past few months I might add, but now all that's over by God it's really over, anyhow I get home and I don't say anything for a start, that is I can't simply say I'm cured and then stop without going on with the sermon which is to illustrate the new guiding principles of our cohabitation, but to make a speech of this kind naturally you have to have the proper atmosphere which at the moment doesn't exist so I sit around grumpy and pensive all day and often I'm even afraid I'll have an attack one of those awful ones that head me straight for the insane asylum, considering this is my first day as a cured man it's not so hot, I even start envying psychopathic types who unlike psychoneurotics aren't burdened by relationships with reality, in any case toward evening I achieve one result in having a fight with my daughter who doesn't know how to do long division and wants her Mamma to do it for her and I insist that her Mamma isn't to do it or otherwise how will our daughter end up in the future when she's got used to her parents' solving all her problems for her, and naturally this isn't the first time that my wife and I argue rather heatedly on pedagogical subjects though things continue the same as before if not worse, still since today I feel myself invested with this new responsibility as a cured man I stand fast and shut my daughter up in her room ostensibly to do her division but in effect to cry over her notebook and then though I am aware the situation threatens to get dangerously out of hand I confront my wife who wants to liberate our daughter and I tell her that until a judge deprives me of my paternal power with a legal decree I am the one to make decisions, and she says if I'm crazy I have to go to the looney bin and not torment her and her daughter, and here is my chance to tell her everything with the proper solemnity, that is without unleashing the usual upheaval that doesn't solve anything, and in fact I start speaking with sufficient calm under the circumstances first making the distinction which for that matter she knows perfectly well between neurosis and psychosis according to which I am not crazy and have very little probability of becoming so, and in the second place I inform her that I am also finally cured of my neurosis in the doctor's opinion and therefore from now on I demand that in my house everyone do his or her duty without flinching or arguing, beginning with myself of course, however she too is going to have to toe the line and especially get it into her head that she can't throw away my money whenever she likes in the thoughtless way she's done till now, and when money is mentioned she always immediately becomes venomous and she says I have to stop saying my house and my money since what's mine is also hers it seems thanks to a law connected with matrimony, and I realize that my just dignity is going all to hell again but this damn woman has a talent for sending me into a fury so I answer hastily that this law doesn't exist and in any case matrimony was my ruination or to be more precise my meeting her was because that's where all my troubles began, and then she stiffens with hatred really I have never seen such hatred in her eyes before and she says repeat that if you're so convinced of it, and at this moment I'm afraid of her and of all the days I still have to live however I can't draw back now so I repeat that marrying her was my undoing, and so now without any hatred but with frightening coldness she says I can then be free and happy since she has another man, and I say what do you mean another man and the zone of compromise comes into my mind, what do you mean another man I ask again, and she confirms what she said another man and if you don't understand you're even stupider than I think, and I am left breathless my spine all ice and stiffness and I keep asking myself what did she say what did she say, I look at her and ask myself what did she say not being able to believe it, thinking that is she was joking or else she didn't say anything and I'm crazy and am hearing things she absolutely did not say, and I now must really look frightening or maybe pitiful because she looks at me terrified with mounting fear and then bursts out crying and as she cries she also makes an effort to speak saying I shouldn't have told you I know I shouldn't have told you, and she says for almost three years I've been keeping this thing locked up inside me and I couldn't stand it any longer, and she says now you're cured and that's why I told you, and at every word she says I lose another shred of hope that she was joking, she wasn't joking at all it seems and the fact that I've been a cuckold for a long time is more and more unmistakable, why I'm a cuckold who would ever have thought it, so I try to save myself as best I can with humor but afterwards what will I do my God what can I ever do, and in the meanwhile she unburdens herself crying and saying that I'll never be able to understand what it means to live for ten years with a man who's sick with a nervous disease, there were times when she felt she was going crazy herself and times she was afraid I was going to kill her like for example when I was convinced she was secretly putting medicines in my soup or when she woke up at night and found me there staring at her wanting her not to be there or after making love when she realized that I felt horror and repugnance at her sex whereas maybe I was the one who had forced her to submit to my desire, in short I had made plenty of mistakes and I knew this but I was hoping I had got at least a few things right, my God a thing like this going on for three years and I never suspected I always thought we loved each other in spite of the fights, because even in the first seven years we were fighting furiously and loving each other at the same time and then for three years it doesn't work this way any more and she is making love with another man and also with me and I don't know it and don't realize it, and of course from a Freudian point of view she has done absolutely right and her only mistake is telling me, this is the horrible error although the Superego promptly springs up to say what shameful compromises are these which mean being cuckolded and content about it, where are you heading, in short taking advantage of the circumstances the Superego tries to unleash a conflict over this contingent event which surely doesn't go back to my earliest childhood unless I am regressing through it to when my mother abandoned me to run after my father in which case I would be suffering at the same time for this grief and for that one, and it's not hard to believe this however I try to cling as best I can to reality so my Ego won't disintegrate maybe forever even if basically there are worse things than losing contact with reality when reality is so disgusting, anyhow my wife now that she's got it all off her chest dries her tears as best she can and looks at me to see how I'm getting on with my psychic health and for a moment it occurs to me that I could strangle her with a bit of an effort to be sure and then in due course the judges would absolve me in view of my mental condition, because while it's true that I was cured only today a man can easily relapse under blows like this, in any case I can't make up my mind and decide on any one of the possible things to do and in short I don't kill her and I don't go crazy and I don't even move I just stand there and look at her trying to think why this lousy whore, and seeing me so inert and almost pensive she asks me what I plan to do, and I tell her what do you expect me to do I'll go off and take a nice trip and I hope that this animal you've been cheating on me with has plenty of money because as far as I'm concerned you may rest assured I'm not even going to leave you the price of a pack of cigarettes, and she answers that this is no more than what she expected of me in view of my base soul and the stinginess I've persecuted her with for so many years however I'll have to provide for my daughter or else she'll take me to court, and now she almost makes me laugh when she says this and follows me around as I gather up here and there at random some things to put in my suitcase, a lot I care about courts and judges and the whole world, and meanwhile I am cursing because it's so hard to shut the typewriter case why haven't they managed to invent something a bit less inefficient, and then I take my three chapters not of course because at this moment I am thinking of going on to the fourth and the fifth and so on but because I don't want to leave them to her, and now I'm ready provided nothing new happens and I am choking with emotion over my daughter shut in her room with her sorrow and her long division and her more than ever uncertain destiny, anyhow I summon up my strength and tell my wife to take out on me whatever venegeance she wants if she can but not on my daughter for the love of God, and she answers what a low coward you must be if you can even think such a thing of me, and maybe she's right to get indignant I won't deny that, however she ought to admit that the event is so enormous it could easily shake my confidence in her in a general sense, in any case I urge her to tell the child I've had to go away for work or because Granny is sick or any sort of lie adding that I trust she won't have too much trouble lying considering the practice she has had these past three years, and then I go out in a hurry not giving her time to answer since I'm sure that my ironic remark will infuriate her, and then I go down in the elevator carrying a not too large suitcase and the typewriter and thinking the elevator is ugly and lousy and there are even some words crossed out which were surely obscene, and then I load the suitcase and the typewriter into the car thinking she is probably watching me from the balcony and will burst with rage when she sees I'm taking the car, but it's mine for Christ's sake I paid for it with my own money although it was my own money also that paid for the frigidaire for example and the furniture and the linen and everything else that I'm leaving her, and so I start the engine and drive away and from the balcony she sees me for a while and then she doesn't see me any more, now she can't see me and I am alone facing the vast and frightening world free as I was when I came back from the wars, or when I left my father's house, my God how did she do it for three years making love with me and maybe thinking of the other man, I know that how she did it should be of no interest to me even unless I want to lose God knows what I can't remember what it is I'd lose if I finally brought out into the light the idea that I married a kind of whore, anyhow the first thing I do is stop at a drinking fountain and take one of those little capsules that help the unfortunate, in fact I take two in view of the exceptional event, my God and I think of that doctor who so many years ago believed I was a drug addict, drug addict hell here I am all to pieces and for example I could drive over to the Tiber and jump in or else I could lose my mind and plunge again into my neurosis even worse than the other times naturally and yet here I am thinking twice before taking two capsules instead of one, what the hell I'll take another at the next drinking fountain, but after the third capsule what shall I do, I could maybe track down my little old doctor and tell him what's happened to me and have him console me a bit in my new misfortune it's not a bad idea but he's probably had a bellyful of me he discharged me only this afternoon and then I show up at suppertime to tell him my wife's unfaithful, and maybe he would bring up the compromise area, no better not especially since things aren't going too badly I believe, that is I know this is the greatest desperation I've ever landed in as far back as I can remember in my life however I feel somehow it's this side of the boundary of anxiety and so I'm not being swept away by it so all in all it's a desperation in proportion to our mortal strength and my Ego is facing up to it in as manly a fashion as possible, and I couldn't ask for better proof than this to persuade me that I really am out of my neurosis so when you think about it there's really no reason for me to go to the doctor, it's better for me to go and eat since it's supper time, no doubt I could go back to one of those restaurants where I went as a bachelor to look for girls and in fact often found them, however what would I do with a girl tonight if anything a tramp from the streets you don't have to talk to if you don't want to, or if you want to you can cry and tell her your wife cheats on you it doesn't matter to her one way or the other, in any case I don't go to a restaurant but to a cafeteria in Parioli since I happen to be in that part of town but then I don't eat anything because I'm afraid of upsetting my stomach and intestine and all I would need at this delicate moment of my existence would be for my intestine not to work, and then I'm not hungry so much as I'm sleepy which is understandable after the three capsules, so I go off to look for a hotel but not right away because I have to think about it, I mean there are plenty of hotels and they're not very full at this season, and I have pleasant memories of hotels from when I was a bachelor and had romances with girls, however I reject all the familiar hotels and go to a priests' hotel near the Vatican that way I'm sure I won't meet anybody who'll bother me, and the bad moment is when I find myself in this alien room and this alien bed and my five lumbars begin to hurt a little and I think what do you bet now I'll jump from this fifth floor where I am unwisely staying what a joke that would be on this priests' hotel and also on her of course because I don't think she would brush it off so lightly if I killed myself on account of her, anyhow the best idea is for me to take another couple of psychoplegics so I'll fall asleep and we'll see about it all tomorrow, the most important thing now is not to let myself be frightened by being alone or by the reason why I'm here because if I had an attack I wouldn't know what to do, my God if I began to see the walls crooked or be afraid of the fifth floor or if I felt that warm sensation moving upwards from my vertebrae, my God maybe I'd be forced to telephone her and she would tell me to go to hell or else she would come and then it would be still worse, now I'll take another capsule and if they were only poison then I'd get it over with once and for all, but they're not poison I think you'd probably have to take a pound of them before there was any likelihood of quietly going off to the next world, in any case I fall asleep thinking that with all my strict and logical pessimism I had never visualized the eventuality of my leaving the house because of a pair of horns on my head, I always thought if anything I would go away because I was fed up with married life, anyhow here I am I've left home and I don't care a great deal what the reason is since I haven't given her much satisfaction I didn't even ask her who this man is who is going to succeed me and perhaps has already succeeded me in the difficult assignment of providing for her wants, and moreover I have time to think that the greatest disaster is for my daughter or rather not so much for her as for me without her, but luckily before I can properly develop this concept I fall asleep and I even have a dream, which is that my father is there in bed sick and maybe it's the hospital bed however there's a washbasin which I don't think

there was in his hospital room and this basin is the very one in the
beautiful bathroom I built at home before I went away but it is in
terrible shape with the faucets loose though they still work, and
moreover it's dirty with some abundant but indefinable substance
and when I ask how it happens to be dirty one of my sisters says
it's my father's vomit and I don't feel the slightest disgust at this
vomit absolutely none at all, and then I wake up because some
damned church bells start ringing right over my head, and I see
that it's just a little past five in the morning and so I could go back
to sleep except that I promptly remember I'm a cuckold and free
and so I surely won't fall asleep again, instead I think about this
curious dream of vomit and I find it fairly revealing though of
course I don't claim to have the ability to interpret dreams in an
orthodox manner according to the doctrine of Freud and the
others who came after him, there's no doubt for example at least
from my point of view that the broken washbasin is the sense of
home that has gone up in smoke, and the vomit also seems fairly
clear to me or rather the fact that I wasn't disgusted it's as if I
were making up for the guilt at having felt disgust at my father
when he was dying and in a broader sense it can also be that this
misfortune which has befallen me is the biggest and most undeserved misfortune that can befall a man like me and perhaps has
appeased my sense of guilt in general and the consequent necessity for expiation, so at present I could even hope to be all square
with everybody including my deceased father and this obviously
makes my inner freedom also more vast though at the moment
I don't know what to do with it except that beyond any doubt I
have to go away, or rather go to the place where I was born and
the house where I was born since I believe a man goes back there
when he doesn't know where else to go, and in fact overlooking
completely the probability that the dream was also a premonition
from what could be deduced from the broken washbasin I set out
and make the long journey swallowing a capsule or two every now
and then to make my anxiety behave if by any chance it starts
threatening me, and indeed I manage to think about my life's
events as if they belonged to somebody else and this is very useful

when you consider the nature of these events and when I am near
my home town I stop at a hotel because there have been changes
in the family after my father's death, that is some have gone one
way and some another and the house where I was born and where
I'm under the impression I'm going back has been rented however
I believe the tenants might also give it up for a modest consideration, and so I go to see this house and the garden is no longer
there of course, now I don't remember too well but maybe my
father himself had given up cultivating it some time before he
died, anyhow at present there are a few somewhat scraggly wild
shrubs and rank grass and it isn't a nice sight but of course
with a little work the garden could be tended again, and then I
ask the people now living in the house if I can come inside and I
find that inside it's ugly as for that matter it always has been
but now it's ugly also in the sense that there's no relationship
between it and me as I'm seeking who knows what, and then the
furniture isn't the furniture my father bought but other things
arranged in a different way from my memory, so I already feel this
journey can't lead to anything good however since I'm here I ask
if I can have a look at the bathroom upstairs and naturally I should
have imagined it in view of the dream however I am upset all the
same seeing it in such disorder, for instance one winter a sudden
freeze burst the pipes and they had to chip away the mosaic to re-
pair them and now it's all patched up with cement, and there's no
hot-water heater since they say it's up to the tenant to furnish that
but this tenant hasn't provided it and so there are more exposed
pipes plugged up and useless hooks stuck in the wall, and so I go
away knowing this is no longer the house for me and I go to say
hello to my mother who is at present living not far from there and
I tell her I can only stop over for an hour to see her because I'm
just passing through and I have an urgent job waiting for me in
Rome, and first off she asks me if I've been to the cemetery to see
my father and I say yes so as not to displease her but I really
haven't been, or rather I went this morning before going to her
house but once I was there I stopped outside the gate and only
peered in toward the new wing in the back where the tombs were

fairly visible though from that distance you couldn't distinguish which one was my father's and which was anybody else's, and for that matter even there at the gate I only stopped for a moment because I happened to think of a strange and similar situation connected with my daughter when she was barely born and in desperation I looked at the undistinguishable cradles inside the nursery at the clinic, and in this way I produced such a sad and ineluctable connection between birth and death that I left the gate as fast as I could, in any case I can't tell my mother these things she's very old now so I tell her I recited a good number of Our Fathers and a *De profundis* at his grave and as I look at her I ask myself in amazement if it's possible that the conflict really began with her with my repose in her womb when she was carrying me and the sweetness of her breast when she nursed me and the love I bore her as I loved no other woman in this life, my God I bet this psychoanalysis is nothing but a pack of lies and I have nothing to do with my mother or her breast absolutely nothing and when two interminable hours have gone by I leave, almost without thinking I head for Rome again however it's soon clear that Rome isn't the place where I can go, nor could I have recourse to a father who after all isn't my father running the risk of hearing him tell me I have to take my productive place in society and rediscover the joy of living, but what can I produce at the moment and as for the joy of living it seems to me that at a certain point a man also has the right to give up any hope of it, for that matter even if I wanted to extend the area of compromise and make it include my horns which is always possible with the help of Christ the Galilean the fact remains that she wouldn't know what to do with an active forgiveness inasmuch as she never even dreamed of asking for it, and in short there are too many insoluble problems facing me for me to continue toward Rome so it's natural to head for other destinations, in general I have the impression that despite the enormity of my suffering it's well this side of anxiety so recourse to the soul doctor would be out of place, and all in all he who has always found good excuses for my mistakes will be able to understand how I must go now toward definitive solutions even if they're erroneous from a certain point of view since in the final analysis they involve a return to the concept of a communion with the deceased which should have reasonably been overcome, however I am not seeking this father to whom I seem indissolubly united in his tomb as was clear but the father of the time when he was myth and poetry, and finally let every man be allowed to seek his peace where he thinks he can best find it, so I will go toward the place where by lifting your hand you can pick the oranges that spill over from the gardens, so it was for my father, as he walked in the dawn along the paths of the Golden Bay and raised his hand towards the boughs that hung over the walls and grandly picked oranges, now I have no home town no place in the world I have only this land of his stories and of my memory, this is the land to which in some way I can still belong, and so for another day I drive along the Adriatic sea and then across the mountains and then again along another sea until I reach the end and the island of the oranges lies on the opposite shore blue and yellow and a little green at its brief distance, and in between there is a little stretch of sea really narrow but I don't have the courage to cross it, father I don't have the courage, it's still a bit of my disease this fear of the island and of the sea and I think I'll be cured one of these days but for the moment I can't go, and for that matter not all of those who desired the promised land could get there, not all were worthy of its lasting perfection, and so toward evening I hunt for a place from which you can look at Sicily, at night the other coast is a long line of light bulbs with red and white signals that blink off and on, and here with my own hands I'll build a refuge of stones and around it I'll have a piece of land to grow a garden, not very big naturally because I haven't the strength in my arms too unacquainted with labor, and I think in the end this might serve well as the place for my life and also for my death if by any chance I couldn't go over there which after all isn't so important since oranges grow on this side too, there's a bit of difficulty with the owner who is a peasant but I'll give him an automobile if he lets me live here, I don't want any deeds or documents or papers of any kind all I ask is that he allow me to live on his

land and to cultivate a very tiny piece of it and to draw water
from the well, and for this purpose I would like to have two
gasoline drums like the ones my father used for drawing water or
for when he emptied the cesspool, except it isn't easy to find drums
of the kind I want you hardly see them any more but the peasant
remembers seeing some and will look for them at Reggio or Catanzaro when he happens to go there, and as for the refuge which
I am planning to build for myself with stones he says it isn't necessary I can stay in the hut which he only uses to store his tools
because for living purposes he has a house in the town on the hill,
and so to this place opposite Sicily I carry my suitcase and my
typewriter and the folder with the three chapters and the envelope
with the photographs of my dead father in it, I know that in these
years since his death despite my efforts I have lost a lot of hair
and now I'm going to lose a lot more since I have brought no lotions of any kind with me of course, and then in the daytime I
work the land trying as best I can to divide it into neat and regular
plots and in the evening I look at Sicily until the lights come on
and even later if it isn't cold, and as for the masterpiece I'm in
no hurry, there it is and I think about it sometimes as something
to do but more often I don't think about it at all, what matters
for the moment or even for always is to stay far away from other
men and the evil they can do and train myself to carry heavier and
heavier containers of water from the well, and then one day a
carabiniere sergeant comes from the town to see what I'm doing
and how I live, and I show him at once what I do and how I live
too, and then he asks me how much I earn since he is also carrying
out these investigations on behalf of the magistrature which has
to decide in a separation plea on the grounds of desertion of the
conjugal roof, but I don't earn anything or rather when it's necessary I write letters for the peasants who have sons off working in
the North or in Germany or at sea on Norwegian tankers, and
the peasants give me bread and oil and wine and figs and grapes
or oranges in return according to the season, and I don't need anything else except a bit of cheese every now and then, but I have
already calculated that with the money I have in my pocket I can

buy my cheese for the next forty-seven years which to tell the truth would be too much, and some time after the sergeant's visit the doctor also comes and I start talking to him with no embarrassment at all about my Ego and my Superego and even about my Id but not too much about this last-named since it seems that I've managed to put it out of commission, and for that matter even the Ego and the Superego don't bother me the way they once did and I imagine that on the one hand the Ego in some way has surrendered at least in the matter of identification to the Superego which on the other hand doesn't have too many demands to make since for better or worse even the carabinieri couldn't criticize my way of life, but I think that this country doctor doesn't have much experience with the intimate subdivisions of the personality and of the sometimes fierce struggles that break out between one part and the other and in fact I see that he is somewhat concerned and then he pretends to go away but in reality he stops and questions the peasant to know if I do any other strange things beyond the obvious one of living the eccentric way I live, and some time after the doctor the priest comes to see how I am fixed with religion, here too things aren't easy to explain and I realize that very well, still I tell him as calmly as possible I think I'm all in order from a religious point of view since I am involved in a normal process of identification with my father, and since I have confused this father of mine now dead for so many years with God in the final analysis I am tending to unite myself with God which unless I am mistaken is the chief end of all religion, however this priest doesn't seem very much persuaded by the validity of my arguments and starts talking to me about the sacraments and the Communion of the Faith which is the Holy Roman Catholic Apostolic Church with all her laws and symbols and institutions, but I ask him to be patient, one day in the not too distant future I hope I'll allow him to bring me the sacraments at least Extreme Unction with its fine list of sins but now he must be patient because I am escaping from my fellow man as he can clearly see so the Communion of the Faithful would be a nuisance to me, and for the rest the Church is not without examples along this line if we think of the anchorites or even the stylites of the desert whose sustenance the Lord himself provided with winged animals or even through his angels, and after the priest a long time goes by I think, various seasons beyond a doubt and in the meanwhile I have become bald at least halfway back on my head and especially on my neck I have many wrinkles and one day if I feel like opening the envelope with the photographs of my dead father I will see how far I've come with the physical resemblance, whereas I believe the spiritual resemblance or identification is just about achieved since the peasant has managed to find me those gasoline drums and I have attached a wire handle to them and now I carry the water from the well with those drums not full of course since I'm old now and it's hard for old men to become accustomed to physical effort, anyhow I think they are already three-quarters full and I keep making progress so I'm almost there, anyhow a long time goes by and then she comes, she is seventeen now and she has passed her *liceo* exams and with some friends other boys and girls she is going to Sicily on a trip, they've taken rooms for the night in a motel not far from here and she has taken this opportunity to come and visit me or rather to know me because she doesn't remember much about when I lived at home, we sit on the bench I have built outside the hut so I can sit down and look at Sicily, and she never knew her grandfather I bet she's never even heard him mentioned and still I think that looking at Sicily is a beautiful thing independently of the quite personal value a person may attach to it, so we sit down to look at Sicily across the water as evening falls and I offer her some fresh figs and she asks why I live like this, and she asks why I don't shave and why I don't wash more, and I know I stink and I know also the terrible consequences a father's stink can have on a child and maybe I would have washed myself with care if I had known she was coming, to tell the truth I have been expecting her for a long time I believe however I couldn't know she would come precisely at this season and on this very evening, and so now I'm ashamed of stinking but what can I do about it only I feel like crying and I have a lump in my throat which makes it difficult for me to speak, and she doesn't have much to say either it seems, and so I'm afraid she'll go away too quickly and then I ask her just to be saying something if by any chance she's happy to be named Augusta and she laughs and says not too much since it's an old woman's name, and then I ask her if by any chance she would have preferred to be named Michaela and she laughs again and says no not Michaela but Michela would have been a nice name, and after this I can't find anything else to say without crying and so a little later even before the lights come on along the coast of Sicily she stands up and goes away otherwise her friends might worry about her she says, and I watch her go off with my heart aching because she is just like her mother that day by the fountain in the Piazza del Popolo when I saw her for the first time, anyhow I light the fire now and I take the three chapters of the masterpiece and I burn them one sheet at a time but without regrets because it's clear that my glory can make no difference to anyone now, and then I also burn the photographs of my dead father without looking at them of course and even turning my head away when I see the envelope curl up from the heat, and then on the coast of Sicily the white beacon at Punta Faro comes on and the red lights of the power station can be seen and the lower ones of the harbor, and I can begin to discern the low rows of lights along the shore, it's late but I will water the garden anyhow and tonight I'll try carrying the two drums filled to the brim the way my father did maybe I will manage it without spilling water or falling down, and then it will be time to say *Nunc dimittis servum tuum Domine*, perhaps the time already has come.

A NOTE ABOUT THE AUTHOR

Giuseppe Berto was born at Mogliano Veneto, near Treviso, in 1914. He won a degree in classical studies at the University of Padua. Later he served as an officer in the Italian army in both the Abyssinian War and the North African fighting of 1941–3; captured at the surrender in Tunisia, he spent two and a half years thereafter as a prisoner of war in a camp near Herford, Texas. Since then he has devoted himself to writing. His first novel, Il Cielo è Rosso *(1947), won the Firenze Prize; it was published in the United States as* The Sky Is Red. *His second book,* Le Opere di Dio *(1948), was entitled* The Works of God *in its American edition. After it came* Il Brigante *(1951), known here as* The Brigand. *Neither his wartime diary,* Guerra in Camicia Nera *(1955), nor his volume of short stories, entitled* Un Po' di Successo *(1963), has been translated into English. The year 1964 saw the publication in Italy of Berto's play* L'Uomo e la Sua Morte, *as well as the present novel,* Il Male Oscuro; *for the latter he was awarded both the Premio Viareggio and the Premio Campiello. Berto, who is married and has one daughter, lives in Rome.*

December 1965

A NOTE ON THE TYPE

The text of this book is set in Monticello, a Linotype revival of the original Binny & Ronaldson Roman No. 1, cut by Archibald Binny and cast in 1796 by that Philadelphia type foundry. The face was named Monticello in honor of its use in the monumental fifty-volume *Papers of Thomas Jefferson*, published by Princeton University Press. Monticello is a transitional type design, embodying certain features of Bulmer and Baskerville, but it is a distinguished face in its own right.

Composed, printed, and bound by
THE HADDON CRAFTSMEN, SCRANTON, PA.
Typography and binding design by
GEORGE SALTER